MISS DIGNIFIED

MISCHIEF IN MAYFAIR—BOOK THREE

GRACE BURROWES

GRACE BURROWES PUBLISHING

DEDICATION

To everybody trying
to come home from the wars

CHAPTER ONE

"That is a kitten." The audacious little beast—a calico—batted at the toe of Captain Dylan Powell's boot as if to herd him out of his own kitchen. "I do not recall giving permission to add another dependent to my household."

If asked, he would have refused. Half of London's disabled and unemployed soldiers already relied on Dylan's hospitality, which was a sufficient challenge for any former officer.

"That," Mrs. Lydia Lovelace retorted, "is a pantry mouser, and you, Captain Powell, are intruding belowstairs unannounced again. We have discussed this. If you're peckish, you may ring for a tray, and I will happily oblige you." In the dim light of the kitchen hearth, she gathered her shawl in a manner that conveyed vexation—with her employer.

Dylan's sisters were equally skilled at wordless scolds, while he had learned to deal in orders, regulations, and precisely applied rules. Mrs. Lovelace dealt in menus, schedules, and clearly defined roles, and thus he and she rubbed along tolerably well.

Most of the time. That Dylan's domestic aide-de-camp would introduce a kitten into the household without gaining Dylan's prior approval was interesting. Insubordinate and presuming of her, but interesting.

"It's nearly midnight," he said, "I would not trouble you over bread and cheese."

"Bread and cheese." She swished past him to the window box. "You hare about London at all hours, on foot, *in this weather*, and think to subsist on bread and cheese." Mrs. Lovelace tossed the longer tail of her shawl over one shoulder with all the panache of a Cossack preparing to gallop across the snowy steppes. "I should let you starve, but then I'd be in need of a post."

While the kitten pounced on Dylan's boots, then pronked away with its back arched, Mrs. Lovelace put together an omelet of ham, cheese, and bacon. At the same time, she had a rack of toast browning over the coals and a kettle on to boil.

For Dylan to sit, even on the hard chair before the kitchen table, was to fall prey to a staggering weight of fatigue. By a London gentleman's standards, midnight was not late. By a soldier's standards, midnight was hours past bedtime. Though he'd sold his commission years ago, Dylan's body had never lost the habit of the soldier's hours.

He rose to turn the toast—when had his hips acquired the aches of an eighty-year-old man?—and the kitten scampered after him. Rather than risk stepping on such a small pest, he scooped up the beast.

"Does it have a name?" he asked. The feline squeezed its eyes closed and commenced rumbling. *More insubordination.*

"She. Calicoes are always female in my experience, and no, she does not. Not yet."

Dylan resumed his seat as the kitchen filled with the scents of good, simple food. "Because you think I'd turn her out?"

Mrs. Lovelace sent him an eloquently skeptical glance. "Even you would not turn away a kitten on such a foul night."

No, he would not, but come morning...

"It's merely raining." Dylan had marched through worse and barely noticed the wet, but this rain was London rain, which could turn to sleet in any season of the year. Welsh rain was well behaved by comparison, usually more of a pattering mist and often bringing rainbows in its wake.

Thoughts of Wales were seldom cheering and never far from his mind.

"Rain with a bitter wind," Mrs. Lovelace retorted, taking the toasting rack off the hearth. She opened the rack and began spreading butter over the warm slices. "River fog redolent of foul miasmas. Footpads on every hand. That you have not succumbed to a brain fever or fallen prey to violence surely qualifies as miraculous."

"Would you miss me?" The question slipped out, not quite teasing. Perhaps Mrs. Lovelace was right—she was frequently right, also somewhat less than respectful of her employer. The late hour, an empty belly, and the dirty weather had taken a toll on Dylan's wits.

"I would miss my post." She cut the buttered toast into triangles and arranged it on a plate with the steaming omelet. "You should wash your hands, sir."

Now she gave him orders, albeit couched as a suggestion served with a side of scowling disapproval. To wash his hands, Dylan would have to stand again, and now that he was finally home and parked on his arse, even crossing the kitchen loomed like a three-day forced march.

He nonetheless set the kitten on the warm bricks of the raised hearth and went to the wet sink to do as he'd been told. Junior officers in particular learned to do as they were told, though half the time the result had been death or disgrace—at least when the orders came from Lieutenant Colonel Aloysius Dunacre.

"Will you join me?" Dylan asked, returning to the table. Mrs. Lovelace had made a prodigious amount of food, more than he could comfortably eat at one sitting.

"I'll see to the tea."

The kitten curled up in a basket on the hearth, looking small and vulnerable all on its lonesome, also sweet, dammit.

Dylan stared at the hot food, an unexpected comfort on an otherwise frustrating night. "For what I am about to receive, I am abjectly grateful. Please do sit, Mrs. Lovelace." He cast around for a means of inducing her to get off her feet. "To have you racketing about will ruin my digestion."

She wore no cap at this late hour, and Mrs. Lovelace did set great store by her caps. She set great store by feather dusters, recipes for lifting stains, and medicinals for every occasion. Dylan had never met a woman so ferociously competent at domesticity, nor so ruthless in her warfare against dirt and disorder.

She brought the tea tray to the table and sat across from him, perched on the very edge of her chair. "The eggs might need salt."

Dylan portioned off a third of the omelet and set it on a saucer. "See for yourself. I cannot possibly finish this, and good food ought not to go to waste." He pushed the plate over to her, then added a triangle of toast. Challenging Mrs. Lovelace to bend a rule was always an intriguing exercise. She was not stupidly rigid, but rather, sensibly well organized.

Had she been running the campaign in Spain, Boney's generals would have been dusted straight back to France within a year.

She deigned to take up a fork. "I am a trifle hungry."

"And this assuredly does qualify as good food." Saved from plainness by the hint of smokiness from the ham and a tangy quality to the cheese. A peculiar thought crossed Dylan's mind. "Did you wait up for me?"

"Of course not, but on such a night, a caller or two at the back door would not be unexpected."

"This late?"

"Not usually, sir. The men would hesitate to disturb your household once the candles are out in the kitchen. Have you heard any more from your sisters about a London visit?"

That maladroit change of subject confirmed that Lydia Lovelace had waited up for him. Dylan was half pleased and half alarmed by such a possibility. In the alternative, perhaps she was plagued by nightmares about cobwebs in the attics.

God knew, Dylan had his share of bad dreams. "My sisters hint," he said, doing justice to his eggs. "They imply. They don't quite threaten."

"You will please inform me if that changes, sir. One wishes to be in readiness for every eventuality."

Mrs. Lovelace ate with the sort of dainty manners a midnight snack did not merit, but then, Mrs. Lovelace was not the typical housekeeper.

She was younger than the usual exponent of her trade and not half so substantial. In the better London domiciles, a housekeeper was a general whose influence was felt in orders followed and inspections passed. She did not ruin her knees scrubbing floors or throw out her back hauling baskets of wet laundry. The housekeeper typically had her own parlor, and from her headquarters, she deployed the maids and commandeered any unsupervised male employees.

The usual housekeeper was a staff officer, in other words, and seldom found herself in hand-to-hand combat with tarnished candlesticks or dusty carpets. Mrs. Lovelace, by contrast, led her troops by example, perhaps a necessity in a bachelor's modest quarters. Dylan had seen her in the garden laying into the hall runner with a carpet beater, dust flying everywhere.

Close and protracted observation led him to two conclusions regarding Lydia Lovelace. First, she got her hands literally dirty because she did not trust others to do the job right without her example. As an officer, she led the charge rather than hang back while others engaged directly with the enemy.

Second—this insight had come up on him only recently—she maintained a prodigious level of activity in hopes that her fine looks would go unnoticed.

She had lovely dark hair shot through with auburn highlights that became apparent only by candlelight. Her complexion would be the envy of any heiress. Her eyes were a gray green that changed hue with her moods and attire. When she spoke French, Dylan wanted to close his eyes and simply listen to her.

She poured them each a serving of tea and added a dollop of honey to Dylan's cup. "Do you mind about the cat, sir?"

Dylan glanced over at the basket on the hearth, only to find that the feline interloper had been joined by a second calico ball of fluff.

"Kittens, you mean?" Female kittens, which could only lead to courtship mayhem and progeny.

Mrs. Lovelace stirred her tea with inordinate care. "The pair of them were on the back stoop, Captain. I suspect one of your men brought them around. Nothing on this earth is as pathetic as a wet, bedraggled kitten unless it's two of them. They huddled together, and when I opened the door, they should have scampered off, but instead..."

"Instead?" To see the indomitable Lydia Lovelace reduced to explanations wasn't as gratifying as it should have been.

"They looked up at me, all fierce and hopeful, and when I stepped back, they darted into the kitchen. I could not turn them out, sir, but I will take them to the church if you insist."

Dylan sipped his tea, mostly to give himself time to consider options. Pets made little sense to him. Livestock had a place in the proper order of things. A well-trained dog could justify itself as a defense against housebreakers, and a personal mount merited appreciation, but cats...

He did not care for cats. They became too self-sufficient, when they finished being too darling and dear. Then they had kittens, made godawful noise, and left a stink about the stables. Children were probably less trouble than cats, not that Dylan would know.

"You would never allow mice on the premises, Mrs. Lovelace, and those two little wretches are months away from being able to defend the pantries."

She pushed aside her plate of eggs, half the food uneaten. Was she saving it for the cats?

"If you insist, sir, I will make other arrangements for the kittens."

Martyrs accepted their fates in such stoic tones. Dylan had sent men into battle and led them into near-certain death. If Mrs.

Lovelace thought he was incapable of turning out a pair of opportunistic little felines when London's alleys were awash in plump, tasty rodents, she had another—

A hard thumping commenced from the direction of the back door. Before the third thump, Dylan was on his feet, mentally reviewing weaponry—a knife in each boot, a third knife secured at the small of his back. His walking stick—mahogany, with a brass handle—sat next to the back door.

"Stay out of sight," he muttered. "That's an order, madam." He chose not to take up a carrying candle lest the *visitor* have warning when the door opened.

The pounding continued, slow and determined. Dylan palmed the knife out of his left boot and secreted his hand in the folds of his coat. He opened the door and stepped back into the shadows.

A sodden, shivering heap of humanity fell across the threshold. "Thank God. I'm s-s-sorry, Captain, but... th-th-thank God." Private Bowen Brook lay on his back, his features almost unrecognizable beneath blood and bruising. "Hadn't anywhere else t-to go. Sorry."

"Get him out of the wet," Mrs. Lovelace said. "We'll need to remove his clothes and get him warm as soon as may be. Use your knife if you have to."

"These are likely the only clothes he has, and I told you to stay out of sight." Dylan got Brook beneath the arms and dragged him back far enough that Mrs. Lovelace could close the door. "Lad, can you hear me?"

"Aye, sir. I'm right enow. Just got m' bell rung."

Bowen was slight, pale, and half lame, but like most career infantry, he was amazingly tough. Somebody had done much worse than ring his bell.

"What the hell tempted you onto the streets at such an hour?"

"Interrogate the poor man later," Mrs. Lovelace said, twisting the door lock. "He needs medical attention now."

Gone was the deference of the conscientious housekeeper. In her place stood the general Dylan had long suspected lurked beneath all those lacy caps.

"Best heed her, sir," Bowen said as Dylan hoisted the man to his feet. "I wouldn't want to get the business end of that poker, if I was you."

Mrs. Lovelace gave Dylan the same sort of look the orphaned kittens had likely given her—defiant, a little hopeful, quite fierce. She kept a steady grip on a heavy wrought-iron poker too.

Of all the confounded, purely female illogic... She had disobeyed a direct order, *thinking to come to his aid*. But then, an iron poker was a formidable weapon.

"Come along," Dylan said, securing an arm around Brook's skinny waist. "Mrs. Lovelace does not tolerate insubordination. To the kitchen with you, and you can make the acquaintance of her palace tigers. I'll fetch some brandy from the library, and we'll have you right as a trivet in no time."

Mrs. Lovelace braced Brook from the other side, and he was soon sitting at the kitchen table, the scent of wet wool perfuming the air.

"He'll need dry clothes, Captain," Mrs. Lovelace said, unbuttoning Brook's coat while he sat inert on the chair Dylan had vacated. "Dry socks, the whole lot. I'd run him a hot bath, but the water will take too long to heat. When you've fetched the brandy, please bring my medical box from the herbal."

Dylan had been given his orders, a curiously comforting reversal of roles. "Mrs. Lovelace, may I make known to you Mr. Bowen Brook, formerly of the 3rd Bicksford Regiment of Foot. I will return directly." He quick-marched for the steps, but paused before ascending. "The kittens can stay, Mrs. Lovelace. I cannot abide the thought of rodents trespassing on your pantry."

She shooed him off, but Dylan's artillery had hit its target. Mrs. Lydia Lovelace had, however faintly, smiled *at him*.

CHAPTER TWO

"I knew Captain Powell wouldn't turn me away," Mr. Brook said. "He's a good sort. Never was much for flogging."

Lydia's hands were steady as she dabbed gently at the blood on Mr. Brook's face. He was a young man, probably not much more than a boy when he'd taken the king's shilling. About the same age as Marcus would have been. Lydia's heart ached, to think of those young men and the many thousands of them who had never come home.

"Quiet for a moment," she said, pressing the cloth to Brook's abused lip. "The gash on your forehead might need stitches." His left eye had swollen closed, and a substantial contusion on his jaw was deepening from red to purple.

"Head wounds always bleed something awful, but they usually heal up well enough. Not like my pretty phiz was going to win me a footman's post."

This philosophical resignation was characteristic of the men—and occasional women—who called at the captain's back door. They lived a truncated existence, from one day to the next, one meal to the next, and larger concerns—appearance, politics, weather—mattered only in so far as they affected survival in the short term.

Was Marcus somewhere in London, his life similarly stunted by his military experience? "Hold this," Lydia said, wrapping Brook's chilly fingers around the cloth.

She made him a cup of tea laced with honey, because getting him warm and dry mattered almost as much as seeing to his wounds.

"It's not terribly hot," she said, setting the cup and saucer before him, "and you probably would rather have rum, but this will warm you up."

Brook passed her the bloody rag and tried to lift the tea cup, but his hand shook rather badly. "Sorry, missus. Battle nerves. I was always fine when Boney's men were firing, but then... I get the shakes. Captain said 'tweren't no matter. Better the shakes than to cast up your accounts like Horrocks did. Regular as taxes, Sergeant Horrible would lose his rations once the shooting stopped."

Lydia held the cup to Brook's lips, in part to stop his recitation. She was fascinated and appalled by the recollections Captain Powell's former associates offered at the oddest moments.

"Did you ever come across a Lieutenant Lord Tremont?" Lydia asked when Brook had drained the cup.

"Never served with Tremont, though my brother did for a time. I always took my orders from Captain Powell. Has a formidable temper, but he never turned it on the undeserving. Saved it for Boney and the generals. Was Tremont your sweetheart?"

Lydia's hands were steady, despite Brook being the first soldier to acknowledge Marcus had even served.

"His lordship is from my home shire. We attended the same congregation for years." Lydia's answer, while true, was not honest. She implied that her curiosity was of the small-talk variety, not that she was waiting desperately for Marcus to come home.

And had been waiting for years.

The distinctive tread of Captain Powell's boots on the stairs had Brook trying to stand.

"At ease," Powell snapped. "Bad enough you're bleeding on Mrs. Lovelace's linen. Bleed on her kitchen floor, and you will be drummed out of the regiment. How bad is the damage, madam?"

"Mr. Brook has a prodigious shiner, a split lip, and a messy gash. The rest appears to be mostly bruises, but I have not examined the patient thoroughly." Nor would she. Lydia was adept at dealing with cuts and scrapes, putrid sore throats, and bee-stings. She had no experience with more serious afflictions.

The captain set the brandy, medicinal box, and clothing on the table. "Take a careful, deep breath, Brook."

Brook complied. "Ribs feel fine, Captain. Got a few hard kicks to my shins once I lost my footing, but they weren't out to kill me."

"They meant to hurt you," Captain Powell said. "To let the whole world know that a former soldier down on his luck took a serious beating for the entertainment of the very people you risked your life to protect." He poured brandy into the empty tea cup. "Drink it all."

Brook looked like he hadn't had a decent meal in ages. His cheeks were gaunt. His clothing hadn't been washed in living memory and might not survive the ordeal. Down on his luck was a vast understatement.

Brook sampled the brandy, though his hand still shook slightly. "You got hold of some fine rations, Captain."

"Colonel Goddard has vineyards in France. He looks after my cellar. Drink, lad. Mrs. Lovelace and I aren't finished with you."

Colonel Goddard was a cousin to the captain. A quiet, decent sort who'd recently married a fancy cook. Another cousin—Alasdhair MacKay—had married a parson's daughter, and Captain Powell seemed genuinely happy for all concerned, or as happy as Dylan Powell ever was about anything.

Brook finished the rest of the brandy at one go.

Lydia took the glass from him. "If you plan to inebriate the poor man, he should eat something. His jaw might well be too tender for anything more than porridge by morning."

"Captain is steadyin' my nerves, missus," Brook said, "and I never had nothin' against a bowl of porridge."

Captain Powell dribbled some of the brandy onto a clean rag. "This will sting, but please recall you are in the presence of a lady." Without further ado, he laid the brandy-soaked linen against Brook's forehead.

"Piss and perdition, Captain."

Lydia had heard far worse, and she tried not to smile. Powell removed the cloth and blew on the wound. "Lip next."

Lydia collected the uneaten food from the table while Captain Powell, with all the patience of a devoted nanny, saw to Brook's various cuts and scrapes. Even the man's knuckles did not escape the captain's notice.

"Mrs. Lovelace," he said, corking the brandy bottle, "perhaps you could make up an extra cot in the footmen's dormitory while I get Brook into dry clothes?"

"Of course, sir. I'll start the fire in the laundry so Mr. Brook can have a hot bath in the morning."

"I'll see to the laundry. Just make up a bed, and don't skimp on the extra blankets."

Lydia made her way through the house that had become her temporary home. From one perspective, the captain was an easy man to work for. His demands were few—hot meals, clean sheets, an honest day's work for generous pay. He informed Lydia of his schedule, invariably approved of her menus, and never entertained.

As gentlemen bachelors went, he was a stranger to vice. From what Lydia had observed, he had no mistress and did not frequent the common nuisances tucked among the clubs of St. James's. He socialized little, mostly with his cousins, though he wasn't reclusive.

In appearance, Captain Powell was several marks short of dashing, being leaner than a properly muscled Corinthian, without clever repartee, and indifferent to fashion. He had nothing of the blond Adonis about him, but rather, was dark-haired, above average height, and blue-eyed. His complexion was weathered, and though his manners were above reproach, he was not a friendly man.

Any passion Dylan Powell had was directed toward looking after former soldiers in need of assistance, managing his family's holdings, and providing for various cousins, aunties, and siblings. Even in those undertakings, his demeanor remained detached, polite, and dutiful.

Lydia stacked two mattresses on one cot, tucked clean sheets around both, and laid not two but four blankets over the whole. She similarly doubled the pillows on the cot and made sure the pitcher on the bedside table was half full of water.

Simple comforts, but they would strike Mr. Brook as luxuries.

When she returned to the kitchen, Mr. Brook was wearing clean clothes, his wounds had been tended, and he was eating what appeared to be the leftover third of the omelet Lydia had made earlier.

"No loose teeth?" she asked.

"No, missus. 'Twasn't that sort of beating. Good eggs."

"What sort of beating was it?" Lydia's question prompted an exchange of looks between Captain Powell and his guest.

"A painful one," Brook said. "I'm not fast enough on me feet, and they knew that."

Another look passed between the two men, one portending more discussion when Lydia wasn't on hand, being female and therefore either untrustworthy or simple-minded. Femininity brought with it all manner of sad deficits in the opinion of those who'd never experienced it.

And, Lydia silently added, in the opinion of many who had. "Captain, will you show Mr. Brook where he is to sleep?"

"I will leave that to you, Mrs. Lovelace. I must go out."

Lydia did not particularly like her employer. She did, however, respect him. Captain Powell's devotion to poor soldiers was genuine and unrelenting. His cousins held him in high esteem, and then too, he'd allowed the kittens to stay.

Lydia had hoped the captain would not notice the cats until they were old enough to fend for themselves or to creditably prosecute the duties of domestic felines. Silly of her. Captain Powell noticed everything. He did not always remark on what he noticed, but he nonetheless perceived all of the goings-on in his household.

He'd allowed Lydia her kittens, though, and if she was to find Marcus, she needed her employer hale and sound.

"Why must you go out at such an hour, Captain?"

"To stretch my legs. Brook, I will expect a fuller report at breakfast."

Don't go. The same thing Lydia had said to Marcus when he'd made the decision to buy his colors. Now, she knew better than to attempt to reason with a grown man bent on his own aims.

"The rain is coming down in torrents," she said. "Do not track mud into my back hallway if you are so fortunate as to return in one piece."

Captain Powell bowed. "Perish the thought. Brook, you will heed Mrs. Lovelace's guidance as if her orders were signed by Wellington himself."

Brook gestured with his fork. "Aye, sir. Good hunting."

Lydia did not like the sound of that one bit. She followed the captain into the back hallway and took down his cloak.

"You are to exercise caution, Captain. No brawling in noisome alleys, no insulting any thugs you encounter in the gaming hells."

"How do you know I plan to frequent gaming hells and alleys?"

Lydia settled his cloak around his shoulders. "Your cousins worry about you." She passed him a top hat, not the one he wore to the clubs, the one he kept at the back door. "If Brook was set upon by miscreants, that misfortune did not befall him on the steps of Carlton House."

The captain fastened a few buttons. "I suspect this was not a casual beating, Mrs. Lovelace. You will lock up after me."

"I lock up every night." She shoved his walking stick at him. "Take this."

"I might need my hands free."

To use his almighty knives and fists. "Then you can drop it, but with a walking stick, you will look more like a gentleman coming home late from his club and less like a demon of the night searching for the bandit who stole his horse."

Lydia was not petite, but she was shortish. When Captain Powell tapped his hat onto his head in the darkened hallway, she felt positively Lilliputian beside him.

"Please be careful, sir."

"I'm only going on reconnaissance, Mrs. Lovelace. I spent years lurking in shadows and reconnoitering by moonlight. Stop fretting. Brook was out looking for his older brother, who has been missing for the past week. They have lost their lodgings because Brook on his own cannot pay the rent. I'm off to learn what I can about a disappearance, not to seek retribution for a beating."

He was off to do both, the wretched man. Lydia fired her heaviest artillery, a single shot of honesty. "I would miss you."

His brows rose. He touched a finger to his hat brim and then disappeared into the darkness. Lydia locked the back door and stood staring for a moment at the gloom.

Had he smiled at her? Something had made the dimple in his cheek flash. A pity the gloom had obscured the captain's features, for Lydia would have liked to have seen him smile, even if only the once.

"What in seven soaking hells has you out at this hour on such a night?" Orion Goddard posed the question quietly, though the kitchen staff at The Coventry Club would never gossip about the colonel's personal business.

Dylan, being cousin to said colonel, was permitted the privilege of using the club's staff entrance when he pleased to. He was not attired properly for the Coventry's elegant public rooms, and he also had no use for the idle and titled.

The Coventry did business as a supper club, though the gambling tables earned the club most of its revenue.

Dylan passed Orion his greatcoat. "Somebody beat the hell out of Bowen Brook, and William Brook is still missing."

"At least let me feed you." Orion hung Dylan's cloak on a peg and gestured to a table set against the kitchen's long window. By day, that window looked out on a small garden. By night, the open clerestory windows allowed for some ventilation in the kitchen.

An apprentice, who could not have been more than fourteen, put a plate before Dylan. Whipped potatoes had been sculpted into the shape of two doves cuddled next to each other. Sprigs of parsley had been fashioned into wings and peppercorns used for the eyes.

Beside the potato doves, thin strips of beef had been wound and curled into something resembling a rose, and another rose had been created from an arrangement of thinly sliced, roasted vegetables dusted with what Dylan's nose suggested were *herbes de Provence*. The plate itself was garnished with more parsley and greenery, creating an impression of a rose arbor for the cooing doves.

Dylan waited to speak until the girl had withdrawn. "I would have been content with a sandwich." Or an omelet served by a scolding housekeeper too softhearted to ignore bedraggled kittens.

"Ann says you need meat on your bones." Goddard accepted a second plate from the same apprentice. "Thank you, Hannah, and the doves are exquisite."

The girl beamed. "I've been working on 'em for weeks, Colonel. Missus Goddard says mine are almost too pretty for the club's buffet. I'm to start on partridges next."

She scampered off, apparently in transports over the prospect of potato partridges.

"One of your former urchins?" Dylan asked, taking up a fork and probing at the edges of his beef rose.

"Hannah is an apprentice to Ann now. Will Brook recover from the beating?" Goddard cut into his vegetable rose and speared a bite.

"He will, this time. He's lost his lodgings because his brother disappeared, and this mischief will likely mean he misses work tomorrow."

"And thus he loses his job. Can you send him to Wales?"

"Bowen claims Wales is too far. I've already sent everybody to Wales who was willing to go. Others have taken posts on MacKay's holdings in Scotland, but the Brook boys..." They weren't boys, and neither were they London born and bred, but Bowen and William were oddly reluctant to leave Town, despite the parlous existence it offered them.

Dylan wasn't in the mood for vegetables—he was seldom in the mood for vegetables—but couldn't quite fathom how to attack his beef.

"Are the brothers Brook your last two?" Goddard used his fork to unwind a strip of beef. For a big man, he had delicate manners. He also had a tender heart, which manifested in his determination that no orphan on London's streets should perish for want of a meal or a safe place to sleep.

A hopeless objective, if noble. "William and Bowen are the last two who came to grief because of Dunacre's stupidity, though I take an interest in any former soldier who needs aid. Bowen lost half a foot. William can barely use his right hand."

"Burns?"

"In William's case." Dylan managed to peel free a strip of beef when he wanted to simply take his knife to the culinary art that somebody had obviously wasted a lot of time creating.

"You still can barely stand to say his name." Goddard took a sip of claret. "Dunacre is dead, your men are all but situated, and the war is over. Go to Wales and marry some pretty lady with a fondness for skinny soldiers."

Goddard, happily married to his lady chef and happily employed managing the Coventry for his in-laws, had become an enthusiastic proponent of matrimony as the great cure-all. Alasdhair MacKay, a cousin who'd also served on the Peninsula, was even more recently converted to the blandishments of wedded bliss.

"I promised those men," Dylan said, trying for another bite of beef, "that if they survived Dunacre's ineptitude, I would see them settled. They would not march, sweat, and suffer just to have to beg for their bread if they made it home."

Many had not made it home. For them, Dylan could do nothing, though it was some comfort that Lieutenant Colonel Dunacre, the author of much misery, had been felled by a bullet at Waterloo.

"If you neglect your potatoes," Goddard said, "Hannah's feelings will be hurt. Ann says your sisters might march on London once the Season gets under way."

Dylan used his knife to slice into the vegetable whatever-it-was. "The ladies will try to see me married off. I want your word you will not abet them, and you will not allow Ann to abet them."

Goddard's smile was particularly fatuous. "Your grasp of a husband's authority lacks an acquaintance with reality, Powell. What is it about Bowen's mishap that bothers you?"

Everything. "He limps. He's scrawny. He's nearly destitute. Nothing was stolen, not his boots, not his miserable infantry coat. He was simply beaten for the hell of it."

"This is London."

"Precisely why I have labored long and hard to see the men set up elsewhere. London is expensive, the air foul, the streets worse than foul. Why beat a man who is no threat to anybody? Why beat a man who served honorably and paid a high price for his patriotism? London is full of drunks, lordlings, and fools. Why single out Bowen Brook, steal nothing, and leave him just sound enough to crawl to my door?"

Goddard popped a sprig of parsley into his mouth. "This was a random beating such as anybody traveling alone on London's streets might receive after dark. Dunacre is dead, and you have grown fanciful. Go home to Wales."

Not until the men were settled. Dylan had promised them that much, and they had relied on his promises. He'd also promised himself not to abandon his cousins until they were settled, which they appeared to be—blissfully so.

"Dunacre is dead," Dylan said slowly, "but where is Marcus, Lord Tremont?"

Goddard scowled at his wineglass, then took a sip and resumed demolishing his doves. "What brings him to mind? Tremont struck me as young, sentimental, and stupid."

"He was Dunacre's toady, but nobody seems to know what's become of him."

"At least try the wine. Fournier sent it over, and he does a fine job with the clarets. I fail to see a connection between a particularly inept young officer whose name apparently should have appeared on the casualty lists and some bad luck for Brook."

"Somebody has asked around at Horse Guards about Tremont. An inquiry by mail, supposedly from his family. Then William Brook disappears, and now Bowen has been beaten."

"Do you plan to eat those potatoes?"

Not while they were billing and cooing at each other. "No."

Goddard reached across the table to scoop the avian sculpture from Dylan's plate. "Good food should not go to waste, and you are sorely in need of a wife."

"Mrs. Lovelace takes adequate care of my domicile. Just because you and MacKay are awash in connubial joy doesn't mean marriage will yield the same result for me."

"If marriage merely stops you from sliding into bitterness and lunacy, I will account your union a success."

"You didn't serve under Dunacre." Alasdhair had for a time, and he'd had sense enough to accept the first transfer that had come along.

"You no longer do. You'd best recall that."

"If you hear of anything, if your urchins hear of anything, you will let me know?"

"I will ask them to keep a sharp eye out for William Brook. I draw the line at watching for Dunacre's ghost."

"As do I." Dylan saw that ghost in his dreams often enough that he need not hunt for shades while awake. "If the sisters come to Town, I will expect your support, Goddard."

"You will have it, and I'm sure Alasdhair and Dorcas will also aid your cause, provided you aren't occupying a private room at Bedlam by then."

Dylan sampled the claret and rose. "I served under Dunacre. A suite in hell would be a comfortable billet compared to that. My regards to your dear wife."

Goddard stood, his gaze full of consternation. "You ate practically nothing. My dear wife will be equal parts offended and concerned."

Goddard's dear wife was running the entire kitchen, which even at this late hour was a barely controlled riot of food preparation.

"The food is too pretty to eat. I'll bid you good night."

"You could stay here," Goddard said. "Or take a bunk at my house. You don't have to march across London at this hour in this weather."

Dylan thought of Brook, aching and bruised as he spent the night on a footman's cot, and he thought of Lydia Lovelace, warning him not to track mud into her back hallway.

"I want to properly question Brook over breakfast, and the walk home will give me time to think."

"Time to brood. Welshmen are the worst for brooding."

"Don't let MacKay hear you say that. He prides himself on his brooding." Or he had before marrying his Dorcas.

Dylan let himself out into the alley that ran behind the Coventry and slogged home through a cold, mizzling rain. He was careful to wipe his feet before he presumed to set a boot upon the floor of Mrs. Lovelace's back hallway, and he resisted the urge to pet the sleeping kittens nestled in their basket on the hearth.

He made his way to bed, already rehearsing the questions he'd put to Brook in the morning, but in the morning, Bowen Brook was nowhere to be seen.

CHAPTER THREE

"Caroline, good day." The Honorable Reginald Glover offered his sister-in-law a nod. Caroline, Countess of Tremont, was one of few women he knew who looked good in half mourning. Pearl gray, lilac, ivory, and violet emphasized magnificent blue eyes and a luminous complexion, though Caroline was well past forty.

A pity she was so venerable, but then, English law did not permit a man to marry his brother's widow. Caroline's faultlessly ladylike demeanor precluded anything so coarse as frolicking for comfort, and she would not remarry until her termagant daughter had found a spouse.

Which, if Reginald had anything to say to it, dear Lydia would shortly do.

"Please have a seat," Reginald said, rising from behind his desk and coming around to gesture Caroline to the wing chair by the fire. "How have you occupied yourself since breakfast?"

Caroline graced him with a smile when she'd settled on the cushion, and all over again, Reginald grasped why his dashing older brother had been smitten. John's widow was, and probably always would be, purely lovely. She moved, spoke, gestured, and even laughed with a sense of poise at once refined and natural. Heads still turned when she walked into a room, and men of all ages grew wistful watching her dance.

She had been an Incomparable, but more than her beauty, her self-possession meant something of that former glory still clung to her.

"I met with Mrs. Bloom regarding the spring fete," Caroline replied. "The weather is always a chancy element, but we will hope for the best and assume the worst. I've also directed Mr. Mortimer to begin moving the hardier plants out of the conservatory. The front terrace looks too dreary without its appointments, and spring is advancing."

She had met with the vicar's wife, and she had conferred with the head gardener. Reginald knew that much to be true, because he knew everything Caroline got up to. She'd also spent two hours tending to correspondence, but not a one of those letters had been sent to her own daughter.

Lydia had left to visit her aunt Chloe prior to the Yuletide holidays, and Reginald was increasingly uneasy about her absence. The girl was not to be trusted, and Chloe's loyalty was to her younger sister and her niece.

"What do we hear from our Lydia?" Reginald asked.

"Precious little. She must be quite enjoying her stay with Chloe, and Chloe is apparently reveling in the role of doting auntie." Caroline smiled at her lovely hands. She still wore John's ring and often wore a mourning brooch that held a lock of John's hair.

An earl's heir would not normally make a love match, but Caroline was an earl's niece, and her settlements had gone a long way toward restoring the Glover family finances. She'd fulfilled any number of requirements with the ease and grace so typical of her, though she had not managed to produce a spare.

Such a pity, that.

"Don't you think it time Lydia returned home?" Reginald asked, taking the second wing chair. "She is your companion in all but name, and without her on hand, you are left to serve as hostess, lady of the house, and general domestic factotum. I worry about overburdening you, my dear."

"Lydia deserves some time away. I miss her terribly, but to know she's happy assuages that ache. Tremont is my home, and I delight in caring for it."

Gracious, selfless, generous... Caroline truly was the lady of the manor, which made Reginald want to shake her—or kiss her. Something to destroy the poise she wore like a bishop's stole. Her daughter had run off to an auntie's house, her son the great war hero was missing at best, and yet, she glided through her days as if village fetes and potted salvia were the summit of her ambitions.

She was enough to drive a conscientious brother-in-law to drink. "I will write to Lydia," Reginald said. "I will remind her of her duty and of all the responsibilities warmer weather will bring. We'll have her back where she belongs, by your side."

Back where Reginald could keep an eye on the girl. Every fine quality Caroline possessed—her quiet, her poise, her warmheartedness—had run amok in the daughter. Lydia was secretive rather than merely quiet. Poise in her had become an indefinable distance from her family, and while she could hardly be called warmhearted, she was exceedingly familiar with the staff and tenants.

Whereas Caroline was classic beauty gracefully matured, Lydia was a dark-haired, gimlet-eyed bluestocking who moved through life with about as much grace as a bullock who'd seen oats dumped into the trough across the barnyard.

And yet, Lydia was fiercely loyal to her mother, which was why this protracted absence to visit an auntie in Oxford made little sense.

Reginald liked good wine, naughty women, and for things—especially the women in his family—to make sense.

"Write to her," Caroline said, turning that smile on Reginald. "She might be shocked enough that you get a reply."

"Wesley misses her." Reginald infused that observation with a bit of grudging admission. "My son would never say anything to me, of course, but he takes Lydia's mare out for the occasional hack, and he sorts through the mail not a quarter hour after it arrives."

"Lydia probably asked him to look after Demeter. The mare is too much horse for me, and Wesley and Lydia are friends, a not-unheard-of situation between cousins."

"And that is precisely why I asked you to spare me a few moments of your time, Caroline. We must face facts. Marcus has not come home, Horse Guards has no idea what has become of him, and I will soon be applying to have him declared dead. I thought you should hear this news from me."

Caroline rose and went to the window, not a gasp or glance gave away what a blow that news must be to her.

"You are in a difficult position, I know, Reginald. Even the most faithful steward cannot take certain steps on his own initiative. Marcus's absence limits your ability to manage Tremont as you see fit. Nonetheless, Marcus has not yet been missing for seven years. Tremont isn't going anywhere, and we're getting by well enough for now."

No, they were not. Tremont was a complicated balancing act, with tremendous value on one hand and tremendous expenses on the other. What was lacking was *revenue*, income generated from all the acres, leaseholds, tenancies, and other property.

Wesley had seen the problem the first time Reginald had shown him the books. The boy would make a fine earl, should that day ever come.

John, Caroline's late husband and Reginald's older brother, had known how to make all the parts of the earldom work together. Times had changed, alas. Rents had fallen, the war had ended, and Reginald was not a magician. If he was to sell off a few parcels of land here and there, he needed for John's son to be declared well and truly dead.

And who was to say Marcus wasn't dead? War was a nasty business, particularly for a dreamy boy who'd never killed so much as a pheasant before buying his colors.

"The problem," Reginald said, getting to his feet, "is the 'for now' part. I might be muddling along adequately with Marcus's power of attorney, but one bad harvest, one boundary dispute with a neighbor, and Tremont will be imperiled." Wesley had seen that too. "Legal machinations take years to resolve, even without opposition, and by the time some judge hears the case, I might well have joined Marcus in the celestial realm. I owe it to Wesley to resolve the matter if I can."

Caroline made a lovely picture by the window. "Marcus is not dead." She spoke quite firmly, for her. "I would feel it if my only son were gone."

"He never resigned his commission, Caroline, nor is there any record of him arriving in London. You say he's alive, and yet, where is he?"

"I know not, but if Lydia were here, she would have a half-dozen arguments for why this step on your part is premature."

Wesley had pointed out the benefit of starting the legal maneuvers in Lydia's absence, though they were expensive maneuvers. For a young man, Wesley was shrewd.

"Lydia will doubtless ring a peal over my head," Reginald said, going to the sideboard to pour himself a finger of brandy, despite the early hour. "Wesley knew you would believe I am being hasty. He holds out hope that his cousin was captured by Corsairs or stricken with a loss of memory. I applaud my son's optimism, but I must be more practical. Care for a brandy? I know this is unwelcome news."

"No spirits, thank you," Caroline said, turning from the window. "I'd best write to Lydia of this development. I esteem you greatly, Reginald, but on this matter, we must agree to disagree. Perhaps word of your decision will bring Lydia home."

The brandy was balm to a parched man's soul. "Wesley would be pleased to have her back where she belongs. I do believe absence has made the heart grow not fonder—Wesley has always been fond of Lydia—but perhaps more determined."

Caroline wrinkled her nose. "John did not approve of cousins marrying."

John was dead. Had been for years. Rest in peace and all that. "We are not the House of Hanover, to intermarry in successive generations, Caroline, and Lydia is not a blushing flower, to attract the notice of every bachelor with a title. Wesley appreciates her, and she likes him."

This was, oddly enough, the truth. Wesley found Lydia's eccentricities charming, or charming enough that, to get his hands on her settlements, he'd cheerfully tolerate her outspokenness and lack of grace. Lydia appeared to like Wesley as well, but then, why shouldn't she?

He was dashing, witty, wellborn, and well liked. If blond good looks, broad shoulders, and bon mots could win a woman's heart, then Lydia should by rights already be Wesley's wife. Then too, if Lydia married Wesley, she'd never have to leave the only home she'd known. Somebody had to benefit from those fat settlement funds. Why on earth would the girl complain that the somebody would be her own cousin?

Though Lydia would find fault with the scheme, of a certainty. She was that most vexatious of tribulations, the discontented female.

"Please do not encourage a match between our children, Reginald," Caroline said, starting for the door. "Wesley will do everything in his power to bring a marriage about if he thinks the notion would make you happy."

"More to the point, Caroline, I believe marriage to Wesley will make *Lydia* happy. You are trying to honor John's wishes, which I respect, but perhaps you should think of your daughter in this one instance. Then too, if I discourage the match, Wesley will take it into his head that Lydia is his one true love. We'll have nothing but drama, heartfelt sighs, and tense meals until Wesley talks Lydia into eloping."

"I will write to my daughter, and I will not support a match between her and Wesley."

Reginald saluted with his brandy. "We will agree to disagree, then, to use your words. Please give Lydia my love when you write to her."

Caroline sent him a fulminating look, one that made her resemble her headstrong daughter, and withdrew.

"You can open the door," Reginald called when her ladyship had been gone a good two minutes. "I think the whole business went rather well."

Wesley sauntered into the study from the library. The door between the two rooms was a panel, barely distinguishable from its neighbors.

"As do I," Wesley said, helping himself to a brandy. "Auntie Caroline will be so busy fretting over my marital aspirations that she'll forget we're having Marcus declared dead." He touched his glass to Reginald's. "I hear wedding bells already."

"As much as I detest the thought of having Lydia underfoot here again, you cannot marry her unless she deigns to return from Chloe's. I want you to retrieve your cousin, Wesley. The sooner the better."

Wesley finished his drink, poured himself another, and considerately topped up Reginald's as well.

"You don't understand Lydia at all, Papa. If I want her to come home, then I look in on her on my way to London. I intimate that we're all doing swimmingly well without her, and Auntie Caroline has begun to ride out with Mr. Roxbury more days than not. Roxbury is a philandering buffoon. Liddie will be back here faster than you can say 'long live the king.'"

"Then do that," Reginald replied. "Charm her, lie to her, press your attentions upon her, but do what you have to do such that your suit progresses swiftly."

Wesley set his empty glass on the mantel. "I have a suit now. Fast work, even for me, though I suppose needs must when the duns are circling. I will write to Liddie and let her know that she's on my itinerary. I can't promise you a grandson by this time next year, but—after I drop in on Tommy Hardwick and pay my respects to the fair

Miss Renfrew—I will look in on Lydia and suggest we'd make tolerable marital allies."

Wesley bowed and sauntered out, while Reginald collected the dirty glass from the mantel. As a father, Reginald was delighted that the boy had so much savoir faire, so much self-possession. Viewed objectively, though, Wesley was a bit too calculating, even when contemplating marriage to a cousin he supposedly liked.

Though, honestly, how could anybody like Lady Lydia Glover? The notion was almost amusing.

In Lydia's opinion, housekeeping had many fine qualities as a source of employment.

One's labor bore immediate and useful results.

A clean house had a certain freshness. The air was more breathable, the light more in evidence. Conscientious housekeeping meant beeswax and lemon oil, fresh flowers, and scented sachets subdued London's pervasive coal-smoke stink.

A clean house was safer than its neglected counterpart, between good lighting, conscientiously trimmed wicks, and proper ventilation.

A clean house required hard, hard work, which meant every night, Lydia dropped off to sleep rather than fret away the dark hours with worries and what-ifs.

Thanks to that hard work, windows, sconces, and mirrors gleamed, though Lydia was still surprised every time she caught sight of herself in a looking glass. When had she become so severe and serious?

Much to her consternation, housekeeping gave her more freedom than she'd ever enjoyed previously. She came and went from Captain Powell's household as she pleased. She ate meals she enjoyed and ate them when she was hungry, not when the kitchen rang the bell. She wore comfortable clothing rather than expensive creations intended to exhibit more of her flesh than she preferred.

She decided whether to start the day with polishing silver, dusting, or a trip to market, and *she* decided if and how to spend her wages.

All those delicious decisions, and yards and acres of privacy to go with them. No lady's maid snooping through her correspondence, no footmen or chambermaids reporting her whereabouts at every hour. No grooms trailing four yards behind everywhere she rode—not that she'd been on horseback since coming to London.

Best of all, no half-soused uncle making constant references to Marcus's absence or Lydia's advancing age. No interminable political dinners watching Mama play the gracious hostess, knowing all the while that political dinners gave Mama megrims.

"Good morning, Mrs. Lovelace." Captain Powell, still in his riding attire, strode into the breakfast parlor. "It's menu day, if I'm not mistaken."

He'd caught her without her cap—again—which explained the smile lurking in his eyes. Fortunately, the sideboard was in readiness for his morning sortie.

"You're up early, sir."

"The days are getting longer, so the sun is up earlier, and a proper London gentleman hacks out at dawn. Please do have a seat, and let me fix you a plate. Where has our patient got off to?"

Lydia and her employer played a game, which she always won. She wasn't sure what, precisely, the captain sought to prove by offering her one courtesy after another, but he was nothing if not tenacious. She invariably refused his mannerly overtures, because housekeepers were not due anything other than civility, and he allowed her to refuse.

Perhaps that was the point. She *enjoyed* rebuffing him, and as watchful as he was, he might sense that. She *enjoyed* scolding him for midnight raids on the kitchen and for the merest scrape of mud on her floors.

"I ate in the kitchen, sir. A cup of tea will do. As for Mr. Brook, he ate in the kitchen as well and mentioned something about going in search of his brother. I asked him to report his findings to you before nightfall and made sure he had two meat pasties and some shortbread to take with him."

Captain Powell held the chair to the right of the head of the table. Lydia permitted him that much, because she'd made her point by refusing to share breakfast with him. His eyes, a startling blue amid slightly weathered features, nonetheless bore a hint of mischief as she took her seat.

She would not have seen that mischief when she'd first taken her post, but she was learning the terrain, and for all his seriousness, her employer did have a sense of humor.

"We have more to discuss than menus," Captain Powell said, taking the place at the head of the table. "I am maneuvering my cannon in place for when the sororal regiment arrives."

This again. Perhaps, despite his unshakable outward calm, the prospect of a visit from family worried the captain.

"The guest rooms are always kept in readiness, sir." Lydia did not look forward to the prospect of visitors, particularly not the young ladies. Ladies knew things. They knew of young earls gone missing, and they would know if the young earl's sister was rumored to have disappeared from the family seat. Then too, the captain, for all his stoicism in the face of battle, apparently did not look forward to hosting his siblings.

He would not complain, of course, but his gaze became bleak when he read the many letters penned by his sisters.

"I would never criticize your efforts, Mrs. Lovelace, but my sisters are not the sort to limit themselves to sniffing the wardrobes. They will be in the attics. They will examine the potted spices growing on the back stoop and pop out to the mews to interrogate my groom. They will be hopelessly disrespectful of my privacy, not only to ensure you are taking good care of me, but also because they are afflicted with curious natures generally."

As was Lydia. "*Am* I taking good care of you, Captain?"

He poured them each a cup of tea, good, strong China black,

exactly as Lydia preferred it. "Fishing for a compliment, Mrs. Lovelace?"

Lydia fixed her own tea, adding a dollop of cream—the captain preferred cream at breakfast—and a half teaspoon of honey.

"You never complain about my work," she said. "An absence of complaints doesn't mean an absence of reasons to complain." And she needed this post for the foreseeable future, because she needed him.

The captain dealt with his own tea, and Lydia realized he would not take his meal while she had only a cup of tea. The overt victories were hers in the battle to maintain proper boundaries, but he managed to subtly gain territory too.

"You do an excellent job, but I don't dare compliment you," he said, letting the honey drizzle into his tea in a golden skein. "If I thank you for the fresh flowers in my study, you rebuke me by telling me how cheaply you bought them. If I mention that I delight to walk into my bedroom and find that even the bed hangings have been washed, you explain that hangings should be washed quarterly. You are never pleased to hear my compliments, thus I hesitate to commend you in my dispatches."

He took a sip of his tea, and the quiet in the parlor was disturbed by the mad chirping of some lovesick robin.

"I am not accustomed to flattery, Captain."

"I do not flatter, I compliment. If you had spent four years living in leaky tents, marching on bad rations, and alternately shivering and sweltering, you would grasp how precious domestic comforts can be."

To think of Marcus in those conditions, quiet, sweet Marcus... He would not have coped well.

Lydia took out the little notebook and pencil she carried with her everywhere. "What was the worst of it?" she asked, laying the paper and pencil on the tablecloth. "The sweltering or the shivering? The bad rations or the leaky tent?"

"The worst of it was the utterly stupid loss of life. The brewer's sons and housemaid's brothers cut down in battle, lost to disease, or felled by the heat. After twenty years of slaughter, we're right back where we started, with France ruled by a monarch and Britain sunk perilously in debt despite all of Bottomless Pitt's taxes. The only differences are that half of France is starving, and London is awash in former soldiers with no jobs to support them."

Captain Powell cared about those former soldiers, for which Lydia should have adored him. Despite his manners and flashes of dry wit, Powell kept a distance, a reserve, that Lydia found both reassuring and disturbing.

Dylan Powell would never trifle with the help, would never steal from a niece's dowry. Lydia had seen his correspondence and handled his laundry. He never came home late at night reeking of cheap perfume—or expensive perfume. His bills were paid on time and to the penny. He gambled rarely, if at all. Lydia saw the contents of his pockets, tossed casually onto a vanity tray. No markers or IOUs were among the detritus of his evenings.

He could play the gentleman convincingly—his family had means, and his manners were exquisite—but he reserved the majority of his energy for the discarded soldiers and their families.

"We are awash in widows and orphans as well, Captain, and though the wars are over, the government still feels entitled to toss the citizenry in jail for expressing honest opinions."

A housekeeper knew that in a way an earl's sister never could. Here in London, Lydia had enjoyed the occasional lady's pint with the senior housemaid and first footman, and the grumblings in the tavern both fascinated and appalled her.

The ale was surprisingly good too.

"Tossing folk in jail is a venerable British tradition," the captain replied, going to the sideboard and filling a plate. "Talk to me of roasts and hams and *haricots verts*, Mrs. Lovelace. I do so adore to hear you speak French."

While she ate the ham, eggs, and toast the captain served her, Lydia prattled on about green beans, soups, and desserts, and all the while, the captain listened politely and did justice to his own plate.

"And for the callers at the back door?" he asked.

"Buttered bread, cheese, ham, and baked potatoes. I thought apple tarts with walnuts would do for a sweet."

"Just hearing you speak makes me hungry," he said, draining his tea cup and refilling it. "You and Ann Goddard could probably wax lyrical about your recipes. You believe my house is ready for guests?"

"I do. I will prepare another set of menus, in case your family arrives unannounced. We can review them tomorrow, if that suits."

The menus were a formality, but one Lydia insisted on. Not only did she enjoy knowing the captain's preferences at table, she liked sitting down with him for a weekly cup of tea—though she would never admit as much to him.

Dylan Powell still had the lean, whipcord toughness of the marching soldier. Lydia had seen him out in the mews, shirt off, a horse's muddy foot resting against his thigh. He'd been muttering in his native tongue, doubtless cursing sprung horseshoes, London streets, and foolish beasts.

A prodigious pink scar ran from one shoulder down across his back, like a sash emblazoned on his skin. He was slender through the middle and through the hips, but his scarred shoulders were formidably broad and muscular. Those qualities, combined with his height and a demeanor that shaded from quiet to silent, made him an intriguing specimen.

She liked looking at him, which was very bad of her. His features were a little too worn to be handsome, his nose a trifle beaky. His hair was plain brown with a hint of curl. The feature she enjoyed most, though, was his voice.

No accent on earth could compare for sheer euphony to a Welshman speaking English. The music of his native language came through, infusing angular Anglo-Saxon words with a lilt that added both subtlety and beauty.

"I love my sisters," the captain said, topping up Lydia's tea cup. "But they will require a great deal of time and attention, and I am not inclined..."

Dylan Powell lost for words was vaguely alarming. "Captain?"

His characteristic reserve slipped for a moment, revealing profound exasperation. "Nobody has seen William Brook for a fortnight. He drinks too much, he's not in good weight, and his landlady demands payment by the week, so he's lost his lodgings and rendered Bowen homeless. William is half deaf from his years with the artillery, and thus he can't hear trouble walking right up behind him. One hand is nearly useless. When I could be out looking for him, I'll instead be mincing through a damned quadrille and discussing the weather. Pardon my language."

"I will ask among the back-door callers. Perhaps William Brook is away to the countryside, thinking to find work at planting." Lydia was learning how to question those men and the occasional woman who came around in need of a meal. Food first, inquiries only as an occasional afterthought, and never ask the same questions of the same person twice.

"Planting is still weeks away, though I thank you for the thought. You are kind, Mrs. Lovelace, though you hide it well. What shall we name our pantry mousers?"

Lydia was not kind. She was desperate to find Marcus, and thus she'd taken employment with the officer most familiar with the former soldiers now cast upon London's streets.

"I had not thought to name the kittens." Guinevere and Mab came to mind—queens and legends.

"Yes, you have. You will inform me of your choices when it suits you to do so. I have another topic to discuss with you, and it wants some delicacy."

If Captain Powell was attempting delicacy, the matter was dire. "Plain speaking will always suit me better than innuendo and euphemisms, sir."

"One has suspected this about you, but one doesn't want to give offense."

One? Now he was a diplomat. "Out with it, sir. I have work to do, and you are intent on finding your prodigal soldier." The captain's plate was empty, as was his tea cup. He'd put off this difficult topic as long as he could.

"For the duration of my sisters' visit, I would appreciate it if you could... That is to say, if you'd be willing to... make a pretense, shall we say, of appearing somewhat..."

A confused bird fluttered against the window, then flitted away.

"Sir?"

"I need to take evasive action, Mrs. Lovelace. To create a ruse, a distraction, such that my sisters cannot steal a march on me when I have much on my mind."

The captain always had much on his mind. "What is it that you'd ask of me?"

He left off gazing out the window and turned a serious expression —more serious than usual—on Lydia. The full brunt of that grave, blue-eyed inspection was somewhat unnerving.

"Mrs. Lovelace, when my sisters are underfoot, might you manu-facture a few superficial indications that you are... fond of me?"

"I am fond of you." Lydia had no idea why those words, of all the words she mentally recited, should leap the parapet of her good sense and fling themselves into audible speech. She did not know the captain well, she did not particularly like him, she did not...

Oh bother. Her words were the truth, and if the captain's measured inspection was unnerving, his unrestrained smile was posi-tively devastating.

CHAPTER FOUR

"You are *fond* of me?" Dylan posed the question as if he'd perhaps not heard the lady aright, which was entirely possible. But then, Mrs. Lovelace's admission had made her blush, and a more charming sight than a flustered Lydia Lovelace did not exist in the mortal sphere.

"I esteem you, Captain. You are conscientious toward your former men and toward your family. Your expectations of your employees are reasonable, and you pay well."

Madam House General was in full retreat, though it was an orderly retreat. That Lydia Lovelace *could* blush was a revelation in itself. "You said you were *fond* of me."

Blushing or not, she could still produce a formidable glower. "Less fond by the moment. Explain this favor you seek from me."

"I do seek a favor of you, you are correct." Dylan seized upon the term with some relief. Mrs. Lovelace was softhearted. She would ignore a direct order if it offended her, but she'd render aid to a shivering, bedraggled bachelor if he asked humbly enough. "The ruse is for the benefit of my sisters."

"The ones with curious natures."

Nosy, prying, headstrong... but not stupid. Dylan's sisters were alarmingly perceptive. "Precisely. I hazard a guess they are coming to Town to find me a wife. I have nothing against the institution of marriage in theory, but no wish to take a wife at this time."

"You don't want a wife of their choosing foisted off on you."

Had somebody foisted a husband on Mrs. Lovelace? House-keepers were addressed as if they were married women, but they were, in fact, not usually married.

"I don't want *any* wife foisted off on me, nor do I seek to be foisted off on any unsuspecting lady. My sisters are convinced that I will come home only after I've taken a wife, but that has nothing to do with it."

"You simply don't care for the country?"

Dylan waited to answer Mrs. Lovelace's question until after the kitchen maid had put a fresh teapot on the table and taken the empty one away.

"I don't particularly care for life in Town," Dylan said, "but I promised a contingent of my men I would see them all securely estab-lished in civilian life. That project is almost complete, and when it is, I will return to Wales and the pleasures of country life."

The beauty, the peace, the old friendships, the satisfaction of hard work, the joy of seeing an estate prosper as a result. Dylan dreamed of home nearly every night and dreaded the waking moment when the dream faded.

Mrs. Lovelace poured them each a fresh cup of steaming tea. "You want me to convince your sisters that you are *involved* with me. I sympathize with your plight, Captain, but not even for the preserva-tion of your bachelorhood will I intimate that I've compromised myself with my employer. A lady's good name is her most precious asset and, once squandered, can never be retrieved."

She recited that last bit with prim conviction, as if reading a sampler, then she added just the right amount of cream to Dylan's tea.

"That's the crux of the matter," Dylan said, momentarily distracted by the grace with which Mrs. Lovelace managed the tea service. "I must appear to be pining from afar, to be alternately contemplating then discarding the notion of an unusual match. You need not do much of anything save tolerate my performance."

"I would be considered a bad match for you." Mrs. Lovelace stirred honey into her tea. "Some would say a disastrous match. Former officers do not marry their housekeepers."

"They do, actually, if that former officer is not titled or particularly well placed. I am gentry, albeit comfortable gentry, and Welsh. Welshmen are expected to take odd notions. Then too, I want to create merely a suspicion of tender regard between us."

Mrs. Lovelace sipped her tea, and that she hadn't dumped Dylan's tea over his head or laughed him to scorn was most encouraging. But then, she was *fond* of him. She would not lie about that, or about much of anything.

"Your objective," she said, "is for your sisters to think they have divined a secret you are almost keeping from yourself, that you pine for me at the same time you try to ignore the inclinations of your heart. If they think they have stumbled upon such an insight, an unlikely romance waiting to blossom, they will shove us together."

Dylan could not have summarized the strategy more succinctly himself. "Do you have sisters?"

"I have a mother. A devoted and dear mother."

Was an aging mama Mrs. Lovelace's entire family? Dylan did not like to think of Lydia so alone in the world, but a dearth of caring family might account for her indomitable attitude.

Also for her kindness toward lame soldiers and stray kittens.

"If this budding attraction is my sisters' idea," Dylan said, "then they will see it as a brilliant stroke against the dictates of foolish conventions. If I were simply to announce that I had decided to marry my housekeeper, they would mutter without end about my having ruined their own marital prospects."

"Will it?" Mrs. Lovelace asked. "If I'm caught gazing at you with unrequited longing, and our hands brush, and all that other foolish whatnot, will that start the sort of talk that could affect your sisters?"

"Who will talk? My staff is loyal, as are, in their way, my sisters. I am not suggesting you stand up with me three times in succession at Almack's." Though Dylan would like to see his housekeeper turned out in some elegant French creation, giving polite society the sort of looks she reserved for dusty mantels and tarnished mirrors.

While turning on him the same looks she'd given those dratted kittens and not the pensive frown she was treating him to now.

"Show me your best worship-from-afar, brooding-bachelor look, Captain. Make it convincing, or this strategy of yours is more doomed than any romance ever could be. Pretend you are fond of me."

She arched an eyebrow, and Dylan was reminded of the pervasive terror of a parade inspection. A missing button would see a man shamed, a weapon out of place could see him flogged.

A fatuous gaze would not do for Mrs. Lovelace, she was right about that. Dylan had to give her something convincing, but mere desire would be an insult. Besides, desire hadn't much plagued him in recent years, another matter to be pondered when he was once again gazing upon the magnificence of the Welsh hills.

What he felt for Lydia Lovelace was certainly respectful, also a little awed. She was formidable and distant, like those gorgeous, magical hills. She held herself aloof by means of her personal dignity, and her caps, and her devotion to some list of duties only she knew. Dylan seized on that sense of distance, of unbridgeable separation, and let her see a hint of his longing to return to Wales, of his weariness.

She returned his regard steadily, and something in her eyes answered him, something hopeful but weary. Dylan had the thought that they were both *lonely*—God above, was he lonely—and so he turned his mind to a wish for her, that her loneliness might find comfort, that someday her list would include a few kisses and smiles, or at least a fond glance and a hug or two.

The silence in the breakfast parlor became laden with odd currents, and some idiot bird thumped again against the windowpanes.

"That will do," Mrs. Lovelace said, though softly, with none of her characteristic starch. "You bring to the exercise a convincing subtlety I had not anticipated."

Did she think he'd take to reciting maudlin poetry beneath her window? "I will be very subtle, the better to be very convincing. Once my sisters realize I am already in contemplation of a union with you, they will content themselves with shopping and terrorizing the eligibles."

"They are well dowered?" Mrs. Lovelace asked. "In my experience, if a lady's settlements are ample, she is beset by the eligibles and fortune hunters alike."

And when had a housekeeper occasion to learn such a thing? Dylan made a note to look over the references the employment agency had provided for Mrs. Lovelace.

"My sisters are not heiresses, but their portions are generous. What is your favorite flower, Mrs. Lovelace?"

"Irises. The scent is delicate, and they don't last long, but they are impressive."

"What do they symbolize?" A devoted swain would know this, while Dylan hadn't a clue.

"Valor and wisdom. What is your favorite flower, sir?"

He hadn't one, but needs must... "Roses?"

"Trite."

Exceedingly. Even a mostly-for-show interest in Mrs. Lovelace deserved a better effort than that. "Daffodils?" Wales was full of them, and they were dauntless, rather like Mrs. Lovelace.

"Chivalry and new beginnings. That suits you. If you will excuse me, I will see about preparing some menus suitable for when we have guests. Good luck finding William Brook. I have cleaned out the governess's room for Bowen. He strikes me as capable of serving in the capacity of house steward."

Interesting suggestion. Bowen, having been transferred to the quartermaster's ranks after his injury, might well prove useful at dealing with ledgers, wage books, and invoices. Dylan rose, because

Mrs. Lovelace was on her feet, and too quickly for him to have held her chair for her.

Who had started that game, and what purpose did it serve? "If we are to be convincingly smitten, Mrs. Lovelace, you must allow me to show you minor courtesies."

"We are not to be convincingly smitten until your sisters arrive, and then we are to be only subtly smitten. Good day, sir."

She curtseyed, Dylan bowed, and then she was off about her appointed rounds. Dylan sat and appropriated her unfinished cup of tea.

Mrs. Lovelace was willing to support his efforts to preserve his bachelorhood. She cheerfully dealt with all the back-door callers and had seen a useful place in the household for Bowen Brook, a post that Dylan would never have thought to offer.

The tea was good and still hot, though Mrs. Lovelace used a light hand with the cream and honey. Dylan sipped Mrs. Lovelace's tea and pondered their exchange until he'd reached and examined a conclusion that appeared to fit the available facts.

Mrs. Lovelace was an *ally*, a partner of sorts, willing to exert herself on behalf of Dylan's causes. *That* was what she'd meant when she'd said she was fond of him. Part of Dylan was wary of such a conclusion, for allies could turn into enemies, but another part of him —the lonely part—was pleased.

Inordinately pleased. For who would not want to have Lydia Lovelace as an ally?

"How do you go about finding a brother missing in London?" Lydia posed the question to Bowen in the quiet hour after supper. The junior staff had decamped for darts night at the local pub, leaving Lydia and the new house steward to a peaceful evening in her sitting room. Captain Powell's dwelling had no servants' hall, so Lydia left her sitting room door open until she retired for the night.

Bowen could not be much above five-and-twenty, but his hair was already more gray than brown, and he had an older man's habit of pausing before he spoke. His manner was quietly cheerful, though he walked with a slight limp that appeared to pain him.

"If a man wants to disappear in London," Bowen said, taking a battered flask from a breast pocket, "you don't find him. Not if he dunna want to be found. I've looked everywhere I know to look and then some, and William hasn't been seen in days."

Press gangs no longer roamed port cities, but gangs of another sort did. "Do you fear he's come to harm?" Lydia certainly feared for Marcus.

"Will's a canny sort. He'd charm his way out of most troublin' situations. He's gone off once or twice before. Always comes back to us with a tale to tell."

Who was *us?* Or was that the rural *us* Lydia had heard so frequently back in Shropshire?

She rummaged in her workbasket for her darning egg and shoved it into one of the captain's stockings. The wool was thick and good quality, the knitting precise. One of his sisters had probably made the stockings, and the captain's relentless tramping around London had taken a toll on the heels. He wore the right harder than the left, but surrendered to the need for mending only when both stockings were worn through.

Marcus had had the same habit.

"What sort of tales," Lydia asked, "cause a man to disappear without notice and stay away for days?" Much less years.

"Tales that usually involve strong drink, stupid dares, wild schemes, or pretty ladies. Will is my lone brother, but he's enough to make me pray that if I'm ever so fortunate to marry, I will be blessed with only daughters in my nursery."

Lydia sorted yarn until she came up with a close match for the captain's navy stocking. "My father wanted sons. I was a disappointment, but Mama eventually rectified the error." She threaded her darning needle and moved the branch of candles on the table a few inches closer.

"Then beggin' yer pardon, missus, but yer pa was an idiot. Sons can work hard, true enough, if they're of a mind to, but they also go off to war, go to sea, get taken up for brawlin', and otherwise create havoc. My mama made me promise I'd look after Will, and now I've lost 'im again."

"He's a grown man."

"He's me brother."

A profound sentiment. Darning was an easy and satisfying task, something even wellborn women learned to do in childhood. The objective was to more or less reweave a patch of yarn over a hole, and while the result was usually an obvious repair, a few minutes' work would render the stocking serviceable again.

"Where would you look for your brother if the captain permitted you to do so?"

Bowen had conferred with Captain Powell before dinner, but the captain had not confided any particulars in Lydia when she'd taken his supper tray to the library.

She needed to ask Dylan Powell directly about Marcus. How to find Marcus, what might have befallen Marcus. That was the purpose of her employment in his household, to gain access to the people who'd known Marcus in Spain and might still know of him. Indirection and casual questions hadn't worked and time was flying.

Lydia worked her needle through the wool of the stocking, creating vertical rows of yarn across the hole, before starting the horizontal weave that would see the item mended.

"I've looked for William in the usual haunts young fellows prefer," Bowen said, "though Will generally hadn't the blunt to indulge such habits."

"You need not spare my sensibilities, Mr. Brook." He'd referred to cockpits, gaming hells, bordellos, and the like. Lydia could not see such venues having sufficient allure to keep Marcus from returning home. "Is William literate?"

"My mother was Welsh. Set great store by her letters, as most of her family did. That's part of why the captain could talk the quartermaster into taking me on, even with my injury. I can read in English and Welsh and a bit of French and Latin too. I can handle the Irish and the Gaelic in conversation. I can cipher accurately, even when I'm not quite sober. Will isn't much for book learning, but he knows all the songs. Our regimental warbler. Despite his injuries, he can still play the harp better than any angel ever did."

"I hope you find him soon."

"He's probably in love again. Springtime has that effect on him. Maybe he took a notion to return to Shropshire."

Well, of course. Lydia hadn't recognized the accent precisely, worn down as it was by years in London, but Bowen's inflections were the sound of home. The music of Welsh ancestors blended with the rounded vowels of Liverpool and softened t's of the Midlands.

A lovely accent, though not as pleasant as the captain's. Lydia finished the first stocking and worked the wooden egg into the second.

"Why haven't you returned to Shropshire?" she asked.

"I will, one day. You've a fine hand with a needle, missus, but I don't believe that's a ball of yarn curled up in yonder basket."

One of the kittens had made a place for herself amid Lydia's mending projects. "That will teach me to leave the lid open." She extracted the kitten from her fabric nest and set the beast on the carpet. "She's the bolder of the two. I believe I will name her Mab."

"Fanciful name for a cat."

"She appeared as if by magic."

Bowen took another nip from his flask. "Does the captain know you've taken in strays?"

"He does. I have his permission to keep them." More magic. That Dylan Powell would turn to his housekeeper to thwart his sisters' matchmaking was also a little magical. Lydia had never met such a self-possessed man. Neither hunger, fatigue, blue devils, nor whimsy deflected him from his chosen course, and Lydia had never heard him complain either.

But she had seen him smile. Seen him absolutely beaming with good humor. All it had taken was making a complete cake of herself.

"Well, this stray soldier is for bed." Bowen got to his feet, something he did slowly, his first steps always a bit gingerly. "Pleasant dreams, missus. I've a mind to write home and see if William turns up there."

"We keep a lap desk in the butler's pantry for staff. Leave the letter on the sideboard in the front hall, and the captain will see it posted for you."

"Will do. Don't stay up too late with your mendin'."

"I'm almost finished. Before you go, might I ask you a question?" Lydia pretended to study her handiwork, the better to present her query casually.

"Of course."

"You mentioned that in your soldiering years, you did hear mention of Marcus, Lieutenant Lord Tremont. What do you recall of him?"

"A lordling," Bowen said, his affable air acquiring an edge of disdain. "One of Dunacre's pretty boys. I transferred to the quartermasters' unit not long after Lieutenant Lord Lacypants joined Dunacre's staff. He was no worse than a lot of them and precious young. Little more than a struttin' boy. You felt sorry for such as him, until he ordered you put to the lash."

Bowen was the first person outside of Horse Guards to even acknowledge that Marcus had served, though Lydia could not fathom Marcus ordering anybody put to the lash.

"Military discipline was strict, I gather."

"Military discipline was murderous under Dunacre. The less said about it, the better."

"Do you know what became of the lieutenant?"

Bowen's smile was bitter. "Probably shoveling coal for Lucifer's forge. He was none too bright, but brave enough. Always spoutin' some old Roman's words or quoting Proverbs. I hope you weren't sweet on him?"

"I have a distant connection with his family, and they are reticent on the subject of his whereabouts. I was simply curious." A version of the truth. When Uncle Reggie was in his cups, Lydia was as distant from him as it was possible to be.

"Ask the captain. He knows more about who went missing and who deserted than anybody. Keeps most of it to himself. Good night, missus."

"Good night."

Lydia had been trying to get up her courage to ask the captain directly about Marcus for more than two months. At first, her employer's nature had been off-putting. Always on his way out the door, relentlessly reserved, and occasionally forbidding. She'd taken some time to see past that demeanor to the man himself.

Dylan Powell was always on his way out the door because he was that conscientious about looking after any man wounded under his command. He had seen and continued to see human suffering on a horrific scale, and he seldom allowed himself adequate rest.

Of course he was serious.

He was also kind, devoted to his cousins, generous with his employees, and hardworking. Few people had Mama's inherently warm heart or Wesley's sunny nature. Once Lydia had decided that she could approach Captain Powell, something—a menu, an unexpected caller, a feud between the first footman and the kitchen maid —always intruded.

The captain would tell her whatever he knew, she trusted him that much. Lately, though, Lydia had hesitated to approach her employer about Marcus because she had realized the truth might well be unpleasant.

Truths such as Bowen had implied: that Marcus had been incompetent, that he'd toadied to incompetent superiors, or worse.

Bowen had also referred to desertion, and for the first time, Lydia had to consider that her brother might be living quietly in France, or

somewhere on the Continent. Marcus might have done the unthinkable and walked away from his duty as an officer. His decision to buy
his colors had been precipitous. Perhaps he'd made an equally precipitous decision to desert.

Surely he would have had good, moral reasons for such a course.
Nonetheless, a man in disgrace would not want his sister revealing
his location.

Lydia would have to tread carefully, then, when she made her
queries of Captain Powell, more carefully than usual. She was
mentally rehearsing various possible approaches to the discussion
when she heard a soft tread in the darkened hallway beyond her
door.

Dylan ought to have found some bread and cheese, poured himself a
glass of cider, and taken his snack up to bed with him. Hours of
walking had left him famished. Nonetheless, if he brought his tray to
his bedroom, he'd probably fall asleep before touching his food.

The sisters would scold him for being too skinny, and they'd be
right. Mrs. Lovelace did not scold him for that particular failing. He
hung up his cloak and hat and set aside his walking stick. A light
coming from the housekeeper's sitting room door suggested she was
still awake.

Dylan had every intention of walking past her door, leaving her
to her embroidery or correspondence, but for reasons unbeknownst to
him, he instead rapped lightly on her doorjamb.

"Might I come in?" he asked. Mrs. Lovelace wore no cap, and as
always, the sight of her hair, all ruby highlights and soft wisps, caught
him by surprise.

"Of course, Captain. Have a seat."

The second wing chair in the room was occupied by one of the
feline intruders. Dylan scooped the beast up, got an owlish perusal
for his trouble, and sat. The cushion had been warmed by the cat, a

profoundly agreeable sensation when the small of Dylan's back was aching.

"How is Bowen settling in?" Having nowhere else to put the cat, Dylan allowed her to curl up in his lap. A slight vibration commenced.

"Have an apple tart." Mrs. Lovelace slid a plate closer to Dylan's side of the small table. Two fat strips of cheddar lay alongside a flaky tart redolent of cinnamon. "You should have something to drink with that."

"You need not—"

She was already out the door.

"Managing woman." Dylan bit into the cheddar and tried feeding a cheese crumb to the kitten, who deigned to partake, then resumed vibrating.

Mrs. Lovelace came back with two glasses of cider. "I am trying to put some weight on Mr. Brook, but he apparently has the appetite of a bird. I will have to consult with the neighborhood cooks for dishes commonly served in Wales."

"He's not Welsh." Not quite, but he was certainly fluent in the language.

She passed Dylan a glass and resumed her seat. "His mother was. He speaks of her fondly. No luck finding William?"

Dylan did not want to revisit the night's failures. "None yet. Bowen likely eats sparingly so he doesn't put any extra weight on what remains of his right foot. That he did not lose the leg is nothing short of a miracle."

"You knew him at the time?"

What did this old business have to do with—? The kitten nudged forcefully at his hand. Dylan obliged with another tiny crumb of cheese.

"I was present for the operation." Somebody, usually several somebodies, had to keep the patient still. "Some French émigré, a volunteer physician who'd been through a medical education in Edin-burgh, was on hand as well. The Frenchman shouted down the

English doctors who were ready to... This is not a happy topic. Bowen can walk, he appears whole when shod, and the situation could have ended much differently."

Mrs. Lovelace took a sip of her cider. "Do you have good memories too?"

Dylan never spoke of his military years, not even with his cousins if he could help it, nor were they inclined to talk of the past.

"I recall very fondly the day when my papa put me on my first pony. I was the King of Wales that summer, also a Viking chief, a Highland laird, a Canadian explorer... No boy ever had more adventures beneath a groom's watchful eye."

"I notice you did not aspire to emulate any English heroes. You have no brothers?"

"None, but I have cousins whom you've met. Goddard and MacKay twice spent summers in Wales, and other years, I spent holidays with them. I was always exhausted by the time my mother retrieved me from Scotland... The summer sun sets only briefly up north, and we cousins were intent on our mischief every hour of the day."

His cousins and their wives liked Mrs. Lovelace, which mattered to Dylan. He wasn't sure why it mattered, but it did.

"Did you buy your colors because your cousins did?"

The cider was good, the apple tart perfection itself. Not too sweet, not too messy. The conversation was on safer ground, and the ache in Dylan's back had subsided. Perhaps he was not lonely so much as he was in want of domesticity, little doses of comfort and companionship at the end of the day...

He set aside that thought, lest he be purchasing himself a dog next. "I bought a commission in part because that was any patriotic fellow's duty and also just to get the hell away from my father. He was determined that I become his steward as well as his heir, and I was determined..."

"Yes?"

To leave. To get away. To be free. More fool he. "Enough of that. Tell me your best memory."

Mrs. Lovelace set a second apple tart on Dylan's plate from the basket in the center of the table. "I well recall the day my brother was born. I was an only child until he came along, and the notion that I would be an older sister was tantalizing. No longer would I be the youngest member of the household, the girl everybody ordered about and corrected and scolded."

"Your parents were stern with you?" Parents sometimes put high expectations on an only child, and thus she put high expectations on herself. Dylan had certainly been burdened with expectations as the only boy.

"My mother was and is the dearest woman you'd ever want to meet." Mrs. Lovelace smiled slightly at the mention of her mama. "I realized, though, when my brother arrived that my failings were beyond salvation by earthly powers. I adored my papa, and he was always patient with me, but when I acquired a brother..."

She sipped her cider, and Dylan realized the late hour had also led her down paths of memories she preferred not to visit.

"When you acquired a brother?" Odd phrasing, but then, most bachelors referred to *acquiring* a wife.

"I realized that I was and always would be a distant second best to a son. I always had been, without even knowing it. My father was tolerant of me, not doting. My mother indulged me to an extent because she knew the burden I carried. I would never be anything but a girl. As children do, I grasped that my brother mattered, while I would only matter if he decided I did. I thus became a very conscientious older sister."

How old could Lydia have been when she'd grasped the realities of her universe? Five? Seven? "And you are conscientious, still." Not a failing, of course, but duty alone didn't leave much room for joy, affection, or apple tarts late at night.

Though duty mattered, of course.

"I was happy," Mrs. Lovelace said. "You were, too, on your pony, summering with cousins. Perhaps childhood has such a rosy reputation because adulthood can be yet still more grim by comparison?"

Dylan ate the second tart and finished the cheese—the kitten in his lap was apparently fast asleep. "Are you happy here, Mrs. Lovelace?" Did she ever long for home as he did, ever wonder if she'd acquire a partner in life to cuddle up with at the end of the day?

"I am abundantly happy," she said, quite firmly. "I have tremendous freedom as your housekeeper, and I see the results of my own hard work. You have hired good people to look after your residence, and you pay me generous wages that I can use as I see fit. Why would I not be happy?"

Because she was lonely. Because she took in stray kittens lest they be lonely too. Because life could not be entirely about gleaming candlesticks and swept hearths.

And someday, for Dylan, life would not be entirely about duty, honor, and the aftermath of war. "Where is home for you, Mrs. Lovelace?"

"The Midlands. You?"

She was prevaricating with a generality that encompassed a third of England. "Glamorgan, though I also spent time in Radnorshire growing up. If we're to be subtly interested in one another, I should know where you hail from, madam."

She set aside her glass. "The Shropshire countryside. I was educated mostly at home, and my mother came from Surrey. We have loftier and somewhat distant relations elsewhere in the county."

More prevarication. Dylan didn't have to be one of Wellington's best reconnaissance officers to notice that Lydia Lovelace wouldn't give up the name of the closest market town, not even the name of an obscure village. Closer investigation was surely warranted.

"Tell me about your fancy relatives."

CHAPTER FIVE

Mrs. Lovelace became interested in rearranging the fabric scraps and yarn in her workbasket. "I've been meaning to ask you about one of my mother's relatives. Marcus Glover inherited the Tremont earldom at a young age and bought his colors after only a year at university. He went off to war and hasn't come home. The family isn't saying much about his whereabouts."

Tremont again? Bad enough that Dylan had brough him up in conversation with Goddard. "Were you fond of him?"

"I am curious. A peer of the realm—if he's extant—should be difficult to misplace, even for the British army."

Dylan had nearly let the men misplace Tremont into an unmarked grave on several occasions. They had refrained, citing his lordship's youth and dimwittedness.

"The kindest thing I can say about Tremont is that I know nothing of his whereabouts, and if he developed a scintilla of intelligence while he held his commission—for he brought little enough with him from England—he will keep me in ignorance of his whereabouts."

Mrs. Lovelace was winding a dark blue mass of wrinkled yarn—

an abandoned project perhaps—into a ball. She ceased her winding. "You would do him an injury?"

"Somebody probably already has. Tremont was inexperienced, too thickheaded to do anything other than follow orders, and assigned to a horror of a commanding officer. I resigned my commission prior to the Hundred Days and only rejoined shortly before Waterloo. I lost track of Tremont, thank the Almighty. Despite commendations from his superior, the men regarded his lordship as no credit to his uniform."

Mrs. Lovelace's hands went still in her lap. "Could he have deserted?"

"Tens of thousands did, on both sides. Why would an earl desert, though? Of all men, he would expect himself to serve loyally, wouldn't he? Nobody accused Tremont of cowardice or disloyalty, not that I recall."

"But if military life did not agree with him, might he have chosen to leave it behind?"

Dylan considered a third apple tart and decided he was, much to his surprise, satisfied with what he'd consumed thus far.

"If Tremont had not yet put an heir and spare in his nursery, nobody would have begrudged him a return to civilian life." God forbid all the wealth amassed by a titled family should revert to the crown.

And whatever else had been true about Tremont, he'd been young. Pathetically, desperately young, in both years and experience. Barely shaving, his voice still prone to cracking at the worst times. Too young, by aristocratic standards, to have left legitimate sons behind, but not too young to die for his country.

"Enough talk of military matters, Mrs. Lovelace. Tell me something about you that only a smitten man would know. What is your favorite sweet? What is your favorite book?"

Mrs. Lovelace resumed winding her yarn. "I ought to say the Bible, but I do enjoy the Waverley novels. What about you?"

"You must make free with my library, then," Dylan said, rather than admit that he hadn't read enough novels to have a favorite. He generally fell asleep before he'd completed the first chapter. "I am more inclined toward agricultural treatises, poetry, and shorter works."

Mrs. Lovelace finished with her ball of yarn. "Tell me of your sisters. What are their interests?"

Dylan wanted to know why Lydia Lovelace had dodged his questions about her home, why she liked Walter Scott's drivel about Highlanders and knights and the Young Pretender. But if Dylan had to prattle on about his siblings to gain Mrs. Lovelace's trust, prattle on he would.

"My sisters. Very well. Bronwen, the youngest, is as bookish as ever. Marged is the family harper, and Tegan, the oldest, has raised her needlework to a high art. Any one of them could run Tragwyddoldeb in her spare time, but I am not about to allow them that honor."

"Duty matters to you a very great deal, doesn't it, Captain?"

"Some duties. I learned in the army that not all duties are equal. A duty to my men does not eclipse my duty to my sisters, but I will rely on you to keep a particularly watchful eye on the back door should my siblings visit." Which they would. Dylan's instincts, which had saved his life more times than he could count in Spain, assured him of that much.

"You've alerted your cousins to the coming invasion?"

"Both Goddard and MacKay have been warned."

Mrs. Lovelace fished around in her workbasket, refolding this, rearranging that. "What of Mrs. Dorning?"

"I beg your pardon?"

"Mrs. Sycamore Dorning is sister to Colonel Goddard and thus also your cousin. She is the widow of a marquess. If your sisters are in Town, then their lady cousin will be well placed to show them around and introduce them to eligible parties."

Dylan absently petted the kitten and realized he'd committed a tactical blunder—an oversight, rather. Jeanette Dorning was married to an earl's younger brother and counted among her in-laws and marital connections roughly half of Mayfair.

"Excellent suggestion." Though how did a man ask his lady cousin to protect him from matchmaking sisters? "Does Lord Tremont matter to you, Mrs. Lovelace?"

She closed the lid of her workbasket, picked up Dylan's half-full cider glass, and took a sip without seeming to realize her error.

"He is family and titled. If he died in battle, that should have been remarked."

Scenes rose in Dylan's memory, not of battle, but of the stinking, dazed, wretched, moaning aftermath. Thousands lying injured among the dead, and each man calling out in his own language for the same thing: *Help me, please. Please, help me.*

"You've heard the term 'missing in action'?" Dylan asked.

She nodded. "I suspect it's a euphemism for 'presumed dead.' Horse Guards claims Marcus was not killed in battle, and he did not go missing. He was assigned to a transport bound for England after Waterloo, and he boarded the ship, but nobody seems to know if he remained in London, was set upon by footpads, or came home with some injury to his mind."

She was on first-name terms with an earl, another puzzle piece.

"You are correct that any of those outcomes should have been properly documented in the normal course, but demobilizing tens of thousands of men is not the normal course. Some officers stayed on in Paris, some came home, some went traveling on the Continent. Some men married wives on campaign who would not be accepted back home. Some soldiers were so badly disfigured in combat or deranged by violence that they no longer sought a return home."

And the military allowed those men the dignity of a quiet retreat to the French, German, or Italian villages of their choice, where many such men from many nationalities were living out their days.

"But an earl," Mrs. Lovelace said, "a man with his whole life ahead of him, why would he not come home to his family?"

Dylan pushed past his abiding loathing for Lord Tremont and

officers of his ilk to consider the question. "War changes people, Mrs. Lovelace. A fellow who was the butt of the apprentices' jokes in his uncle's shop could become a sharpshooter, lethally accurate even under fire, the pride of his regiment. A lord's son, given every advantage in life, might be overcome at the sight of a dead horse's entrails. That man longs to be brave and tireless on the battlefield, but he can't even stay on his feet if he cuts himself shaving. If Tremont is alive, he might well dread the day his family finds him."

She watched as Dylan petted the kitten snoring in his lap. The little creature liked to have the top of her head stroked, and she was surprisingly soft given her lowly antecedents.

"You never did tell me your favorite dessert, Mrs. Lovelace." She had instead brought the conversation back to Dylan's military past and to her *distant relative*, the earl.

"I am quite fond of a cup of *chocolat chaud*, particularly served with a dollop of whipped cream."

Not a typical dessert. "I am quite fond of apple tarts." Too late, he realized that his word choice might embarrass his housekeeper. She was *fond* of him, a ridiculous notion. Because she was fond of him and because Dylan was still tired but no longer aching and famished, he made an offer he would doubtless regret.

"Shall I see what I can find out about your missing lordling?" The peer whom she'd referred to as *Marcus*, though she was only passingly curious about his years-long absence?

"Please. My mother is concerned about him, and not knowing his fate is hard on her."

Dylan rose and passed Mrs. Lovelace the sleeping kitten. "I cannot promise anything. A man who doesn't want to be found usually has reasons for protecting his privacy. I thank you for the conversation and sustenance, Mrs. Lovelace, and you *will* avail yourself of my library. That is a direct order."

She rose as well. "Thank you, Captain. For the library, but also... Marcus's family has worried about him for too long. His heir is a bibulous uncle. I suspect that fellow isn't very interested in discovering his nephew's whereabouts."

She made a fetching picture by the light of the candles, the kitten snuggled against her shoulder. A fetching, worried picture. Dylan bowed and withdrew, though sleep eluded him more determinedly than usual.

Mrs. Lovelace was being vague about her past and her connections, she was comfortable using French phrases in regular conversation, and she'd had access to books and the leisure time to read them. Moreover, she considered that a housekeeper had "tremendous freedom" and was delighted with the simple fact of controlling her own wages.

Lydia Lovelace was hiding something. Dylan had yet to decide if she was lying per se, or simply guarding her personal dignity. He drifted off on the thought that he must instruct the kitchen maid to ensure chocolate was kept on hand at all times, for despite whatever secrets she kept, Mrs. Lovelace was entitled to some pleasure in life.

Wasn't everybody?

"May I use the lap desk when you're through with it, Mrs. Lovelace?" Bowen Brook asked, leaning against the parlor's doorjamb.

"This is my traveling desk," Lydia replied. "The one in the butler's pantry ought to be available, but you are the house steward, Mr. Brook. The library and office writing supplies fall within your purview."

In the morning light slanting through the windows, Bowen Brook was a very different man from the weary soldier who'd fallen at the back door days ago. His bruises were fading, and given the opportunity, he'd proved to be a fastidious fellow. His attire wasn't fussy—Lydia had altered some of the captain's clothing to suit Mr. Brook—but his person was scrupulously clean and his bearing that of a former military man.

Even his speech had become more genteel, at least around Lydia.

"Has the captain explained to you where it is I am to execute me duties, missus?"

The captain, after that late-night conversation earlier in the week, had barely been in evidence. "He might be leaving the decision to us. I have an idea." Lydia set aside her latest letter to Aunt Chloe and led Mr. Brook up the steps.

By the time Lydia had located the items in the attic that would transform an old warming pantry into a steward's office, the morning post had arrived. She took the mail to the library for sorting as she always did, because certain expenses were hers to pay from her household budget, and the remainder of the mail went to the captain.

Between what looked to be a tailor's bill and an invoice from a bootmaker, Lydia found a letter from Aunt Chloe.

By agreement, Chloe was not to contact Lydia in London unless a dire situation had arisen.

Lydia used the captain's letter opener to slit the seal and took Chloe's epistle to the windows. The news was not quite catastrophic, but it was worrisome. Wesley was planning to visit Chloe a fortnight hence. That was doubtless meant as a warning from Wesley to Lydia herself that she was to be escorted home to Tremont on her cousin's arm.

Why? Why would Uncle Reginald demand her return when he regarded Lydia as little better than a poor relation?

"You look as if you're running out of rations, and you've received word of massed enemy forces in the next valley."

The captain lounged with a hip propped on his desk, his riding jacket open, the tips of his boots dusty. How long had he been observing her, and why hadn't she heard him come in?

And besides all that, did any man in the whole of England look half so delicious as Dylan Powell after a morning hack?

"Family squabbles," Lydia said, folding the letter and tucking it into a skirt pocket. "Why are you looking at me like that?"

"You aren't wearing your cap." He pushed away from the desk and prowled closer. "I'm taking your advice."

Lydia put a hand to her hair. She'd forgotten her cap, so absorbed had she been in drafting her letter to Aunt Chloe and then setting up Mr. Brook's office.

"What advice would that be?"

"Paying a call on Jeanette Dorning. At first, I thought to drop in after my ride, as family might, but then I thought no. Better to pay a morning call in proper morning attire."

He was asking Lydia's opinion. "You clean up nicely," she said. "Do the pretty, and if her husband is on hand, he will be more favorably inclined toward you. The Dorning menfolk are protective of their womenfolk and of family generally."

Too late, Lydia realized her mistake. A housekeeper did not refer to an earl's siblings as "the Dorning menfolk." She had stood up with the earl once or twice and also with one or two of his brothers. A big fellow—the Dornings were all big fellows—Hawthorne, maybe? And a smiling dark-haired charmer with a shorter name. Ash, Oak, Beech... Lydia could not recall.

"Has Goddard been complaining about his in-laws?" the captain asked, joining Lydia at the window.

"The colonel would never be so disloyal. Like everybody else, I occasionally peruse Debrett's. I know Mrs. Dorning was married to the Marquess of Tavistock before she was widowed, for example."

"Why would you know that?"

Because I am curious about anybody connected to you. "Because she is your cousin, and thus..."

Humor lurked in the captain's blue eyes. "Yes, Mrs. Lovelace?"

Lydia fell back on what she hoped was a credible lie. "One wants to use proper address, if the occasion ever arises. When a former marchioness marries an earl's brother, what becomes of her honorific? We haven't much occasion to discuss such matters belowstairs."

The captain reached past Lydia to twitch at the sash holding the curtain open. He squeezed the sachet affixed to the sash and released the scent of bergamot.

"She technically lost the honorific when she gained a second husband," he said, "and I gather Jeanette is content with her bargain, though informally, she is likely still referred to as her ladyship. Did the letter upset you?"

A loud thump sounded from beyond the door, followed by cursing in Welsh. Something about a lackwitted bullock's backside.

"We're setting up an office for Mr. Brook in the old warming pantry," Lydia said. "I hope you do not object."

"And if I did?"

"Then I would ask you to assign Mr. Brook a proper space to do his job. A desk in the library, a corner of the schoolroom. One needs a place of one's own, especially if one is handling wage books and other sensitive documents."

"One does. Today is my day to commit oversights, apparently. You've rearranged the artwork in here."

"I put the portraits where they'd suffer less damage from the sun."

This explanation apparently amused the captain. "Where I don't see them unless I go looking for a biography. Instead, my desk gives me a view of the Brecon Beacons and a landscape of Tragwyddoldeb in summer. Where did you find it?"

"Leaning against the wall behind the great harp in the music room. I gather your sister Tegan sent it to you, and you never hung it after you'd had it framed." The painting of the family seat was the embodiment of rural repose, a pretty stone manor nestled among stately trees and rolling hills. Something in the landscape nonetheless hinted that this was not the tame, tidy English countryside. This was the wilder, more remote reaches of Wales—higher hills, a denser forest, sharper light—and the captain's birthplace.

"Why hide such a glorious prospect," Lydia asked, "and put in its place some dour old ancestor who looks as if smiling would break three Commandments?" She sidled around the captain and swiped a finger along the bottom of the landscape's frame. By next week, the paintings would need a careful dusting, a task she reserved for herself.

"Perhaps I did not want the sun to damage Tegan's work," the captain said. "You never did tell me about your letter, Mrs. Lovelace. I gather it's bad news."

He was tenacious. If Lydia knew anything about Dylan Powell, it was that he did not give up on an objective, ever. She admired that about him—usually.

"My family did not approve of my decision to go into service." Aunt Chloe had been appalled, though Mama had supported the plan. The measure was desperate and temporary, or should have been. The longer Lydia remained under the captain's roof, the less she wanted to return to Tremont.

The captain resumed his perch against the desk. "You were to serve out your days in rural Shropshire, I take it. Too smart to settle for a yeoman's son and not ruthless enough to try for a squire's heir."

"Your view of rural spinsterdom is not particularly flattering, Captain." Though it was accurate.

"Do they want you to marry a cousin?" he asked. "A second cousin? I bought my colors in part to avoid such a match. Everybody —excepting myself—was certain the young lady and I would suit marvelously. I know how family can be."

Stick as close to the truth as possible. Every lying schoolgirl knew that rubric. "They want me to come home. I wasn't supposed to be gone this long. I wasn't supposed to manage this well in Town."

The captain stalked across the room, and while Lydia had never been afraid of him, she was tempted to take a step back.

"You cannot leave me," he said, not stopping until he was close enough that Lydia caught the scents of shaving soap and horse. "No deserting the regiment just as we hear the enemy's drums in the distance. Tegan's feelings would have been hurt had she found her painting behind the harp, but I honestly forgot where I'd put it. A steward needs his own office, but Bowen would never have mentioned that to me. I will not answer for the fate of your palace tigers if you retreat to Shropshire now, Mrs. Lovelace. I want your word you will not abandon your post."

Lydia could not give him her word, and yet, she was loath to lie to him—to lie to him again. "You can hire another housekeeper, Captain."

"Of course I can, and she won't serve me apple tarts late at night, or hang sachets to chase the bugs from my library, or scold me for tracking mud into the back hallway, or wash my bed hangings even once a year."

What was he going on about? "I'm simply doing my job."

"I've grown *quite fond* of how you do your job, Mrs. Lovelace. Promise me you won't quit."

Lydia would quit. As soon as she figured out what had become of Marcus, if not sooner. "I will stay at least long enough to see your sisters settled in, but I doubt my family will relent."

Chloe could tell Wesley that Lydia was in Town doing some shopping or catching up with friends as the Season got under way. A whole sampler of lies would have to be stitched to support that fiction —an escort to Town, some friends to stay with—but Wesley would accept half-truths at face value, because Lydia frequently did the same for him.

"I will not relent either, Mrs. Lovelace. You have turned a command post into a home, and that means more to me than you can fathom."

Captain Powell was not an affectionate man, at least not that Lydia had seen. She was thus entirely unprepared for him to lean close, kiss her cheek, and bow over her hand.

"My chief intelligence officer's advice is not to be ignored," he said. "I'm off to change into my best morning attire."

He strode from the library, leaving Lydia smiling at nothing in particular, for no reason at all. She'd never been anybody's chief intelligence officer before, but then, neither had she been a housekeeper— or a liar.

How dare they? How dare Lydia Lovelace's family try to summon her back to rural obscurity when she'd barely had time to find her feet as Dylan's housekeeper? She'd taken the post only at... Yuletide? Already, it felt as if she'd been managing Dylan's domicile since he'd moved to London, she was that competent at the job.

Competent was the wrong word, not superlative enough.

Dylan strode along the walkway, mentally remonstrating with a lot of Shropshire yokels who hadn't appreciated Lydia when they'd had her—trying to marry her off to a clodhopping cousin, for God's sake—and now that she had found herself a respectable London position, they missed the treasure they'd scorned.

Served the lot of ingrates right. Dylan traveled several streets, composing sermons to the dunderheaded Lovelaces, before it occurred to him that he was upset. On a tear. Charging headlong, bayonets fixed, at Lydia's relatives, who, for all he knew, were the very same maiden aunties who'd taught her so much about the domestic arts.

"*Uffern a'r diablo.*" Dylan had marched nearly to Jeanette's door, but had little recollection of his travels.

"What has you invoking Old Scratch on such a fine day?" Hughie Porter tucked his fiddle into the crook of his arm and brandished his bow. "I hear you aren't getting enough sleep, Captain." He played a bit of a lullaby. "Yer London cousins are all married, and you're the last bachelor standing."

Hughie was plying his trade on a busy corner where mercantile and residential neighborhoods intersected. He dressed the part of the wandering minstrel, with a jaunty top hat and lacy neckcloth, but his clothing hadn't seen an iron since Moses went up to the mount, and his boots were seriously down at the heels.

"Since when is this your regular patch?" Dylan asked, flipping a coin into the fiddle case open on the walkway.

"Since better surrounds mean better earnings." Hughie played a few spritely notes. "I hear you're looking for Will Brook."

"I am, as is his brother."

"Mayhap Will doesn't want to be found." Hughie started on a waltz, which made a curiously apt accompaniment to a busy London morning. "Will's a big boy, and Bowen tends to hover over him."

"Will's a big boy who can hardly hear his own harp tunes. If trouble walked up behind him, he'd be ambushed, and he has only the one good fist."

Hughie hadn't served under Dylan for long, but he'd been a good soldier. Tireless, as the pipers and drummers had to be, and brave. He was also far too fond of drink for a man who often plied his trade in pubs and taverns. For all his cheerful ditties and pretty tunes, Hughie was not a happy man.

"Do you know something of Will's whereabouts?" Dylan asked.

"If I did, and Will told me to keep my gob shut, I'd keep my gob shut." Hughie played on in lilting triple meter. "Bowen's biding with you now?"

"He has accepted a post as my house steward." A solution of sorts, and one that had been sitting right under Dylan's nose.

"A former quartermaster's clerk will like all that ciphering and so forth. What should I tell Will if I come across him?"

"To stop being an idiot. Bowen lost his lodgings because Will piked off, and then Bowen lost his job at the livery. He's worried about his brother."

Hughie brought his little waltz to a conclusion, tipping his hat to a beldame who'd put a copper into the fiddle case.

"Will was a soldier. He can look after himself. Seems to me Bowen has come up in the world since Will cut him loose."

"Will didn't cut him loose, Porter. Will disappeared like a thief in the night. Like a man with something to hide, and then Bowen was beat to flinders for no apparent reason. If I did not know Will Brook to be an honorable fellow, I'd think he deserted his family."

Hughie extracted a chunk of what looked like dark amber from his pocket and rubbed it along the bow hairs. "Will is honorable, and he's not stupid. If I see him, I'll tell him Bowen's asking after him, but, Captain, heed me. Standing up for the men was how you earned our loyalty in Spain, and we loved you for it. We're not in Spain anymore."

"And I promised Will Brook I'd see him settled. If he's come to harm, I want to know about it, and I want to know why."

Hughie put his fiddle to his chin and laid his bow on the strings. "But nobody has to follow your orders anymore, do they, Captain? A body might almost think the war was finally over." He smiled and launched into Niel Gow's "Lament for the Death of His Second Wife."

A sadder and more beautiful fiddle tune had not been written. The strains followed Dylan as he made his way to Jeanette's door and was admitted by the lady herself. The encounter with Hughie Porter had been unsettling. The hug Jeanette bestowed on Dylan threw him off-balance in an entirely different direction.

"Cousin, you are a naughty, naughty man," Jeanette said, squeezing him hard. "You play least in sight as if I'll try to marry you off now that Orion and Alasdhair have found women to put up with them. You forget that, of all people, I am the last who would force anybody to the altar."

Jeanette bore the scent of flowers, she hugged fiercely, and she didn't merely squeeze and let go. For a progression of instants, Dylan was *held*, unable to politely escape and bewildered about how to respond.

She stepped back and plucked Dylan's hat from his head and his walking stick from his hand. Jeanette had been all angles and elbows as a girl. As a woman, she'd become terrifyingly self-possessed, rather like Lydia Lovelace, oddly.

"You are not as peaked and wan as usual," Jeanette said, casting a critical eye over Dylan. "Mrs. Lovelace must be feeding you adequately."

"You and my housekeeper are acquainted?" Why did that unnerve him?

"You tasked her with putting Alasdhair's house to rights before he and Dorcas married. My path crossed with Mrs. Lovelace's then, and I was favorably impressed. I dare hope she was as well. Come sit with me. Sycamore has abandoned me to meet with the head gardener at our Richmond property. They get to talking about mulch and trellises and compost, and I feel an irresistible compulsion to nap."

She linked her arm with Dylan's and escorted him—she did not quite march him—to a parlor overlooking the thoroughfare. The Coventry Club sat across the street, its façade as staid and respectable as the buildings on either side of it.

"How fares the club?" Dylan asked, for want of a wittier conversational gambit.

"The Coventry is thriving. Orion and Ann manage the day-to-day activities, Sycamore keeps a hand in, and I am available to assist with the ledgers, inventories, and whatnot. You did not deign to call on me to discuss the club, Dylan."

Jeanette sat with all the grace of a monarch and gestured for Dylan to take the wing chair next to hers. The parlor was comfortable. Framed drawings of pretty plants hung on the walls. Enormous ferns held pride of place before the windows.

The parlor was also unique to Jeanette and her spouse. A cork target hung between the framed prints, the center heavily pitted. A pair of throwing knives, one larger than the other, lay on the low table atop a bound volume of what appeared to be risque prints.

Dylan was abruptly aware that he hardly knew his lady cousin. Jeanette had married a much older man when she'd been barely out of the schoolroom. By the time Dylan had come home from war and sorted his affairs out, Jeanette had been a retiring widow. Now she was married to Dorning, and apparently finally happy.

"I called on you because..." *Because we are both grown up now, and soon we will be grown old?* He could not say that. "How are you, Jeanette?"

"I am thriving. Sycamore spoils me without limit, and that... You have no idea, Dylan, what a relief it is to have somebody to love."

"Surely you..." She could not possibly have loved the strutting martinet she'd been matched with in her first marriage. "Dorning loves you, too, I take it?"

"Madly. He exasperates and delights me, but mostly, he listens to me. Sycamore is affectionate and honest—appallingly so, sometimes— and he talks to me. To have another's trust is a heady responsibility, but I flatter myself that Sycamore feels equally honored to have mine. Finding husbands for your sisters will not be easy, not if we're to make a proper job of it."

"About my sisters..." A soft rap on the door bought Dylan a few moments to marvel at what had already passed between him and his cousin. Jeanette had been a shy, determined girl often overshadowed by a boisterous older brother.

Nobody overshadowed her now. She had become blunt, charming, confident, and somehow radiant. Dylan suspected the same could be said of her spouse. Of *all* the spouses—Orion and Ann, Alasdhair and Dorcas, Jeanette and Sycamore.

For the first time, being the odd cousin out was not a status to be treasured and guarded, but rather, cause for consternation. Dylan had assumed that once he was finally back in Wales, he'd find a suitable wife. She'd be cheerful, organized, well liked by the neighbors and staff, and affectionate toward her husband under appropriate circumstances.

Dylan would esteem her and see that she wanted for nothing— and nobody would be radiant or exasperated or doting. To think of Lydia Lovelace consigned for life to the arms of some cheerful, industrious cousin whom her aunties had chosen for her was an intolerable notion.

When had a pragmatic union of lukewarm mutual esteem become not only tolerable for Dylan, but an assumed eventuality?

CHAPTER SIX

"You are opposed to a match between me and Lydia."

Wesley offered Caroline a smile with that statement, and his smile, as always, gave her a moment of confusion. John had had just that same winsome expression, as if he and Caroline shared a secret joke about life.

As charming as Wesley was, the calculation never left his eyes. That hint of assessment in his gaze warned Caroline that Wesley was not John, not Marcus, and not to be trusted.

She cut a half-dozen sprigs of lavender and placed them in the basket Wesley carried for her. Nights were still chilly, but the walled garden on a sunny day was already lovely. She'd hoped to be alone here, and Wesley had likely chosen his moment for that very reason.

"I do not favor cousins marrying in the general case," Caroline said. "We have royal examples of that folly."

"Do we?" Wesley strolled along at Caroline's side. "Or do we have royal examples of the folly of strangers marrying?"

They had both. The House of Hanover sat upon the English throne, and Georges the First, Third, and Fourth had all married

ladies largely unknown to them. Three of the four Georigan consorts
had also been cousins to their bridegrooms.

"Lydia esteems you," Caroline said, "but not as she should esteem
a suitor." Caroline cut off more lavender and passed it to Wesley.

"We esteem each other well enough," Wesley said. "We also *like*
each other. I am quite fond of Liddie and flatter myself that she is
fond of me too. Surely, Aunt, you cannot find fault with liking as a
basis for marriage?"

Wesley was likable by design, not likable by nature, as John had
been. He had John's height and something of his nose and jaw, but
John had never had the sly quality Lydia attributed to Wesley. Caroline had not put that label on her nephew, but Lydia's term was
accurate.

Wesley was forever jaunting off to *visit friends* in the same weeks
the major race meets were held. He exchanged knowing glances with
the local widows, and he misplaced invoices from his London tailors
as a matter of course. Reginald claimed that was all standard behavior
for a young gentleman of means.

Lydia had pointed out years ago that Wesley had no means of his
own, and his behavior constituted a poor example for Marcus. Caroline should have seen that herself, and perhaps the whole debacle
with Marcus buying his colors could have been avoided.

"If you marry everybody you like," Caroline said, "you will soon
have more wives than King Solomon."

"Would that I could." Wesley sighed dramatically, his comment
doubtless meant to be humorous. "Alas, any wife of mine deserves to
be kept in fine style, and while I might share Solomon's appreciation
for a pretty face, I do not share his resources."

Or his wisdom. "If Lydia is so fond of you, why did she remove
herself to visit Chloe?" Caroline wanted to tell Wesley to take
himself off, to dismiss him, as Lydia would have known how to
dismiss him, but she hadn't Lydia's way with a command.

"Absence makes the heart grow fonder," Wesley said. "Liddie is
giving me a chance to consider my options while she looks in on the

old guard. Papa has deputed me to retrieve her, though. We know how you value Liddie's company."

Caroline did value her daughter's company, very much. Lydia knew how to deal with the staff such that squabbling was kept to a minimum, hard work was rewarded, and meals arrived to the table hot. And yet, John would not have wanted Lydia to become the unpaid chatelaine of Tremont, no matter how much easier that arrangement made Caroline's life.

And thus, Caroline treasured Lydia's freedom even more than she treasured Lydia's company.

"Reginald oversteps if he thinks to order my daughter about," Caroline said. "She is of age. She has means. I am sure Chloe would welcome a visit from you, but do not expect to collect Lydia like another trunk to be tossed onto the boot of your coach."

The traveling coach was actually Caroline's, part of her trousseau, and the means by which her own mother had made certain the new bride could visit home at any time. What would Mama think if she could see how infrequently Caroline now ventured away from Tremont's sheltering walls?

What would Mama think if she knew that the settlements she had insisted on when Caroline had become engaged to John were all that allowed Lydia to be so independent?

"Let's cut some daffodils, shall we?" Wesley said, moving ahead. "They are such a cheerful flower, and their scent doesn't overpower as the lavender does."

That was the point of lavender. The scent was so strong that it banished bugs, blue devils, and foul miasmas alike. Rather like Lydia in the midst of spring cleaning.

"Daffodils don't last long in the vase," Caroline said, tarrying at the lavender border. "If you'd like some flowers for your room, then you should take your bouquet inside immediately." *On the instant.*

Wesley used his penknife to slice off a half-dozen yellow blooms and laid them in the basket. "You can put them in the family parlor where they will cheer you up in Lydia's absence."

"I am not in need of cheering up. In fact, I enjoy having this garden to myself from time to time." More blunt than that, Caroline could not be.

"The garden reminds you of Uncle John?" Wesley cut three more daffodils, taking them all from the same part of the bed rather than choosing with an eye to maintaining the beauty of the planting. "I want that for Lydia, Aunt. I want her to have happy memories of wandering with me here, riding out with me to call on the tenants, and presiding with me over the holiday open house. Why would you begrudge your daughter the same lovely life you so enjoyed as a younger woman?"

Caroline moved away from the flowering beds, lest Wesley chop down every blossom. "What you want for Lydia is lovely. It's the life I treasured with my late husband. My mother made sure that the late earl and I would not only suit, but regard ourselves as most fortunate in our choice of spouse. I want that for Lydia more than I want to see her step into shoes that might not fit her as well as they fit me."

Wesley helped himself to four more blossoms before following Caroline to a birdbath fashioned to resemble a stylized ceramic sunflower. The water in the bath was dirty, the ceramic in need of a good scrubbing with weak white vinegar.

If Lydia were on hand, the birdbath would be sparkling clean. But Lydia was not on hand, Marcus was not on hand, and John was not on hand.

Caroline set aside her shears and hefted the heavy bowl of brackish water from its stand.

"Aunt, we have gardeners..." Wesley fell silent while Caroline dumped the dirty water into a pot of salvia.

"We have gardeners," Caroline said, setting the sunflower back on its base, "but without Lydia here, nobody reminds them that spring means regularly scrubbing out the birdbaths. I notice the flowers, while Lydia notices everything. If Lydia sought to marry you, she would have married you by now, Wesley. I'm sorry to dash your hopes, though honesty is generally the kinder course in the long run."

"If Lydia seeks to marry me, she needs me to propose to her, and in that regard, I have been remiss. I cannot remedy my oversight if Liddie continues to sulk at Aunt Chloe's."

"Lydia has never sulked a day in her life," Caroline said, taking the basket of flowers from Wesley. "That you know your cousin so little is more proof that she ought not to marry you. Shall you join me for some weeding?"

She aimed her Gracious Lady of the Manor smile at him, all the while wishing him to perdition, or to his London clubs, or to some race meet or other.

"Liddie sulks," Wesley said. "She doesn't sulk in the normal way. No fulminating glances, no brooding silences at meals. She sulks by nattering at Papa to repair the tenant cottages and to look for Marcus."

"Reginald should be looking for Marcus, and I have wondered, Wesley, if you are part of the reason he does not."

The whole reason, though Reginald would enjoy his turn at being the earl too, of course.

"No doubt Papa has predictable ambitions for me," Wesley said, taking one of the daffodils from the basket, twisting off most of the stem, and tucking the bloom into his lapel.

"I cannot help that Papa wants to see me well settled," Wesley went on. "Regarding Markie, I have made such inquiries as I can among my London connections and any friends who bought their colors. Their best theory is that the boy thrives in rural obscurity in Provence, maybe even enjoying a stipend from a grateful French government, and the company of a lovely French wife. I nearly called out the fellow who suggested that possibility to me, but as you say, Aunt, honesty is often the kindest course in the end. I thought you should hear the rumors from me."

The temptation to cosh Wesley with the basket of flowers took Caroline by surprise. He was taunting her and insulting her son while pretending false outrage on his cousin's behalf. What would Lydia do in the face of this disclosure? She would think, she would consider, she would analyze, and she would do all of that in the time it took Wesley to fluff his cravat.

"I cannot help that military gossip is so disrespectful of a man who served loyally," Caroline said, "just as you are powerless to force Lydia to the altar. She receives her competence whether she marries or not. You will have to do more than crook your finger at her to earn her hand, Wesley."

"I am prepared to do much more than crook my finger, Aunt. I am prepared to endure dear Chloe's hospitality for as long as necessary to inspire Liddie to come home. I might even jaunt down to London to have a listen in the clubs. If Markie-boy is kicking his heels in France, Lydia's best strategy is to marry me now, before she's proved to be the sister of a traitor."

Wesley spoke calmly, even pleasantly, as if the topic was of no more moment than a birdbath full of brackish water. But he deliberately described Caroline's missing son as a traitor, and Caroline felt all over again a widow's powerlessness.

Except that she wasn't quite without resources. Not yet.

"If you are traveling on to London to look for Marcus," Caroline said, "you will need means." She slipped a bracelet from her wrist, one her grandmother had given her upon the occasion of her come out. The jewelry was heavy, ugly by modern standards, and a constant reminder that the women in Caroline's family were not faded, spineless creatures.

Most of the women.

"This is worth a small fortune," Caroline said, though Wesley likely knew to the penny what the bracelet would bring. "If you can sell this bracelet and use the proceeds to learn the truth of Marcus's situation, however painful, I will be in your debt, as will Lydia."

Wesley took the bracelet, the amethysts and emeralds sparkling in their gold settings. "Are you sure, Aunt? This is a lovely antique." His words were hesitant, the look in his eyes positively jubilant. This was not the first time Caroline had financed his jaunting about, all in hopes he'd meet somebody to distract him from the notion of marrying Lydia.

"Anything that aids me to learn the truth of my son's situation is worth more than an old bracelet, Wesley. I do not mean to criticize Reginald's efforts, but we must admit his perspective is not entirely selfless." Neither was Wesley's. Far from it.

He slipped the bracelet into his pocket. "I will do all in my power to find out what has become of my cousin. I never wanted Marcus to buy his colors, but Papa said Uncle John would have wanted Marcus himself to make that decision. Suffice it to say, Papa is not infallible. Marcus was too young and too tender of heart to go for a soldier."

A pretty speech, and true enough as far as it went. "Find my son," Caroline said. "Lydia would ask the same thing of you, if she hasn't already."

An odd expression crossed Wesley's features, a little amused, a little chagrined. "I will send her back to you as my intended and then find our Marcus. See if I don't, Aunt." He bowed and strode off, a man very much on a mission.

Wesley disappeared into the house, and the whole garden felt more peaceful in his absence.

"I'm sorry, Grandmama." Caroline had acquired the habit of addressing the deceased after John had passed. At first, she'd been self-conscious about such an eccentricity, but John would not have judged her for it. "Wesley will make a flying pass down to London, pawn your bracelet, and spend the proceeds on a new wardrobe." Or worse. "I could think of no other way to buy Lydia more time."

Chloe would be very upset at the fate of Grandmama's bracelet, but needs must.

Wesley might yet think to look in on Lydia on his way to Town, and that would create all manner of awkwardness. Caroline considered remaining in the herbal and indulging in a good cry, but no.

Somebody had to remind the gardeners to clean the birdbaths, and that much at least, Caroline could do.

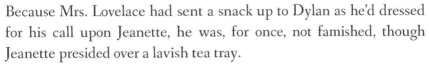

Because Mrs. Lovelace had sent a snack up to Dylan as he'd dressed for his call upon Jeanette, he was, for once, not famished, though Jeanette presided over a lavish tea tray.

"So tell me how your sisters are getting on," Jeanette said after she'd poured them each a cup of tea. "Their letters are all about spring lambs, daffodils, and double rainbows."

That simple recitation sent a pang of longing through Dylan. Home in any season was beautiful, but springtime had been made for Wales.

"As far as I know," he said, "my sisters are thriving. I have not seen them since I mustered out, save on their previous visits to Town, though they are faithful correspondents. They might well be dancing naked under the full moon and holding orgies in the ballroom."

Orgies. He had mentioned orgies to his lady cousin. Jeanette merely smiled and sipped her tea. "Sycamore shares your gift for a colorful turn of phrase. If the Powell ladies were hosting orgies, I would have heard of it, and Wales would have gained considerable cachet as a holiday destination."

Dylan reviewed what he knew of each sister's current occupations. Bronwen was drafting a novel. Marged was collecting old ballads to arrange for the harp. Dylan honestly did not know what occupied Tegan, but as the oldest, she was doubtless responsible for the decision to storm London.

The conversation reached a lull, and still, Dylan had not broached the topic of avoiding a match for himself. Jeanette doubtless had a thousand things to see to, and yet, she remained in her wing chair, as contented as a cat.

Dylan rose, prepared to take his leave.

"Was that the purpose of your call?" Jeanette asked, getting to her feet and slipping her arm through his. "You simply wanted to let me know the cousins are planning to visit Town?"

Dorning could have told her that much, and probably had.

"I have neglected you. I wanted to remedy that oversight." *Ask her about the bachelors and wallflowers. Get the dispatches from the ballrooms, enlist her aid.* The words refused to come, but a different question did. "How did you know, Jeanette, that Dorning was worth marrying? You had a miserable time of it with the marquess, and yet, you put your foot in parson's mousetrap a second time."

"Sycamore isn't everybody's cup of tea," Jeanette said. "I like that about him. He demands notice and refuses to be brushed aside. That fascinated me, when I'd devoted myself to living behind veils and shadows. Having so many older siblings—and especially older brothers—he refused to be ignored. That takes courage and tenacity."

Or it took a penchant for histrionics. "But he didn't simply catch your eye, he caught your heart. How did he do that?" And why had Dylan wandered onto this odd topic? He was not contemplating marriage, and his sisters were hardly the kind to need advice about their own preferences.

"Are you considering courting somebody, Dylan? Before you answer, please recall that I have no secrets from my husband, though he will take my confidences with him to the grave."

"I am not in contemplation of any courtships. I'm simply curious. Dorning is a good enough fellow, but what did he *do* that a dozen other bachelors haven't done as well or better? Is he the best dancer? The greatest wit? Does he have a store of *bon mots* second to none?"

Jeanette's gaze turned puzzled. "None of that matters in the least, Dylan."

It certainly didn't matter to him. "Then what does matter? Goddard told us you'd never remarry. That the marquess had been very uphill work, and one marriage was enough for you. Then you become Mrs. Sycamore Dorning. Dorning is not titled, he owns a questionable if elegant establishment, and he likes to play with knives. Something convinced you to take him on as a spouse."

Jeanette eased away and peered at the corkboard target hanging between two renderings of flowering plants. "Sycamore sees me."

This version of Jeanette would have been impossible to overlook. Dylan waited in hopes of further explanation.

"Sycamore," she said, wandering over to one of the ferns enthroned before the windows, "has been watching his family fall apart since he was a small boy. The older brothers went off to school, the old earl died, a sister disappeared into service and then married a virtual stranger. As the youngest boy, Sycamore could do nothing about any of it, and nobody took the time to explain to him that these developments were normal. His brothers would come back from school, his sister was only married, not gone to darkest Peru. He became vigilant where the welfare of his loved ones is concerned. He *pays attention.*"

Picturing Dorning as a lonely, anxious boy took imagination, but the narrative made sense. "Now he pays attention to you?"

"And I pay attention to him. I told myself I was concerned about my step-son's behavior, but Sycamore saw that I was worried sick. I pretended that widowhood was peaceful, when Sycamore could see that I was lonely in my soul and bored to wretchedness. I cannot deceive myself when he is on hand to listen to me and observe my behaviors.

"He knows when I'm tired," she went on. "When I'm out of patience. He listens to what I do say and to what I don't say. He knows *me,* and he loves the woman I truly am, not the woman polite society expects me to be. I have never been so free, Dylan, as I am now because of one man who accepts me as I am."

That explanation raised more questions. "You describe your spouse as if he were an ever-welcoming refuge."

"He is, and I aspire to be that for him, though we have regular and vigorous differences of opinion. We are also partners in mischief. I suspect Orion and Alasdhair would say the same about their wives."

"After a few drinks, they say exactly that, though not as eloquently as you do." And still, the whole business made little sense to Dylan.

Jeanette walked with him to the door and was soon handing him his hat. "You will know, Dylan. When the right person comes along, she might not be the easy person, the convenient person, or the available person, but if she's the love your heart has longed for, you will know."

Jeanette kissed his cheek when he would have offered her a bow, and then Dylan was back out in the chilly afternoon, having made no headway in any direction. He considered turning his steps for home, but then recalled Hughie Porter's odd remarks.

The men had struck a bargain with Dylan more than a year ago, when more of them had yet bided on London's streets. They would tolerate his attempts to help them, from a coin tossed into a fiddle case to a position offered and accepted, but he was not to venture into the worst slums after dark without them.

He could lead a charge, but he could not volunteer for a forlorn hope. Will Brook was the last man left in London whom Dylan had personally promised to help, and Will was missing in action. The afternoon was not well advanced, and the days were getting longer.

Dylan turned his steps for the stews.

Lydia hadn't cried since Papa's death. All of her tears hadn't brought him back and hadn't made her miss him any less. They hadn't inspired Marcus to bury himself any less in his studies, and they hadn't stopped Uncle Reginald from sermonizing at everybody about looking to the future and accepting God's blasted will.

Lydia's tears had made Mama only more sad, which should not have been possible. Hard work pushed grief aside. Weeping, by contrast, was stupid and pointless and...

Lydia stopped lecturing herself long enough to have a good look around the library, but the errant kitten wasn't there. Still wasn't there—Lydia had searched the library twice previously. Mab wasn't belowstairs. She wasn't in the attic. She wasn't in Mr. Brook's new office. She wasn't anywhere Lydia had looked.

Mab's sister had curled up in the hearth basket and gazed at Lydia with subtle accusation, as if Lydia had done away with the prodigal rather than mounted a search from attics to cellars. The last place to look was the captain's quarters. He hadn't come home for dinner, and the hour was growing late. Lydia had hoped she'd find her stray hiding in the butler's pantry or sniffing about Mr. Brook's office, but no.

If the captain found the kitten under his bed, he would banish all felines back to the alley, and that would inspire Lydia to profanity and tears both. She regularly cleaned in his sitting room and bedroom rather than leave that to the maids, but she was loath to trespass on his privacy for her own purposes.

"Needs must, as Mama always says." She missed Mama's quiet humor, missed her serene outlook on life. Lydia wasn't homesick for Tremont itself, which ought to bother her, except that, increasingly, Tremont was Uncle's domain rather than Lydia's home.

"And yet, I am homesick for something," she muttered, opening the door to the captain's sitting room. All was ruthlessly neat here, with a desk by the windows angled precisely to catch the most sunlight. The hassock before the reading chair was at the exact distance between the chair and fireplace to ensure the captain's feet were warm, but not too warm.

He'd explained that to Lydia when she'd inadvertently moved the hassock to dust the mantel. He hadn't quite scolded her, but she'd never again moved the hassock—or anything else in this apartment—without returning it to its assigned location.

"Here, kitty, kitty, kitty..." Lydia called softly, but she hadn't trained the kittens to come to their food bowl with that call. "Please come, please."

She lit the candles on the desk, hoping to see a furry paw sticking out from beneath the sofa, but no such luck.

"Nothing for it, then." She opened the door to the captain's bedroom, a place she rarely ventured after dark. The room held his scent, a combination of orange blossom, a touch of cinnamon, and an undernote of something woodsy. Lydia had never come across its like elsewhere and found the light, warm fragrance an intriguing choice for such a serious man.

He would be very serious indeed if Mab had trespassed on his personal domain. "Here, kitty, kitty, kitty. Won't you please come out?"

Nothing. Lydia lit a candle on the bed table and opened the door to the wardrobe. The captain's scent was stronger here, and his inherent sense of order was abundantly displayed. Everything—boots, coats, shirts, breeches—was neatly organized, not so much as a cravat hanging over a doorknob.

His life was so... so *in hand*. What must that be like? No missing brother, no eternally grieving mother, no uncle pilfering from estate coffers...

"No missing kitten, no cousin threatening to destroy the only viable plan I've come up with to find my sibling." Chloe's letter had weighed on Lydia's mind all day, demanding a reply—or demanding that Lydia go haring back north, abandoning the search for Marcus just as glimmers of hope shone.

Tears threatened again, and this time, Lydia couldn't force them away as easily. She sank onto the dressing stool, wanting to be surrounded by the captain's personal effects where nobody would see or hear her weakness.

She missed her brother. She missed her mama. She missed the time in life when she'd been part of a family, not a resented spinster trying to keep an estate from floundering.

"Mab, where are you?"

The little room remained still and shadowed. "Please, for the love of God, show yourself." *Don't you disappear on me too. Don't die, don't buy your colors and never come home, don't fade into endless grief...*

Perhaps this was why the captain had no dogs underfoot, why he remained distant from his siblings. Grief could not invade a life free of attachments, though loneliness could. Lydia rose from the dressing stool, weariness adding to her sense of despair.

Things would not look better in the morning—they seldom did— but the kitten might deign to come out of hiding after the household settled for the night—if she was hiding. The notion that Mab might be trapped in a drawer, or that she'd slipped out into the garden and gone exploring down the wrong drain was too awful to contemplate.

Lydia closed the wardrobe door—captain's orders—and returned to the bedroom. She was blowing out the candle on the bedside table when she saw the bed skirt move ever so subtly.

"Mab?" Hope and relief tried to shove aside despair. "Mab?"

Again, nothing. Lydia set down her candle and knelt on the carpet. "It's safe to come out. I'm worried about you. I've missed you. You make the kitchen a more cheerful place, though your sister is a bit grumpy because you went exploring without her."

Lydia kept her voice cheerful, but for a ridiculous tremor. Kittens were as ubiquitous as pigeons in London, and Mab would in all probability grow up and take to the alleys where she'd been born.

"Mab? Will you please...?"

The kitten poked her nose out from under the bed far enough to peer up at Lydia.

"Don't be afraid." Lydia extended a shaking finger in the cat's direction, the sight of that little nose bringing forth all manner of emotions. Mab bestowed a curious sniff to Lydia's fingertip.

"There you are." Lydia scooped the kitten into her lap. "I was worried about you." She cradled the cat against her chest, which provoked silent purring, and just that—the slight, warm, furry, vibrating sensation—wrecked the last measure of Lydia's self-possession.

When Captain Powell came into the bedroom a few minutes later, he found a teary-eyed Lydia, sitting on the floor, the kitten snuggled against her heart.

CHAPTER SEVEN

Military camps were full of tears. Women cried for their fallen soldiers, soldiers cried for their fallen comrades. Letters from home could cause tears, a lack of letters from home could as well. Life—and war—went on nonetheless.

Dylan had learned to deal with the tears, because when a lady could not cry for her deceased swain, when a soldier no longer reacted to the death of a friend, then trouble worse than sorrow was afoot.

Nothing in his experience had prepared him for the sight of Lydia Lovelace, sitting cross-legged on his bedroom floor, her cheeks damp with tears.

"Don't s-scold me," she said, her usual starch barely in evidence. "If you scold, lecture, or order me about just now, I will not answer for the consequences."

Two candles burned on the bedside table, a taper and a carrying candle. In the flickering shadows, Dylan's housekeeper looked both fierce and vulnerable, probably much as the damned kittens had first appeared to her.

She was not a kitten. Dylan lowered himself to the floor, an undertaking that his hips protested, and took the place beside Mrs. Lovelace, his back braced against the bedframe.

"The wee beast deserted her post in the kitchen?"

"I c-could not find her."

"Ah."

The rumbling grew louder.

"What does that mean? Ah?"

Dylan stroked a finger over the top of the kitten's head. "It means, when we can't find those we care about, we become a bit unhinged. I cannot find William Brook." He hadn't meant to say that, but then, Lydia Lovelace probably hadn't meant to succumb to tears on the floor of his bedroom, much less allow him to find her in such a state.

"You were out looking for Mr. Brook tonight?"

The kitten went on purring, oblivious to the upheaval her wanderings had caused. "Out wasting time. I came across Hughie Porter earlier today, and his comments suggested Brook was in hiding. That's plausible. A fellow runs up a few debts to the wrong people, or angers some girl's father, and hiding becomes a sound strategy."

"Hughie is the fiddler with the sad eyes?"

"The very one, though I would have said he has shrewd eyes." Dylan produced a handkerchief and passed it over. An exchange followed, wherein he was handed a kitten, and Mrs. Lovelace took his linen.

What was he to do with...? The kitten rubbed her head against Dylan's chin.

"One can be both shrewd and sad." Mrs. Lovelace dabbed at her cheeks. "I could not find Mab."

"And you left my rooms for last when you searched." No doubt after spending the whole day turning the house upside down.

She nodded. "I was reluctant to intrude."

Dylan's thigh touched Mrs. Lovelace's. She did not seem to

notice as she finished blotting her eyes with his handkerchief, then took a sniff of the wrinkled fabric.

"I arguably broke my word to the men tonight," Dylan said. "I was in the stews, alone, after dark."

Mrs. Lovelace regarded him steadily, tears adding a sheen to her gaze. "Why disobey orders like that?"

Dylan was tempted to make up a tale, about catching wind of a rumor, hunkering down in a dodgy tavern, and patiently standing watch until the establishment had closed. That lie would flatter him, but subtly insult him and Mrs. Lovelace too.

"I got lost. I don't know some parts of London well, and the men have extracted a promise from me that I won't venture into those neighborhoods alone after dark. I'm to have their escort."

"But most of your men are settled, aren't they? Some will come by for a meal, but I suspect they are checking up on you as much as they are filling their bellies."

Interesting theory. Dylan nudged her with his shoulder. "Or they are flirting with my pretty housekeeper."

"I have it on the best authority that I am not pretty."

"You are not a schoolgirl trussed up in silly frocks, your hair tormented into ringlets, your every thought bent on marriage or gossip. I rather like that about you, but who said you aren't pretty?"

Lydia flattened his handkerchief against her thigh and smoothed out the wrinkles. "This is not my first sojourn in London."

He liked sitting on the floor next to her, exchanging confidences. He liked that she trusted him, liked that she wasn't bustling off to dust or polish or make a list. Jeanette's words came back to him, about the powerful tonic of being listened to and heard.

"You stayed with some widowed auntie for a time when you left the schoolroom, and she introduced you to all of her spotty godsons?"

"And their bachelor uncles. I was a rousing failure." Her fingers smoothed the abused linen over and over, their rhythm entrancing.

"I was a failure as an officer. Bungled my orders regularly."

She glanced up at him. "You did not."

"Got stripped of rank for it at one point. You notice Goddard is a perishing colonel. MacKay is a major. I am a lowly captain. I was in consideration for lieutenant colonel, then I was ordered to lead my men into what I knew was an ambush. The ambush was intended to be a diversion, to keep the French distracted while some supply wagons meandered out from headquarters. I learned the supply wagons hadn't even left yet, and still, my commanding officer told me to dangle my men before the French."

"Why?"

"He wanted me dead or disgraced. I felt the same way about him, but I wasn't about to desert my men." Dylan did not speak of this to his cousins. He didn't have to, and he didn't want to.

"Your commanding officer was rotten?"

"Rotten to his soul. A great advocate of flogging the men over nothing. A fine one for keeping them drilling in the heat by the hour. He killed them with his version of discipline, and I desperately wanted to kill him, too, slowly and painfully."

Dylan had never said those words before, but oh, he'd lived them.

"What happened with the French ambush?"

"I got lost then too. The day was overcast, so the sun wasn't in evidence. I missed a turn so to speak."

She nudged him with her shoulder. "You did not."

"No, I did not, but nary a man in the company would betray me. They marched according to my orders and lived to march another day. I was given the option of a transfer or demotion, and I chose the demotion."

"Because you would not abandon your men. You still haven't. Has Will Brook abandoned his brother?"

The question of the hour. "I don't know. He's gone to his covert for some reason, and I am being warned not to meddle."

"But meddling is what you do, isn't it? I have been referred to as a meddler. A busybody. My uncle is probably pleased that I've removed to London."

Dylan thought back to his call upon Jeanette, to the changes in her that she'd attributed to marrying a difficult, if doting, man.

"I am pleased that you removed to London. The whole time I was wandering around the battlefield of the stews, I thought, 'Mrs. Lovelace will wonder what's become of me if I can't find my way out of here. Mrs. Lovelace will scold me for worrying her. She will be *disappointed* if I cannot even manage to find my way to the river.' One doesn't disappoint a lady who is fond of one."

"Are you teasing me?"

The kitten's purring was so subtle as to be a mere whisper of warmth against Dylan's chest. "No. I am not teasing."

Mrs. Lovelace folded his handkerchief and held it out to him.

"Keep it, madam. I have, as you know, many others."

"All plain. Tell me about the stews. You used the word 'battlefield.'"

Words came, slowly at first, about how London's downtrodden and inebriated reminded Dylan of battlefield casualties. They even sprawled in the same undignified positions. He spoke of how angry a simple walk through St. Giles had left him, how despairing. He spoke of Dunacre's cruelty, never using that hated name, but using other words—*evil, vile, disgusting, contemptible, dishonorable.*

The recitation surprised him, as Lydia's tears had surprised him. Perhaps the two were related. Mrs. Lydia Lovelace never cried, and Captain Dylan Powell never complained.

But he mourned, apparently. By the light of two candles, stroking a purring kitten, sitting next to his housekeeper on the bedroom floor, he raged and lamented and grieved.

The carrying candle guttered out before he fell silent, leaving only the taper to illuminate the room.

"You were right, Captain," Mrs. Lovelace said. "I would have scolded you sorely had you spent the night on the streets. I know your men do that, or they have, but I do not keep house for your men."

"You are not fond of them?"

Her smile was slight and gorgeous. "You will not let me forget that, will you?"

He would never forget her words, and after the conversation they'd just had, he was compelled to be honest with her in one more regard.

"I am fond of you, too, Lydia Lovelace, and while I would never presume on your person, I would like to kiss you again."

She considered him as he petted the cat, her expression unreadable. Dylan wanted to explain—he was not like those employers who treated a housekeeper or comely parlor maid as a convenience. He was fond of her, *respectfully fond*, and she'd just heard more from him about the war than his whole family put together had.

"I think not," she said, gently easing the kitten from his grasp.

Well, hell. He was apparently to blunder his way through the whole day. "I understand. My apologies. We needn't—"

With some arranging of skirts, Lydia settled closer. "This time, I will kiss you." She leaned in, such that the cat was nestled between them, and the moment when she pressed her mouth to Dylan's, the rumbling from the cat became more palpable.

The confluence of sensations and emotions was the sweetest Dylan had ever felt, and he wished the kiss would never end.

Lydia knew how to kiss—or so she'd thought.

Hostilities with France had ensured that an endless stream of fellows from the Tremont surrounds had kissed Lydia farewell. No dashing soldier was judged for taking such liberties, some of which Lydia had actually enjoyed.

When those same fellows came home on leave, they'd kissed her in greeting. At quarterly assemblies, more kisses had been stolen beneath various full moons, until Lydia considered herself thoroughly schooled in the overrated business of kissing.

She had the knack of it now. Swoop in, pucker up, land about thirty degrees off-center of the other party's mouth to avoid bumping noses. Tilt to the other side, repeat. Linger a moment mouth to mouth, but not long enough for the fellow to get untoward ideas. Sigh. Linger again about two inches from his mouth. Retreat. Lean for a moment. Step back. Sigh and step back farther if he looks to be getting ideas.

Not complicated. The actual kissing part could be kept quite brief, particularly if the fellow hadn't recently used his toothpowder. Denying some men a kiss was an invitation for them to become more importunate, and besides, Lydia hoped that one day, she'd meet a man she *wanted* to kiss.Logic decreed that bringing some experience to that happy encounter would enhance her chances of succeeding at it. To find a man worth kissing only to put him off with ineptitude would not do.

Her strategy had served her well both at Tremont and during her sojourn to London under Aunt Chloe's chaperonage. The change of location had not changed the characteristics of the men Lydia had kissed. Some were sweet, some were bold, some were bothersome.

None were particularly memorable.

Straddling Dylan's Powell's lap, Lydia could not remember what day of the week it was.

He did not merely press his lips to hers or try to breathe into her mouth. He stroked her hair, her shoulders, her nape. His touch was slow and sweet, as if merely caressing her arm filled him with wonderment.

He didn't mind a little nose bumping and, in fact, nuzzled at her throat, then her ear—that tickled—then kissed the place where her neck and shoulder joined, which gave her the shivers.

Lydia's list—pucker, tilt, press, whatever—melted straight into a puddle of pleasure as the captain's hand slipped around her waist and traveled over her back. When he eased away from her, without allowing her more than that initial pucker-and-press, she grabbed him by the hair.

"More."

He rested his forehead against hers. "The kitten, Lydia. Let me set aside the kitten."

What? "Oh, of course."

The captain passed over one purring little ball of fur.

"Up onto the bed," he said. "She can't get into trouble there."

Lydia set Mab on the coverlet and gave her a little push toward the center of the bed. "Explore, cat." The kitten blinked and made for the pillows.

"You explore too, Lydia."

Lydia's brain could not make sense of that command, as if she'd overslept on a rainy day and could not orient herself to the hour of the morning. "Explore?"

"Explore me." The captain took her hands and placed them on his chest. "To your heart's content."

Some vague, officious voice in the back of Lydia's mind tried to warn her: She would have to face this man over menus, make his bed, and curtsey to his sisters. She would return to Tremont, hopefully with Marcus in tow, hopefully soon, and resume the duties of an earl's sister.

But all of that was *later*. Another day, another life.

The captain cradled her cheek against a warm, callused palm. "Go on reconnaissance, Lydia. Scout the terrain. Gather intelligence. Inventory the stores in the armory."

She ran her fingers through dark, silky hair. "I can skirmish with you. I cannot allow you to take me captive." Though she longed to surrender all, and the novelty of that sentiment did infuse her with a little caution. "I am your housekeeper."

He brushed his thumb over her brow, and she wanted to purr. "Right now, you are the lady I hope will get to know me a little better."

"Only a little?" That was some relief, also a disappointment.

"We are not the sort of people who seek a casual tumble and think nothing of it. I don't recount my military history to just anybody. I don't kiss just anybody."

Lydia would certainly be much more selective going forward. "I like kissing you. Leaves me all muddled and warm inside."

"Let's muddle each other a little more."

Dylan Powell should never be allowed to kiss a lady when both of his hands are free. That was Lydia's last coherent thought before his mouth settled over hers, and all her previous kisses were revealed to be so much bumbling.

Kisses—real kisses—were a balance of patience and consideration with curiosity and desperation. Lydia settled onto the captain's lap and realized that tasting was involved too—mutual tasting and flirtations too intimate to bear. At the same time, the captain's caresses traveled farther afield, to her lower back and thighs, until she resented her clothing and positively loathed his.

This was kissing as kissing was meant to be. A dangerous, reason-stealing delight.

"Settle a bit." The captain cradled Lydia's nape and urged her against his chest. "Please."

She cuddled close, her sigh entirely genuine. "I am... astonished."

"Good word." He rested his cheek against her hair and kept one hand moving over her back. "Once upon a time, a horse was shot out from under me. The beast lived, but the moment was disconcerting. This is... the most marvelous ambush imaginable."

"I am ambushed too, Captain."

"Dylan. Your kitten is in my bed, Lydia. You can call me Dylan."

Oh, how she liked to hear him use her name. "My kitten and I should be going."

"Not yet, please. I need to calm my animal spirits."

He was being delicate. Lydia had been raised in the country, had caught any number of grooms and dairymaids frolicking. His animal spirits were pressed against her intimate flesh, and she liked how that felt.

The captain simply held her and stroked her back after that, and Lydia eventually succumbed to the temptation to close her eyes. Tomorrow was soon enough to make sense of this folly, if folly it was.

"I'm falling asleep."

"Shall I carry you down to your bed?"

"I can walk." Lydia could not think, though. She was too relaxed, too happy and amazed. Before she realized exactly what the captain was about, he had her sitting on the bed. He'd gathered her up as she'd straddled him, risen, and simply deposited her on the coverlet as if she were a stack of clean linen.

He sat beside her, *on the bed*, and when Lydia ought to have been alarmed, she was pleased.

"You will think this to death," he said. "I will think this to death."

"Brood," Lydia said. "Men brood. Don't brood, please. I am not, as you've noticed, a blushing schoolgirl."

"Sensible," he said, taking her hand. "But passionate. Interesting combination." He kissed her knuckles. "I don't know what to say, Lydia. I should probably lecture myself about overstepping and ungentlemanly behavior—I am your employer—but... we are fond of each other. Also attracted to each other."

"That surprises you?"

"Bewilders me. You are all that is lovely, but I did not... I *do* not bother with frivolous pastimes. Neither do you. I would also never impose myself on a woman in my employ."

Kissing was all well and good—kissing Dylan Powell—but Lydia liked even more that he would talk with her, that he would hold her hand and speak what was in his heart.

"I had regarded kissing as some peculiar fixation men have, a little odd, sometimes pleasant, sometimes not, but with you..."

He looped an arm around her shoulders. "With me?"

A wild impulse seized Lydia, to tell him everything, about Marcus, about Uncle Reginald, about years spent watching Mama become Tremont's living ghost. But no. She was exhausted, the captain's view of Marcus was dubious at best, and the past hour had been, as the captain had said, bewildering.

Also lovely. "With you, I will ponder what has passed between us," Lydia said, "and I will smile. I am fond of you, you are fond of me—"

"Quite fond."

"Quite fond, and we need not panic or fly into the boughs over a kiss."

"Will there be more kisses, Lydia?"

She *adored* that he would leave the decision to her. "That is up to us. For now, I am content to marvel and smile." Mama needed her, Marcus needed her, Tremont needed her. Lydia had come to London looking for her brother—she was still looking for her brother—but she'd found something unexpected and precious with the captain instead.

What to do about that unexpected treasure, if anything, was a question for another, more sensible and well-rested, day.

"I will see you down to the kitchen," the captain said.

Lydia sat up. "That won't be necessary. I know my way through the house, sir."

"What you know and what I need are two very different articles." He rose, scooped up the kitten, and offered Lydia his free hand.

She took it and held hands with the captain as they navigated the darkened house. When he might have made some grand little speech outside the door of her parlor, she eased the kitten from his grasp, kissed his cheek, and wished him sweet dreams.

"If I'd wanted to throw money away," Sycamore Dorning said, ambling along beside Dylan in the darkness, "I could have played patience against my niece. I would suspect Tabitha of cheating, except her aunties have the same skill. They can recall the location of any card they've seen, and they have an uncanny knack for turning over pairs."

Dylan had consented to a night of cards among the cousins. Dorning, because he was married to Jeanette, had joined Goddard and MacKay to make up a fourth. Dylan's excuse for an evening of pointless diversion had been the need to take his mind off last night's encounter with Lydia.

An impossible objective. She was so blazingly honest, so forthright, and so astonishingly kissable. She had the knack of being held, too, of resting in a man's arms as if no place on earth could afford her as much comfort.

"Next time we play," Dylan said, "partner MacKay. He's all pleasantries and domestic chitchat while he picks your pocket and robs you blind."

"Sounds like Goddard, and most of my brothers. Jeanette says you're sweet on your housekeeper."

Years of marching, despite heat, enemy fire, downpours, and drifting snow, kept Dylan from betraying his surprise at Dorning's observation. That, and having survived many an ambush from both the enemy and his superior officer.

"Why would Jeanette conclude such a thing?"

"Because you delegated that housekeeper to spruce up MacKay's house before he got hitched, and you would not entrust such a mission to just anybody."

"Who else would I entrust it to?"

"Powell, you sent her as your intelligence officer, not simply to dust the windowsills. Jeanette says you also get a look in your eyes when you mention her name, and do not ask me to describe the look, because my lady wife did not elucidate. What do we know of the fair Mrs. Lovelace?"

"*We* know you will leave Mrs. Lovelace in peace, Dorning. None of your legendary tactless blundering, please. You are not to interrogate her, intimidate her, or investigate her."

Dylan nodded to old Andy Bean, a former drill sergeant lounging idly against a lamppost across the street. Bean returned a two-fingered salute and broke into a song about some naughty little boy who fell into a stream and came down with a cold.

"I do not tactlessly blunder." Dorning sounded amused, which was fortunate. With his size, muscle, and guile, he'd be lethal in a fight. Then too, he liked to play with knives. "I boldly sally forth when others are too fainthearted to join the affray. It's a gift."

"It's a bad habit, otherwise known as meddling. Stay away from Lydia Lovelace."

"Jeanette says Mrs. Lovelace sings beautifully."

Oh, she did. Little art songs while she dusted, snippets of lyric arias when she polished, the occasional folk tune as she beat a carpet runner. Her voice was nimble and sweet.

"Why would I have any occasion to notice how a housekeeper passes the time when at her chores?"

Dorning sauntered along, twirling his walking stick. "She sings in French and sometimes in Italian."

How had Dorning's six older brothers allowed him to reach adulthood? "If a song is written in French, one generally sings it in French."

Dylan did not increase his pace, but he wanted to. He wanted to be rid of Dorning's thick-witted prying, and he wanted to be back under the same roof as Lydia. Was she having second thoughts about kissing him? Had she found excuses to spend more time than usual in his room today, or avoided his apartment altogether?

"Mrs. Lovelace is skilled with a needle," Dorning said. "Jeanette had occasion to observe her handkerchief, the borders of her gloves, the stitchwork on her bonnet."

"Most women are skilled with a needle. My sister Tegan has raised embroidery to a high art. What on earth are you getting at?"

Dorning paused on a street corner and propped his walking stick across his broad shoulders. "How did Tegan become so skilled with a needle?"

Dylan felt as if he were a recruit being schooled by a particularly pedantic corporal on the basics of firing a long gun.

"Tegan has been at her stitchery since she was a child, Dorning. The hour is late, and I'm sure you long to return to your lady's side. I'd bid you—"

Dorning shrugged, or something, and the walking stick was in his hand. "Mrs. Lovelace quoted Wordsworth, according to Jeanette. Also, Shakespeare:

I rather would entreat thy company
    To see the wonders of the world abroad,
    Than, living dully sluggardized at home,
    Wear out thy youth with shapeless idleness."

Dylan had to think for a moment, mentally reviewing his sisters' parlor dramas. *"Two Gentlemen of Verona.* Lydia is from Shropshire, and a post in London qualifies as seeing the wonders of the world abroad. Her family resents the initiative she's shown and wants her back home stepping and fetching for them. If you will excuse me, the day has been wearying—"

"You are not thinking, Powell, and you have no brothers to do your thinking for you, so I will put the case to you as simply as I can: You have a housekeeper who at some point had a singing master. She studied long enough that her voice is at least as trained as any self-respecting debutante's. Shropshire's dairymaids and alewives do not learn French chansons. Mrs. Lovelace has also had time to sit by many a sunny window, perfecting her fancy needlework, not simply repairing torn hems. She quotes the Bard and not the usual that-which-we-call-a-rose drivel."

"You are taking rather a long time to make some obscure point, Dorning." A point Dylan had glimpsed for himself days ago and promptly ignored.

"If you are smitten with Mrs. Lovelace, then those who care about you have a right to become interested in her particulars. Who are her people? Why did she leave them to come all the way to London? Is there a Mr. Lovelace, and if not, what became of him?"

"There is no Mr. Lovelace." Lydia would never hide such a thing.

Not after last night. She wasn't hiding anything of significance, except a passionate and wonderfully affectionate nature.

"If she provided characters, who wrote them?" Dorning went on. "Has she had any callers or paid any calls the whole time she's been in London? With whom does she correspond, if she has such devoted family in Shropshire? Does she even *sound* like she comes from Shropshire?"

William and Bowen Brook came from Shropshire. Lydia didn't sound much like them at all, but then, they were the sons of a yeoman.

"Lydia Lovelace is an exceptionally talented housekeeper, Dorning. She has the knack of putting a place to rights and keeping it that way. She could be Napoleon's daughter, for all I care, and I'd see no reason to inquire into her antecedents."

"I will give you a reason, Powell: You referred to her by her given name. 'Lydia is from Shropshire.' You trust her to gather intelligence for you on your own cousins. You have potted violets on your office windowsills."

And they looked quite cheerful on that windowsill, which had nothing to do with anything.

"My office has east-facing windows, which is the best exposure for violets, apparently. I will deal severely with MacKay for bearing tales." MacKay had to be responsible for spreading this nonsense. Goddard hadn't been in Dylan's office for months.

"Powell, if MacKay noticed your east-facing violets, it's because his own office has likely been kitted out similarly, *by his new wife*. I'm not saying you need to sack *Lydia* without a character, but if she *is* Napoleon's daughter, you deserve to know that before your firstborn is Napoleon's grandson."

"You have me already married and a father? What a fanciful imagination you have, Dorning." Lydia would be a wonderful mother. Loving but firm, affectionate, warmhearted, good-humored, patient...

"I told Jeanette that reasoning with a man in love is futile, but she said I had to try."

"I am not in love, but I am in anticipation of a visit from my sisters. If you or Jeanette or the archangel Michael do anything to vex Lyd—Mrs. Lovelace, I will have you drummed out of the regiment."

Dorning took an idle swipe with his walking stick at some ivy trying to climb a lamppost. "I'm a-tremble with dread. I am also a happily besotted man, so if you ignore everything else I said, please heed me on this: Jeanette was keeping secrets when I began courting her. She was trying to protect herself with her reticence, but she was also protecting those she loved. That number included my darling self, for which novel sentiment, I was compelled to marry her. Certain aspects of Mrs. Lovelace's situation do not tally and crossfoot, Powell."

Oh, perhaps they didn't. Minor, inconsequential aspects. Perhaps Lydia's uncle had been a singing teacher. Perhaps an aunt had taken particular pride in her needlework. A grandfather might have been interested in literature, or done some acting in his youth. A few lines of Shakespeare did not an intrigue make.

And there was no Mr. Lovelace, of that Dylan was certain. Lydia had not kissed like a wife, not that Dylan made a habit of kissing wives.

"Are you finished, Dorning?"

Dorning smacked him on the arm. "That's the spirit. Chin up, soldier on. It's merely your heart that's in peril. No risk to anything of value. If Jeanette asks, tell her I tried and met with an absolute granite wall of Welsh pride. Thank you for a pleasant evening, Powell. I'll give Jeanette your regards."

Dorning sauntered away into the night, swinging his walking stick and whistling some jaunty tune.

Dylan turned for home, moving quickly as he mentally set about cataloging everything he knew regarding Lydia Lovelace's life prior to her joining his household.

She'd not disclosed the name of her village.

She'd never mentioned any family member by name, other than to admit a distant connection with that idiot Marcus, Lord Tremont.

She'd never paid any calls or received any callers that Dylan knew of, and the only mail she received was a rare note from an auntie in Oxfordshire—not Shropshire.

Dylan's steps slowed, and he was seized by a sudden urge to pummel the hell out of Sycamore Dorning.

CHAPTER EIGHT

"The captain played cards until about midnight, my lord. Walked partway home with Mr. Dorning, what owns the Coventry and is married to the captain's cousin."

William Brook still had the habit of standing at attention when he made a report. Marcus, Earl of Tremont, hated that mannerism. The war with all its inane posturing was over, and the information was the same whether a man stood, lay on the floor, or slouched.

"And then?" Marcus asked.

Brook continued to stare unwaveringly at a water stain on the opposite wall. "Andy Bean said the captain went home, let hisself into the house, and took hisself upstairs to his own bedroom."

As a younger man, Marcus had felt awkward having to rely on a lot of reprobates and scalawags to keep him informed—also to keep him alive—but they had proven to be wily and loyal reprobates when he'd needed them most.

And he was in no position to judge anybody. "No light appeared in the kitchen windows?" Or in the windows of the houseckeeper's parlor?

"Nary a light belowstairs, sir. Straight up to bed, candles snuffed thirty minutes later. Appears the captain enjoys a clear conscience, and as much as he's been pokin' about lately, he deserves his rest."

Brook's loyalties were divided, which was understandable. His brother Bowen now worked for Dylan Powell, and Powell was fiercely protective of his former subordinates.

Was he protective of Lydia, indifferent to her, or something else entirely? "When did his housekeeper go to bed?"

"Mrs. Lovelace turned in a couple hours before the captain came home."

Lydia's typical bedtime, though she'd stayed up later than usual the previous night. Why? She was looking for Marcus in London, asking discreet questions of the men, but why conduct that search as a housekeeper in Captain Dylan's Powell's domicile, of all places? Why leave Shropshire at all?

The whole situation was far too puzzling for a mere disgraced earl to fathom.

"Beggin' yer pardon, my lord, there's something else you need to know."

Marcus had asked, ordered, reminded, and begged Brook not to refer to him as *my lord*. "My uncle is trying to have me declared dead." A clerk in the solicitors' office had passed along that much in exchange for a bit of coin. He'd thought Marcus a clerk from the offices of the countess's solicitors, but heavens above... if a man would betray a legal confidence for a few shillings, what would he betray for a few pounds?

Brook's eyes-front, blank expression turned quizzical. "I thought you wanted to be dead?"

"I want to be disappeared," Marcus replied. "I thought I still had some time before I must choose whether to be dead. It hasn't been seven years, and that is the minimum necessary to create a rebuttable presumption of my demise."

"Whatever that means." Brook ambled across the room to crack a window. "Goddamn chimney fumes will kill you, sir."

"So will the goddamn cold."

"This ain't cold. Cold's behind us for the nonce. The flue ain't drawin' proper, and that's a worse hazard than fresh air."

There was no fresh air in London outside of Hyde Park. Brook was right, though—the chimney likely hadn't been cleaned since Queen Anne had held court, just one of the many charms of life in St. Giles. Before residing in London, Marcus had had only the vaguest notion that dirty flues were a health hazard—in addition to being a fire hazard—and not the first inkling how to remedy the problem.

An earl's heir had to be among the most useless, ignorant creatures ever to strut about the earth. "What is this other news I need to know?"

Brook remained by the window, gazing through the grimy glass to the alley below. "Captain was on reconnaissance yesterday not two streets over."

"Blast and damnation." If Dylan Powell found Marcus, Marcus would likely not live to see another sunrise, and yet, returning to Shropshire was impossible.

"He weren't lookin' fer you, my lord. He were lookin' for me. Seems everybody's lookin' for me of late. The lads gave the captain enough wrong directions that he got proper turned around, but he won't make that mistake again."

Powell seldom made *any* mistakes, damn him. Dunacre had delighted in trying to outsmart the captain and had failed unless Powell—for reasons Marcus had never entirely grasped—had wanted Dunacre to succeed. Even when Powell had lost his major's rank, Marcus had suspected that had been Powell's objective.

All very complicated and deadly, when the French were supposed to be the enemy. "Who would the lads choose, if they had to fight for me or for Powell?"

Brook speared him with a look that was anything but respectful. "You and the captain keep clear of each other, and there won't be any fightin'. Be a lot easier to keep clear of him if you'd just leave Town until he goes back to Wales. His sisters won't bide here much past June, and by then, he'll have given up on me."

"I tried leaving Town. Villagers all know who the outsiders are, and even the posting inns on the Great North Road know who's a regular and who ought to be just passing through." This stinking, gloomy little room had come to represent safety, which made no sense at all.

"Go to Scotland," Brook said. "Take a coastal packet, skip the inns, bide in Edinburgh. My cousin says it smells even worse than London."

The Old Town part of Edinburgh did. The New Town was quite nice. Marcus had visited there with Mama when he was twelve.

"If I'm in Edinburgh, I can't keep an eye on the solicitors." Or on Lydia, who'd had no business leaving Shropshire. "Then too, I make money here in London." In St. Giles and the East End, the ability to read and write was worth coin. The tavern owners paid Marcus—in pennies, pints, and plates—to read the newspapers aloud to the patrons.

The patrons paid to have any mail read to them and to have replies penned when necessary. Skills Marcus had mastered by age eight were supporting him adequately, which called into question what all that other schooling—and drinking and whatnot at university —had been in aid of. The great Marcus Aurelius had said that drunkenness pained both the body and the purse, and he'd been right.

As usual.

"Sooner or later, somebody will slip, my lord. Somebody will mutter into their beer about a handsome young peer hiding in the stews. You should go home."

"I cannot go home." Powell could call Marcus out and observe the standard rules in any ensuing duel, though a peer really ought not to be dueling with a commoner. The contest would be nominally fair. In Shropshire, Marcus would get a noose slung from the nearest oak, or worse—arrest, trial, and then the noose.

"You cannot bide here forever, sir."

"Many do."

"Many are not perishing earls, trying to fool family into thinking they're dead."

That had not been the plan, not at first. It still wasn't the plan. The plan was for Uncle Reggie to die, Wesley to become the heir, and Marcus to dwell in Italy on quiet remittance—presumed dead, proved dead, it didn't matter if Uncle was gone—until Wesley could take over the earldom. In an ideal world, Wesley would marry Lydia, and nobody at Tremont need ever mention Marcus's name again.

Uncle was not to be trusted, but Wesley was resourceful and loyal. He'd proved that beyond any doubt. Perhaps it was time to contact Wesley? That decision wanted thought—a lot of thought.

Marcus did not dare prop a hip on the rickety antique that served as his desk. He instead took the lone chair in the room, a hard, ladder-back article missing half its rungs.

"What you aren't saying, Brook, is that *you* cannot bide here forever. You have more than repaid any debt you ever owed to me in even a theoretical sense, so decamp for the shires whenever you are so inclined."

Brook shook his head. "You talk like that, sir, and a stumbling drunk whore will know you for a nob. The innkeepers already do, unless I miss my guess, but you keep folk comin' around to hear the news, so the publicans don't ask questions. You ain't safe on yer own. Not here."

"Not yet," Marcus said, "but I'm learning. I'm not completely hopeless." He had been completely hopeless when Dunacre had first got hold of him. Then Marcus had taken to studying Powell's tactics, listening to the men grumble at mess call, and chatting up the other officers.

"What are my orders, sir?" Brook ambled away from the window and made for the door. "I'll keep mum about your situation, but I'd like to let Bowen know he needn't worry about me."

"Family is supposed to fret about us." Though Lydia coming to London to work as a housekeeper was the outside of worrisome. She would never abandon Mama unless matters at Tremont were growing dire. "Subtly indicate to Bowen that you yet enjoy good health. I will carry on as before, but I must ask you to do something for me."

"I'll not betray the captain, sir. I don't like causing him extra worry, come to that."

"This has nothing to do with the captain. You will go to the Haymarket and procure a bouquet of speedwell, if you can find it this early in the year, but any pretty posy will do. Have the flowers left on the captain's back stoop along with this note."

Marcus used a pencil to write six words on a scrap of paper, then passed the note and a coin to Brook. "Secret the note among the flowers, and mind nobody steals the bouquet." As soon as he'd heard that Lydia was in Town, handing out sandwiches and shortbread at Powell's back door, Marcus had pondered what to do.

Lydia needed to go home, bless her, the sooner the better. Of all the households she could attach herself to, Powell's was the worst choice in the whole of London.

"Nobody would steal from the captain's back stoop, sir. The men wouldn't allow it."

Powell had spent the past several years seeing those men set on their feet. A former marksman might not hear well, but he could earn his keep working for the night-soil man. Another soldier might have come home with a game leg, but serve well and happily as a gardener. Yet another could have lost the full use of an arm, but be particularly talented at walking dogs for Mayfair's elderly widows.

Powell was resourceful and quietly relentless once he'd set a task for himself. That he might take it upon himself to find Marcus, whether on Lydia's behalf or because Powell finally ran out of soldiers to look after, was deuced alarming.

～

Lydia was neither panicking nor flying into the boughs over her kiss with Captain Powell, but she was inspired to sing more. She had forgotten to don her cap two days in a row, and she was also—as predicted—smiling more.

"You are cheerful," the captain said as Lydia set a vase of daffodils on the library mantel. He did not remark her lack of cap, but then, unlike some men, Dylan Powell wasn't compelled to bleat and carry on about his every opinion or perception.

"The sun is shining, your sisters are to arrive within the week, and the house is showing to good advantage. I have reason to be of good cheer. Luncheon approaches, sir. Would you like a tray in here, or will you dine in the breakfast parlor?"

"Don't flit away." He rose from the desk and came around to take down the vase Lydia had just set on the mantel. "I love the scent." He put the bouquet on the blotter and propped his hip on the desk corner. "Elegant and sweet, also unique. How are you?"

Lydia was in a complete, flummoxing muddle, but a happy muddle. "I am well. You?"

"I am distracted," he said. "I should be finding William Brook, looking in on the men, explaining the household accounts to Bowen, and otherwise preparing for the upcoming siege, but instead..."

He regarded the flowers, while Lydia regarded him. Dylan Powell was no downy youth, hadn't been for some time. He was weathered and worn, unsentimental, and battle-hardened. And yet, he kissed with more tenderness than Lydia had known a man was capable of.

He'd talked with her, held her hand, and escorted her through the darkened house. In the past two days, not by word, glance, innuendo, or hint, had he offered Lydia anything approaching disrespect or presumption—or encouragement, drat the man.

"Instead?" Lydia asked.

"I stare off into space and marvel, but I also ponder the demands of honor."

That did not sound encouraging at all. "In what sense?"

"You work for me, madam."

Lydia set off on a round of tidying, starting with the newspapers on the reading table. "That is my happy privilege."

"A gentleman does not impose his attentions on those he employs."

She arranged the newspapers in date order. "I don't recall anybody doing any imposing. In fact, I find your observation ironic." She moved on to the books stacked on the reading table, two of which came from the history shelves. She returned them to their proper places and took up a bound libretto from some old masque by Handel.

"Ironic how?" the captain asked.

"You did not kiss me, sir. I kissed you. A first, unless you count the times I've kissed my mare. On every other occasion, the gentleman assumed the initiative, though some of them did not behave as gentlemen, and my assent was apparently irrelevant. Now I find a man whose attentions I enjoy, a man I esteem—"

"And of whom you are quite fond."

"And of whom I am quite fond, and he's enthroned himself on some philosophical toadstool to ponder trivialities having nothing to do with anything. This is the same fellow who asked me to tolerate the fiction that he was enamored of me, and now he's gone for a Puritan."

Lydia had spoken civilly, but the urge to shout was nearly over-whelming. Finally, and in the least likely place, she'd found a man who held her interest and esteem, and he was turning up *missish*?

"Your dignity and livelihood are not trivialities, Lydia."

She pretended to leaf through the libretto while trying to sort logic from longing. The captain believed her to be a housekeeper, and assenting to a fiction of interest was very different from acting on a real attraction.

She ought to esteem him for his blasted scruples.

The captain eyed the libretto, which she'd rolled up like a news-paper. "Do you plan to smack me with that, Mrs. Lovelace?"

"I would like to smack you with something, Captain. You have decided to be uncomfortable with what passed between us. Rather than acknowledge the true source of your unease, you reach for the fig leaves of gentlemanly honor. Not well done of you. You are supposed to tell me that I caught you in a weak moment, that my confidence overpowered your common sense, and as delightful as the interlude was, I must not presume again. We retire to neutral corners and speak no more of the matter."

One corner of his mouth quirked up. "Is that how it's done?"

Apparently, nobody had ever had to pin his ears back in that fashion. "I grasp, Captain, that I have been insubordinate or violated orders or somehow threatened your command. You need not be delicate. I will execute my duties as conscientiously as I always have, and you will find no bouquets left on your pillows." Better that way, considering that Lydia hadn't planned to tarry in London even this long.

"You leave the bouquets in my library instead."

"And in your formal parlor, and I keep one blossom for my own parlor." Lydia shoved the abused libretto onto the shelf reserved for music. She had not anticipated that the captain would blow retreat like this. She'd expected—she'd hoped, more fool she—that their flirtation might continue or mature into friendship or the pleasures that came after admitting a flirtatious warmth toward another person.

The captain stood, and whatever else was true about the military, it gave a man spectacularly impressive posture.

"Am I really so fragile as all that, Mrs. Lovelace? My entire command can be upset by"—he waved a hand in upward circles —"some expressions of fondness?"

Lydia had come to London to find Marcus, not to become entangled with a difficult Welshman, and yet, the captain was not difficult. He was... different. She had begun to hope he was different in a wonderful way.

"You need no one," she said, gathering up a stack of three almanacs. "You are ever available to your cousins, to stand up with them when they speak their vows, aid their causes, or make up a fourth at cards for their convenience. You never rely on them to do likewise for you."

She reshelved the almanacs and started on the Welsh periodical newspapers sent in from Swansea.

"We played cards hour after hour in Spain. I hate playing cards."

Lydia organized the newspapers by date and added them to the stack on the shelves. "Then tell your cousins you'd rather play billiards. You could have one of your sisters manage this house for you. Instead, they visit you when they're of a mind to buy new frocks. You could have hired Bowen or one of his ilk at any point to act as your house steward. Instead, you bury yourself in the ledgers every Wednesday and mutter about the cost of paper."

Lydia had tidied what needed tidying and hadn't thought to bring her duster with her. She took up the broom from the hearth set and began sweeping what did not need sweeping.

"You look after a battalion of tattered and lame soldiers," she went on, "but they are not permitted to look after you. They could be your gardeners, your footmen, your grooms, but you never hire the men who fought under your command for this household—save for Bowen, and I had to goad you into that."

The captain watched her wielding the broom and said nothing.

"I keep this house immaculate," Lydia said, "but you never entertain. We are a temple to pointless industry belowstairs, while you racket about London, getting lost in the very slums, where thievery and worse are rampant, and—"

She stopped because the captain had stalked over to the hearth to stand immediately before her.

"You were worried about me."

"Will you have me court-martialed if I say yes?" Lydia's reply was not merely insubordinate, it was angry—upset. She was never upset. She was determined, focused, occasionally annoyed and sometimes puzzled, but not upset.

Losing one's composure accomplished nothing.

The captain gazed down at her, his expression unreadable. "The men took enough orders from me in Spain. I don't want them having to take orders from me as my gardeners, footmen, or whatnot. In Wales, they won't have to put up with me personally, because the estate is large and managed by familiar retainers. When I finally see the last of the wounded settled, I will close up this house and decamp for home. Hiring the men for this household makes no sense."

When that day came along, he would no longer need a London housekeeper. Well, no matter. Lydia had always intended that her post be temporary.

"You dislike playing cards," she said, "and you want your men to have long-term situations. That does not explain why you never impose on family or friends, Captain." Or why a single kiss with his housekeeper had him making a belated case for gentlemanly scruples.

Even as Lydia posed that query, the logical, never-upset part of her had to wonder what had caused her outburst. All she and Captain Powell could ever be to each other was a temporary pleasure, a passing preoccupation.

But she wanted that pleasure, had been starved for it. A hand to hold, somebody to talk to, a shoulder to lean on. She craved those comforts and had not even known what she'd longed for.

"I conclude," the captain said, "that nobody has ever taken your welfare to heart, Lydia Lovelace, else you would not rip up at me when I fear to cross the honorable line. You are correct that a shared kiss can be set aside, the memory ignored."

He took the broom from her—gently—and set it back on the stand. "But I am also correct that a personal connection between us presents different risks for you than for me. I can turn you off without a character, for example, and then you are a woman alone, cast on your own resources far from home."

An earl's daughter did not have to think in these terms. If the captain turned her off without a character, she would collect the wages she'd saved, toddle off to the solicitors' offices, and have them arrange either lodgings or a short-term rental for her.

But the captain did not know that, and Lydia wasn't about to tell him lest she lose her post before sundown.

"I have some means," she said. "I would not be destitute, and my family is all but demanding that I return home as it is."

"You truly don't understand." He glanced at the open library door, then took Lydia's hand and led her to the far end of the room, where they were less likely to be overheard. "A commanding officer exercises the power of life and death over his subordinates."

"I thought those powers were reserved to the Almighty." *And you are not my commanding officer.* Uncle Reggie was, for the nonce, or believed himself to be.

The captain brushed his fingers over her knuckles. "You enjoy that happy misconception because you never served under Lieutenant Colonel Aloysius Dunacre. He was a viscount's younger son, not even the spare, and keenly felt the indignity of his station. When he tired of sending me out to die, he turned to sending MacKay out to die, simply to taunt me. MacKay transferred after yet another heinous incident involving Dunacre, mostly because the alternative was to murder his commanding officer."

In the midst of a war infamous for the scale of its violence, what constituted a *heinous incident*? Lydia had the sense that Dylan would not disclose particulars to her, even upon pain of death.

"People in powerful positions can commit powerful trespasses," Dylan said. "I refuse to be among them. In the general scheme of things, I'm of little import, but with respect to you, I am in a powerful position."

He was not of little import to his family, to his men, or to Lydia, but she grasped his point. "Because you respect me, you will keep your distance?"

She did not like that solution at all. Selfish of her, which ought to have made her ashamed rather than frustrated.

"Because I respect you," Dylan said, dropping her hand and pacing several steps away, "I will make a suggestion. I would like to write you a glowing, accurate, though undated, character. I will put that character in Bowen's keeping, along with a sum intended as severance. I will instruct him that both are to be given to you upon your request, whether you provide notice to me or leave in the middle of the night."

"You are making it easy for me to desert the regiment."

He sent her a peevish look. "My intention is to make it possible for you to further your fondness for me, should the impulse strike you. Will you accept my suggestion?"

Lydia looked about the library for something to tidy up, but the room was quite in order. Dylan was right that consideration of her needs had never ranked with much import in the eyes of her family, and maybe not in her own eyes either.

"I hate that you served under this Dunacre person. He was a contemptible excuse for a human being."

"He's dead. Took a bullet at Waterloo. He lies in a hero's grave, which is more than he deserves."

Dunacre's ghost clearly walked in Dylan's dreams and was at least partly responsible for this quibbling over terms. And yet, Lydia sensed that, for Dylan, ensuring that her decisions were free of coercion was not quibbling, but rather, the sine qua non of *his* version of fondness.

She had the odd thought that Uncle Reginald and even clever, worldly Wesley would be baffled by Dylan Powell.

"I accept your suggestion," Lydia said, and because she had her own honor to tend to, she added, "I did not intend a permanent remove to London either, if we're being painfully honest. I'm seeing to some family business while I'm here, and I've already made progress with that task."

Not enough progress, but some.

"You will at least warn me before you retire to Shropshire?"

"I will give you plenty of notice, and by the time I'm ready to leave Town, you might be halfway to Wales."

He looked like he might say more, but Bowen chose then to rap on the doorjamb. "Post is in. Letter for you, Mrs. Lovelace."

Lydia took the epistle from him with a sense of foreboding. Aunt
Chloe writing twice in the space of a week was not good news.

"Lunch is almost ready," she said, stuffing the letter into her
apron pocket. "I can have you gentlemen served in here, at your
respective desks, or in the breakfast parlor."

"I'll nip around to the pub for my nooning," Bowen said, passing
a stack of letters to the captain. "Ask after Will, check in with the
lads." He saluted and left, his limp almost indiscernible.

"Did you have him fitted for new boots?" Lydia asked.

"I sent him to a cobbler who has accommodated other men whose
feet are the worse for having marched off to war. Will you join me for
lunch, Lydia? Take a tray with me on the terrace?"

She ought not. She ought to take herself back downstairs, don her
cap, and come up with more recipes to delight his sisters—and him.
But that would be ungracious of her, and the captain's household was
not Hampton Court, to be run according to endless protocols and
pomposities.

Then too, he'd called her Lydia, and this whole business with a
character and severance was his idea of gentlemanly deportment.

"I will take a tray with you, and we will not speak of the war or
honor or glowing characters."

The slight quirk had returned to the corner of his mouth. "What
shall we speak of?"

Lydia cast around for a topic that would be interesting and cheerful. "Wales. You will tell me about growing up in Wales, because that
is the sort of discussion fond friends would have."

"And you will tell me about growing up in Shropshire?"

"There's not much to tell."

"Tell me anyway."

～

Dylan had been studying maps of London when Lydia had come
humming along with her daffodils.

For him to have lost his way in the stews had been unforgivable. He'd gone so far as to ask Corporal Miles Bamford for directions and had still ended up turned around. With Henry Sutherland, Dylan had simply asked which way to the river, and Sutherland had apparently been confused himself.

But then, Sutherland's wound had been to the head, and he was reported to be unable to recall the name of his sovereign when a megrim was upon him.

Dylan never got lost, not in open terrain. His misfortune had been authored by a combination of worry for William Brook, fretfulness caused by the sisters' upcoming visit, and the foul London air that obscured even the path of the sun.

Also by fondness for Mrs. Lydia Lovelace. A gentleman did not importune women in his employ, and the conundrum of how to be a gentleman and also be fond of Lydia—and her kisses—had vexed Dylan sorely.

He considered that conundrum unresolved, but he'd at least raised the issue with her. She had not admitted that a conundrum existed, which struck Dylan as odd. A woman in service had to guard her reputation more fiercely than did a highborn lady.

Damn Sycamore Dorning for planting a seed of doubt where only curiosity had been.

When Dylan joined Lydia on the terrace, she allowed him to hold her chair, but had brought one of her preferred weapons to the meal.

"I am not discussing another menu with you," Dylan said. "You can plan all the meals you like, but Tegan and Marged have been known to wander the kitchens and pantries. They have recipes without limit and will likely ask for some of them to be prepared, despite your menus."

"I will inquire about your favorite dishes," Lydia said, taking a spoonful of pepper pot soup. "It's not really warm enough for a picnic yet, is it?"

"Two months from now, such a day would not be warm enough,

but coming off winter, we are inured to the cold. Tell me about your mare. Did you ride hell-bent all over Shropshire?"

Lydia had referred to kissing her mare. Not *our* mare, not *the* mare, but rather, *my* mare. Horses were endlessly expensive and required care, shelter, fodder... A squire's daughter might have her own horse, but a yeoman's would not.

Lydia patted her lips with her table napkin. "Her name is—*was*, rather—Demeter, but I call her Demi. *Called* her. Her name was a joke, because she was quite up to my weight. Seventeen hands and endless bottom. My brother got first pick of the mounts on offer, and when he instead took a black gelding for his own, I was relieved. Demi was the best of the lot, and my brother couldn't see that, because she was a mare and a bay rather than a dashing black."

Lydia's family had the means to keep not one but at least two saddle horses. "Do you miss riding?"

"Terribly. What of you? Did you have a favorite mount in Spain?"

The soup was not excessively spiced, an improvement over the usual pepper pot before Lydia had taken the household in hand.

"One learned not to get too attached to any mount. There was one game fellow of the golden breed the Spanish regard so highly. He was given over for army use because of some spectacular scars around his chest and neck. His name was Lobo—wolf—so I assume the scarring was a result of tangling with a pack."

"And living to tell about it. What became of your Lobo?"

"When MacKay transferred, I asked him to take the horse with him. The last I heard, Lobo was enjoying a life of relative ease pulling a gig for some Spanish general's mama. What became of Demi?"

Lydia finished her soup and set the bowl aside. "You asked MacKay to take the horse so the beast would be safe from your commanding officer."

And MacKay had obliged, thank God. "Dunacre would ride his horses to death. In the heat, over the hard terrain, that was easy to do if the animal was denied rest and water. The lieutenant colonel thought it gave him a reputation for toughness to be able to outlast his mounts."

Lydia took a sip of cider. "Why didn't it give him a reputation for stupidity or abusiveness? Horses are expensive, and if Wellington impressed one thing upon Parliament, it was the need to keep his soldiers well supplied."

How would she know that? The duke's published dispatches were often little more than lists of commendations for his direct reports. His Grace's grumbling, lecturing, and importuning was reserved for letters to his peers and their official parliamentary committees.

"Dunacre was charming when he wanted to be," Dylan said, "and the senior officers saw him only in meetings or at banquets."

Lydia held out an epergne that had sandwiches arranged on one level and fruit tarts on another, a prettier presentation than a mere tray.

"I know the type," she said. "All polished manners and clever quips in the buffet line, but not to be trusted with a waltz. Take two, because you will doubtless go off looking for your lost lamb again, and the food in some taverns is not to be trusted either."

Dylan took two sandwiches, because he was hungry, and she was right. "Would you tell me if you had a husband, Lydia?"

Without helping herself to any of the epergne's offerings, Lydia returned it to the center of the table.

"Yes, I would tell you, and no, I do not have and have never had a husband. I have adopted the standard form of address for housekeepers. Are you being honorable again?"

"I hope I am always honorable." Dylan was also in that moment profoundly relieved. "The sandwiches are good. Not too heavy a hand with the mustard." Another improvement since her arrival. "Tell me about this brother of yours. Was he a perfect pest growing up?"

She rearranged her linen on her lap, took another sip of her cider, and studied the epergne.

"I have only the one sibling, and he didn't come along until I was in the schoolroom. My parents doted on him—the only boy—and he wasn't as robust as some young fellows. He liked his history books, liked to elude his tutors to ramble about the park, liked chess and old Latin philosophers. He beat me at chess for three straight years, and because I am his older sister, I felt it my duty to let him win at first. Then I got serious about the game, and he stopped playing with me."

"He was faint-hearted, then. Could not stand to be beaten by a mere sister. My sisters regularly best me at any number of undertakings." Making small talk at the top of the list.

Dylan had meant for this shared meal to be pleasant, a light-hearted counterpoint to the day's earlier discussion of severance and propriety. Matters, as was so often the case, were not going as he'd planned.

"Would you enjoy an occasional game of chess?" he asked, moving the epergne closer to Lydia's plate.

"I would." Her smile was shy, not like any of her previous smiles. "I have not played in years." She reached for one sandwich, then apparently decided to take a different one.

"Where is your brother now?"

She set the sandwich on her plate. "Traveling. Mama misses him terribly."

And a family that could afford to send its only son off on travel was a family with some means, as was a family with the leisure to play chess or hire tutors for the only son.

"Do *you* miss this odious brother?"

"Do you miss your sisters?"

"I do, until they threaten to descend, then I am unaccountably willing for them to continue biding in Wales."

"Don't you miss Wales, Captain? I'm told it's beautiful."

"Wales is so far beyond beautiful that words fail. You've never been?" Shropshire bordered Wales, and many an older denizen of Shropshire's western villages still claimed Welsh as their native tongue.

"I haven't. Are you truly waiting to see William Brook settled before you allow yourself to leave London?"

"If my cousins asked, I would say I had a few more men to look after. Until recently, I was in truth more concerned for Goddard and MacKay, who both have found solid footing with their respective ladies. Brook's disappearance is troubling, though, and now I've created a post for Bowen that won't survive my eventual remove to Wales."

"Would he travel to Wales with you?"

"Not without his brother. Where has your brother decided to wander? Is he larking about the Continent with the fashionable crowd?"

Lydia picked up her sandwich. "Every time I mention Wales, you change the subject, Captain. Why is that?"

"Guilt, I suppose." The words were out, unplanned and damnably honest.

"Can you explain?"

Dylan had never tried to before, but for her, he made the effort. "I come from Dissenting stock. The irony of that status is that those who grasped the wisdom of rebelling against Rome, and who then rebelled against Canterbury, are often the least tolerant of rebellion in their children."

"You were a naughty boy?"

Dylan was glad they were eating out of doors, where nobody could overhear, glad for the relatively fresh air this close to the parks and for a chance to think this topic through before the sisters arrived.

"I was an only boy, like your brother, and expectations were heaped on me like pots on a tinker's cart. I was to be well educated but humble, hardworking but joyous, sober but good-humored... nothing in excess, nothing spontaneous. I grew impatient with my father's endless sermons and exhortations, impatient with my sisters expecting me to constantly charm their acquaintances. I had never aspired to be a paragon, and all of my friends and both of my cousins had already bought their colors."

"You ran away from home."

"In a word, yes. I scraped together every groat I could get my hands on and begged my father to come up with the rest of what I'd need to buy a commission. The nation was at war, and Papa expected me to spend my days as his unpaid bailiff. Running off to Spain was the furthest thing from the great lark I expected, but one cannot resign a commission simply because one ends up serving in hell under a commander who by comparison made the enemy look like..."

Dylan fell silent, having once again made a hash of what should have been a pleasant, informal meal. Goddard had the whole family's complement of social self-possession, and MacKay had got all the charm. That left... honesty, perhaps, for Dylan.

Not exactly a gift, if it gave the lady a distaste for him.

Lydia offered him the epergne again, but he shook his head. "No sweets, thank you."

"No sweets and no sweetness?" she replied, putting a lemon-iced tea cake on his plate. "You have banished yourself from your home because you were among thousands of foolish, patriotic boys looking for adventure in uniform?"

"I will go back to Wales when matters are settled here in Town. The property is well managed, and my sisters would tell me if my presence was required at home."

Lydia chose a cake decorated with raspberry glaze. "I gather you have inherited the property?"

Dylan nodded. "I see now that when my father sent me around to collect the rents and inspect the tenant properties for needed repairs, he was trying to familiarize me with land that would become mine. At the time..."

"At the time, you had probably just put up with several years of useless instruction at university—Greek, Latin, and natural science, which appeared to have nothing to do with anything—and you were convinced that you alone could make the difference that would send old Boney packing. You would be a hero."

She had paid attention to that younger brother, apparently. "I was a fool."

Lydia held up her glass of cider, as if making a toast. "Be it hereby known to all by these presents that Dylan Powell, at an age infamous for foolishness, succumbed to the same temptations that lured his peers into uniform, which is exactly where their king wanted them to be."

She took a sip and looked straight up. "The sky has not fallen, no pigs are soaring around in the heavens. Apparently, your great foolishness has not stopped the planets in their orbits either, though Napoleon did get buttoned up eventually. You will have to do better if you are trying to take a first in foolishness, Captain."

She munched her treat, and Dylan wanted to kiss her. Not a kiss that would lead to passion, but a kiss that would lead to smiles and cuddles and sweet sighs. He hadn't known there were such kisses, but with Lydia...

"Have you ever been foolish, Lydia?"

She finished her cake. "No, I have not. I have been a daughter to be proud of, a conscientious sister, a dutiful niece, a fine neighbor, and a handy dancing partner for awkward bachelors and portly widowers. I have done all that was asked of me and much that wasn't, because I am a paragon, and I can tell you, Captain, paragoning is hard, thankless work. Before you know it, people expect you to fulfill that office without complaint—*or remuneration*—and then you aren't a paragon anymore. You are simply Lydia—or Liddie, a nickname I do abhor—and you have become the most boring, proper..."

"Yes?"

She held his lemon cake up to his lips, and he took a bite before she continued.

"You have become the most lonely, invisible cipher ever to count the silver, month after month, for no reason except that it has been a month since the last time you counted it. Then you take a wild notion to behave outrageously, but it's no use. Because you have become invisible, nobody even notices your scandalous lapse."

Lunch with Lydia was not like any meal Dylan had ever shared with another person. He'd failed miserably to make small talk, *and so had she.*

"I have never kissed a paragon before," he said. "Is the condition contagious?"

"Why don't you kiss me again, and then we'll find out?"

CHAPTER NINE

Aunt Chloe's letter had brought good news. Wesley was still tasked with retrieving Lydia, but his itinerary would take him first to a house party or two—or what diversions passed for house parties in Wesley's lexicon of idleness.

He might well be coming straight to London to indulge in a spate of debauchery, and sparing himself the immediate burden of collecting his cousin.

Perhaps relief accounted for Lydia's improved mood. More likely, proximity to Captain Dylan Powell had that effect—or closeness to him. He shared his memories and regrets with her, and that trust *was* contagious.

She had *complained* to him, about life at Tremont and a little bit about Marcus too. She had admitted to loneliness. A lonely woman could more easily leave her family, could journey far from home and consider it an adventure rather than a tribulation.

Could leave the family seat and not look forward to returning home.

"I am not about to kiss you," the captain said, "when we are doubtless being chaperoned by every person on my staff save Bowen.

His nose would be plastered to a window as well, but he's off the premises. If you are through with your meal, I will accompany you to your parlor, there to take a final look at the one dessert menu you neglected to bring with you."

He spoke in his usual crisp, impersonal tones—even his recitations about leaving Wales had been rendered more like a report than a reminiscence—and yet, his eyes danced.

"Silly of me to forget the desserts," Lydia said. "I was flustered by the prospect of sharing a noon meal with my employer. He can be imposing."

Dylan chose the last raspberry tea cake, Lydia's favorite. She begrudged him that tea cake, because Betty, the kitchen maid, usually ate all the raspberry ones.

He held it up to her mouth. "You must keep up your strength as the Welsh horde approaches. I insist, Mrs. Lovelace."

She bit into the tea cake, and he ate the remainder. The moment was foolish and precious, and the tea cake was the best Lydia had ever eaten. The captain rose and held her chair for her—more foolishness—and then offered his arm.

"I can walk to the kitchen unassisted, sir."

He glanced around the terrace as if inspecting the trees and garden for signs of the advancing season. "I cannot go another moment without touching you. I do not dwell on the past."

"You do not *discuss* the past." She took his arm, and they moved into the house.

"I will have to ask my cousins if soldiers from Shropshire had a reputation for fierceness, or perhaps insubordination. There is a fine line between the two."

Lydia and her employer toddled down the steps, and because it was the noon hour and because most of the staff preferred a pint at the pub to another hurried meal in the kitchen—or preferred to linger abovestairs spying—the kitchen and pantries were deserted.

"You think I'm fierce?"

"Admit me to your parlor, and I will add graciousness to fierceness on your list of virtues."

He could have kissed her on the stairs or pulled her into the butler's pantry and been assured of privacy. "Why my parlor?"

"I want to see your demesne by daylight, with you on hand."

The kittens were awake and having a wash on the raised hearth in the kitchen. They watched Lydia go by as if well aware why she would allow the captain a private audience in her parlor.

"A modest chamber," the captain said, glancing around and making no move to pull the door or draperies closed.

"Small spaces are easier to heat, and I do have a window." At ground level outside and slightly higher than usual from within, as was typical of half basements.

"And a parlor stove for warmth. Is this your aunt Chloe in her youth?" He peered at a sketch Lydia had brought with her, the only sketch. "She was a very pretty young lady. Has your nose."

"My mother, who is a paragon's paragon." Lydia had done the sketch last year. "I've wondered why you have no renderings of your sisters on hand. I can do some while they're here if you like."

"You did this?" He studied the little portrait, a three-quarter profile of Mama half smiling in that serene way of hers. He drew his finger down Lydia's nose, a glancing touch and maddeningly brief. "Maybe her chin too."

"Like all paragons, Mama can sit patiently for hours. She wasn't even embroidering. She just held that pose because I asked her to."

"A woman given to introspection, perhaps. A terrifying thought, though I suspect the trait has bred true." He ambled over to the bedroom door and pushed it open. "At least your bed is decent size. Did you bring that quilt with you?"

Once a reconnaissance officer, always a reconnaissance officer, apparently. "I did not, but I did the embroidery around the border. Gave me something to do as we waited for winter to pass."

The captain stepped into her bedroom, and Lydia wasn't sure how she felt about that. Her washstand, her clothes press, her wardrobe, her *everything* was always tidy. But this was her *bedroom,* and abruptly, it seemed a very small space indeed.

And very personal. Her nightgown lay folded across the foot of the bed. Her slippers sat near the hearth, awaiting the warmth of a fire. Her traveling desk was on the windowsill, there being no other place to store it. Lydia's trunks and valise were under the bed, and because her initials were embossed on that luggage, she did not want anybody seeing it. Bad enough the Glover family crest was carved onto the side of the traveling desk.

"I would like to tarry with you in this bed," the captain said, running a hand over the quilt. "That admission shocks me. I hope it doesn't surprise you."

Lydia said the first thing to come to mind. "We'd be more comfortable in your bed, Captain."

Heaven defend her, that smile. That smile of his was knowing and full of mischief.

"Comfort has its allure," he said, bringing a pillow to his nose for a sniff, then returning it to the precise place he'd found it. "But I want you to go to bed each night recalling my warmth beside you, my head beside yours on these pillows. I want to know the exact creak of your bed ropes when two people occupy that mattress, and those two people are thee and me."

His tone was cool, while heat ignited in Lydia's middle. "Is that a dare, Captain?"

"A confession." He took one last look around the room and returned to the parlor. "I should be off on my rounds."

"You truly wanted only to see my apartment?"

"What I want, and what you allow me, could be quite different, Lydia."

Insight dawned. "I have had quite enough of your honor for one day, sir. You expect me to make all the overtures?"

"I expect you to make the important ones, after suitable negotiation. I've already stated where my ambitions would take us."

He had also made certain Lydia would have memories of him, his head nearly brushing the lintel of her bedroom doorway, his hand stroking over her quilt. She ought to resent him for placing the burden of the initiative on her.

One more thing to manage... Except it wasn't. He'd come down here, to her personal quarters, he'd stated his wishes, and he was waiting, with that maddening smile lurking in his eyes. He'd wait all afternoon for her to choose what came next.

All week, all month... He'd put her *in command* of this undertaking and a little bit in command of him.

Gracious heavens. "You are mine to kiss?" she asked, needing to hear the words.

"At least that, provided you have a care for my dignity. No accosting me on the street, if you please, or bragging of your conquest to the other ladies."

"I understand dignity, Captain." She drew the curtains closed and moved the parlor door so it was ajar only a few inches. "I am not sure I understand exactly how to proceed with you, but I know you will be patient with me."

"With you, I will become the patron saint of patience." He was too expert at speaking dispassionately while imbuing his words with all manner of implications. Intriguing implications, about self-restraint, a lady's pleasure, and a gentleman's ability to delay his own satisfaction.

Lydia stepped close enough to run her hand over his lapel. "When you are not pressed for time, we must have a discussion."

"Regarding?"

"That time when I decided to not be a paragon." That *other* time. "Might I kiss you, Captain?"

"Dylan." He looped his arms around her shoulders. "If you are broaching the topic of kisses, you will please use my name."

Lydia wasn't certain who kissed whom first, but the result was lovely. Dylan did not plunder so much as he explored with his kisses, and with his hands. He was a toucher, much to her delight. All that

starch and dispatch he exhibited in the normal course went straight
into the dustbin when he held her.

He brushed his thumbs over her cheeks and brow, and she
wanted to push into his caresses like a greedy cat. All the while, he
sipped and teased at her mouth, until Lydia had him by the hair and
was demanding less delicacy and more passion.

He laughed and tucked her close. "Have mercy, madam. I am to
go forth into the world, and I must be able to walk upright when I
do so."

"You will smile when you go forth. I delight in the notion that
I've made you smile for a change."

"You will smile, too, and I will not be on hand to see it. Expect me
back in time for supper, and then perhaps you will join me in the
library this evening for a game of chess."

He would remember that. He'd probably remember every word
to ever come out of her mouth. "I will look forward to besting you."

And maybe over the chessboard, she could gently, gently probe
him for how to find Marcus. Not by name, not with specifics, but in
the general case. That Lydia was embarking on both a flirtation and a
deception bothered her—*sorely*—but she had been honest with Dylan
that her sojourn in London was temporary and motivated by family
business.

Or it had been. Lydia wasn't sure where her path would take her
once Marcus had been found, but that was a complication for another
day.

She stole one more moment in the captain's arms. "Where will
you go this afternoon?"

"Back to the stews. I have the map in my head now, and I won't
get lost, but neither will I tarry past sunset. If William Brook has left
London, somebody might know why and where he went."

Had Marcus left London? Though where better to hide than the
metropolis? If he was still alive. Another call on the solicitors was in
order, and Lydia's next half day came tomorrow.

She walked with the captain to the back door, reluctant to see him go, but needing time to consider what had just passed between them.

"You will eschew your greatcoat?"

"It's warm enough to do without if I keep moving, and some brisk air will aid me to regain my composure." He took a slightly worn hat down from a peg and took up a brass-handled walking stick with a few nicks on its shaft. "Think of me as you polish my candlesticks, Lydia."

Dylan kissed her cheek, opened the door, and crouched down. "Somebody has left you a token."

He rose, holding a bouquet of forget-me-nots tied with a blue ribbon. "I am apparently not your only admirer."

Lydia took the flowers, though they made her slightly uneasy. "One of the men, I suppose. Though if a fellow down on his luck has coin to buy posies, he ought not to be wasting it on silly gestures."

"There's a note among the flowers."

Lydia's foreboding increased, because many of Dylan's former subordinates were illiterate, and her presence in London was supposed to be kept secret from any man who knew her. She extracted the little slip of paper.

"Somebody offers thanks for sustenance given when needed." The note did nothing of the sort and wasn't even in English. "I should put these flowers in water, and you should be on your way."

The captain saluted and winked—the rascal—and marched off down the garden path. Lydia was still watching his departure when he stopped before the gate and blew her a kiss.

She pretended to catch it and laid her palm against her cheek. Utter nonsense, of course, but it was the best she could do when her heart was hammering like a war drum.

As Dylan disappeared from view, Lydia closed the door and retreated to the kitchen, where she found a vase and, with shaking hands, arranged the flowers and gave them water. While the kittens looked on like disapproving godmothers, she tossed the note onto the coals in the kitchen hearth.

Marcus had written in Latin and added a little sketch of a tree on a hill, lest Lydia mistake the identity of the note's author. The name Tremont meant something like *across the hill* or *over the mountain*.

As a little boy, Marcus had devised the tree and mountain sketch as his "secret" signature to Lydia when playing his brave-explorer and fierce-pirate games. For a time, he'd also sketched a glove—more complicated than a tree or a hill—to signify the family name rather than the title.

The message translated easily: *Bene sum. Ite in domum suam.*

I am well. Go home, and the verb *go* had been rendered as a command.

Lydia set the flowers on the windowsill and considered two very different men. Dylan had told her in several ways that he would not presume on her person or her time, that *she* determined the manner in which their dealings proceeded, if at all. That her dignity mattered to him.

Marcus, after a protracted and unexplained silence, gave her six words, no explanations, and a direct order. *Go home.* A command given to collies by shepherds and drovers.

That he was alive should have been cause for undiluted joy. Should have been. What Lydia felt mostly was relief—and annoyance.

"Marcus is the earl," she informed the kittens as the note curled and blackened into ash, "but he's also my baby brother and a complete gudgeon if he thinks I will allow him to behave like this. I'm supposed to scuttle back to Tremont, thrilled to know he's alive—and I am thrilled, after a fashion—and await his pleasure."

The bouquet had flowers going every which way. Lydia got out a knife and evened up the stems, which resulted in some improvement.

"I am owed an explanation," she said, not a conclusion she would have reached before coming to London and earning a wage in the captain's household. "I am owed the courtesy of an explanation, as is Mama. We deserve some idea of what to expect from Marcus going forward."

One thing was clear. Marcus had not suffered one of those blows to the head that obliterated memory. Mama had presented that somewhat fanciful explanation whenever the subject of Marcus's absence had been raised.

Lydia moved the flowers to Bowen's office, where she would not have to see them much, and still, they troubled her. She was polishing the mirror in the captain's bedroom before she admitted the basis for her upset.

For this particular upset.

The flowers, and their imperious little note, made Lydia's deception of the captain more real. He sought intimacies with her—intimacies she longed to grant him—but she was not who he thought her to be. She was an earl's sister and, more significantly, the sibling of a man whom Dylan despised.

Lydia took a final pass over the mirror's glass and beheld the reflection of a woman who had many reasons to rejoice and just as many reasons to despair.

"Why would a man hide from his own kin?" Dylan asked as he pretended to study the chessboard.

Lydia sat across from him, candlelight finding garnet, bronze, and gold highlights in her hair. Despite her plain gray dress, she looked of a piece with the library's learned tomes and landscapes.

She touched a pawn, then withdrew her hand. "I beg your pardon?"

"I poked about St. Giles for much of the day, and though I knew precisely where I was at all times, on three occasions I asked former soldiers for directions."

"To strike up a conversation?"

"To test a theory."

Bowen Brook was ostensibly reading an agricultural pamphlet in a chair by the fire. Gentle snoring suggested the mysteries of contour plowing were less riveting than the temptations of Morpheus.

Lydia moved the pawn, which was puzzling. One game had been enough to show that her chess was shrewd—shrewd enough to best Dylan's cautious strategies—but that move was either a sophisticated feint or a mistake.

"What theory did you test, Captain?"

"Yesterday, I somehow got turned around, more than once. I have studied maps of London generally, and in the usual case, that is enough to orient me. St. Giles isn't that large an area, and I've walked the surrounding neighborhoods often enough."

"And?"

"And on all three occasions today, I was given inaccurate directions from men who've spent considerable time on London's streets." The first time, Dylan had been surprised. The second, puzzled, and the third, disappointed.

And the third fellow, Andrew Bean, owed Dylan his life.

"Are they scolding you for trespassing?" Lydia asked, sitting back. "You have essentially disobeyed a direct order by going into the stews on your own."

"I have not. My agreement is to avoid the slums alone after dark." Dylan shifted his queen's rook a few squares. "They are protecting William Brook, would be my guess, but why?"

"Has he broken the law?"

"If so, nobody—not MacKay's streetwalkers, not Goddard's urchins, not the constables I'm on good terms with—has heard of it. William is in hiding and does not want to be found." Hughie Porter had all but told him so, and Dylan hadn't listened. "The question is why. Solve the why of it, and William Brook can come out of hiding."

Lydia should have been studying the chessboard, but was instead frowning at Dylan. "Perhaps the why of it cannot be solved? Perhaps that way lies Newgate, or worse."

"Then leave London."

"Your men tell me there are few jobs to be had in the shires, and wages are abysmal outside of London. How else could you go about looking for William if he does not want to be found?"

"Post spies, which I've done. Goddard's juvenile henchmen are keeping a lookout, as are MacKay's ladies. The constables, lamp-lighters, night-soil men are putting the word out. They are looking for a fellow who has a bad hand, doesn't hear well, and resembles a sturdier Bowen."

"I could make you a sketch. I met William on several occasions. He has a dimple..." Lydia stared off in the direction of the hearth. "His face is broader than Bowen's, but Bowen could assist me with my sketch. Would a likeness help?"

"Your move, Lydia, and yes, a likeness would help show people which man I'm looking for, but it won't explain why some of my former direct reports are now lying to me. That bothers me as much as William's disappearance. Somebody could be holding a threat over the men, the same somebody who might have authored William's disappearance and Bowen's beating."

"Sad thanks, after all you've done for them, to refuse you their trust." She moved the knight that had been protecting her queen, then put him back where he'd been.

"Do you still have the note that was in that bouquet we found earlier?" Dylan asked.

"I tossed it on the coals. Why?"

"Bowen would know William's handwriting, and the words might have included some sort of hidden message."

Lydia did shift the knight in what might well be a bid for Dylan's king, leaving her queen unprotected. "Your move, Captain."

Dylan's hours of walking had given him time to think, and to worry. Lydia had not been pleased at the sight of the flowers, and she'd all but crammed the note into her pocket after the merest glance. Now she admitted to not merely consigning that little message into the dustbin, but destroying it. The flowers were not in her apartment—Dylan had done that reconnaissance—but rather, in Bowen's office.

Dylan weighed all the ramifications of taking her queen and, finding no consequences of particular concern, executed the move.

"You have become distracted, madam." She'd won the first game with a brisk dispatch that had caught Dylan unaware. Now she was bungling the second. Sycamore Dorning's questions about French songs, Shakespeare quotes, and fancy needlework came to mind.

"Resting on my laurels," she said, scowling at his rook. "Or tired. I should have seen that coming three moves ago, but I was too focused on your king in the corner. I believe that puts you just a few moves from checkmate."

"Four. Shall I escort you to your parlor?" Dylan expected argument, for form's sake if nothing else.

Lydia began removing pieces from the board. "I meant to tell you that I'll be out and about some tomorrow afternoon. I'll take the market cart, if that's allowed?"

"This is that family business you alluded to?" Dylan put away his army as well. "I'd be happy to escort you, Lydia, or lend you the coach. It's not fancy, but it will spare you exposure to the elements."

"The market cart will do, thank you. I won't be going far."

She did not want him tagging along, whatever her errand. Dylan considered having her followed, but put the decision off. Perhaps Lydia would tell him the nature of her outing, and perhaps it was none of his damned business.

Except that she was in his employ, and her safety was thus his business if it was anybody's.

Complicated. Like the politics of moving an army across occupied Spain.

"We must have a rematch," Dylan said, returning the chessboard to the shelf behind the library desk. "We've each won a game, and that is no place to leave matters."

"Your soldier's heart demands a victor and a vanquished?" Lydia asked, yawning behind her hand and rising.

"My sense of fair play means I should not have kept you up so late, and you must be permitted to trounce me for my presumptions."

She gave him a look that said she knew balderdash when she heard it, then moved about the library, blowing out candles. "Do we leave Bowen to spend the night in a chair?"

"He's spent the night in much worse surrounds." Dylan banked the fire and gently extracted the agricultural treatise from Bowen's slack grip.

Bowen stirred enough to twitch at the arm of the chair.

"At ease, soldier." Dylan spoke softly, and Bowen went still.

Lydia draped an afghan over Bowen's lap. "You give commands, and they are followed even in sleep. I envy you that." She tucked in the blanket as one might tuck in the bedcovers for a child. "Sweet dreams, Mr. Brook."

"Don't you give commands as well?" Dylan asked, holding the library door for her. "To the maids and footmen and fellows at the back door?"

"I make requests, Captain. Not the same thing at all."

Dylan did not take Lydia's hand, because she didn't seem to be in a hand-holding mood. Also because his conscience plagued him. His venture into Lydia's private apartment after lunch had been in part simply to share a moment requiring discretion. One did not kiss one's housekeeper on the back terrace for all the world to see, after all.

But some ungentlemanly part of him, a part he'd been loath to acknowledge at the time, had also wanted to inspect her quarters, to *spy* on her. He'd delighted to see her pretty little writing desk—good quality, only slightly used. To see her slippers by the hearth—also good quality and beautifully embroidered.

He'd wanted to open her wardrobe and sniff her shawls and touch her chemises. He'd been tempted to lie on her bed, to learn what she beheld in that sweet moment when she stretched out on the mattress at the end of a tiring day.

Bad of him, just as feeding her a tea cake on the back terrace had been bad of him. A lapse, a weakening of defenses. Not quite a breach of the city walls, but... significant. Now he was vexed by the puzzle of why a lady whose Shropshire family had means, who was distantly related to at least one title, was dusting windowsills in London for her daily bread.

He had looked about her room for answers, not once but twice in the course of a day. Once in her presence and more recently without her permission, ostensibly in search of the bouquet of forget-me-nots.

Dylan was still searching for a means of confessing his transgression, and the concern and curiosity behind it, when Lydia drew him into her unlit parlor, closed the door, and kissed him within an inch of his sanity. As he kissed her back with equal ardor, his mind presented him with an inescapable conclusion.

This flirtation, affair, whatever it was, with Lydia was serious. He worried for her, and he carried her in his thoughts when he left the house. He wanted to make her burdens his own and resolve them by any means necessary.

Jeanette's little homily came back to him: *When the right person comes along, she might not be the easy person, the convenient person, or the available person, but if she's the love your heart has longed for, you will know.*

Lydia tugged Dylan toward the bedroom, and another thought followed him into that private space. A woman whose family had some means, who'd been raised with a riding horse and singing lessons, was not the most likely candidate for the post of London housekeeper, but she might be ideally suited to become the wife of a comfortably suited Welsh landowner and former officer.

Lydia resumed kissing him with a fervor that would soon put rational thought into disorderly retreat.

"Wait," Dylan said, resting his forehead against hers. "Wait, we have time."

"Your sisters will be here in mere days, Captain, and with them underfoot..."

"Dylan," he said. "If I am about to tear the clothes from your body, you can call me Dylan."

Lydia whipped around, sweeping the hair from her nape. "No tearing, if you please. Unhooking would be appreciated, though."

That request filled Dylan with consternation. He desired Lydia madly, and she was willing, but... the haste was troubling. Both Goddard and Powell had courted their ladies only briefly, but what Dylan contemplated in this moment with Lydia made those undertakings seem like prolonged sieges by comparison.

She deserved a siege. She deserved flowers that made her smile rather than frown. She deserved cherishing and bliss and wooing, dammit, and Dylan was just the man to give all of that to her. He slipped the first half-dozen hooks free and pressed his lips to her nape.

CHAPTER TEN

Lydia was in four different kinds of a muddle.

She hated to see Dylan so weary in spirit and so sad. The lodestar in Captain Dylan Powell's personal constellation of virtues was that soldiers should be loyal to one another, and yet, his men had betrayed him three times in the course of an afternoon.

She was awash in guilt, for deceiving Dylan, for—in her way—showing him a far greater disloyalty than the soldiers had with their inaccurate directions.

And she was angry. Dylan's observation, that Will Brook did not want to be found, forced Lydia to examine the same conclusion where Marcus was concerned. She had assumed that her brother *could not* come home, if he was alive. That an illness of body or mind plagued him to the point that returning to Tremont was beyond him. He might long for home, but he lacked the ability to make the journey or face his old life.

Dylan's remarks raised the possibility that Marcus was *choosing* not to return to Tremont. Given Marcus's penchant for drama and self-absorption, that explanation was as plausible as it was infuriating. How could Marcus ignore the strain on Mama, the awkwardness for

Uncle Reggie and Wesley, the uncertainty every tenant and employee faced daily...?

And the burden Marcus's absence put on Lydia herself?

Beneath her simmering ire at her brother—he'd had no compelling reason to run off to war in the first place—lay the worst muddle of all: Lydia's whole situation was growing too complicated, and because of those complications, Lydia had little hope of any future with the first man to truly earn her notice.

That notion—that she had found a man to treasure, but must part from him too soon—made her reckless. She'd all but dragged Dylan to her boudoir, and that was the tamest of her intentions where he was concerned. She would regret her rash behavior, but she would regret even more letting the moment pass her by.

"Hurry, please," she said when Dylan had undone only the first half-dozen hooks.

"Why embark on a forced march when a leisurely stroll will afford a greater opportunity to appreciate the scenery?" He appreciated the back of Lydia's neck with his lips—and tongue?—and sent a shiver down her spine.

"I am not a rural shire, Captain, full of fluffy sheep desperately in need of sketch—"

He'd looped an arm around her waist and snugged her bottom against unmistakable evidence of ardent desire.

"And I am not a plundering vandal, to heedlessly gobble what should be savored—this time. Tell me about when you weren't a paragon, Lydia."

She had no idea what he... "Oh, that."

"That." More hooks came undone, and Lydia felt the subtlest of tugs as Dylan undid her laces. "Did you give him your heart?"

"I gave him about a quarter hour of my time."

Dylan purely hugged her from behind. No arousing caresses, no kisses to shivery places. "Why give him that much?"

Lydia focused on the question, not one she'd made herself face squarely, though on the perimeter of her mind, she'd puzzled over it.

"I had spent three years interned at the most boring, silly, vapid excuse for a select academy you can imagine. Then I wasted more time parading around with Aunt Chloe. I was finally home, and all anybody could talk about was the war and the *boys* in their regimentals, as if war was an undertaking for children. I wanted attention, I suppose, and he offered that." Childish *of her*, in hindsight, but also understandable.

"Fifteen minutes of attention?"

"He wanted a precious memory to take back with him to Spain. He wanted... I don't know what he wanted, but there was some strong punch involved, and I had vowed to learn what all the fuss was about. He could oblige me, and thus I spared him a quarter hour."

"Fuss?"

Lydia eased from Dylan's arms and faced him, though the coals on the hearth gave her little light to see by. "Are you laughing at me? I refused to trot up the church aisle without some idea what I was getting myself into. At the time, I fully expected to be married before I turned two-and-twenty."

Dylan took her in his arms. "I am laughing at the select academy. They did their best to turn you into a demure, marriage-obsessed twit, and you emerged from your ordeal full of self-possession and determination. I'm sorry your reconnaissance mission lasted only a quarter hour and was undertaken with a varlet in uniform, but you doubtless did give him a very sweet memory to take back to Spain."

Lydia let go of some of the tension that had hounded her since the forget-me-nots had arrived. "I was awful. He wasn't a varlet. He was simply a somewhat dishonorable young man, doing what soldiers on leave are notorious for doing. I got shed of some ignorance, also some arrogance."

At some point, the discussion had gone from a conversation to a confession. Lydia liked that Dylan could visit this topic with her, and that his reaction was regret for her—and understanding. No dramatics, no outrage. She'd be able to put that long-ago interlude aside now in a way she hadn't previously.

"You consider a single encounter with an opportunistic bounder educational?"

"I was opportunistic, too, and maybe the lieutenant sensed that in me. In any case, the experience was not worth repeating. My curiosity was duly satisfied, and I was none the worse for it. Had I not peeked beneath the covers, so to speak, there's no telling whose suit I might have accepted."

Dylan kissed her cheek. "I'm sorry."

"Sorry?"

"First intimate experiences are probably all too commonly disappointing, especially for young ladies, but I wish better for you."

Lydia snuggled closer, reveling in the simple pleasure of a warm embrace. "What of your first encounter?"

"Her name was Jane, and she was my sisters' elocution teacher. An English widow highly regarded in the village. She has since remarried and moved to Scotland, which I account a relief. I was at risk for nervous exhaustion by the time our affair concluded, though I was probably the happiest young fellow in Wales for a time. My English pronunciation was improved for the experience as well."

He'd had an *affaire de couer*, while Lydia had had a quarter hour of fumbling and poking. Perhaps, if Dylan said a leisurely stroll was the better approach, she should heed his suggestion.

"What happened to your naughty soldier, Lydia?"

"I don't know. My cousin Wesley knew the lieutenant from university or Town, and invited him to attend our New Year's ball. My brother subsequently had a falling-out with the lieutenant, as young men do—drama over nothing, according to my cousin. The next thing I knew, my brother bought his colors, and an unimpressive quarter hour at the ball was the last thing on my mind."

"Did your brother come home?"

How gently Dylan asked the question. "Yes." That much Lydia knew. Marcus had boarded the transport ship, and that ship had made port without any mishaps at sea. She ought to move the conversation to some other topic—any other topic—but instead, she undid Dylan's cravat and breathed in his lovely scent.

"I've done something larcenous," she said.

"Under my roof?"

"In your bedroom. I put a few drops of your scent onto one of my handkerchiefs. I'm an idiot."

Dylan kissed her temple. "Do you know why I really wanted to see the note that came with your flowers, Lydia?"

"Because William Brook—"

He kissed her to silence. "I am jealous that some other fellow thought to leave flowers for you before I could bring you a bouquet myself. Forget-me-nots, of all the cheek. Whoever he is, I resent him bitterly. I suppose this makes me an idiot as well."

"Assuredly, Captain."

They fell to kissing, a sweet, unhurried introduction to a gradual and mutual disrobing. Where Lydia's anxieties had been, hope blossomed, for surely a man this patient and considerate would hear her out when she made her awkward explanations? Surely he would understand sibling loyalty as well as he understood loyalty among soldiers?

Lydia set aside the last of her worries when Dylan scooped her up and laid her on the mattress.

He came down over her, a warm blanket of nearly naked male. "I want your word on something, Lydia."

"That sounds serious."

"You tolerated the fumblings of some randy officer to satisfy your curiosity."

"Not the behavior of a paragon, I—"

He treated her to an openmouthed, tongue-twining kiss that stole the thoughts from her mind.

"Precisely the behavior of a very young paragon when she's intent on banishing a dangerous sort of ignorance, but please be a different sort of paragon with me in this bed."

Dylan's ardor had waned as they'd spoken of past encounters, but he was once again quite obviously aroused and making no effort to spare Lydia awareness of his desire.

"What sort of paragon would you have me be?" she asked, tracing his eyebrows with her fingertip. "I cannot compete with your elocution teacher for skill, Dylan."

"Be a paragon of courage," he said. "Trust me enough to be honest with me. If I'm too heavy, and you can't breathe, if I'm making you uncomfortable, or if you need me to touch you somehow differently or more or less, then tell me. My objective is to please you, but I'm scouting new terrain, Lydia, and you will have to help me get the lay of the land."

"You make it sound as if we are learning some complicated new dance together."

"We absolutely are."

"Will you be honest with me too?"

He spoke very near her ear, so she could feel the shape of his words in his breath. "Does that mean I must confess that I would love to see you without your chemise?"

"Yes, and that you will allow me to see you without your breeches." Though the bedroom was all but dark, and Lydia's need was more to touch Dylan's naked flesh than to actually see him unclothed.

Dylan lifted off her and peeled out of his breeches.

Lydia shifted up and back against the pillows and scooted about with her hips until the hem of her chemise was bunched around her waist. Dylan had been right to ask her to summon her courage, because she had not thought to associate bravery with what transpired between men and women in bed.

Indignity, embarrassment, haste... not this nearly solemn unveiling and quiet sharing of memories. She lifted her chemise over her head and stuffed it under the nearest pillow.

"Will I do, Captain?"

He surged over her, gently pinning her to the mattress. "I have wanted you since you first scolded me for intruding belowstairs in search of a sandwich. You have brought warmth and comfort to my home and to my heart, and yes, Lydia, you will do. You will do splendidly."

Besiege her, Dylan ordered himself. *Besiege her with kisses and tenderness and patience...*

Lydia curled herself around Dylan as if she were intent on laying siege to his self-restraint. "You cannot know, Dylan, what it means to me that you listen, that you do not stand in judgment of me."

Who in his right mind would judge this woman, and what on earth could he judge her for? "You steal a few drops of my scent," he said, shifting to nuzzle her breast. "Then you confess the crime. I'll drench you in that scent if you like, Lydia."

The urge to join, to mate, and thrust, and rush to pleasure was nigh overwhelming, but Dylan had set for himself the challenge of being a paragon of intimate consideration. Lydia had had one encounter with a lout, regardless that she refused to cast him as such. A young lady overimbibing and intent on breaking rules deserved protection, not potential ruin, and any male old enough to wear a uniform knew that.

Dylan tried a few caresses to the sides of Lydia's breasts, and she went still. "Do you like that?"

"I hardly know. You'd best do it again so I might give the matter protracted study."

By the time he was using both his mouth and his hands on her breasts, she was thrashing beneath him and tugging at his hair.

"You are diabolical," she panted. "Watching you eat a tea cake will henceforth put me into a fever."

"And I'm supposed to stand idly about while you polish my silver and change my sheets?"

"I like polishing your silver." She'd worked a hand between their bodies and gave Dylan's shaft a glancing caress to emphasize her words.

He let her play for a moment, though it required conjuring thoughts of cold boiled turnips and other army fare.

"Enjoying yourself, Lydia?"

"Yes, if you must know. Are you?"

And to think he'd challenged her to bring *her* courage to the affray. "I am having trouble forming complete sentences. I'll spend if you keep that up."

"Isn't that the point?"

"The point..." Dylan mentally cast about for words that made sense, but all that came to mind was something Lydia had said earlier, about envying him the authority to give commands. "The point is whatever you want it to be, whatever would please you. Tell me what you want, Lydia. Give me my orders."

She'd got the knack of brushing her thumb over the spot under the tip of his cock, and Dylan's control began to unravel.

"I'll... God in heaven, Lydia."

"Spend. Let yourself spend."

Her whispered imperative was superfluous, but added to Dylan's desire. He barely managed to swipe a handkerchief from the night table before he was kneeling up, his hand around Lydia's as he brought himself off—as *they* brought him off—in a spectacular implosion of sensation and wonder.

When he'd shuddered and bucked through more satisfaction than one mortal man could bear, he crouched over Lydia, panting like a spent steeplechaser.

"*Duw yn y nefoedd.*"

Lydia's hands idly winnowed through his hair. "Did you just curse at me?" She sounded pleased with the possibility.

"I prayed to *God in heaven* for strength." An expanded translation. "I am slain."

"You followed orders."

"I am in bed with a fiend. A darling, daring fiend. Let me hold you."

Lydia was apparently willing to be held, because when Dylan

spooned himself around her, she took his hand and tucked his arm about her waist.

"I've never done that before." She faced away from him, though Dylan could hear bewilderment in her voice.

"I don't make a habit of it either."

She sent him a curious look over her shoulder.

"I pleasure myself regularly," Dylan said, "but if I am fortunate enough to share a bed with a willing partner, I generally don't... That is..."

"Are you frequently in bed with a willing partner?" Lydia's question was carefully neutral.

"No, I am not." Dylan considered that answer and considered the utter passivity of the woman around whom he was draped. "Until recently, I haven't considered the distraction worth the reward. Then some managing female in lacy caps came along, adding kittens to my domain and forcing regular meals on me. My priorities have changed."

He ought to propose. The notion popped into his head, as all his best ideas tended to. Careful study of the maps, long hours in the saddle learning the terrain, and much staring off into space trying to think like a Frenchman had yielded one clever strategy after another.

In Lydia's case, Dylan found himself thinking like a suitor, a very determined suitor.

Except that winning Lydia's heart was not exactly like battling across Spain and up over the Pyrenees. That had been a fairly straightforward exercise in claiming territory, town by town and valley by valley.

What did Lydia crave that she would never ask for? What did she *need*? Dylan pondered that question as his body recovered its equilibrium, and Lydia's breathing slowed.

He shifted his hand experimentally upward to close gently around a bare breast. Lydia moved into his touch minutely, a mere whisper of an invitation, and Dylan had his answer.

Lydia drifted, wrapped in the warmth and strength of her almost-lover, and in puzzlement. Why had she chosen to limit intimacies with Dylan as she had? Was her decision the result of guilt, because she had not been honest with him about her connection to Marcus, or was some more complicated motivation at work?

Had she been driven by a need to remain in possession of her wits, or to for once give the orders and set the expectations? Dylan had offered her exactly that. And yet, he had not surrendered *to* her, he had surrendered *with* her.

Rational thinking was made difficult by unabated desire, a yearning both soothed and enflamed by Dylan's embrace. Lydia was lecturing herself about the necessity to get adequate sleep when she felt a sweet, subtle caress to her breast.

Dylan's breathing was regular, and he hadn't stirred. Lydia arched into his touch ever so slightly, unwilling to awaken him if he'd fallen asleep.

His touch became a caress. "Did you think I'd simply nod off and leave you unsatisfied, Lydia?"

She could feel his voice rumbling from his chest. "I like sharing a bed with you, but we need our rest, and..." And she wasn't sure what he'd alluded to when he'd referred to satisfaction. One kissed and enjoyed the kissing, in the best case. Caresses were lovely, and desire was... Desire was not something Lydia had much experience with. Halfway between an itch and an ambition, of both the body and the spirits.

Dylan sat up and began rearranging pillows. "If you give a man pleasure like that, Lydia, you inspire him to return the favor. I have an idea I'd like to try."

"A naked man with ideas." Lydia eyed him, though he wasn't in a state of great arousal. "What sort of ideas?"

"Scoot up." Dylan knee-walked to a place behind her so she sat in the V of his legs, her back to his front and a hairy male knee on either side of her. "Let me be your pillow." He urged her against his chest, which was... odd. Intimate, but frustrating.

"I can't see you," Lydia said. "I can't touch you. I don't know what you're about." She could feel him, though, a bulwark of masculine muscle and bone.

"I'm *about* tending to your pleasure. Pull the covers up if you like, and tell me if I'm doing it right."

He palmed both of her breasts at once, and Lydia's question —*doing what?*—flew straight from her head.

"This position has possibilities, don't you think?" Dylan punctuated his query with a kiss to Lydia's shoulder. "The view is lovely too. Next time, I'd like at least one lit candle, Lydia."

"Hush." Lydia wanted silence in which to concentrate on his caresses, on the slight percussion of his heartbeat against her back, on the exquisite sensations he created with his hands.

Dylan ceased chattering, but what he did instead... One hand remained on Lydia's breast, while the other stole south, over ribs and abdomen, provoking crosscurrents of longing and restlessness to go with the pleasure he'd stirred up.

"Spread your legs, Lydia. Please." He stroked her curls lightly, and a notion that had been unthinkable ten minutes before became an inspired suggestion.

She arranged herself so Dylan's thighs cradled her own, and while the faint voice of modesty suggested pulling the covers up, Lydia was more interested in pulling Dylan's head down so she could kiss him.

He was tall enough, and determined enough, and ye gods... *skilled* enough. As he stroked her intimate flesh, Lydia felt at once the need to scramble off the bed and gather her wits and the need to consume a man whose touch conjured such fire.

When Lydia broke the kiss, Dylan had both hands between her legs, so he held her immobile at the same time that he caressed her in a manner more arousing than she could bear.

And yet, she did not, could not, and *would* not tell him to stop.

Her breathing became harsh, and she delighted in the room's chill as Dylan's touch shifted, and the pressure increased. One moment, she was writhing in the grip of a need that eclipsed comprehension, and the next, yearning coalesced into sensations of stunning, silent pleasure.

Lydia gave in to the clamoring of her body, no dignity, no words, nothing but need and glory and wonder. Dylan held her through it all, until Lydia had curled to her side, panting against his chest. He kept a hand over her sex in a grip both firm and oddly comforting. A connection of sorts, an anchor.

What did one say? How did one even discuss...?

So this is what the fuss is all about? did not seem adequate, and yet, Lydia felt as if the greatest secret in all of creation—the secret of her own body's capacity for pleasure—had just been put into her keeping.

"Sleep." Dylan kissed her crown and drew the covers up over her. "For now, sleep."

A stronger woman might have extricated herself from that tender embrace, might have given up the protection and solace it offered. Lydia had no strength. She had no will. She had only a nameless fullness of the heart and the certain knowledge that she loved Dylan Powell.

Orion Goddard would have spent his evening at the Coventry, given a choice. He enjoyed the role of host, or ringmaster, to use the more apt term. Ann always had the kitchen firmly under control, the head dealer kept matters on the gaming floor in hand, and Sycamore Dorning—as owner and dispenser of bon mots, good cheer, and naughty asides—dropped around just often enough to keep both staff and patrons interested in his comings and goings.

Rye's job was a lot of bookkeeping and also spotting problems before they blossomed into issues. A dowager playing a bit too deeply for her means, a widow quietly pilfering from the buffet, a young sprig courting disaster by virtue of drunken accusations.

The whole business put him in mind of his army days, dealing with bored recruits, opinionated mules, and squabbling generals. Rye loved the challenge and variety, but he loved his family as well, and thus when Ann told him to go share a few hands of cards with Alasdhair MacKay and Sycamore Dorning at the Aurora, Rye obliged her.

The problem threatening to become an issue at the card table was their fourth—Monsieur Xavier Fournier. He was charming, easy to look at in a substantial, Gallic, dark-eyed way, and he was winning. Fournier was also a successful wine merchant and thus a competitor of sorts for Rye's champagne vineyards.

"You fellows are tired," Fournier said, raking in another pot. "No challenge. This is the problem with happily married men. No focus, or no focus on anything but domestic pleasures. I will console myself with your coin, and you will go home and console yourselves with a much more substantial source of comfort."

Fournier was at least half French, though Rye hadn't been able to learn much more about his antecedents. Given that England and France had been at war for most of twenty years, personal histories could require discretion, as Rye himself well knew.

"Maybe," MacKay said, accepting the deck from Fournier, "if you spent less time blethering and more time doing the pretty, some female would take pity on you too. Why isn't there a Madame Fournier? You aren't destitute, and you're only half ugly."

"I am all that is charming, unlike you heathen Highlanders, but I am also a man of discerning tastes when it comes to the ladies. In my gentlemanly acquaintances, I am not as particular, witness present company."

"You have brothers," Dorning said. "That ability to annoy with every pronouncement is one honed by a surfeit of male siblings."

"A French auntie is the equal of five English brothers in terms of polishing a man's humility, Monsieur Dorning, but I humbly suggest the lot of you are worried about your Welsh cousin." Fournier picked up his cards and began calmly arranging them.

"Explain yourself." MacKay flicked the next card at Fournier with particular force. Alasdhair was the sweetest of men, but he had a convincing growl and a positively eloquent pair of fists.

"Please do elaborate," Rye added. "We take the welfare of family members seriously."

Fournier sent him an ironic smile. "One hears this, and considering that Monsieur Dorning has more family than Mad George has German cousins, one makes allowances."

They permitted Fournier a few more moments of posturing—he was French, after all—before Dorning rose to bring the decanter to the table.

He set the decanter on the table with a *thunk*. "If you do not, in the next two minutes, unburden yourself of whatever is troubling you, there won't be enough of you left for your French aunties to scold."

Fournier topped up his glass of brandy and passed the decanter to MacKay, who declined and then passed the decanter to Rye.

"We are worried about Powell," Rye said. "Our *ladies* are worried about Powell, and thus you will oblige us with whatever triviality you think you know."

"Powell goes everywhere safely," Fournier said. "He has the freedom of the city—the whole city, not simply the mercantile district —in a way no lord mayor ever will."

"Because," Dorning said, "he's always within shouting distance of some old soldier or former regimental laundress. They keep an eye on him."

Fournier nodded. "As do their brothers, grannies, and pet hounds. He passes as quietly as the breeze, walking the streets by the hour, but they watch out for him. He has been breezing about the slums of late, looking for one William Brook."

How Fournier knew this was probably a matter of his own network of former soldiers, former prisoners of war, and aunties of the French variety. The émigré community was close-knit and, at the same time, tightly integrated with London's English population at all levels of society. Then too, Fournier sold a more pedestrian champagne than Rye did, as well as some exquisite clarets.

The Frenchman was thus connected to inns, taverns, and shops Rye would never frequent.

"Brook was one of Powell's direct reports," MacKay said. "The fellow doesn't hear well and has an injured hand. Powell would worry if Brook went missing."

"He is not missing." Fournier pretended to study his cards. "He is hiding, and one suspects that if Captain Powell continues his perambulations, even his honor guard might not be able to protect him."

Dorning poured himself half a finger of brandy. "And you couldn't simply have a word with Goddard about this? You had to wait until we needed a fourth so you could drink my brandy and lighten our pockets?"

"Do forgive me," Fournier said. "I am still trying to learn the ways of an English gentleman. I tried riding in the park this morning at the ungodly and frigid hour after dawn, but you sluggards refused to oblige me with your presence. I tried fencing at Angelo's for half the afternoon, but still no luck. I am reduced to accepting Goddard's invitation to make up a fourth."

He put down his cards and finished his drink. "After politely watching you three consult the clock every quarter hour and handle your cards with all the finesse of eight-year-olds, I am reduced to playing the role of your French auntie. Powell needs assistance. He is a good fellow. He helps the occasional former prisoner when he can, and nobody dares criticize him for aiding a Frenchman, because he is Captain Powell. He needs your aid now. I have said what I came to say. I bid you *bonsoir*, and thank you for an amusing evening. My regards to your ladies, who are doubtless missing the company of such estimable gallants."

He rose and bowed elegantly, then sauntered from the room.

"By God," Dorning said, "he left his winnings. That was a splendid exit. If he keeps that up, I might have to like him."

"Ann likes him," Rye said. "They talk about sauces and spices by the hour. Jeanette would probably enjoy him too."

MacKay collected Fournier's abandoned cards. "Dorcas says he is something of a fairy godfather among the émigrés. They try not to abuse his generosity, but when somebody is arrested or unexpectedly widowed, the family turns to him. He does not protect the guilty or indulge the profligate, but he does what he can."

MacKay's wife was something of a crusader regarding London's downtrodden. "Dorcas has crossed paths with him?" Goddard asked.

"Charitable committees are one way a cit or émigré can gain entrée to a more genteel circle." Alasdhair shuffled the deck into a neat stack and put the cards aside. "Dorcas includes duchesses among her acquaintances thanks to those committees. Gives a man pause, to think of all those ladies putting their heads together. What shall we do about Powell?"

"Nothing," Dorning said. "If I read him correctly, he hasn't asked for any aid, and that all but ties our hands."

Our hands. Dorning was a cousin only by virtue of his marriage to Jeanette, but he'd apparently decided not to quibble over details.

"Right," Rye said. "We are honor-bound to do nothing. That settles it. Gentlemen, I will bid you good night."

"What do we do with the winnings?" MacKay asked, rising. "We did not play for farthing points."

Not in front of the Frenchman they hadn't. More fool them.

"We donate the funds in Fournier's name to whatever charity Dorcas suggests will most directly benefit the émigrés," Rye said, "and send the receipt for the donation to Fournier, along with a case of my best champagne."

"All very honorable," Dorning said. "Jeanette will approve." He stood, stretched, and yawned. "Shall I walk out with you, Goddard?"

MacKay rose. "You fool nobody, Dorning. You will take the

shortest route home, the same as I will, and Goddard will repair straight to the Coventry, because that's where his Ann is at this hour."

"Because," Rye said, holding the door for the others, "doing nothing to interfere with Powell's situation means we each embark on a lengthy and immediate consultation with our wives."

"For starters," Dorning said. "And if the situation grows dire, I will even consult a sister-in-law or two, or perhaps—as a last result—a few brothers. Don't quote me on that."

MacKay smacked Dorning on the back of the head, Dorning elbowed MacKay, and Rye shoved them each on the shoulder.

"March, you idiots. Annie was making profiteroles for tonight's buffet, and I am famished for sweets."

That earned him a pair of reciprocal shoves, and then each man was off to consult with his respective commanding officer.

CHAPTER ELEVEN

Dylan rose to awareness with the single thought that he was safe. Not in camp. Not on campaign. Warm, cozy, and secure, with an operatic robin somewhere nearby heralding the start of a new day.

A spring morning without birdsong was a morning when the French lurked in the undergrowth.

His next thought was that roses never bloomed this early in the year, and then the woman around whom he was snuggled wiggled her backside lazily against his erection, and his mind went still.

Lydia.

Lydia's bed.

Lydia's bedroom.

He'd *spent the night* with his housekeeper.

While one part of him allowed that it had been a spectacularly lovely night, and he'd never awoken feeling quite so refreshed, another part of him was court-martialing his witless self for having done just that.

The sun wasn't yet risen, and Dylan had some hope he could tiptoe up to his own quarters unobserved. He eased from the bed, drew the covers around Lydia's bare, delectable, entirely too kissable shoulders, and silently pulled on his breeches and shirt.

"Don't go." Lydia hadn't opened her eyes, and Dylan doubted she was awake.

He kissed her cheek. "Dream on, my lady. Duty calls." He permitted himself not so much as one more caress—that way lay the most blissful folly—and collected the rest of his effects. He made it through the kitchen and past the pantries.

By the time he was up the steps, Dylan was congratulating himself on passing through dangerous territory undetected, until he noticed Bowen Brook observing him from the door of Brook's office. Bowen was dressed, holding a cup of tea and looking puzzled.

"Not like you to bend a rule," he said, sipping his tea, "though Mrs. Lovelace would tempt many a man to sell his soul. She's not beautiful in the usual sense, but she's formidable and decent."

Dylan set down his boots. "My intentions toward her are honorable, if she'll have me."

"But you stand before me, boots off, your shirt undone, not certain she will. What has the world come to when Captain Powell is wandering about headquarters barefoot and smiling?"

It's not what you think. Dylan didn't bother protesting, despite the fact that he and Lydia hadn't even made love. They'd been intimate, though. Spectacularly intimate.

"I can trust your discretion, I hope," Dylan said.

"Oh, of course." Bowen saluted with his tea cup. "But more to the point, *she* can trust my discretion. Going to be some sort of hell to pay if you're still on covert missions belowstairs when your sisters arrive, Captain."

Sisters. Dylan swore in Welsh. Bowen, good Shropshire lad that he was, doubtless understood him.

"I have some time," Dylan said. "We have some time before they arrive. I spent most of yesterday in St. Giles, by the way."

"Why would you do a buffle-headed thing like that?"

Bowen's adjustment to civilian life was proceeding apace.

"Looking for Will, and he's there, Bowen. He's there, and he's either threatened the lads into providing him cover, or somebody else has. Nobody gave me honest answers to any question I put to them, though they were all concerned for poor Will and eager to assist me."

"Like asking the Spanish locals about the movements of the French?"

The analogy was dauntingly apt. "Precisely. They all know something, and they are all as pleasant and helpful as they can be, but nobody's *talking* to me. That tells me Will is still alive, which is progress."

"I could have a look."

"We know what happened last time you went nosing around, Bowen. Between Goddard's urchins and MacKay's ladies, I am under constant guard, while you are not." Not to mention the former soldiers reduced to begging on nearly every street corner.

Bowen sipped his tea. "Have you tried asking the ladies to nose about? I found my way to your doorstep when I first mustered out, because one of the streetwalkers told me you were always good for a free meal. I got not only a meal, but a decent pair of boots and some coin here, Captain. I was too ashamed to ask my old mates for aid, but the ladies knew a weary soldier when they saw one."

Bowen was being polite, allowing Dylan's sortie belowstairs to earn him a mere scolding before permitting a change in topic. This suggestion, though, to rely on intermediaries and noncombatants wasn't one Dylan had considered.

"If I involve the ladies and the urchins, then I involve my family. This is not their fight."

Bowen eyed him up and down, from tousled hair, to rumpled shirt, to bare feet. "Might not be your fight either, Captain. Will's a big boy and a decent brawler, for all that he has a bad hand. Our mother would say to leave him be and give him time to sort himself out."

"But your father said to keep an eye on him, because he's not as smart or formidable as he thinks he is."

"Is that what your papa told you about your cousins?"

Papa had said exactly that. MacKay was heir to the Scottish equivalent of a barony. Goddard came from English gentry, had risen to colonel, and been knighted. Men of standing needed to know they could rely on family at least.

"My papa told me," Dylan said, "not to trifle with a lady unless I intended to marry her. That objective requires Mrs. Lovelace's cooperation."

"Earning her cooperation. Is that what they call it now?"

"You're fired," Dylan said, gathering up his boots. "Drummed out of the regiment, stripped of rank, a disgrace to His Majesty's army."

"You forgot insubordinate and on latrine duty until Judgment Day. We knew when you trotted that one out you were truly vexed."

"I'm not truly vexed." Dylan started up the steps, realizing he wasn't vexed at all.

"Captain, you should know that your sisters' baggage coach arrived last night."

Well, maybe Dylan was vexed, but only a little. The sisters would aid his cause, and Lydia Lovelace would soon be Lydia Powell. Had a wonderful sound, that did.

"You dealt with the coachman and groom?"

"As your steward, of course I did. Put the coachy and groom up in the carriage house, and the lads and I will start unloading the trunks once we've had some breakfast."

"You will stand about making a list and looking steward-ly," Dylan said. "Mrs. Lovelace will direct the lads. She has assigned rooms and parlors and whatnot for the visiting dignitaries." The invading horde. No matter, Lydia would have them all in hand.

"John Coachman gave me a letter for you from your sisters." Bowen passed over a sealed epistle. "Marching orders, no doubt. Should I be looking for another post, sir?"

Dylan spied Tegan's elegant hand on the missive. "Why would you do that?"

"If you are intent on marrying Mrs. Lovelace, she'll want to go to housekeeping in Wales, won't she?"

I dearly hope so. "The siege is just beginning, Brook. There are trenches to dig, artillery to bring forward, negotiations to be held. Abandon your post now, and I am sure to fail."

"Can't have that," Bowen said. "Honor of the regiment, latrine duty, and so forth."

"Precisely." Dylan resumed his progress up the steps, feeling an unaccountable urge to laugh. Yes, he was ever so slightly vexed. The sisters were on the march, Bowen was insubordinate, Will was still missing, and the men were behaving oddly.

But Dylan was also in charity with all of creation and feeling particularly benevolent toward his newly married cousins and their spouses. He was in love with Lydia, and that reduced all annoyances, woes, and vexations to mere details.

Lydia had made an appointment with Mama's solicitors upon first arriving in London. The firm of Sigafoose and Sigafoose had shown her every courtesy and dealt with her financial requests swiftly. She'd also, however, asked Mr. Robert Sigafoose, the elder brother, pointed questions to which he'd replied with much throat-clearing, desk-tidying, and sighing.

When Lydia had silently stared at him through that entire performance, he'd asked for time to undertake some research. Mr. Sigafoose had put her off last month with a pompous little speech about delicate matters not being rushed and inquiries having been put in train.

She needed answers now, and she needed even more desperately to clear the air with Dylan Powell. She found him in the breakfast parlor looking as neat, self-possessed, and handsome as ever—or perhaps more self-possessed and handsome than ever.

Her assessment had lost any pretensions to objectivity. "Captain, good morning."

He rose and bowed. "Mrs. Lovelace, good day. Please do have a seat."

He held a chair for her, as courteous as always, while Lydia felt a blush creeping up her neck. Only hours ago, she'd been *naked* with him, utterly abandoned to all propriety. She'd been *eager* for his excruciatingly intimate caresses and had touched him in unbearably intimate ways too.

She summoned every iota of dignity she possessed, swept past him, and took a seat. "I forgot my cap again."

Oh, *that* was an impressive way to start a difficult conversation, but since last night, she'd misplaced her wits, her common sense, and her ability to focus on anything but her next sighting of Dylan Powell. This business of being in love was not at all convenient.

Dylan poured her a cup of tea. "I spent five minutes this morning looking all about my room for Papa's pocket watch. I never go out without it. I had aired my best army curses—which are reserved for only the most annoying of circumstances—when I caught sight of myself in the cheval mirror and happened to notice the damned thing was already affixed to its fob and mocking me from my pocket."

He stirred cream and honey into her tea. "I also generally take a pair of reading spectacles with me when I have business calls to make. This entailed another search." He set the toast rack and the jam pot by her plate, along with the butter dish. "My spectacles were atop my head. Need I go on?"

"I tripped on the carpet in my parlor," Lydia said, feeling marginally less mortified. "A lady should be at all times graceful, and I also nearly walked into the kitchen table."

Dylan began buttering a slice of toast. "I am frequently off-balance with the world. I am irritated with my cousins, impatient with the men, and otherwise out of sorts, but I could not stand to be off-balance with you, Lydia. Last night..."

He glanced at the parlor door.

"Was lovely," Lydia said quietly. "Astonishingly lovely. One had no clue how delightful such dealings could be. One is gobsmacked with wonder."

Dylan took inordinate care spreading the butter over the toast. "Precisely. Gobsmacked, befuddled, and grateful. Very, very grateful. Perhaps tonight you'd allow me to expound on that feeling of gratitude?"

Tonight was both eons in the future and quite soon. Lydia hauled back hard on her anticipation and forced herself to take a sip of tea.

"We have matters to discuss, Captain, and I refuse to put them off any longer."

He added jam to the toast. "My sisters' baggage wain has arrived, along with sealed orders. I am to convey to you a request to schedule fittings for them at the modiste of their choosing, along with a tailor— Tegan needs a new riding habit—bootmaker, and glovemaker. I am to leave my afternoons free to escort them to Gunter's, and Bronnie is planning to dress up as a lad so I can take her around to Tatts and my clubs."

"Is that an idle threat?"

"The clubs, yes—I hope—Tatts, no. And how I'm to do all this and also track down Will Brook, I do not know. What is this discussion we must have?"

Dylan passed over the toast, a symbol of all the careful rules and boundaries Lydia had put in place with him and how those rules no longer applied.

"I have not been completely honest with you."

She expected him to poker up, as only he could, but instead, he merely regarded her. "Are you married?"

"I am not."

"Is there a child, Lydia? Did one foray past the bounds of paragonhood result in a permanent reminder of the occasion?"

His tone was gently curious, not a hint of judgment in his words. If Lydia weren't already in love with him, she would be smitten by the patience and understanding in his gaze.

"Nothing like that, thank God. It's about the family situation that inspired me to take a post in London."

"Eat your toast. You will need your strength."

She took a bite because she was in good appetite, not because he'd given her an order. The jam was excellent, and Dylan hadn't skimped on the butter. "I will need my strength because your sisters are soon to arrive?"

He swept her a look that should have sent the curtains up in flames. "That too. Tell me of this family situation."

"Finish your eggs, Captain. We will both need our strength."

He gave Lydia a smile that inspired her first serious case of the female flutters—for the day—and then dutifully tucked into his eggs.

"I am trying to sort out a matter of inheritance." Lydia had come upon that gratifyingly brisk opening gambit while braiding her hair. Not the most direct approach to the topic, but factually accurate. "An heir has gone missing several branches over on the family tree, and the logical parties are trying to have him declared dead. I believe they are being hasty and self-interested, and my mother has asked me to consult with the lawyers and ask what questions I can."

"Questions of whom?"

"The lawyers, first, both to ensure Mama's funds are thriving and to inquire regarding this other matter." Horse Guards thereafter, and then Mama had had no more ideas other than, *You are clever, Lydia. I'm sure you'll get to the bottom of this in no time.*

"This is the distant maternal relation you mentioned? Lord Tremont? Why not send his brother, uncle, or male cousins to make those inquiries?" Dylan's question was more puzzled than accusatory.

"His lordship has no brothers, and his uncle and male cousin— note the singular—both stand to benefit from his disappearance."

"If you suspect foul play, Lydia, then investigating the situation could be dangerous for you."

"I do not suspect foul play," she said slowly, except that on some unspoken, unacknowledged level, she had. Why else make a secret of her remove to London? Why else the elaborate pretense with Aunt Chloe? Uncle Reginald was draining Tremont's coffers, and that had started shortly after Marcus had bought his colors.

Uncle Reginald *of all people* would not want Marcus to come home and demand explanations.

Dylan set aside his empty plate. "You did not discuss with your mother the possibility of foul play because you were loath to upset her, but you have made little progress with your inquiries. London is an incomprehensibly big place, and you are but a housekeeper trying to investigate the disappearnace of a peer. The longer you think on the matter and the longer you get nowhere with the solicitors, the more worried you become."

A reconnaissance officer would excel at grasping fundamentals quickly. "I am off to meet with the lawyers in part because I want to assure myself—in detail—that Mama and I will not suffer should the earl be declared dead. I am of age, and my mother is widowed, but the law does not respect women generally, and Mama is too sweet for her own good. She relied on Tremont as the head of the extended family to safeguard her interests."

A silence bloomed, one that begged to be filled with further truths. *The missing peer is my brother, and you dislike him intensely, almost as intensely as you dislike liars...*

"Your prodigal earl might have fallen prey to nothing more nefarious than rotten luck, Lydia. Anybody can come to harm merely crossing London's streets. I had a passing acquaintance with Tremont when we both reported to Dunacre. Lieutenant Lord Tremont was forever spouting Latin, and he could get lost between the mess hall and the armory. He bungled everything from direct orders to shaving himself, and I once saw him fall off a horse that was moving at a sedate trot. London would finish off a man like that in less than a week. If the street gangs didn't get him, the card sharps or dysentery would."

Lydia choked on her last bite of toast, which resulted in Dylan thumping her gently on the back.

"Have a sip of tea." He obligingly held her cup to her lips, and Lydia sipped, but she wanted to dash the cup away.

Marcus rode like a demon. Yes, he spouted Latin—he was much taken with the Stoics—but he was neither clumsy nor dimwitted.

"Could Lord Tremont have suffered a blow to the head?"

Dylan set down her tea cup. "I would not necessrily know of such an injury. Nobody knew many details where he was concerned, except that he'd come into his title in adolescence and bought himself a commission despite having no heir of the body. I admired his willingness to serve, but not much else about him."

Lydia's throat still ached from where the toast had got stuck. "You speak of him in the past tense. Did he fall in battle?"

"I have no idea. He was still answering to Dunacre as we prepared to meet Bonaparte at Waterloo, but I was detailed elsewhere on the day of battle. I haven't seen or heard of Tremont since, which is to the good for all concerned. His lorsdhip was the worst sort of sycophant, and toadying only encourages a tyrant to believe his own lies. Shall I accompany you to the solicitors' office, Lydia? I will lurk at your elbow looking capable of violence toward any who disrespect you."

"You are capable of violence." Was he capable of violence toward Marcus?

Dylan finished her tea. "We all are, if driven too hard for too long. I don't like to think of you having to humor a lot of unctuous lawyers who take your money and do nothing to further your interests."

Lydia sat very still, trying again to gather the courage to reveal the last, most damning fact to a man who professed protectiveness toward her. *I am not who and what you think I am.*

"Beg pardon, Captain, missus." Bowen Brook stood in the doorway. "Colonel Goddard and Captain MacKay have come to call. I put them in the family parlor."

Lydia rose. "Please have Betty send up a tray." The hour was ungodly early for a social call and the timing ungodly inconvenient.

Something had to be amiss. Bowen hustled off, though it wasn't a steward's place to give orders to the kitchen maid.

Dylan was on his feet as well. "We will chat more later," he said. "If you could see to setting up my sisters' requested appointments, I'd appreciate it."

"Of course." Lydia could send off the requisite notes before leaving on her legal errand. "Captain?"

"Dylan, when we are private."

"The door is open, *Captain*, and your cousins are on the premises. I have more to tell you, and you won't like it."

His gaze held humor and blatant affection. "Have you concocted a lecture for me, Lydia? A little homily about decorum, proper behavior, and mistakes that must be put firmly behind us? If so, please be informed that I've been mentally rehearsing a proposal of marriage since the moment I left your bed."

Lydia frankly gaped. "Marriage? *To me?*" He'd utterly flummoxed her, left her befuddled and baffled.

"Men do marry their housekeepers, Lydia. You needn't goggle at me so. I'm merely gentry, and you seem to be as well, for all your despair over missing caps."

Worse and worse. "Why would you think me gentry?"

"You sing in French. Your embroidery is exquisite. You have a portion in the keeping of family solicitors. You had a mare of your own growing up. Your extended family boasts a missing earl, and the working folk of this world do not trouble themselves over missing earls. Don't look so panicked, my dear. I aspire to be your intended, and your secrets are safe with me."

"Powell." A large Scotsman whom Lydia knew to be Major MacKay appeared in the doorway. "Stop whingeing at a busy woman who knows better than to listen to your nonsense. Goddard and I need a moment. Mrs. Lovelace, good day. My Dorcas sends her regards."

Dylan bowed to Lydia. "The press gang has arrived. Until this evening, Mrs. Lovelace." He marched out, and Lydia sank into the chair he'd vacated, unwilling to trust her knees to fulfill the office of keeping her upright.

"'I aspire to be your intended, and your secrets are safe with me.'" MacKay quoted Dylan's intent word for word, but he also laid on a Scottish burr rife with incredulity.

Goddard turned from the parlor window to regard Dylan with brooding censure. "You *said* that? To Mrs. Lovelace?"

"And what's this about a missing earl?" MacKay added, closing the parlor door. "You'd best tell us, because even Dorcas would concede that beating the answers out of you would be allowable in the circumstances."

Dylan's cousins were worried for him. He was touched at their concern, also annoyed. "Eavesdropping is beneath you, MacKay."

"All but proposing in the breakfast parlor with the door wide open and to a woman who did not look enraptured with your maundering, is not only beneath you, Powell, it's *stupid*. You have sisters. Is that how you want their dashing swains to court them? Pass the butter, and shall we be married?"

Nobody conveyed ire as well as a fretful Scotsman. "Speaking of those sisters," Dylan replied, "their luggage has arrived."

"Don't even try your diversionary tactics." MacKay paced the confines of the room. "What are these secrets you have offered to guard for your housekeeper?"

Marriage had made MacKay more like his old self, which was to say, a rubbishing nosy pain in the arse. A relief, that, to see him back on his mettle.

Also a nuisance. "Mrs. Lovelace's personal matters are none of your concern," Dylan said. "Her family situation is a bit delicate, and the lawyers might get involved."

Goddard took a seat on the sofa and crossed his long legs at the ankle. "Housekeepers are not typically embroiled in litigation, Powell."

"I gather Lydia is investigating matters on behalf of her mother..." Though Goddard, damn him to eternal latrine duty, had a point.

Goddard and MacKay glowered at him as one. "*Lydia*," they said in unison, making a perfectly lovely name into an accusation.

Goddard took up the verbal lash. "Since when did your position as honorary guardian angel of the regiment expand to include resolution of legal matters that do not concern you and about which you know almost nothing?"

"Since I spent the night in *Lydia's* bed. I mean to marry her if she'll have me, so you can leave off strutting and pawing and tell me why it is that you've disturbed my peace at the crack of doom. My plans for the day include lurking in a number of disreputable taverns, idling on noisome street corners, and generally listening at keyholes. You two louts were not on my schedule. Finding William Brook—before my sisters arrive—is."

Goddard and MacKay both looked as if they'd been caught filching sweets from the pantry.

"In her... *bed?*" MacKay asked nigh timorously.

"For the night." Lydia would not thank him for making that disclosure, but Goddard and MacKay needed to cease their nannying and deal with facts. "You can draw lots to see which of you stands up with me, or you both can. A ceremony needs two witnesses at least."

"Ask Dorning to stand up with you," Goddard said. "He likes that sort of thing, and it will save me a sore shoulder from arm-wrestling MacKay for the honor."

"Dorning?" Powell did not care for Mr. Sycamore Dorning. He was loquacious, self-important, and, at the most inconvenient times, right. "I think not."

"His brother is an earl," MacKay shot back. "Another brother paints half of fancy London's portraits. Two others have married into some other earldom's family of Vikings. His older sister is married to

Worth Kettering. A family like that could do a lot for your lads, Powell."

An unreasonable anger blighted much of Dylan's joy in the day. "*I* do a lot for the lads. When they need something, they come to me, not to Sycamore Damned Dorning."

Goddard and MacKay pointedly did not look at each other, or at Dylan.

"My apologies," he said. "I will ask Dorning to stand up with me, should the happy occasion arise, but you will forgive my protectiveness toward the men. We had only each other to rely on, and now something untoward is afoot. I fear for Will Brook."

"We ran across Fournier last night," Goddard said, pretending to study a portrait of Great-Grandmama Beulah Powell in her widow's weeds.

"I thought you were assembling for a hand of cards." To which Dylan had for once sent regrets.

"He made up our fourth," MacKay said. "Dorning's suggestion. Fournier volunteered that he's heard of your search for Brook and heard as well that you'd best desist."

Dylan said the first thing that popped into his head. "Fournier is French." Sold a very good claret at a reasonable price, but his champagne hadn't a patch on Goddard's.

"And you are Welsh," Goddard observed. "Some things cannot be helped." Goddard was half French, hence the note of umbrage in his observation.

"Don't be ridiculous. I meant, why would a Frenchman hear of my ramblings about the stews? The émigrés and I rarely cross paths, for understandable reasons. I am puzzled and intrigued."

MacKay smacked him on the arm. "You are warned, ye bloody fool. Fournier indicated that whoever has sent Will Brook into hiding is in a position to shorten your life. Give it up, Powell, or at least let the lads do your looking for you."

"The lads are lying to me." Even the words hurt. "Probably trying to keep me safe. Do you trust Fournier?"

"Yes," Goddard said. "He noted that you've helped the occasional former prisoner of war or French soldier. He feels he owes you a debt on their behalf, and Fournier pays his debts to the penny and on time."

"He went to some effort to convey the warning," MacKay said. "If Brook has borrowed money from the wrong people, if he got the wrong woman with child, you can do little for him."

Those problems were relatively straightforward—if expensive—to deal with. "If he committed rape, then he's put himself beyond the pale, but short of that, he's one of ours, and we do not leave a soldier to fend for himself in enemy territory."

"If you won't desist," Goddard said, "then at least let us help you."

"It's not your fight."

"But you are our cousin."

MacKay stepped close. "You aspire to be Lydia Lovelace's intended. Hard to do that if you're being measured for a shroud because you were too pigheaded to accept aid when you needed it."

That argument gave Dylan pause, as did the particular battle light in MacKay's eyes. MacKay had transferred rather than remain under Dunacre's command, and once, in a semi-inebriated fit of remorse, MacKay had berated himself for deserting his cousin.

A meddling pair of cousins was bad enough, but cousins driven by old guilt would be impossible to wave off.

"Let me see what I can find out today," Dylan said, "and I'll let you know if assistance is needed."

MacKay looked like he wanted to say more, about stubborn Welshmen, hopeless battles, and soldiers who could not be saved from their own recklessness.

"We tried," Goddard muttered. "The ladies said we had to try."

"And I thank you for trying, but it doesn't feel dangerous yet." The memory of Bowen's battered face rose in Dylan's mind. "Not seriously dangerous."

"A bullet's not seriously dangerous if it misses you," MacKay said. "What of your housekeeper and her secrets? Are those dangerous?"

Beyond the parlor window, a groom steered the pony-trap around from the mews and parked it before the house. The shaggy creature in the traces would make slow progress in Town traffic, but Lydia apparently felt confident of her ability to drive London streets.

"She's dealing with a family squabble. The scion of the house nipped off to Canada or ran afoul of the law. Nobody really knows his fate, but they are happy to divide up the estate in his absence." Dylan was reluctant to disclose exactly who the scion was. MacKay had dealt with Lord Tremont for a time, and Goddard had known of him. Neither cousin had formed a good impression of his lordship.

"A housekeeper whose family has an estate to divide up." Goddard could not have spoken with greater disinterest. "Be careful, Powell. Be exceedingly, relentlessly careful."

"I always am."

MacKay smiled. "You spent the night in *Lydia's* bed, Cousin. That is not the behavior of a careful man."

No, it wasn't, and Dylan didn't particularly care that it wasn't, which only underscored Goddard's warning twice over. Now was no time to be stupid, because Dylan very much did consider himself Lydia Lovelace's intended.

This explained—mostly—why, when she climbed into the pony-trap ten minutes later, Dylan discreetly followed her halfway across London and watched while she entered the offices of Sigafoose and Sigafoose.

As far as Dylan knew, that firm dealt only in civil matters and handled only clients of considerable social standing. He could hear Powell, Goddard, and even Dorning mentally reminding him that gentry would have to be very wealthy indeed to wrangle representation from the brothers Sigafoose.

Dylan turned his steps north and west, back to the part of Town where the only standing to be had came from quick wits, a sharp knife, and a pair of swift fists.

CHAPTER TWELVE

"Captain Powell won't give up," Willaim Brook said. "He won't quit."

Marcus had devoted considerable thought to Powell's recent penchant for ambling about the stews. For most of an afternoon, Powell had sat nursing a pint in the snug of one of Marcus's most lucrative taverns. He'd asked after William Brook, presenting himself as an old army comrade, and this time, the publican had disavowed any knowledge.

Continued silence would come at a cost, and Marcus's means were exceedingly limited.

"Powell hasn't made any progress," Marcus said. "If he continues to lurk in doorways and stroll about aimlessly, he'll find himself missing his coat and a few teeth." Marcus did not want such a mishap on his conscience. Powell was an honorable man and a good man.

Unfortunately, he was also as tenacious as an underfed hound on the scent of a rabbit. Then too, the men would take it very much amiss if Marcus's games resulted in harm to their captain, and the good opinion of the men had saved Marcus's life many times over.

"I don't like leading the captain on a dance, sir." Brook wasn't standing at attention today. He was pacing back and forth before the cold hearth. Dunacre had been a pacer, and Marcus had learned to hate—to abhor, despise, loathe, and revile—the results of his pacing.

Dunacre would pace himself into high dudgeon over some imagined slight—the wording of an order, the seating at an officers' banquet—and the result, unless something or someone distracted him, was misery for all in his ambit.

Powell had rarely witnessed the pacing, but he'd frequently earned Dunacre's ire. Marcus had eventually puzzled out that Powell antagonized his superior by design and had taken the resulting punishment rather than let Dunacre's temper rain down on the men.

Powell was brave, for which Marcus had both esteemed and resented him.

And Marcus did not pace. He remained in his rickety chair behind his dilapidated desk and forbade himself to think of Tremont, Mama, or the mischief he and Wesley used to get up to.

"Powell may not even be looking for you," Marcus said. "He's asking after you, but in a casual way, probably as a pretext. He's canny like that." Marcus was not canny. Never would be. "Your brother can't tromp about all day searching for you, so Powell takes on that thankless task, but in truth..."

Brook came to a halt at the grimy window. "Sir?"

"In truth, Powell might well be looking for me. Why else would Lydia still bide in his household unless she's set Powell to looking for me?" Brook had brought word that Lydia yet remained in London and had shown no signs of returning to Shropshire. She'd received Marcus's note, and her Latin was in excellent repair. She was, as usual, thinking independently, at which she excelled.

Brook shot Marcus a look over his shoulder. "So have a quiet little reunion with your sister, explain the situation to her ladyship, and then send her home. And as for you... Italy is cheap, I'm told."

A substantial portion of polite society was living cheaply on the Continent, particularly the former officers, heirs presumptive, and younger sons whom Marcus was avoiding at all costs. That Brook would suggest Marcus leave the country was indicative of waning patience on the part of a soldier kept on watch too long.

"I can earn my bread simply by reading and writing here," Marcus said. "I'm an oddity in the stews, but not a foreigner. In Rome or Lisbon, I would have no ability to blend in." No ability to hide, to state the disgraceful truth.

Why must Lydia still be so damnably stubborn?

Marcus felt the old frustration welling, the frustration of a man who was not clever, who had no gift for quick stratagems. He was a practical sort content to follow the rules—usually. If people could not read or write, he could do that for them and be paid a pittance for the task. That sort of transaction made sense to him.

All this subterfuge and skulking about...

"There's more, sir."

"With you, there is always more, Brook." None of it good.

"Her ladyship called on the solicitors again this morning."

"Collecting funds, no doubt." But then, would Lydia need funds if she had a housekeeper's salary, lodging, and the usual allowance for candles, tea, and beer? Marcus longed to simpy talk to her, to hear her crisp, confident voice, to again catch a whiff of her rosy fragrance.

She'd been a protective big sister, and Marcus had looked forward to the day when he could be her protective adult brother. He'd bungled that as badly as he'd bungled everything else.

"If Lydia has asked Powell to search for me, then sooner or later he will find me," Marcus said. "We'd best break ranks, Brook. Make up some tale of being coshed on the head after imbibing too freely. Contrive to look convincingly disheveled and suffer a few judicious lapses of memory."

Brook peered at him. "You want me to lie to my own brother?"

If it is not right, do not do it; if it is not true, do not say it. Excellent guidance from Marcus Aurelius, though impractical when a fellow wanted to live to draw another breath. The philosopher had also said that the best revenge was to never be like one's enemy.

How did one apply that guidance when one was one's own worst enemy? A conundrum for the ages.

"Bowen will want to believe what you tell him," Marcus said, "and he'll know enough to not ask awkward questions."

"The captain will ask awkward questions. You can send me out waving a white flag, and if the captain is searching for you, he'll only look that much harder when I try to bamboozle him."

Meaning Powell would ask awkward questions *of Brook*, and Brook, being human and half in awe of Powell, would eventually give something away. Marcus wanted to bang his head on the desk, but that would solve nothing.

"I need time to think."

"You've had years to think, sir, and what you did wasn't so very wrong. Stupid perhaps, though we all understand why you did it, but the war is over, and Powell isn't the kind to—"

"Powell was and is the regimental conscience," Marcus snapped, abruptly out of patience with Brook, Powell, Lydia, and life in general. "He of all people, *of all officers*, would not understand." And Brook did not understand that one terribly bungled moment on a battlefield was not the worst of Marcus's lapses of honor.

"Fine, then," Brook said, "I will offer my brother a Banbury tale, which he will see through as easily as the captain does, but you need to know this, sir: I took up bodyguard duty where you are concerned because somebody was asking around about you before I supposedly went missing."

Marcus's annoyance congealed into dread. "Explain yourself."

"The questions were casual and quiet, but they were aimed at finding men who reported to you directly. I decided somebody ought to keep an eye on you—why search out your direct reports, if not to eventually locate you? I was your batman, while Bowen served under Powell. I suspect whoever gave him such a beating simply got the wrong Private Brook."

"I don't like this." The situation, which had been complicated before, was growing convoluted.

"I don't like this at all. Somebody was nosing about and interrogating the men... about me?" Lydia wouldn't have nosing-about connections in London, but Wesley or some of his unsavory friends might.

"So I hear, and I would like to discuss this with Bowen. He's shrewd, and he may have heard things I haven't."

"Discuss it quietly and report back."

"Bowen won't lie to the captain, sir." *And neither will I.* A reproach lay in Brook's unspoken words. One did not have to cite Marcus Aurelius to know that truth was preferable to a lie.

"Then the captain learns that somebody was looking for me in low places and mistakenly tried to beat some answers out of an innocent party. My own sister is apparently trying to find me, as is—I suspect—Powell himself on her behalf."

"Powell will find you," Brook said. "Your best bet is to leave while you can."

A disorderly retreat was the worst disgrace that could befall an officer. Better to be taken captive on the battlefield, best of all to fall in victorious battle.

Except that Marcus had never wanted to be an officer. He'd wanted to be a philosophical sort of peer, pondering eternal questions at length, while tending his acres and finding some pleasant female to while away the years with.

Those wants had died early one winter morning in Tremont's vast deer park. Now Marcus wanted two things, the first being the courage to admit the wrongs he'd done and to atone for them as best he could. An impulse that honorable would surely get him killed, and he frankly dreaded to die on the end of a rope with a crowd gleefully jeering to see a peer hanged.

The second longing, the one so painful and constant he never spoke of it, was simply to see his mother again. To feel her embrace, to one last time behold the love in her eyes, even if that love was clouded with disappointment.

Soldiers expiring of mortal wounds invariably called for their wives or mothers. Sick to death of the poverty, stink, and danger of the stews, Marcus knew exactly how they felt.

"Go to your brother," Marcus said, "do as you must. I will make arrangements to take ship."

"Don't tell me where you're off to," Brook said, heading for the door. "I suspect I will enjoy a longer life if I'm allowed to march along in ignorance of your plans. Good day, sir. Shall I carry a message to your sister?"

Brook was anxious to clear the air with his brother, while Marcus had spent years perpetrating a lie on his family.

"The less Lydia knows, the better." That was self-serving, and Brook's scowl said he saw it as such too.

Oh, very well. Sentimental farce it shall be. "Tell her, if you can do so discreetly, that I love her, that she was the best big sister a lad ever had, and that I'm sorry."

"She will want to know for what, sir."

"Then don't tell her that part. I am fresh out of cleverness for the day, Brook. Be off with you, and if you have anything to report, you can leave word at the Goose."

"The Goose, sir? That's little more than a..."

"Common nuisance with a taproom, I know. Nobody will think to look for me there, and everybody who patronizes the place is busy trying to not be seen. They won't notice if I do my best Captain Powell imitation and slouch over a pint in a dim corner for an evening." The Goose rented rooms by the hour to the game girls and their clients, did not believe in wasting money on too many candles, and managed to serve a palatable, if humble, ale.

Then too, the game girls needed somebody to write letters for them—pathetic fictions about posts in grand houses—and Marcus undercharged them for his work.

"Try to stay out of trouble," Brook said, tapping his hat onto his head, "and consider simply explaining your situation to Powell. The war is over, and every soldier has regrets."

"Powell doesn't."

"Why do you think he's still in London when he longs for Wales? Why do you think he's looking for me, when ninety-nine other sheep are safely drowsing in the fold? He has regrets. Depend upon it."

Brook left, and Marcus sat for a long time staring at a cold grate and a grimy window. He could confess to Powell all day long about the many ways he'd bungled being an officer, and Powell might, for the sake of Marcus's family, turn a blind eye.

But a bungled command was not the worst of Marcus's sins, and even the upright and much-respected Powell could not forgive him all of his trespasses.

Nobody could. The time had come to contact Wesley, explain the situation to him, and wish him the best of luck at keeping Uncle Reggie from bankrupting the earldom. Marcus took up a precious piece of foolscap and sharpened his best quill pen.

"Madame, you know you are among my most-valued customers."

Xavier Fournier could say that honestly. Sybil Fontaine was a successful courtesan, and when she bought wine, she did so in quantity. She demanded fair value for her coin, which Xavier aspired to provide all to of his customers.

She also, however, expected a miracle from him and was subtly offering her favors as an inducement, as if that would hasten shipping between Bordeaux and London.

"I am among your most devoted customers," Sybil replied. "I praise your wine to all and sundry. Not too effusively, not too timidly, because the English regard passion in any form as suspect."

"The English profess to suspect passion while indulging in excess as frequently as possible." Some English. In Fournier's experience, Englishmen were not so different from their French cousins. Some good, some bad, mostly in between, as he was.

"Have you taken to vice, Xavier, that you are now an expert on

English overindulgence?" Sybil drew her finger along the back of his hand, letting her nail lightly scrape his skin.

That was supposed to be an erotic caress. Xavier wanted to push her hand aside, as he would a cat purposely flicking its tail in his face.

"I am no expert on anything, and I cannot produce case after case of claret by the end of the week merely because a beautiful and beguiling lady asks it of me."

Sybil's hand disappeared. "If I am so beguiling, why won't you fill my order, Xavier? An earl's heir has certain expectations of his *chère amie*, and Wesley Glover will be in London by Monday."

Fournier rose and came around his desk to take the seat beside his guest. He'd received Sybil in his home rather than at his wineshop, and he'd not shown her to a parlor. To treat her as a guest would have made the identity of his caller known to any passerby gawking in the window.

The last thing Sybil would want, if this Wesley Glover fellow was on the verge of becoming her protector, was for rumor to imply that she'd been dispensing favors in Fournier's direction. The issue here in the midst of good English Society would not be that she was plying her trade, not even that she'd done so with a fellow French national, but that she had done so *indiscreetly*.

"Tell me of this Mr. Glover," Fournier said. "Perhaps something other than claret will appeal to his discerning tastes."

Sybil sat up straighter, like a schoolgirl called upon to recite, though no schoolgirl had ever sported such curves or worn fashions that showed them off to such elegant advantage.

"He truly is an earl's heir, or very nearly. His cousin was the last earl, but that fellow did not come home from the war. Such a pity, you know? Wesley's papa has stepped in, but the papa is older, and not"—her dark brows knit prettily—"not *adepte du maniement de l'argent*. Wesley will aid his papa to manage the money. He comes to London on business, in fact, and wrote to me that he looks very much forward to enjoying my company. He specifically instructed me to see to my wine cellar, and he's quite fond of his claret."

"Is he fond of you?"

She touched Fournier's arm. "They are all fond of me, Xavier."

A howling misstatement, but Sybil's definition of fond was likely a professional one. "What I mean is, if you told him that claret is a fine drink for the unimaginative, but sophistication and elegance call for adventuring beyond the dependable reds into the more complicated and alluring whites, or even a charming rosé, would Monsieur Glover heed your guidance?"

"Englishmen must have their steak, and that means clarets."

"Champagne goes surprisingly well with steak, and you will find it easier to procure in quantity on short notice. Champagne has become a drink for celebrations, and those occasions do not always arrive predictably."

Sybil wrinkled a delicate nose. "I like champagne."

"As it happens, I have a quantity on hand. A Mayfair customer with a preference for champagne punches could not hold her annual spring event due to an unexpected death in the family. I graciously accepted the return of my wine and offered my most sincere condolences."

True, but not the whole story. Fournier's vineyard had only recently adopted Madame Clicquot's technique for producing a clearer, lighter wine, and his product was not competitive with the best champagnes on the London market—Orion Goddard's, for example.

Fournier's clarets were in demand everywhere, while his champagne was... not. Not yet, but a loquacious courtesan could do much to address that little problem.

"I will be charming," Sybil said, as if charm were a dress that could be put on or taken off depending on the occasion. "Wesley has missed me, and his responsibilities at the Tremont estate have not allowed him to spend much time in London. I will tell him champagne has become the drink of Society's darlings."

Very likely, the Glover fellow hadn't been able to *afford* to spend much time with Sybil. "How well do you know this Englishman, madame?"

"I do not kiss and tell, Fournier. If a man snores or has nightmares, that is private."

"Allow me to be a little indelicate, for I am a Frenchman protective of a lady who finds herself far from home. Which particular earldom will your dashing cavalier inherit? Some of these aristos are rolled up and living on credit. This man is asking you to spend *your* coin for his enjoyment. That is not how the game is played, and a gentleman in line for an earldom should know that."

Sybil regarded him owlishly. "We must be practical, those of us far from home. You are correct about that, and I will make some inquiries, as the English say. Wesley's title will be Earl of Tremont, a good Norman name for a title, don't you think?" She offered a painfully bright smile.

"A fine name, and I hope he is a fine man, and smart enough to know how lucky he is to have gained your notice."

Her smile became bashful. "He could not afford me, not regularly, but his fortunes have improved, and immediately, he writes to me. He hopes I will smile upon him, too, but I will make him earn his privileges."

"As well he should." Fournier dickered a little longer for form's sake and tossed in two cases of a serviceable merlot to soothe Madame Fontaine's pride. In the end, he had unloaded a quantity of less than impressive champagne for a reasonable price, but the whole conversation troubled him.

With the peace after Waterloo had come a frightening degree of civil unrest in London. After twenty years of sending their sons off to fight and die, English shopkeepers and farmers were out of patience with their profligate monarchy. The middling sorts could not control their country's politics or rid it of parasitic peers—yet—but they had taken to asserting their power over its morality with a vengeance.

Englishmen able and willing to openly support a mistress in grand style were growing fewer and fewer, and Sybil's opportunity to earn a lifetime of security was waning. One wealthy earl could change her fortunes considerably.

And one rotten bounder could ruin them.

Fournier would make what inquiries he could and send along what he learned for Sybil to do with what she pleased. Not, of course, that he moved in the same circles as an earl's heir, but he knew people who did, and those people—Englishmen, all—would be honest with him.

"How was your call upon the lawyers?" The captain posed that question to Lydia while setting out the black army on the chessboard.

She busied herself with the white pieces, but doubted she'd acquit herself well. "The senior partner informed me that my mother's funds are doing splendidly." Mr. Sigafoose the Elder had reassured Lydia that her own portion also remained secure in the cent-per-cents. No need to worry on either account.

Not a' tall! Everything quite in order!

"His reassurances were not to your liking?"

Lydia put her king on a white square, then realized her error. The king always opened opposite his own color so that beside him, the queen would start on her own color.

"My paternal uncle, who is not a client of the firm, has also made recent inquiries. The solicitor offered my uncle the same reassurances he offered me." Though Uncle Reggie had certainly not sent along a letter of introduction from Mama, such as Lydia had to present to the solicitors at every appointment. That letter empowered Lydia to speak on Mama's behalf, and the solicitors—conscientious about demanding to see it—never seemed pleased when Lydia produced it.

Perhaps Reggie *had* forwarded such a letter, but it would have been a forgery.

"Meaning," Captain Powell said, "the solicitor gave your uncle specific totals to the penny, while affording you what amounts to a pat on the head."

Lydia sat back, having put only her king and queen on the board. "They are an old and respected firm. I conclude that is a euphemism for a collection of doddering nincompoops. I am most unhappy that they broached the topic of Mama's finances with her brother-in-law *at all*, and they spoke to me as if I should be grateful to have a meddling uncle nosing about matters that are none of his business."

The captain rose, went to the sideboard, and poured a scant inch of libation into each of two glasses. "Does your mother have brothers or uncles on her side of the family who could deal with the attorneys on her behalf?" He passed Lydia a drink, which turned out to be brandy.

Very good brandy. "She does not. Mama was an heiress, and the firm handling her money is her family's firm. Uncle has nothing to do with them, and Mama gets regular reports. Uncle's prying served no purpose."

The brandy was a comforting blend of subtle aromas and smooth fire. A lady did not take strong spirits—in theory. In reality, she nipped from a flask in the hunt field, swilled patent remedies that made strong spirits look like nursery punch by comparison, and downed toddies to ward off the chill year-round.

She also, if she was Lydia, drank brandy because Dylan Powell offered it to her at the end of a trying day.

"So your mother gets regular written accountings from the solicitors by post, but you felt you had to confirm those reports?"

"Yes."

The captain held out his hand to Lydia. "You are not in the mood for mock battles with toy soldiers. Come sit by the fire and tell me of your difficulties. I got precisely nowhere in the stews today, but I did confirm my theory that the men are purposely lying to me."

"You spent all afternoon confirming a theory?"

"Theories can be wrong. When the French retreated over the mountains, they were desperate to know through which passes we would follow them. We'd bribe informants to convey supposedly false information to the French, the French would out-bribe us and get what they thought was the truth, but we of course had *mostly* lied to our informants, and so forth. Appearances can be deceiving."

Housekeepers could be deceiving, and yet, there never seemed to be a good time for Lydia to unburden herself to the captain. She was either too angry, too muddled, or too impassioned.

She had to try anyway. "I asked Mama's solicitors if they'd heard any rumors regarding that other matter—the missing earl—how his estate is getting on in his absence, any legal gossip concerning the handling of the property or its revenue. They gave me what amounted to another pat on the head."

And had all but shoved her out the door immediately thereafter. Sigafoose had been similarly unforthcoming about how one declared a peer dead and whether the lawyers employed by the Tremont estate were being paid regularly for their services.

That combination of rudeness and reticence spoke volumes. Uncle was proceeding with his rotten plans, and Lydia could do nothing to stop him—unless she could find Marcus. Her own efforts thus far had been unavailing, earning her nothing but orders to retreat and a bouquet of silly flowers.

The captain led Lydia to a comfortable sofa situated before the library's fire. More than once, she'd found Dylan dozing on this sofa, sprawled full length with his sister Marged's sketchbook clutched to his chest. Boots off, coat off, he'd been the picture of a gentleman in casual repose.

Lydia had always left him in peace. The last sentiment Dylan Powell would admit to was homesickness, but studying those sketches left him looking wistful and lonely, even in sleep.

"If you had all the troops," he said, coming down beside her, "all the horse and cannon in the world at your command, any resource you needed, how would you foil your uncle's meddling?"

Lydia did not need all the infantry, cavalry, and artillery in the world, she needed only her brother. Holding Dylan's hand wasn't exactly a need, but to do so comforted nonetheless.

"I cannot best him, only the missing earl can. I have to hope that Lord Tremont lives and that he's in London."

Marcus had erred badly when he'd sent those flowers. First, he'd expected Lydia to meekly slink away on the say-so of a younger brother. Second, the fact of Marcus's survival had become an unassailable truth. Lydia had sent word to that effect to Mama through Aunt Chloe, using a prearranged reference to having found the perfect bonnet.

Marcus wasn't much given to deviousness—or he hadn't been—while Lydia was becoming adept at it.

She was tempted to plead fatigue and put an end to the evening. Instead, she remained on the sofa, casting around for the next particle of truth she could offer Dylan. The drapes had been closed for the night, the door was shut to keep in the fire's heat, and the library had become a cozy haven at the end of the day.

"The flowers were from him?" Dylan asked, looping an arm around her shoulders, "from Tremont?"

Lydia nodded, both dismayed and relieved that Dylan could reach that conclusion, but then, a reconnaissance officer excelled at observation and deduction.

"How did you know?"

"I guessed because, as you said, the men who've come to the back door regularly enough to feel inspired to such a gesture can't afford flowers. You were not pleased to receive them, and you destroyed the note rather than keep it as a memento of a thoughtful gesture."

What else had Dylan surmised on the basis of passing observations? "Tremont told me he was safe and ordered me to go home."

"Which leads you to conclude he is not safe, and you must search all the harder."

Lydia allowed herself the comfort of Dylan's embrace, drawing up her knees and curling against him. She was exhausted, physically and emotionally. Tired of trying to solve the family's problems, tired of polishing silver, tired most of all of lying.

"I tell myself," she said, "that his lordship can have no concept of the hardship his absence has created for others, no notion that his own family might betray him. He left an uncle in charge of Tremont, and that uncle like a second father to him, the uncle's son was Tremont's best friend."

"You don't trust Tremont's cousin?"

Lydia had to think about the question because keeping straight what she'd admitted and what she'd withheld was becoming difficult. Her eyes were growing heavy, and she was increasingly aware that she faced a choice—a hard choice—where Dylan and Marcus were concerned.

"Tremont's cousin is in a delicate position. On the one hand, he is his father's only offspring and mindful of his filial duty. On the other hand, he's Tremont's friend, and—I think—a good friend, more like a brother. Choosing between loyalties like that is nearly impossible."

"My commanding officer delighted in forcing me to choose between following orders and putting my men at needless risk of harm. I tried to be both dutiful toward Dunacre and decent to the men, but the object of the game—it was a game to Dunacre—was to break me. To break my honor as an officer and a gentleman."

What had the cost to Dylan been of enduring such games? "I am worn out," Lydia said, "not quite broken. My mother and others are depending upon me, but if I turn my back on them and do as I please, they have no one else."

If she married Dylan, assuming he would have Lady Lydia Glover in the place of his Mrs. Lovelace, Reggie would prevail, and the Tremont estate would be ruined.

"I eventually gave up," Dylan said. "I reasoned that I would let Dunacre win, and then he would leave me alone. I was wrong. He saw me stripped of rank when I disobeyed an order to scout terrain we knew was securely held by the French. Even that wasn't enough for Dunacre. The games, the tests of honor and loyalty, went on and on. I hated him and those who toadied to him more ferociously than I ever hated a lot of French farm boys conscripted into the Corsican's army."

Those who had toadied to Dunacre included Marcus, of course. Especially Marcus.

Lydia wanted to weep, but tears never solved a problem. She instead sat up. "I have a few things to tell you, things you won't like."

"This again. You don't want to marry me?"

"I do want to marry you." That much she could say honestly. Breathtaking passion aside, Dylan was kind, tenacious, devoted to family, self-sacrificing, and so endlessly, relentlessly decent. If Lydia's life had been a desert of truly honorable men and filled instead with an endless expanse of knaves, charlatans, and self-serving twits, Dylan was a lush oasis of integrity.

She longed to dwell with him for all her days *and all of her nights.*

"You want to marry me?" He spoke softly, his tone clearly antici-pating all the *buts* and *notwithstandings* and *nevertheless* that turned hope to despair.

"I want to marry you, and dwell with you in Wales, and make a home and a family with you. I have not known you long, but I know you well, and I adore the man you are."

He hugged her. "Hush. Cease prattling before I have to kiss you."

Dylan did kiss her, or Lydia kissed him, though it was a kiss of contradictions. She could feel the joy in him, the relief and wonder, because she had expressed a desire to accept his proposal. True, he could be taciturn, and he had his rules and routines, but what did that matter next to his lovely and caring soul?

No woman who had shared intimacies with Dylan Powell would reject his proposal.

Lydia had not, however, accepted his offer of marriage. She could not, and thus for her, the kiss was one of yearning and heartache. She indulged as long as her conscience could bear the strain, then eased back.

"Tell me," Dylan said, still hugging her. "Tell me the awful weight on your heart, and I will kick it into the Channel, and then we will be married."

Lydia's heart made a slow, painful drumbeat as she extricated herself from his embrace and rose. She paced over to the chess table, where her king and queen still stood alone on their respective squares.

"That missing earl," she said, putting the royal couple back into their box, "Lord Tremont, the distant maternal relation who sent me flowers—"

A commotion sounded outside the door, followed by loud knocking.

"We know you're in there, Dylan. We're coming in on the count of five. Put away your naughty prints and prepare to defend yourself."

The door opened immediately—no count of five—and three young ladies swept into the library, all three wreathed with smiles and making straight for Dylan, who'd bolted to attention beside the couch.

To hear Marged threatening on the other side of the door had inspired an exquisite confusion of joy and frustration for Dylan. His sisters barreled into the library on a cloud of floral scents and softly rustling muslin, moving toward him like a summer downpour of fragrance and smiles.

He'd been on his feet more swiftly than if Wellington himself had appeared for parade inspection. Marged led the charge, squeezing him soundly about the middle. Tegan followed up with a stout hug, and Bronwen—dear, no-longer-little Bronnie—looped her arms about him and sighed as if she'd walked every step from Cardiff in her bare feet.

"You have been exceedingly naughty, Dylan," Tegan said.

"Expect to make amends at length. We have new cousins-by-marriage to meet, and we are years behind in our fashions."

Tegan, oldest and tallest, was the sororal general. Marged, the most outspoken sibling, was her aide-de-camp, while Bronnie was simply herself. Quiet, diminutive, astonishingly well-read, and sweet, but like Dylan, also possessed of a rare and formidable temper.

The sisters were stair-stepped in height. In terms of coloring, Tegan was possessed of Titian locks, while Marged was a lovely chestnut, and Bronnie had inherited Papa's fiery copper hair.

"Ladies, you look well." Dylan wanted to hug them all at once, forever, and to shoo them out the door so he could finish his conversation with Lydia. "My prayers are answered by your safe arrival, though, Marged, we must work on your counting skills. May I introduce you to my housekeeper, Mrs. Lydia Lovelace..." He marched through the introductions, and the ladies dutifully bobbed serial curtseys, but Lydia had retreated beneath her figurative cap.

She was polite, she was dignified, she was deferential, and then she was gone, intent on alerting the kitchen to the need for a substantial tray. The temptation to yell, *Don't leave me*, warred with Dylan's admiration for how swiftly she'd made an orderly retreat.

He spent the next hour being regaled with stories from back home about every neighbor and stray dog in the shire—Mr. Jenkins's daughter had immigrated to Canada to take a post as a schoolteacher. Old Maudie Perkins had celebrated her ninetieth birthday by dancing all the young bachelors under the table, and that handsome Rhys Campbell was off to Scotland to be a gamekeeper, of all things.

To hear those names, to hear Welsh swirling around in all directions, was both painful and sweet. Dylan had missed much, and yet, to know that home was still home, that life was going on, was also reassuring. The whole war had been fought not to re-open European ports to English trade, but to safeguard the British way of life from destruction at foreign hands.

Or so the recruiting sergeants had claimed.

The sisters demolished the tray carried in by the kitchen maid, and in due course, they demanded that Dylan light them up to their rooms. Lydia had explained the arrangements to him, though where was Lydia, and why hadn't she brought up the tray herself, or at least accompanied Betty on some pretext?

Lydia was Dylan's intended, but he would not announce that happy development to his sisters without her permission.

Which he would obtain, without delay, just as soon as he'd lit the candles in Bronnie's bedroom.

"Dylan?" Bronwen had not raised her voice, but a note of impatience had Dylan pausing before seeking out his housekeeper. "You know we have missed you?"

"I have missed you too." In the flickering candlelight, Bronwen looked too solemn for a young lady about to storm London's modistes.

"Then why didn't you come home? Not even for a visit. Marged and Tegan said we must not confront you regarding your choices, that war takes a toll, but being without our brother has taken a toll as well."

This was not Bronnie in a temper. This was something Dylan had not encountered from her previously. Some sort of scold crossed with an interrogation and underscored with a lament.

"My men needed me, our cousins needed me. You ladies are spectacularly well suited to managing the property in my absence, and I expect I will be returning home shortly." With a bride, he hoped.

Bronwen gave him a skeptical perusal. "I will believe you mean to come home when you are seated at the head of the table, and Tegan and Margs are arguing about whether there's too much pepper in the soup. Off to bed with you. Our sisters will run you ragged if you allow it, and you will need your rest."

Dylan bowed his good-night, both amused and slightly uneasy that his baby sister had just dismissed him as if he'd brought disappointing news back from a reconnaissance mission.

Little girls grew up. Dylan's papa had often said as much, and not with any glee.

Nor did Dylan feel much glee as he made his way through the darkened house to Lydia's quarters. The remains of the tray sat on the kitchen table, apparently to be dealt with in the morning, and the kittens were curled in their basket, little bellies doubtless full for the night.

Feeble candlelight shone from beneath Lydia's bedroom door. Dylan knocked softly, thanking heavens for small mercies. Maybe she hadn't waited up for him, though she wasn't avoiding him either.

"Come in." Lydia sat on a vanity stool, her dark hair unbound and cascading down to her waist. "You should not be here, Captain."

That barely qualified as a rebuke, given the lectures and perorations she was capable of.

Dylan came into the bedroom, scene of his dearest memories, and closed the door. "May I serve as your lady's maid?" He held out his hand for the brush, and Lydia surrendered it. "Your first impression of my sisters is correct. They don't quite play fair—no counting to five —but they don't quite cheat either, and everything they do, they undertake with a fixity of purpose that steals one's breath."

"Rather like you."

Dylan drew the brush through abundant tresses, the movements soothing him, as he hoped they soothed Lydia.

"And like you, usually, but you quit the field in quick time, Lydia. You will like my sisters, once you get to know them."

"I already like them. They clearly love you and would take exception to any slight to you."

"Siblings," Dylan said. "I've often wondered if having brothers would be different, but I suspect not. I have Goddard and MacKay, and they are as dear and vexatious as any brothers could be. Shall I braid your hair?"

"Please, one braid will do." Lydia met his gaze in the mirror, and Dylan was put in mind of Bronwen's seriousness. "This is not prudent, Captain. Not while your sisters are visiting and probably not—"

"Stop," Dylan said, making quick work of fashioning a thick

plait. "You are not beating retreat now, Lydia. You've said you want to marry me, and I want to marry you, and we will not take back those words just because the sororal mob has descended for a few weeks."

Lydia passed him a length of plain white cotton, which he secured around the end of her braid. "We never finished our discussion."

How he treasured the sight of her in her nightclothes, her hair in a simple plait, her gaze luminous by candlelight. A husband saw his wife thus, and she saw him in similar dishabille. The notion of ending every day with Lydia for the rest of his life overwhelmed him with gratitude.

He bent near and wrapped his arms around her shoulders. "There is nothing we have to say to each other, nothing you could tell me, that would make me one iota less desperate to share that bed with you tonight."

He had not come here intending to importune her, but something about her remoteness, about the haste with which she'd withdrawn, made him reckless.

"Your sisters..."

"Will sleep soundly tonight, two floors away. Tegan is a restless sort, though, and I will not presume on your privacy again while my sisters are underfoot." They noticed things, those three. Dylan could have been parted from them for twenty-five years, and his sisters would still notice details about him others never would.

"Now or never?" Lydia murmured, rising and slipping her arms around Dylan's waist. "Do or die?"

"Now, or I am at risk for pitching my sisters back into the traveling coach, and they will take that very much amiss." Dylan was unable to read Lydia's mood, but then, his own mood also refused to admit of a neat label. He was eager to become Lydia's lover in the fullest sense of the word, also worried that the arrival of his sisters would ruin his chances, which made no sense.

Lydia cuddled closer, her hold on him gratifyingly snug.

"Shall I leave you in peace, Lydia?" Dylan stroked her hair, willing to decamp if she asked it of him. "The decision is yours."

Lydia was utterly passive in his arms, though he could feel her thinking.

"I choose you," she said, stepping back. "I choose you, and tonight, and now. We will talk later, Dylan, and it will be a difficult discussion, but I choose you."

That was not quite what an adoring swain wanted to hear as he contemplated an irrevocable step with a woman he cherished.

"Tell me again you have no husband."

"No husband, no jilted fiancé, no legal reason on earth why I cannot share these intimacies with you." She kissed him, a sweet little introduction that only hinted at the fire and passion she was capable of, but it was enough. "And I have many reasons to seize the moment and the man when the opportunity comes knocking at my door."

Dylan scooped her into his arms, laid her on the bed, and in the next instant started unbuttoning his jacket.

CHAPTER THIRTEEN

Maybe the fact that Lydia was *sister* to Marcus, Earl of Tremont, would not matter to Dylan. He had all but promised it would not signify *one iota*.

Dylan had siblings and cousins. He well knew one family member could not answer for the actions of another. He knew Tremont was related to her somehow. He had promised Lydia a sympathetic hearing—not merely a fair hearing—and she simply did not have the fortitude to embark on a discussion of hard truths at this late hour.

A discussion of *more* hard truths. Recounting the visit to the solicitors' office and admitting that Marcus had sent the flowers had been difficult enough.

And yet, Dylan had guessed most of Lydia's situation and calmly listened to what she had to say. He was just as calmly pulling his shirt over his head and folding it neatly atop his jacket on the vanity stool.

To think of enjoying this display every night for the rest of her life... Lydia wiggled out of her dressing gown and scrambled beneath the covers.

When Dylan emerged from behind the privacy screen, he wore only his breeches. "I borrowed your toothpowder."

"And you lost your boots and stockings, sir."

He peered at his bare feet. "Apparently so. My breeches go next, so if you're having reservations or doubts, speak now."

He stood beside the bed, his manly charms quite on display, and the wretch likely knew the impact his naked chest and shoulders had on Lydia's composure.

"The candles, please."

"Your wish, my lady."

He could not know that Lydia had been addressed by that honorific since birth and that his use of it tainted the pleasure of watching him amble around the bedchamber. He blew out all but the candle on the vanity and brought that one to the bedside table.

"I'd like to leave this one burning," he said. "The decision is yours."

"I am torn between the modesty afforded by darkness and the pleasure I will take in seeing you drop those breeches."

Dylan unbuttoned his falls and peeled out of his breeches and underlinen, adding them to the pile on the vanity stool.

"Does this make the decision any easier?" He was gorgeously naked, half aroused, and not at all self-conscious about either circumstance.

Lydia had assured him—and herself—that they would sort out her true situation come morning, and she was certain Dylan would grasp why she'd done as she had. He would be unhappy about her close connection to Marcus, but not unduly so.

And yet, the corner of her mind that had been disappointed over and over, by Marcus, by Mama's inability to confront Reggie's mismanagement of Tremont, by Reggie, Wesley, and people in general, warned that even Dylan might prove less than steadfast.

"Leave the candle lit for now," Lydia said. "I will feast my eyes on the bounty of your masculine splendor."

Dylan climbed under the covers as casually as if he and Lydia had been cuddling up regularly for years. "Masculine splendor. That sounds like something Sycamore Dorning might say about himself, but coming from you, I like it. Budge up, and get comfy."

Lydia most assuredly did not *get comfy*. She got bothered and aroused and so frustrated with Dylan's slow caresses and sweet kisses that she was ready to bellow at him to *be about it*. Quick time, forced march. Whatever the term was for consummating relations with a lady.

"You are in a hurry," Dylan said, stroking his fingers over her brow, "but I promise you, Lydia, anticipation is part of the pleasure."

He lay on his side, while Lydia was on her back. Somewhere along the way, her nightgown had bunched above her waist, and she was abruptly desperate to be rid of it.

"Get this thing..." She wiggled, Dylan drew back, and then she had the last, offending article of clothing off and stuffed under her pillow. "Now, Dylan. If you value your manly splendidness, you will stop dithering."

"My masculine splendor," he said, easing himself over her on all fours. "From the Latin, *masculinus*, and *splendor*, meaning bright—"

Lydia kissed him, feeling an urge to both laugh and weep. She feared, in the small part of her that was always on the alert for the next disappointment, that this would be her last encounter with Dylan. She also hoped, in the equally small part of herself still prone to such foolishness, that he and she would frequently laugh in the course of lovemaking.

Dylan joined Lydia in the kissing, his tongue a wickedly subtle weapon parting her from her wits. She began to move, seeking him and seeking to part him from his wits too. The first near occurrence of joining was almost by happenstance, stilling them both when Lydia almost gloved him with a random roll of her hips.

"Steady there," Dylan said, his voice a trifle raspy.

Lydia did not know if he was speaking to himself or to her, but that slight, glancing penetration only whetted her appetite for more.

"You be steady," she said. "I cannot bear to hold still."

Dylan grasped her suggestion and remained motionless while Lydia took him into her body on increasingly luxurious undulations of her hips. To share such intimacy with him was a pleasure and a wonder, also a maddening frustration.

"You too," Lydia said, locking her ankles at the small of his back. "Please, Dylan."

He began to move, and Lydia's body became a firmament of starbursts. The pleasure he'd given her before had been magnificent, but this... this defied words. She gave herself over to his loving and to him, until the fading of one pleasure ignited the beginning of the next.

Lydia became a stranger to herself, wanton in the best sense, spontaneous, unrestrained, free of shame and self-doubt. Dylan was hers. He was declaring himself bodily, and Lydia responded with reckless joy.

From time to time, he would go still, holding himself inside her and stroking her hair while Lydia caught her breath. His generosity was as sumptuous as his tenderness, and when he finally withdrew to find his own satisfaction, Lydia had not the strength or the will to stop him.

He saw to the tidying up and blew out the candle—in that order, which should have been mortifying—then climbed into bed and spooned himself around her. She laced her fingers with his, wallowing in the pleasure of skin-to-skin closeness and wishing she had the resolve to remain awake.

"Thank you, Dylan."

"One doesn't thank a man for indulging his every selfish dream to the utmost." He sounded both pleased and self-conscious. *Now*, he was turning up bashful?

"Yes, one does. Masculine splendor is an understatement for the glory you embody."

He nuzzled her ear, which tickled. "Any claim I have to splendor or glory is thanks entirely to the inspiration of present company." He rested his cheek against Lydia's. "I was worried. Worried I'd be too hasty, too headlong. I was desperate to climb into this bed with you."

"I have been just plain desperate." Desperate to keep Mama happy, desperate to keep Reggie from bankrupting Tremont, desperate to find Marcus, desperately weary, and desperately lonely.

"You are," Dylan said, kissing her cheek and easing back to the pillow, "splendid and glorious and mine to love, and I know of no more sincere prayer than the gratitude I feel now for having shared the past hour with you."

Mine to love. Lydia rolled over to face him and wrapped her arms around him. That passionate, courageous declaration moved her to tears, and she fell asleep clinging to Dylan, and to hope.

Dylan awoke awash in benevolence. Beatitude beat in his veins, and good cheer filled every particle of his being. He *felt* splendid because, in Lydia's considered opinion, he *was* splendid. She was beyond splendid. She was fierce and passionate and bold and affectionate and... *his.*

He had torn himself away from her in the middle of the night rather than take advantage of all the wonderful things she was. A lady needed her sleep, and she needed time to compose herself before facing the smitten swain she'd loved witless in the cozy hours of the night.

Lydia would have to face her future sisters-in-law as well, whom Dylan was counting on sleeping late on this most delightful of mornings. He found Lydia in the breakfast parlor, cap in place, a shy smile turning a lovely day transcendent.

And what tender effusion came out of his mouth? What clever greeting did he offer the woman whom he esteemed above all others?

"Good morning, Mrs. Lovelace." He bowed. "May I fix you a plate?" Had she been waiting for him? Looking forward to seeing him with equal parts glee and trepidation, as he'd been looking forward to seeing her?

"Captain, good day. I'll stick with tea for now. I trust you slept well?"

Dylan glanced at the door, dismayed by the hint of misgiving in Lydia's eyes. "I dreamed the most unbelievably lovely dreams... of splendors unimaginable to a mere mortal man. Breathtaking, exhausting, glorious splendors."

Lydia frowned at him. "You sought to allow me my rest by abandoning me?"

Marvelously blunt speaking. "We would still be abed if my selfish nature had anything to say to it." He took the seat beside her rather than sit at the head of the table. "How are you?"

She took a sip of her tea. "Gobsmacked. Again. Double-gobsmacked."

Dylan poured for himself. "Likewise, and happily so." He watched the steam rising from his cup and debated the wisdom of taking Lydia's hand beneath the table. He needed to touch her, he wanted to consume her, and he wanted to sit across from her such that he could simply *behold* her.

"I hope you will not feel unhappily gobsmacked," she went on, "when I tell you that Marcus, Earl of Tremont, is my brother."

Dylan set his tea cup down slowly. "I beg your pardon?"

Lydia brushed a glance over him. "I am Lydia Glover, sister to Marcus, Earl of Tremont. He never came home from France. As far as we know, he was on a transport ship that docked in due course at Deptford, but—"

"Lydia *Glover*?"

"Lovelace is my mother's maiden name. Mama and I got exactly nowhere making polite inquiries regarding Marcus's whereabouts, so I thought approaching the problem from a different angle made sense."

Nothing *made sense.* "If you are Tremont's sister, then you are *Lady* Lydia Glover. Your mother is the Lovelace heiress."

Lieutenant Lord Tremont had once mentioned that about his

mother. Dylan took a sip of his tea, though he tasted nothing. Lydia had lied to him. *Lydia* had lied to him.

He'd sensed she was keeping secrets, but this... Even Dorning and the cousins had warned him of the same possibility. Why tell him now? Why not tell him over a game of chess? When taking a meal on the terrace? Why not tell him *before last night*? If she sought to find *her own brother* why not openly ask for aid?

"Uncle Reggie is bankrupting the estate," Lydia went on. "The same Uncle Reggie making a pest of himself with Mama's solicitors. Our cousin Wesley—Tremont's and mine—can do nothing to stop him. Mama retreats into planning the village fete. The lawyers are circling, starting the process for having Marcus declared dead, when I know he's alive, if perhaps unwell. I had to do something."

"Did you have to lie to me?" Dylan kept his tone civil with effort.

"Yes," Lydia said, quite firmly. "Had I marched up to your doorstep as Lady Lydia Glover, asking for your aid because you are Captain Powell, guardian angel of former soldiers, you would have been polite, reserved, and useless."

"Useless, Lydia?"

Dylan had despised Tremont, thought him the most scurrilous, inept sycophant ever to don a uniform, which was saying a great deal. That Lydia was his sister was troubling, though one sibling did not necessarily cast the die for another. That she would *lie* to Dylan, join his household under false pretenses and a false name, then take him to bed...

"You made it plain that Marcus disgusted you," she said. "Why would you help a woman you don't know to find a man you don't respect?"

She was growing annoyed, which baffled Dylan. "Because I am honorable, for God's sake. You cannot help that your brother is a scoundrel, but that doesn't excuse your behaving like one too."

Dylan's temper, which plagued him rarely but spectacularly, was threatening to take over the discussion. He knew this feeling, this bewilderment and fury, for they'd befallen him frequently when Dunacre had been alive. Dunacre had lied with such regularity and so convincingly, that Dylan had been hard put to know truth from fiction.

"I have tried to be honest with you," Lydia said. "The moment was never right, or I'd get my courage together and then we'd be interrupted—by your cousins, by Bowen, by your sisters' arrival. I did try, Dylan."

Dylan mentally reviewed last night's conversation with Lydia and recalled her admitting that the flowers were from Tremont. Tremont, her supposedly distant maternal relation, who was larking about London somewhere. Why hadn't that disclosure resulted in a thorough interrogation from Dylan rather than...?

But Dylan knew why. Dorning had claiming that reasoning with a fellow in love was pointless, and Dorning had been right. Dylan hadn't wanted to see the clues or notice the patterns. He'd wanted to take Lydia to bed and arise as an engaged man.

"This was the conversation you sought to have with me," Dylan said. "The one that would make me unhappy?" The one she'd repeatedly warned him would make him unhappy.

She nodded. "And my prediction has proven accurate, though you also assured me that whatever I had to tell you, you would pitch my worries into the Channel, and then we'd be married."

"This is not a worry, Lydia. This is a great, ill-timed falsehood."

She closed her eyes and bowed her head, as if weathering bad news. The sight cut through Dylan's ire, and he resented the guilt it brought.

"Then we both spoke untruthfully," she said, "for apparently, now that you do know the truth of my last name, you aren't about to help me find my brother. Horse Guards would not help. My father's former friends would not help. I even tried writing to Wellington, because Marcus's commanding officer fell at Waterloo—you reaffirmed that much for me—but nobody knows where Marcus is, and nobody cares either, except Mama and I."

Lydia sounded so forlorn, so weary, but could Dylan trust

anything she did or said to be honest? "So you sniggled your way into my household, thinking that such a subterfuge would somehow win you my aid?"

"What few people I spoke with who tried to be helpful said you know the former soldiers in London better than anybody. Those men come to you as a last resort, and I hoped that you could be my last resort too. No matter. Marcus is here somewhere. I can hire runners, or inquiry agents, or..."

"They will take your money and pat you on the head, Lydia." And as angry as Dylan was, as bewildered as he was, he didn't want that for her.

"At least they won't accuse me of being a scoundrel simply because I want to find my brother." A spark of anger crackled through that observation. "You have lied, Dylan. You lied when you were a reconnaissance officer the better to gain trust you hadn't earned from the local populace. You lied to your sisters, telling them repeatedly you'd be home soon. You've lied to your cousins, telling them you bide in London for your soldiers, when it's your cousins whom you've worried about the most."

Had she shouted at him, Dylan might have shouted back—and brought all three sisters on the run. Shouting would get them nowhere, and some inconvenient vestige of a conscience whispered to Dylan that Lydia had made a valid, if peripheral, point.

"I am ambushed," Dylan said, "and disappointed and not at my best. I saw indications that your station was not as lowly as you pretended, and I ignored that evidence. I know better than to ignore what's before my own eyes." And yet, he had wanted too badly to rescue Lydia from the drudgery of housekeeper-hood and ride off with her to his castle—a manor house sort of castle—in Wales.

"I will be gone by sunset." Lydia tugged off her cap. "I am sorry, Dylan. I never meant to fall in love with you, and I hoped... I am just so sorry."

"What, precisely, are you sorry for?" Dylan asked, because in a general, uneasy way, regret figured into his feelings, too, which was deuced bewildering.

"I am sorry for lying to you. I am sorry to have disappointed you. I am sorry for much, but I am not sorry for last night."

Whatever did that mean? Dylan felt as if he was again in the midst of a pitched battle, the noise and smoke creating such confusion that even trumpets and drums were hard to hear. Delayed orders were overtaken by new orders, and nothing made sense after the first half hour of fighting.

"Where will you go?"

"The lawyers will find me suitable lodging until I can arrange to leave London."

Dylan did not like the sound of that. "Do you want to leave Town?" A stupid part of him asked a different question: Did she want to leave *him*? What had all that passion been about, because in that much at least, Dylan believed Lydia had been sincere.

"When has what I want mattered to anybody?" Lydia asked wearily.

That question doused the fire beneath Dylan's simmering ire. Horse Guards hadn't taken her seriously, her lawyers brushed her off, her uncle was stealing her brother's birthright, and her mother apparently thought sending an earl's daughter into service was just a fine idea.

And somewhere in London, Tremont was kicking his handsome heels and probably memorizing more Latin inanities.

"You'd leave your post without notice?" Dylan asked. "Just as my sisters have arrived? Hardly cricket, Lydia."

She waved the hand in which she clutched her cap. "Contact the agencies. They are awash in candidates for the post of housekeeper. You, yourself, gave me leave to quit without notice." She sounded defeated, and that more than anything confirmed to Dylan that she was in no condition to march off on her own.

"The Season is getting under way," he retorted. "No candidates will be available who are worth the post, and none will be up to my standards. My sisters expect me to entertain at least my cousins and their ladies. Damned Sycamore Dorning will wedge himself into those gatherings, and his brother is an earl. Standards must be maintained now more than ever, and you cannot desert your responsibilities because we are at odds."

"I can," she said, glowering at her tea. "What do you want, Dylan? I have been dishonest with you, and you are disappointing me. If I stay on here, we will have to deal with each other civilly. I will not be subjected to pouting and sneering from you."

Dylan had no idea what he wanted, but he knew that he did not want Lydia to leave. Not yet, not in anger, not until he'd had time to sort himself out. She had been wrong to lie—and to join him in bed before telling him the truth—but she had apologized, and she'd had what she thought were valid reasons.

"I am..." He cast around for honest words, because some fool was making a great issue out of sticking to the truth. "I am muddled, Lydia. I don't care who your brother is, and I have said as much to my cousins, but I am uncomfortable with the idea that we became lovers under false pretenses."

More than lovers, though not quite engaged. She had refused to allow him that explicit expectation, a fact Dylan recalled with some relief.

"The only fact I withheld from you was my familial association. Everything else was the truth." She rose and curtseyed and made it halfway to the door before Dylan thought to stop her.

"Will you stay—for now?" he asked.

She set her cap back on her head. "For now, and if I leave my post, I will give you notice."

"Fair enough," Dylan said as the patter of feminine feet above warned him that his sisters were about to descend.

Lydia left at a dignified pace, while Dylan fixed himself a plate of food he wasn't hungry for. Then he recalled Lydia's words: *The only fact I withheld from you was my familial association. Everything else was the truth.*

Everything else left a great deal. Dylan was still pondering that conundrum when his sisters joined him and informed him that his day would start with a visit to the British Museum, followed by ices at Gunter's, and a protracted stop at Hatchards bookshop.

Dylan let the sororal chatter swirl around him, passing over the teapot and the butter and jam as he was directed, and still, he turned over in mind what it meant that *everything else* with Lydia had been the truth.

What saved Lydia from utter despair was a small tower of oranges advertised as fresh from Spain. They were big, bright, enticing specimens sitting outside the greengrocer's stall at the market, and Lydia longed to hurl them all against the nearest stone wall.

She had left the breakfast parlor in a welter of miserable emotions. Dylan had not given her a fair hearing, much less a sympathetic response. He had not offered to help her find Marcus. His concern had been over menus for his perishing family dinners.

But then, she had lied to him about a matter of significant weight.

She marched along the rows of stalls, the chatter and bustle of the market humming all around her. Then she'd come upon that tower of oranges, stacked like cannonballs, begging to be hurled in anger.

Standards must be maintained. Nobody ever said why, and the person making that declaration was seldom responsible for the hard labor involved in the maintenance. Staring at the tower of handsome, succulent oranges, Lydia's ire grew, past guilt, past shame, past weariness even.

Certainly past tears, for tears never solved anything.

The oranges were perfect, while Lydia was a failure. She hadn't found Marcus. She would not have a future with Dylan Powell. She might not like the words Dylan had used, but part of what drove her anger was the fact that, from a certain narrow perspective, he'd been right.

She'd been a little bit scoundrelly, taking a job no earl's daughter would hold, taking a false name, and taking Dylan's coin while encouraging his advances.

Maybe more than a little bit scoundrelly, and Lydia resented the admission. Scoundrel or paragon, she was tired of not being enough. Not comfort enough for Mama, not clever enough to salvage Tremont's fortunes, not shrewd enough to find Marcus, and not perishing honest enough for Dylan.

"Shall I buy you an orange?"

Sycamore Dorning stood at Lydia's elbow, eyeing the tower of fruit. "Ann Goddard says the best produce is always gone by nine of the clock. I finished my hack and bethought myself to have a snack on the way home. How are you, Mrs. Lovelace?"

I'm not Mrs. Lovelace. "Mr. Dorning, good day. If you'll excuse me, I have shopping to do." The next week's menus were rattling around in Lydia's head somewhere, though for all she cared, Dylan could serve his sisters raw potatoes and boiled turnips.

"Help me pick out an orange," Mr. Dorning said, pulling off his riding gloves. "Ann says she sniffs them, but I will not be caught in public sniffing fruit."

He was exceedingly presuming, and yet, as Dylan had said, he was brother to an earl. Rank had its privileges, and Mr. Dorning was also married to Dylan's cousin.

"You expect me to sniff the fruit for you?"

"No, I expect you to tell me why a woman who has earned the lasting esteem of her employer is looking like the wrath of Mayfair on such a fine spring morning. My wife and I are very much in each other's confidence, and Powell is family to her, ergo, any upset in his household merits my notice."

Lydia had the sense everything merited Mr. Dorning's notice, everything except a lady's need to be left in peace. Though that wasn't quite fair. If she told Mr. Dorning to take himself off, he would.

"I want to smash the oranges," Lydia said, apparently having lost all self-restraint thanks to one short and disappointing discussion with Dylan.

Mr. Dorning bought three oranges and handed one to Lydia. "That wall should do nicely. The birds will thank us. Shall we count to three?" He'd put a second orange in his pocket and was tossing the third like a cricket ball.

"Don't be ridiculous."

"I am never ridiculous," Mr. Dorning said. "I am dramatic, but sometimes a little drama is necessary to make a point. Let's sit, shall we?"

How was this happening? Lydia had come to the market first as an excuse to leave the house and walk off the dismals or the furies— whatever she was feeling. Second, she honestly needed to stock her larders now that the Powell ladies were on hand. Third...

Third, she'd wanted solitude, in as much as London's crowds and bustle afforded that precious commodity. Instead, here she was, sitting on a bench in the morning sun, her market basket at her feet and Sycamore Dorning beside her.

"Powell is not an utter lackwit," Mr. Dorning observed. "And yet, he has apparently bungled with you. Tell me all, and I will put it to rights if I can."

"You will meddle? The captain does not care for meddlers, Mr. Dorning."

"The captain *is* a meddler of the first water. He is the field marshal of meddlers, the grand duke of meddlers... Care for a bite?" Mr. Dorning held out a section of orange.

In her present mood, Lydia understood why dogs nipped at presuming humans. "No, thank you. The captain does not meddle."

"He sees a former soldier down on his luck, and the captain meddles until that fellow has decent lodging, some sort of employment, and a few mates keeping an eye on him. He sees a soldier's widow begging, and the next thing you know, that woman is employed as a scullery maid in my own establishment. Two of my club's footmen, the largest two, are former soldiers. They are scary fellows, but when Powell wanders around to check on them, they are new recruits eager to pass inspection."

"The captain cares about his men."

Mr. Dorning offered her another section of orange. "It's quite good, and you, Lady Lydia, have the look of a woman who skipped her breakfast."

She'd been too nervous to eat. Too damned hopeful. Lydia took the orange section and then realized that Mr. Dorning had addressed her by her honorific.

"You recognize me."

"And you recognized me. I have not called at Powell's household, and yet, you know exactly who I am. MacKay pointed you out to me as we rode past the market earlier in the week. Dare I hope that a waltz shared a few years ago left an indelible impression?"

He munched his orange, not a care in the world, while Lydia wanted to smash the fruit on his handsome head.

"We never waltzed. A quadrille perhaps. They go on forever."

"We were introduced, my lady, back in my eligible days, and we danced. I recall you because you did not chatter, did not flirt, and did not cling to my arm when I led you back to your auntie. I was intrigued by your indifference, fickle creature that I am, and by the fact that we are both the offspring and siblings of earls. Now you are housekeeper to the royal meddler, and I am intrigued again."

This was not good, but given how the day had started, Mr. Dorning's excellent memory ought not to have been a surprise.

"The captain has been apprised of my family connections. I doubt I will remain in his employ much longer." A few weeks at most, long enough for Dylan to hire a replacement. Standards could go to blazes.

"You note that Powell cares about his men," Mr. Dorning said, sitting back and crossing his booted feet. "He cares about his cousins, about his sisters... He's a paragon, but I suspect our paragon has not gone on as he ought with you. Last I heard, he was all but courting you, and now you are glaring daggers at oranges."

The orange was good. Dorning had been right about that. "We are not courting."

"Shall I offer the captain a lesson in manners?"

The offer was both pointless and touching. "He'd beat you silly, Mr. Dorning."

"No, he would not. True, he bested the French, but I learned to hold my own against six older brothers and two sisters. The French were so many pesky midges by comparison, I promise you. Let me help, my lady. You need reinforcements, and I am apparently the only option to hand. Powell does not particularly care for me, but that's of no matter when one is family. My wife would like to see him happy."

"My brother is a complete gudgeon." Lydia should feel disloyal for saying that, except it was the truth. "Lord Tremont is biding somewhere in London when we need him back in Shropshire."

A subtle shift came over Mr. Dorning. His posture did not change—he was still idling at his leisure on the bench—but he was more alert.

"My older sister went into service," Mr. Dorning said. "She declared that if she was to drudge for a pack of louts—meaning her devoted brothers—she would at least be paid for it."

"Lady Jacaranda..." Lydia said, mentally reviewing Debrett's. "She married Worth Kettering." Lord Trysting, now.

"She married *her employer*," Sycamore said. "I was too young at the time to do more than miss my sister and fret because she was angry with me, but I am well placed to aid you now. If you need somewhere to stay, funds to leave London, or a certain captain brought up to scratch, I am your man."

Lydia wanted to hold on to her anger, wanted to stomp and storm all the way back to Shropshire and stomp and storm yet more when she arrived home. Sycamore Dorning's offer—his meddling—was deflating at least some of her ire.

"I appreciate the offer, Mr. Dorning, but I need neither coin nor lodging. The captain and I have reached a truce of sorts."

"A ceasefire to deal with the wounded is not a truce, my lady. Think about what I said. Use the ceasefire to gather reinforcements and call upon me in that capacity if you need to. Loutish brother or dunderheaded captain, I will happily trounce either one."

"No trouncing," Lydia said. "I cannot find my brother, and if you lay a hand on the captain, I will tattle to your lady wife and the captain's male cousins as well."

Dorning finished his orange and tossed the peels to the pigeons ever present in a London marketplace.

"If you don't want me to trounce the captain, and you don't want me to intervene on your behalf, perhaps more than reinforcements, you need to patch up whatever has gone amiss with your favorite paragon?"

Mr. Dorning rose, bowed, and strode off, while the pigeons swarmed the discarded orange peels. Lydia sat on the bench for a good twenty minutes, pondering Mr. Dorning's suggestion—that she needed to patch matters up with the captain.

Simply not possible, and if ever there was an excuse for tears, that might be it. Lydia instead tended to her shopping and arranged for most of the produce to be delivered to the captain's house before noon.

CHAPTER FOURTEEN

"I came as soon as I could." Wesley whipped off a stylish high-crowned beaver and ran his hand through artfully curled hair. "Clever of you, to send word through Sybil."

Marcus had not been clever. He'd followed orders. Before Marcus had taken ship for Spain, Wesley had told him that if ever Marcus needed to reach his cousin discreetly, he was to have Miss Sybil Fontaine of Ambleware Court post what appeared to be a tailor's bill to Wesley at Tremont.

When Marcus had been sweating and marching himself to death in Spain, that scheme had seemed like some schoolboy subterfuge, but then the war had ended, and life as Marcus had longed to live it had ended as well.

"Your Sybil is sweet," Marcus said. "The Goose serves surprisingly good ale, if you've a mind to partake."

Wesley looked about the inn's dingy common, his expression more curious than repulsed. "Pretty tavern maids always bode well for the quality of the ale, regardless of how humble the institution might appear." He led Marcus to a table in the corner, and they both took seats facing the common.

Marcus remained silent as one of those pretty maids served the drinks. When Wesley had done the requisite flirting and ogling, Mary Ellen—sixteen, illiterate, and as shrewd as any barrister—flounced away.

"My Sybil," Wesley said, "is very expensive, but also well worth the coin. You do not look to be prospering, old man."

Wesley had dressed in the first stare of gentlemanly morning attire, a rare miscalculation for him. Even Marcus knew to dress for the occasion, whatever that occasion might be.

"In these surrounds," Marcus said, "the prosperous are soon relieved of their trappings. You will be left in peace because you are with me, but a handsome tip to Mary Ellen would not go amiss."

Wesley took a sip of his ale. "These are your regular associates now? I did try to find you, you know. Had a few inquiries made of some of your former subordinates, as best I discreetly could. Spent some coin on trying to track you down, all for naught. One worried."

Had *one* inadvertently caused the beating of the wrong Private Brook in the course of those discreet inquiries? Marcus declined to kick that hornet's nest.

"I try not to associate too closely with anyone, but I am allowed to ply my trade as reader and amanuensis here at the Goose. Unfortunately, given the regular clientele, that means some of my former subordinates have indeed recognized me." Those former soldiers also thought they knew why Marcus lurked in the stews, but they did not know the whole of it.

Wesley did not know the whole of it either, but he knew enough.

"Will they keep mum, old chap?"

"I cannot afford to trust to their discretion indefinitely. They are good fellows, but they like a pint or three when they can afford it, and they were never very impressed with me as an officer."

"Then they are idiots, judging their betters. What would a lot of riffraff know of an officer's duties?"

Marcus took a drink rather than reply. Wesley was clever, articulate, charming, and handsome. Quick-thinking, never at a loss. Would have made a good officer. In this case, however, Wesley was wrong. The enlisted men knew best when an officer was incompetent. They lived and died as a result of that officer's abilities.

Another odd miscalculation on Wesley's part, but one doubtless meant to bolster Marcus's spirits.

"Fortunately," Marcus said, "I am no longer an officer. I am, however, in want of funds." He blushed to make that admission, and the blush embarrassed him almost as much as the truth of his statement.

"In want of funds? I thought you said you were employed? Lavish spending will only draw attention to you, and we can't have that, can we?"

The cajoling note in Wesley's tone grated, particularly because one of Marcus's last acts before leaving England had been to establish a generous allowance for Wesley. At the time, he'd felt he owed his cousin. Now, he wasn't so sure.

"I must take ship, Wesley. Lydia has taken it into her head to search for me, and you know how she is."

Wesley patted Marcus's wrist. "You need not tell me how she is. I expect I'll have to marry her. I listen to Papa's rants many a night over the port. Headstrong widows and interfering spinsters are among his favorite themes, with an occasional nod to slacking tenants. I'll give Liddie some babies, and she can spend all her days managing them and their nurserymaids and leave the rest of creation in peace."

The notion of Lydia and Wesley married did not sit well. Wesley was a capital fellow, full of charm and so forth, but Lydia had little patience for foolishness, and Wesley did love a good lark.

That Marcus would not be on hand to discuss the match with Mama and Lydia, that he would never see the nieces and nephews Wesley contemplated so casually, hurt. *Accept the things to which fate binds you...* The great philosopher had excelled at taking his own advice, while Marcus wished fate had bound him to some pleasant country manor and a smiling wife.

"I know Lydia claims to be visiting Aunt Chloe," Wesley said, "but my informants tell me that's not the case. Auntie offered me some taradiddle about Liddie nipping down to Town to do a spot of shopping. If so, the Tremont solicitors haven't any idea where she's got off to, though she might well have been shopping since Yuletide. One doesn't know whether to worry for Lydia, or reserve one's concern for greater London."

Marcus had given himself orders to carry out at this meeting, and those orders did not include disclosing Lydia's whereabouts. Had Wesley not been so jocular, so cavalier, about the woman he intended to marry, Marcus might have deviated from his orders.

But Lydia always, always meant well, and Wesley was choosing a poor time to be a bit silly.

"Never mind about her for now," Marcus said. "The time has come for me to make an orderly retreat from Albion's shores, and I need the blunt to make that happen."

Wesley took a sip of his ale, his gaze on Mary Ellen as she bent to scrub a table across the room. The vigor of her actions reverberated through her frame, making her nether end jiggle, perhaps intentionally.

"If you know where Liddie has got off to, old boy, you should tell me. I'll fetch her home to Tremont, and Papa will stop haranguing me about unbiddable females. Aunt Caroline got all the biddableness in our family. Liddie's lack of the same quality is unnatural. Babies, I tell you. The woman needs babies, and lots of them. The sooner the better, and it shall be my happy privilege to get them on her."

The beginnings of impatience nagged at Marcus. Wesley was the older, wiser cousin, cool under fire, utterly trustworthy—not some lust-obsessed fribble. To maunder on like this about Marcus's own sister was in poor taste.

"Lydia has had to think for herself precisely because Mama became so meek." Marcus had puzzled that out somewhere in the middle of the Pyrenees. The insight had occupied his mind for days, dazzling him with his own perceptiveness and hinting that he, too, had been affected by Mama's retiring personality.

Mama, to whom he would never offer even a proper farewell, much less an apology. "You will promise to look after Mama?"

"Of course. I treasure Auntie Caro, you know I do. The problem we face, dear boy, is Papa."

Uncle Reggie had always been a bit overbearing, a bit too impressed with himself, but he was Papa's brother, and he'd conscientiously stewarded Tremont's resources in Marcus's absence, if his letters were any indication.

"What's amiss with Uncle now?" Marcus asked.

"Liddie bothers him exceedingly, and your absence bothers him. I grasp why you want to turn tail and run, Markie, but you need to know that Papa is trying to have you declared dead."

The words made sense—Marcus had known such a legal petition was in the drafting stages—but to hear Wesley so blithely bruit the plan about... "I am not dead." Marcus had never, in his darkest moments, wished himself dead. That would be cowardly.

And he had never, since leaving for Spain, turned tail and run.

"And thank heavens you have not been gathered to the arms of our forefathers," Wesley said, patting Marcus's wrist again. "Perish the thought and so forth. But Papa can only do so much to preserve the Tremont fortune and so much to look after the ladies, unless he well and truly becomes the earl in your stead."

Marcus had not read law, but he knew a few things. "It hasn't been seven years yet." Even after seven years, the courts could dither and delay, particularly where a wealthy peer was concerned. In Marcus's wildest dreams, the courts delayed for twenty-one years, and after that length of time, no prosecutions for murder could attach.

"It has not been seven years," Wesley said, "but we all know how slowly the wheels of justice grind forward, and sooner begun is sooner done. I had thought you'd be relieved."

"Relieved to be *dead*?"

"Not *dead* dead, but dead enough that you no longer have to look over your shoulder every time a constable walks past. Dead enough that in a few years you could come back from your little tour of the Continent under a different name, and nobody would suspect your true identity. For you to be declared dead would advance your cause considerably, Marcus. I have given the matter much thought and have encouraged Papa's efforts on your behalf."

Marcus stared hard at the table, a scarred antique too heavy to be easily stolen. "I cannot like the notion of being dead. Mama and Lydia would grieve all over again. They have grieved enough. At least now they have hope."

Marcus had hope, too, that somehow the whole business might come right. A superstitious man would have worried that to play dead tempted fate to make the lie a reality. Marcus was not superstitious, but he was loath to cause his mother and sister any more sorrow. Mama, especially, still grieved Papa's passing.

Wesley swilled half his ale and set the tankard down. "I did not want to tell you this, but we've always been honest with each other. I fear Papa's efforts to safeguard Tremont's interests have been less than successful."

Marcus had not *always* been honest with Wesley. Marcus felt bad about that, but Wesley had taken on enough burdens for the sake of a foolish younger cousin.

"The peace has brought many adjustments," Marcus said. "Harvests haven't been reliable. I do not expect Uncle to perform miracles."

Wesley leaned forward, as if imparting betting advice. "He hasn't the head for it, Marcus. The younger sons never do. They gamble and whore and wager until somebody finds them a bride, and the result is fellows like my own darling self. Insurance for a title I'll never inherit. Papa might even be, shall we say, a bit greedy about how he's handling Tremont."

For Wesley to insult his own father had to be difficult. "A bit greedy is understandable, Wes. Uncle is still living on an allowance, for pity's sake."

Wesley shook his head. "That allowance went out the window before you landed in Spain. The solicitors did not expect you to survive the war. You were very young when you bought your colors, and they considered your decision to join up, with only Papa to secure the succession, proof of a reckless character."

Marcus would never have been clever enough to think of buying an officer's commission as a pretext for leaving Shropshire. That suggestion had been Wesley's, though Marcus could not argue with Wesley's further insult to his character. He had been reckless.

Murderously so, and *then* he had turned tail and run.

Reading Marcus's expressions was like watching a Drury Lane actor convey emotions so clearly they were visible to patrons in the royal box seats. The poor fellow had no guile and fewer brains. A touchingly vulnerable combination in a peer of the realm.

"Uncle is my heir for now," Marcus said, "and Wesley, you are also on hand to secure the succession. I take great comfort from that. Uncle Reggie is doubtless indulging himself financially to some extent, but that is to be expected of a younger son given responsibility for the finances."

No saint had ever had a purer heart or an emptier head than dear Marcus. "Papa is behaving as if he's already the earl, I am sorry to say. Lord of all he surveys. He's talking of breaking the entail on some of the tenancies and selling off the acreage."

Wesley had had to work up to that plan slowly. The estate proper was not that large, but over the centuries, the Earls of Tremont had expanded the family holdings by purchase, until Tremont's tenancies included some of the best farmland in the shire.

Papa had been hesitant to sell any parcels, but Wesley was bringing him 'round one glass of Marcus's excellent port at a time.

"That doesn't make any sense," Marcus said slowly. "Without rents, without crops to sell, without control of water rights, Tremont will have less income and most of the same expenses. My papa's own steward drilled that lesson into my head before I went off to public school. You must stop Uncle, Wesley. In five years, he can ruin an estate that took generations to build."

Wesley finished his drink—how else was he to tempt the buxom barmaid back to the table?—and sent a suitably worried glance heavenward.

"I am concerned for Tremont, Marcus, but I am more concerned for your mother. Aunt Caroline knew how your papa loved that estate. She'd be heartbroken to see it wither and fade. She doesn't need any more heartbreak."

Marcus was the quintessential good boy. He loved his mama and sister and could be manipulated into committing any folly if he thought his actions were for the sake of his womenfolk. Once Wesley had figured that out, his path to the earldom had been a matter of time and patience.

Marcus, bless him, was looking bewildered. "And my supposed death would not cause Mama and Lydia heartache? Mama is sweet and dear and deserving of every good thing. Life has handed her sorrow, and she has not weathered the blow well."

"She already fears you gone, a casualty of war or London's violence. To confirm your demise will give her peace, and more significantly, it will allow me to combat the worst of Papa's excesses."

Wesley let a silence build, during which Marcus doubtless envisioned his fragile mama once again consigned to wearing weeds, once again drifting about Tremont as silent as a wraith, suffering again...

Marcus aimed a puzzled expression at Wesley. "How can you combat Reggie's excesses if he becomes not merely my attorney in fact, but legally the earl?"

Well, well, well. Wartime experience apparently gave even the dimmest fellow a few glimmers of common sense, glimmers Wesley had come prepared to snuff out.

"The heir must consent to break any entails, my boy. *I* will be the heir once you are declared dead, and I will not consent. My word on that. Papa and the solicitors will have to reckon with me. Papa is not, alas, a young man, nor has he lived a temperate life."

Wesley had not lived a temperate life, though he wasn't the complete sot Papa was becoming. When Marcus had dwelled at Tremont, Wesley had set himself up as the sophisticated, casually wicked older cousin, only too ready to explain to Marcus how to get on at university and what to expect on jaunts down to Town.

That investment had paid off many times over when an opportunity had arisen to send Marcus packing.

Marcus looked unconvinced, which Wesley should have expected. What God had denied his lordship in brains, He had made up for in a generous allotment of stubbornness. Lydia was just as bad, and for a woman to be that pigheaded was most unattractive.

"Whether or not I'm declared dead," Marcus said, "I need funds to vacate England, Wesley. I have been recognized here, and Lydia has all but ferreted out my location. If she finds me and asks me what I'm about, I will have to tell her something of the truth." The poor fellow looked like a martyr gazing upon the scaffold. "I don't fancy lying to the courts either, but if I'm not on hand, I won't have a part in the lying, will I?"

"You will have no part in any legalities whatsoever," Wesley said, saluting with his empty tankard. "You are a weary soldier, too sick at heart to resume civilian life, so you wander the world in search of peace. Perhaps you suffered a blow to the head somewhere along the way—war being a violent business—and have no recollection of who you are. Leave the rest to me."

"'Accept the things to which fate binds you...'" Marcus muttered, which had to be some of his old Roman drivel. "The philosopher also said, 'There is but one thing of real value—to cultivate truth and justice and to live without anger in the midst of lying and unjust men.'"

"That's awfully deep, Marcus. Personally, I find philosophers a confusing lot. I'm far more comfortable with the company of friends and family." And whores. Wesley positively treasured the company of an enthusiastic whore, though Sybil was strongly hinting that he ought to be looking about for his own quarters.

"You have always been a good friend, Wesley, and a very dear cousin. I will miss you and Uncle Reggie sorely, but the time has come to change my billet. When might you bring me some funds?"

Like a dog on a bone, now that his lordship had finally turned up. "Soon," Wesley replied as the curvy little maid approached the table. "Another for me," he said, holding out his glass. "You serve fine libation, for such a humble establishment."

The maid took his tankard and poured an expert portion, spilling not a drop, despite the foaming head.

"And we expect honest coin in return." She sauntered off, and that was a sweet view too.

"She's comely," Wesley said. "Perhaps life in the stews has a few consolations."

"Life in the stews is hard and dangerous," Marcus said. "Much like life at war. I am ready to start over someplace where I don't have to fret that my throat will be slit every time I pass some noisome alley. When can I have the money, Wesley?"

This next bit was delicate, and the whole reason Wesley had decided to heed Marcus's summons. "I'll need a little time, but I'll also need something else."

Marcus gave Wesley a peevish look. "Stop being coy. Specific orders are less likely to be misunderstood, Wesley."

"Write one of those last will and testament letters soldiers write the night before a battle. It has to be in your hand, and it has to be full of impending doom. 'The deadly foe awaits me yet again on the morrow' and so forth. Toss in a premonition of death or a fatal dream."

Marcus stared off across the common, doubtless trying to make the ponderous wheels of his reasoning powers turn.

"I have a will," he said. "I made mine before Papa had been gone a year, and every British officer is required to have a will too. When I reached my majority, I validated the arrangements set forth in that will and re-executed it. All very legal. I don't see the need for any letter."

Thank heavens the military had taught Marcus a bit of caution. He'd need it, wherever he landed.

"The first purpose of such a letter is to make your final farewells to your mama and sister, which seems to matter to you."

"Of course it does."

"The second purpose of such a letter is to allow me to make the case that you gave this letter to your commanding officer, who fell at Waterloo, if I recall. I will contend that if the letter surfaced, it was because your superior saw you fall on the battlefield before his own unfortunate demise. We'll get some former soldiers to opine vaguely about your possible last moments, with a lot of references to smoke, noise, confusion, and a facial wound if need be, and you will be as good as dead in no time."

For the first time, Wesley beheld true disapproval on Marcus's handsome phiz. "You're ghoulish, Wesley."

The observation was irksome. What Wesley sought, in truth, was simply to preserve an old and respected lineage from complete ruin, while affording himself a well-deserved comfortable life. Papa was a bumbler, and Marcus was nearly simpleminded. Aunt Caro had taken on the role of frail blossom, and Lydia—who might have made a very fine earl—was lamentably female.

Wesley was willing to take on the thankless task of marriage to Lydia, which ought to be proof everlasting of his honorable nature. Of course, his consolation would be her settlements, but her consolation would be babies. A more than fair trade, assuming she survived her various travails.

Wesley was the only party in a position to preserve the Tremont title from disgrace, and he was surrounded by ingratitude.

"I am not ghoulish," Wesley said, allowing a touch of true impatience to color his words. "I am determined to save your birthright. If it's a new start you want, then a new start I will get you. I am nothing if not loyal, and you of all people should recall that."

"I do recall that, and I thank you for it, but I cannot approve of deception in the general case."

Wesley did not dignify that pomposity with a reply. Did Marcus but know it, Wesley would sleep much more soundly with Marcus out of the country. Marcus would get his remittance, eventually.

"I will write the letter you ask for, Wesley, though I doubt it will be sufficient proof of my demise."

"It won't be." Wesley rose and tapped his hat onto his head. "But add some tearful testimony, let a bit more time go by, bribe a judge or two... we'll see this thing done for you, Marcus. You can count on me."

Marcus rose as well, gentleman that he was, even in this stinking rathole. "When can I have my money?"

The note of worry in his voice was ever so gratifying. "Get me my letter, and we'll talk about money. I'm actually a bit flush right now, thanks to some luck, so the money won't be a problem. Where do you expect to end up?"

The hook was set now. No money without a letter written in the deceased's hand. The wonderful irony was, the money Marcus had asked for was technically his already.

"I thought I'd try my luck in Philadelphia," Marcus said. "The city of brotherly love and all that."

"Excellent choice," Wesley replied, grinning. "First-rate choice. If you pay the shot, I will sally forth first. Would not do to be seen strolling the surrounds together. I'll leave word for you here when I have some news, and you can drop a note to Sybil when the letter is ready for me to pick up."

Wesley bowed—he did not shake hands—and winked at the buxom maid on his way out the door. The meeting could not have gone better, unless Marcus had expired in the common before half a dozen witnesses.

"Spring is advancing," Tegan said, accepting the lemon ice Dylan handed her. "The sun isn't quite warm, but the light is lovely."

"Lovely and bright, before the leaves all unfurl," Marged added, taking her barberry treat.

Bronwen had decided not to partake, which was of a piece with her generally quiet and reserved nature. Something about Bronnie's mood, though, smacked of discontent. Dylan took the place beside her, leaving Marged and Tegan to share the next bench over.

"Raspberry?" Bronwen asked, aiming a glance at Dylan's ice.

"Would you like one?"

"No, thank you."

Perfectly polite. Annoyingly polite. Dylan had spent nearly a week squiring his sisters about Town. Lingering at the bookshops, driving out in the park, doing the pretty. All the while, Lydia had played the role of housekeeper, barely speaking to him, while his sisters never ceased their chattering, shopping, and hauling him about.

Dylan's dwelling, which had acquired the quality of a haven in recent months, was no longer *homey*. He took a spoonful of cold sweet and reviewed his situation while Marged and Tegan began debating the moral implications of the waltz.

Dylan's sisters, whom he'd long missed, were biding under his roof. His cousins were calling frequently, and last night had been the first occasion of a family dinner in years, with all four London cousins and their spouses at the same table with the Welsh sisters.

Dylan should have felt a sense of satisfaction to be hosting a regimental dinner and one with a damned impressive menu too. He should have been relieved to know winter's grip had been cast off once again, making life easier for his former subordinates in London.

He should be happy.

"Your ice is melting," Bronwen observed, taking the bowl and spoon from him. "You never used to like raspberry."

Raspberry was Lydia's favorite. "Tastes change."

"Yours apparently have. You never used to allow embroidery on your waistcoats. Undertakers were more fashionable than our sober brother. We concluded you were trying to be more Puritan than Papa was."

Dylan ran his fingers over the hem of his waistcoat. The stitchery was mostly blackwork over black silk, but Lydia had added a few golden daffodils to her design. Discreet, exquisite, and delightful, because the work was hers.

"We've been meaning to ask you something," Tegan said, spooning up a bite of her lemon ice.

"Ask. I will be coming home when the Season concludes, or shortly thereafter." Dylan had made that decision two days previously. Bowen had received a note purportedly from his brother, claiming William had recovered from a bender and found himself in Portsmouth, where he planned to look for work along the docks.

A man with one functional hand should not have to seek such employment, but Dylan's heart for that fight was waning. William had a strong back and sooner or later would leave his brother's watchful eye.

"Dylan is planning to come home," Marged said, waving her spoon as if to summon attention from the pigeons strutting on the walkway. "Alert the *Times*."

"Send for the fatted calf," Bronwen muttered. "Again."

"I am being ambushed." Dylan folded his arms, crossed his legs at the ankle, and closed his eyes as if to cadge a nap, though he was in truth spoiling for a good sibling row. "Fire away, ladies. I know I've tarried in London longer than anticipated, but I've had my reasons."

"We gave up on your promises to come home two years ago, Dylan." Tegan spoke with patient amusement, and that grated more than Bronnie's or Marged's sneering. "We're more curious now as to why you have an earl's sister employed as your housekeeper."

Dylan had been shot twice. Once a graze, once a more serious wound where a ball had passed through his arm. On both occasions, his body had known of the wound a few instants before his mind had accepted the truth of the injury.

Tegan's words cast him into the same lacuna, where his reactions lagged behind reality. On the battlefield, that gap could be fatal. Sitting on a bench beneath the maples of Berkeley Square, Dylan told himself not to panic. He kept his eyes closed and his posture relaxed.

"I did not know Mrs. Lovelace was an earl's daughter when she sought the post. She executes her duties conscientiously, and that is all you need to know of the matter."

"She takes a very great risk," Tegan observed, setting aside her empty bowl, "dusting your parlors and blacking your andirons."

Dylan sat up and swiveled his gaze at his oldest sister. "What risk?"

"I recognized her," Tegan said. "While you were off at war, I was subjected to a London Season. I noticed Lady Lydia then because she was different. She wasn't dimwitted or vain, she never gossiped, and she was seldom asked to dance despite being an earl's daughter. She has a certain presence, a presence that does not suffer fools, and I envied her that."

"Cousin Jeanette," Marged said, scraping her spoon against her bowl, "who gained something of a reputation as a matchmaker, recognized her ladyship, or perhaps Cousin Sycamore did. Those two are very much in each other's pockets, and you'd think an earl's son would know of other earls' daughters."

"You'd think,"—Bronwen took up the narrative—"that a man renowned for his reconnaissance skills would realize that polite society's vigilance, when it comes to searching out scandal, has no limit."

Dylan wanted to pace, but he would not give his sisters that satisfaction. "As ambushes go, this one is proceeding in the usual fashion. Surprise the unsuspecting, attack in force, storm the opponent before he can get organized, and overwhelm him with numbers and strategic advantage. I must ask myself, though, what sort of surrender do you seek from me? Lady Lydia is free to leave my employ at any time, and she took the post of her own volition."

"Typical," Bronwen muttered. "You see an attack where we offer only support. Dylan, what are you about, employing Lady Lydia as a domestic? What is *she* about? Why must she hide in your pantries, and *what have you done to aid her?*"

Dylan considered dodging and dissembling, but these were his sisters, and he hadn't done anything wrong.

Not truly, awfully wrong. Lamentable and regrettable, yes, but not *wrong*. "She did not disclose her identity until after she gained my trust. I do not approve of self-serving liars."

"Papa would be proud of you," Marged said, taking the last spoonful of her ice. "So sure of your principles. So upright and steadfast."

Papa, may he rest in peace, had been a rigid, righteous old pedant. "You insult me because I expect honesty from those who take my coin?"

"How many times," Tegan mused, "have you lied to us, Dylan? You tell us you'll come home with us, but something always necessitates that you tarry yet longer in London. You meant to pass Yuletide in Wales, but that hasn't happened all three times you've proffered such a plan. You intend to return in time for harvest, when the weather improves... Lie after lie after lie."

"And do you know," Marged said, "what results from your lying?"

"I do not lie."

"We lie too," Marged went on, as if Dylan hadn't spoken. "We invent excuses for you, regimental business, difficulties for our cousins, bad weather to the east, a bout of ague—you are very prone to the ague since Waterloo. We've become adept at supporting the fiction that you yearn to come home soon, always soon."

"I do expect to go home. I long to go home. Why would you lie about my reasons for staying in London?"

The silence that ensued felt very much like the silence that had followed when Dylan had reported seeing French forces where

French forces were not supposed to be. Pained, incredulous, profoundly disappointed.

"How can you not know," Bronwen said, "that without your consequence, we are a trio of increasingly pathetic spinsters? Rhys Campbell left for Scotland after trying to compromise me. His efforts failed, and I made it known we were off to London to fetch you home. I might have mentioned that you are a dead shot and in some ways as old-fashioned as our papa. And no, Dylan, he did not violate my person. Margs prevented him from transgressing to that extent."

"He tried it with me too," Tegan said. "I'm old enough to be desperate, of course, or perhaps my darling brother has spent my settlements living the high life in London. I had no idea that having found me unreceptive, Rhys would simply keep opening cupboards so to speak. He's handsome and charming. I was supposed to be flattered."

"I'll kill him."

"He's not the first," Marged said quietly. "Osian Jones has been pestering me for ages, no matter how firmly I dissuade him. The lazier tenants are cheating you, and your steward is too old, or too weary, to put a stop to it."

The Hundred Days had felt like this, when Napoleon, exiled after nearly twenty years of wreaking death and hardship on a whole Continent, had slipped the leash and advanced through France. The very army that had repudiated him less than a year before had flocked to his side, and town after town had welcomed him as a returning hero.

Britain and her allies had watched with incomprehensible dismay piled atop growing horror.

"My tenants are cheating?"

"They claim they have only sixty spring lambs when, in fact, they have seventy-two. They poach, Dylan, and they sell the game, which means the professional sorts of poachers have also been seen in the area. If Lydia Glover has fled the protection of her family seat to hide in service in a London household, she is not off on a lark. She is in trouble, and *of course* she would wait to secure your trust before she confided in you."

"She is not in trouble. She is merely trying to find her..." Dylan shut his mouth, because he'd sounded exactly like Papa launching into a sermon. Lydia would never admit that her own situation was becoming perilous. She'd alluded instead to an estate falling into disrepair, relatives with their fingers in the earldom's pockets.

"Merely trying to find her brother?" Tegan suggested airily. "We well know what a thankless undertaking that is. Tremont inherited quite young, ran off to play soldier, and hasn't been seen since. Lost on the battlefield, so they say. The drunken uncle's running matters back in Shropshire."

I am not lost. Dylan kept that protestation to himself, because he suspected his sisters would hear it as another falsehood. "How do you know this?" Lydia had not mentioned that her uncle was a sot, but then, Dylan hadn't given her a chance to mention it.

"Reconnaissance," Marged said, "is not a skill limited to the male of the species. We have little else to do on rainy days, but correspond with friends and distant relations, and Wales has its share of rainy days."

Some years, rain blessed their part of Wales every other day on average.

"Nobody likes a liar," Marged went on, "and we know you miss home, but even fewer people care for righteous prigs. Witness, Papa's bleating piety and probity were what sent you off to Spain in the first place. I've always wondered how he reconciled 'thou shalt not kill' with driving his only son off to war. Not very well, I gather."

"He had regrets," Tegan said, getting to her feet. "I expect you will too." She gathered up her bowl and spoon. Marged and Bronwen similarly held empty bowls.

"Might you ladies return to the house without me?" Dylan said. "I feel a need to stretch my legs rather than take the carriage."

That was a lie—another lie—but one he needed to tell.

"Of course," Tegan said. "It's a pleasant day for a walk."

Tegan kissed his cheek, and Marged patted his arm. Bronwen stood before him, her gaze as solemn as Dylan had ever seen it.

"Come home soon, Dylan, or we might not be there when you do. We hardly have a brother as it is, and we are tired of playing steward and squire in your place." She touched his shoulder, then Dylan's sisters left him alone beneath the maples, without a map, compass, or clue.

CHAPTER FIFTEEN

Lydia was balancing the household accounts, a task she usually enjoyed, except that today her mind refused to focus on the numbers. The kittens weren't helping. Regular meals and the passage of time were working their magic, turning a pair of bedraggled strays into energetic and playful young felines.

"I will miss you." Lydia spoke the words softly, trying them on aloud. The kittens, tackling each other, wrestling, and racing about the kitchen, ignored her.

She would miss so much. The pleasure of having the authority to put a house to rights. The joy of earning a wage that she could do with whatever she pleased. The comfort of simple clothing and a measure of privacy she'd never had at Tremont.

She would not miss the odd moments when she'd caught Dylan regarding her with a veiled sort of puzzlement. She would not miss sleeping in the bed where he and she had become lovers—though she would miss *him*.

She would miss the Dylan who'd taken such pains to ensure that his advances were welcome. She'd miss hearing his boots thumping about on the floor above, and even more, she'd miss those boots thumping down the steps, presaging another raid belowstairs.

The kittens ceased their antics and stared at the steps a moment before Lydia heard the measured tread she used to take such delight in. Boots first, then breeches, morning coat, and broad shoulders appeared as the captain descended into the kitchen.

He looked weary, though Lydia could not read his mood. She rose and curtseyed, because in this house, she was Mrs. Lovelace the housekeeper, as far as anybody other than the captain was concerned.

He visually inspected her, from her mobcap, to her shawl, to her hands. "I no longer know what to call you," he said. "May I sit?"

Lydia nodded, prepared to be civil. Clearly, Dylan had come to ask for her resignation, and she had been steeling herself to proffer exactly that.

"Ladies first," he said, standing behind the chair Lydia had occupied.

She allowed him to seat her, though the courtesy put her off-balance.

"I have been thinking," Dylan said. "I was a good reconnaissance officer."

"I'm sure you were."

"One thing a reconnaissance officer cannot do, not if he wants to remain alive, is become lost."

Lydia closed the ledger before her. "I beg your pardon?"

"Somewhere along the way, somewhere in Spain or France or perhaps not until I came back to London, I went missing in action, like your brother. I became obsessed with matters not strictly under my command."

Lydia had never heard Dylan Powell speak with less than perfect self-assurance, and yet, he sounded reflective now. Introspective rather than commanding.

"Dylan, are you well?"

"No. No, I am not. I have behaved badly toward you and toward my sisters, and if I do not make amends, I will be drummed out of the only regiment that matters. And yet, I cannot reconcile myself to the notion that you had to lie to me... Do you know what a reconnaissance officer's greatest skill is?"

Lydia had not been forced to lie to Dylan. She had chosen to lie to him—and chosen to make love with him too. She had pondered the matter at length and in hindsight did not see that other choices would have yielded appreciably better results.

"I suppose a reconnaissance officer relies most on his sight," she replied. "His ability to notice details."

Dylan shook his head. "His hearing. His ability to listen carefully, to ask the right questions, to notice what isn't being said, or what's being offered in jest what isn't humorous at all. I could ride the countryside all day, noting what was in plain view—crops, cows, terrain— but what I heard and overheard in the taverns, in the churchyards, at the farrier's forge gained me the most useful information. I would like to hear from you why you came to London and why you could not tell me who you really are."

"So you can call me names again?" Lydia asked. "Reassure yourself that I am a scoundrel and liar?"

Dylan scrubbed a hand over his face. "I am sorry for those words. I spoke in anger, and I was wrong. You are not a scoundrel, and you are no more a liar than I am. You are right that I would go forth under false colors myself, pretending to be a tinker or a deserter or some other convenient character. There was a war on, and I want to know what war you are fighting, Lydia. You are not simply searching for a wayward brother, are you? Your uncle is some sort of threat, and your mother depends on you."

What was the purpose of this discussion? What was Dylan's objective? Did that even matter, when for her own sake, Lydia wanted only the truth between her and Dylan?

"After Waterloo, my brother, as you know, apparently traveled as far as London. He resigned his commission and then just... disappeared. You know Marcus. You may not respect him, but he is conscientious to a fault, much concerned with honorable behavior, but not... not quick. He will think a matter to death, and unless some old Roman has a quote precisely relevant to the situation, Marcus will dither and equivocate."

Lydia was dithering and equivocating, while Dylan remained silent.

"I do not trust my cousin," Lydia said. "Wesley expects to marry me, though I've never given him encouragement. My settlements are generous, and when I marry, my husband will have control over a substantial sum. Wesley isn't awful, but he's lazy. My mother has taken to losing jewelry in recent years, and whenever a piece goes missing, Wesley shortly thereafter decamps for a visit to London, or Brighton, or someplace where idle young men waste great sums of money."

"Your mother is an heiress," Dylan said. "The Lovelace heiress."

"Yes, and she has a large and lovely collection of jewelry that she owns personally, or she did, but she's a widow and has few occasions to wear her better pieces, so how are they going missing?"

"Precisely the sort of question a reconnaissance officer asks. Go on."

"My uncle has no head for business, and he relies on my cousin's guidance. Wesley has never managed his allowance well, much less had responsibility for a huge estate. I fear Uncle and Wesley have both borrowed against expectations, mortgaged tenancies, and otherwise helped themselves to Tremont's wealth, and I cannot stop them. Uncle has raised rents, but he's not keeping up with repairs. Our best tenants have gone elsewhere, and some land agent in Oxford is now responsible for replacing the farmers who leave."

"A land agent who's also helping himself to Tremont's bounty?"

Lydia nodded. "The lawyers won't talk to me. Horse Guards won't talk to me. My father's friends reply to my letters with avuncular nonsense about trusting to my uncle's judgment. My home is being plundered before my eyes, my mother is fading, and my cousin has been subtly harassing me to accept a suit I want no part of. I feared if I remained at Tremont, Wesley would engineer some sort of scene, and my choices would be limited to ruin or marriage to a man I cannot trust."

This recitation flattered nobody. A more clever woman would have found a means of taking the situation at Tremont in hand, putting Wesley in his place, and getting some answers from His Majesty's military. Lydia was fresh out of cleverness.

Was this how Marcus had felt? Dull-witted? Inadequate, slow to see the obvious?

"Do you trust anybody, Lydia?"

"I tried to trust you."

"And I disappointed you, called you names, and then expected you to meekly return to polishing my windows. Tegan recognized you."

"So did Sycamore Dorning. I danced with him at some point during my misspent Seasons, maybe at several points."

"Him."

A world of male reproach lay in that single word. "Dorning is your cousin by marriage now, Dylan, and he told me he was willing to serve as my reinforcements. To take you to task."

The kittens had worn themselves out and returned to their basket. They made a sweet, peaceful circle of sleeping felines, curled up with each other. For no earthly reason, the sight brought a lump to Lydia's throat.

"Dorning thinks to offer me a good pummeling."

"You'd pummel him worse. He's arrogant, while you are..."

A ghost of a smile lit Dylan's eyes. "I am...?"

"You have the courage of your convictions. You do not back down. You do not give quarter. Mr. Dorning strikes me as pragmatic. If he were losing a fight, he'd cry pax and try to charm his opponent into sharing a pint."

The smile faded. "You would have made a good reconnaissance officer, my lady, and you are an excellent housekeeper, but it was wrong of me to ask you to continue in the post."

Now he would ask to her leave, though Lydia dreaded a return to

Shropshire. "I have not yet found my brother, and I, too, refuse to quit short of my objective. I know Marcus is here, and I know I must find him."

Dylan rose and took the morning's tray of raspberry tarts from the bread box. "I suspect William Brook found him." He set the tray on the table. "Cider, tea, or milk?"

"Cider goes well with these tarts." Then the import of Dylan's words sorted itself in her mind. *"William Brook* found Marcus?"

Dylan poured Lydia a mug of cider and resumed his seat across from her. "I suspect so, and your brother…"

"Marcus."

"Lord Tremont," Dylan said. "William served under him for a time. He would recognize Tremont easily. I will try to find your brother for you, Lydia, but am not among his admirers. I admit that nobody serving under Dunacre had it easy, and your brother was young, but I could not like or respect him."

"You don't like or respect me much at this point either." She did not dare reject this offer of assistance, but she wanted to. Marcus had been a boy when he'd joined up, barely seventeen, with a single year of university to his name. How on earth was he to have known how to deal with the same commanding officer who'd made a game of putting Dylan's life at risk?

"I respect you enormously," Dylan said, "and I have disappointed you, so I will make right what I can, but time after time, Lord Tremont—whom you love fiercely—supported Dunacre's lies, failed to stand up to him, and toadied to a monster. That truth will always be between us. I'm sorry for that, my lady. I'm sorry I judged you, and sorry my temper got the better of me. I'm exceedingly, abjectly sorry."

He rose, kissed Lydia's cheek, and left her sitting before a plate of raspberry tarts while battling the useless urge to cry.

The answer came to Dylan the next morning as he ate a solitary breakfast and recalled the kittens scrapping and wrestling in Lydia's kitchen. The inspiration for their contention, besides plain feline high spirits, had been a small, hard pinecone. One kitten would bat the toy away, then chase after it. The other would pursue her sibling and try to reach the toy first.

Keep away. Boys played the same game in every schoolyard in Britain, and some people played a version of it in the ballrooms.

While Lydia had been recounting fears and worries that would have felled a lesser woman, some silent part of Dylan's mind had been pondering the game of keep away. He'd kept away from Wales, unwilling for the war to be over until he'd satisfied himself that all the men he'd protected so poorly in Spain were well set up in London.

Until the cousins he'd also been unable to protect in Spain were comfortably settled.

Until he'd punished himself with homesickness for so long that even hearing his sisters speak Welsh nearly brought him to tears.

William Brook and his friends had been playing keep away in the stews too.

Dylan went to the library, got out a map of London, and recalled every time he'd been given "directions" by a helpful former soldier.

"There," he said, tapping a short street in a warren of twisting byways near Seven Dials. The men had always directed him *away* from that little street, and they'd been posted on every corner that led to that location.

"On picket duty," Dylan muttered, "and I didn't even notice." He still had not sorted out why former soldiers would be so loyal to Tremont. About the only compliment his lordship could honestly be given was that he hadn't been mean. Dunacre's cruelty had appalled Tremont, but he—a belted, if young, earl—had done nothing to confront Dunacre or hold him accountable.

"You barely touched your breakfast." Lydia stood in the library doorway, looking very much the housekeeper, wearing both a pristine cap and a full-length starched apron. "Are you well, sir?"

Dylan was not well. Hadn't been well for years. "I know where your brother is."

She put a hand to her throat. "You are certain?"

"All but. The situation wants some reconnoitering, and I will be about that now." He'd need to change into less-conspicuous attire and most especially don a waistcoat that bore no golden daffodils.

"I am coming with you."

"Lydia, I will be on foot in one of the worst slums London offers, which is saying a great deal."

She advanced on him, figurative bayonet clearly fixed. "Marcus is *my brother*. He will be well aware that you hold him in no esteem whatsoever. What do you think he will do if he sees you marching on his domicile? He might well leave England, and then I will never find him, because you could not be content to lead the charge. You had to go alone into enemy territory, the same as always."

For a sheltered lady turned housekeeper, she had phenomenal aim. "I am trying to keep you safe, and I have said I will find him for you. I mean Tremont no harm, despite his military record."

Lydia kept on marching until she and Dylan were nearly toe to toe. "Marcus is a dead shot. He practiced and practiced until he felt he lived up to my father's legacy as a marksman. I am trying to keep you safe, too, but you are too dunderheaded, stubborn, and *male* to contemplate your own mortality."

Her fragrance assailed him, all rosy and fresh, a soft counterpoint to the frustration in her gaze.

"Tremont could not hit a stationary target at point-blank range if somebody loaded and aimed the pistol for him." Marcus had seen Tremont bungle an easy shot any number of times and nearly put a bullet through his own foot as well.

"I am his sister, and I know my brother, and I am coming with you." Lydia pivoted, giving Dylan her back. "Please, Captain, for the sake of all concerned, I must accompany you."

She clearly believed her brother to be handy with a pistol, though

Dylan knew otherwise. She also had a point that Tremont would hardly expect Dylan to be making a social call.

"Dress in your oldest cloak and most battered hat. Bring no coin. If I give you an order, you obey instantly and without question. Before we leave the garden, put some loose soil in the pocket of your cloak to fling in the eyes of any assailant."

She nodded. "I will meet you at the back door in fifteen minutes, but you should eat something if we're to hike halfway across London."

Spoken like an experienced officer. "I must change as well, so let's say thirty minutes."

Dylan heeded Lydia's guidance, stopping by the breakfast parlor to finish a cold plate of eggs, toast, and bacon, then choosing attire that would be considered finery in St. Giles and fit for rags in Mayfair. When Lydia met him at the back door, she wore a patched, wrinkled cloak that was nonetheless clean. Her millinery was a plain straw hat such most ladies would not wear beyond their own garden.

"My pocket is half full of dirt," she said, preceding Dylan out the door. Her tone suggested any thief stupid enough to try to pick that pocket would not live long to regret it.

"I would offer my arm like a proper escort," Dylan said as they set off in an easterly direction, "but I need my hands free. If I tell you to run—"

"I will pelt off like a rabbit pursued by hellhounds. You even walk differently in those clothes. No military bearing, no brisk stride."

Dylan had taken a moment to dirty his hands with some ashes from the hearth and had streaked yesterday's limp cravat with a hint of ash as well.

"Reconnaissance is largely a matter of becoming who and what people expect to see, knowing which piece of small talk—the weather, the price of bread, the latest royal folly—is the one they expect to hear. You, for example, should allow yourself to show all the weariness you feel. No more maintaining appearances where we're going."

The neighborhood had already changed, from genteel if modest homes, to dingier shops and narrower streets.

"I am not weary," Lydia said, "not in the sense you mean. I am worried."

"Then show that, because to blend in believably, some of your disguise must be genuine."

They walked the length of two more streets before Lydia spoke again. "I hate that you know these games, that you know so well how to hide in plain sight. I suspect that the stratagems you employed at war to keep you alive have only led you astray now that we're at peace. You wore so many disguises that you no longer recognize your own reflection."

Dylan could not afford to focus on her words in the dodgy surrounds they'd reached, but Lydia had put her finger on something that merited further thought. Of necessity, he'd learned the habit of dissembling while at war, and that habit had, indeed, kept him—and often his men—alive.

They walked for another twenty minutes before Dylan slowed his pace yet further. "The only lodging to be had on this street is in that building, the one housing the gin shop. I'm told the rooms above are humble, but as close to clean as—"

Lydia jerked his arm violently, pulling him around to face her. "That man coming out of the door beside the gin shop and stuffing a folded piece of paper into his breast pocket is my cousin Wesley."

Dylan stepped nearer, as if trying to quietly placate a woman who'd taken umbrage at something he'd said.

"Dressed like that, your cousin is all but begging to have his pocket picked and his clothing stripped from his back. Do we see him escorted back to safe territory, or assume he was calling on your brother, and Tremont is thus at home?"

"Wesley is looking entirely too pleased with himself. Leave him to the pickpockets, and let's find Marcus."

The rest was fairly easy. Half of the rooms above the gin shop had no doors, and being young and fit, Marcus would have gone for the cheaper lodging on the highest floor. Dylan stopped a boy on the last landing and asked which was the fancy gent's room. The lad pointed to a closed door and scampered off before Dylan could pass him a coin.

"Smart fellow," Dylan muttered, rapping on the door. "Glover." Even Tremont wouldn't bother with a title in this neighborhood. "You have callers."

Sounds on the other side of the door indicated an occupant moving around. "A moment."

The door opened, revealing a thin, less than spruce version of the Earl of Tremont. The boy had aged into young manhood, gangly youth giving way to a spare, muscular frame.

"Powell and... *Lydia?*" He retreated and left the door open. "I had hoped... Well, do come in. Can't exactly ring for tea, but neither can we have this discussion on the stair. I was not expecting... That is to say... If you intend to rip up at me, Lydia, have at it, but please tell me first how Mama is getting on."

Another woman might have dissolved into tears, but Lydia merely marched into the room and walked a circle around her brother, leaving Dylan to close the door. Tremont stood at attention, chin up, looking more like a resentful schoolboy than a former officer.

And not at all like a long-lost brother.

"You had more growing to do," Lydia said. "You are taller than Papa was. I cannot... It's good to see you, Marcus."

Tremont nodded. "Good to see you too, Lydia. Good, but also... I had hoped to leave England without causing you and Mama further upset."

She came to a halt before him. "Why leave England?"

"How is Mama?"

Still, she did not embrace her brother, and Tremont did not embrace her. Did not take her hand, did not in any way show evidence of sibling affection, and Dylan knew Lydia to be an affectionate woman.

"Mama is miserable. She still misses Papa, and now she frets endlessly over you and over the havoc Uncle is wreaking with Tremont. She does not want me to marry Wesley, but Tremont will need my settlements before too much longer."

Whatever Dylan had expected of the sibling reunion, it hadn't been this painfully awkward, cool exchange. Appreciation for his sisters tugged at him, for their blunt honesty, their patience, and their caring. He owed them an apology, at least.

And somebody owed Lydia an apology. A woman ought not to be this composed when reuniting with a brother thought lost to the battlefields. For that matter, Tremont, barely of age, coping with straitened circumstances, ought not to be so reserved either.

"You confirm Wesley's report," Tremont replied, "and he shares your fears regarding Uncle's bungling. I hope you do marry him, Lydia, because Wesley has Tremont's best interests at heart."

Lydia looked her brother up and down. The earl might have gained height, but he was doubtless still very much Lydia's little brother.

"Wesley just called on you. What was he doing here?"

"He's helping me make arrangements to leave England, and he will do what he can to stay Uncle's hand. I'm sorry, Lydia, but I am trying to do the right thing. I have always tried to do the right thing."

And that little sermon was vintage Tremont. Reeking of pompous nobility and absolutely wrongheaded.

"The right thing is to come home," Lydia said. "Tremont is your birthright and your duty."

The earl sent Dylan a pleading look. "No, Lydia, it's not. Well, it is, or it was, but it's not my only duty. Tell Mama not to worry, tell her that I'm willing to work hard and turn my hand to any honest labor. I wasn't worth much as an officer, but I do well enough in a humbler role. I will write if I can, though I will have to change my name."

Lydia's expression was absolutely composed. "You turn your back on the family who needs you, you go larking off to God knows where, and tell me you are pursuing the honorable course? Marcus, has war left you deranged?"

Finally, Tremont tried a pat to Lydia's shoulder. "I am doing the honorable thing, Lydia. You just don't know it. Ever since the business with the Finchly scoundrel, I have tried to do the honorable thing, and the results have been... challenging, not as I intended. But I did the only thing possible in the circumstances. Wesley was right about that. I never wanted to join up, much less leave you and Mama, but 'nothing happens to any man that he is not formed by nature to bear,' and I carry on. You and Mama must carry on too."

Lydia stepped back. "You quote Aurelius *now*?"

Tremont drew himself up with a curious dignity. "The philosopher has seen me through many a dark day, Lydia. I am sorry to disappoint you, but I must ask you to leave and not come back."

Lydia stood motionless, staring at her brother as if she'd see into his soul. Her heart had to be breaking into a thousand jagged pieces, and yet, this priggish stupidity was exactly what Dylan would have expected from Tremont.

The young earl had debts, or had angered some jealous husband, and was fleeing the consequences.

"When do you sail?" she asked.

"Ten days hence. Wesley is arranging it all, and I will travel under an assumed name. Don't try to find me, but I will write if I can."

Dylan waited for Lydia to fly at her brother with her fists, to unleash torrents of sororal vituperation upon him, but she only curtseyed.

"Safe journey, my lord. I will miss you."

Tremont bowed. "I'm sorry, Lydia. I did the best I could. Powell, I trust you will see my sister safely from the premises."

Tremont was still so very young, and clearly, he believed he'd set himself on some version of an honorable path. His demeanor wasn't quite martyred, but rather, nobly resigned.

Why? "Is there anything I can do to help?" Dylan asked, though his own question surprised him. He did not like or respect the

Tremont he'd served with, but Lydia's brother was miserable and about to part from his only home and everybody he'd ever loved.

"Look after Lydia and Mama. Please, for God's sake, somebody look after Mama. I was clearly unequal to that honor. Lydia, you should not have come, but it has been good to see you." Tremont held the door open, eyes front, and Lydia swept through without sparing her brother a glance.

The door closed, and Dylan expected Lydia to throw herself into his arms and commence a fit of weeping. In this tired, old building in this sad, crowded neighborhood, nobody would remark the sound of a woman's heart breaking.

Lydia descended the steps at a good clip, leaving Dylan to follow in her wake.

"I want to know what the hell Wesley was doing here," Lydia said when they were standing outside the gin shop. "Why does Marcus think his only course is to banish himself, and what could my ancient and sorry history possibly have to do with this whole business."

Dylan thought back over the strange scene in the dingy little room above. "Who is Finchly?"

"My lapse from paragon-hood. That was years ago, and Marcus didn't even like him because he was stealing Wesley's attention from Marcus, or something." Lydia started walking, and Dylan fell in step beside her. "I had no idea what 'whole business' Marcus alluded to regarding Finchly. Gambling debts, I suppose. Stupid wagers. Male folly all mixed up with Marcus's overdeveloped sense of honor."

Lydia did not speak again all the way back to the house, but Dylan was sorting through what he'd heard and seen, even as he waited for some outburst from Lydia. The outburst never came, but Dylan did reach three conclusions.

First, Lydia was absolutely correct that Cousin Wesley was up to something. Wesley had known where Marcus dwelled and said nothing to Marcus's family about that discovery. He was further arranging for Marcus to leave England, a maneuver that put Wesley much closer to holding the title himself.

Second, Lydia's ancient history, her *lapse*, was somehow the root of all these troubles. Whoever Finchly was, wherever he was, he was the key to solving Lydia's problems and the clue Dylan would pursue.

Third, Lydia had reserves of composure that Dylan found frankly unnerving. Soldiers were supposed to calmly gaze upon the battlefields where comrades had fallen hours before, except that few soldiers could be that stoic. They cried, they raged, they drank, brawled, swived, and cursed God. Sometimes they deserted or took their own lives rather than face another battlefield.

Lydia was dry-eyed and determined, but somewhere in that large and courageous heart of hers, she had to be carrying years' worth of hurt.

And Dylan, guardian angel of the regiment and all that, had added to her pain.

Walking back to Dylan's house, Lydia pondered a new appreciation for the sheer effort required for effective reconnaissance. Without in any way conveying watchfulness, Dylan had walked across much of London on highest alert.

He'd silently acknowledged a half-dozen former soldiers, whom Lydia recognized from their calls at her kitchen door, but would have passed by on her own without even noticing.

He'd twice gently tugged Lydia closer to the street, and only then had she realized they'd been approaching some shadowy doorway in which a beggar or streetwalker slouched. Dylan had known exactly where he was going, while Lydia had lost her bearings fifteen minutes from home.

And all of this—maps, destinations, perils, potential ambushes, possible allies—Dylan had carried in his head while appearing to be nothing more than another down-on-his-luck Londoner ambling through the morning throng with a tight-lipped woman at his side.

What must it be like to carry a whole war's worth of such

missions in his head, sorties into dangerous territory a daily duty, death and torture ever-present threats? Perhaps Dylan's past was the deadly version of what Lydia faced at Tremont—Uncle's sniping and stealing, Mama fading into vapid agreeableness, Cousin Wesley circling like a hound on the scent of Lydia's fat settlements, the servants spying, the neighbors gossiping...

Marcus's deceitfulness had been a rude shock, and Lydia had been ready to cosh her brother with her reticule, except she hadn't been carrying a reticule. Marcus might be taking the only course available to him, but in the moment, Lydia had felt furious, dismayed, caught off guard, *betrayed*...

She had been one increment of self-restraint away from accusing her darling baby brother of acting like a scoundrel.

And Dylan and Marcus had both had a flaming scoundrel for a commanding officer.

"I am tired," Lydia said as she and Dylan traversed a quiet street lined with oak trees in the pink-fading-to-green phase of leafing out. "You were right about that. Not physically tired. I do sleep, but..."

"You are worn out," Dylan said. "Weary of spirit. Shall we sit?"

The street fronted a bit of bricks and greenery in an oblong shape with a three-tiered fountain at the center. No iron fence declared the tiny space private, and the sound of trickling water imparted a sense of repose.

The fountain was flanked by two benches. A pigeon strutted about on one, like a footman keeping the seats free for anticipated dignitaries. The other bench was unoccupied, and Lydia sank onto it gratefully.

"I wanted to hug Marcus, and I wanted to hit him," she said. "That man we met is both my dearest brother and a complete stranger. He did not even..." Lydia fell silent, trying to recall who had not hugged whom. "He was always so dignified, even as a little fellow. He once told me he could at least comport himself like an earl, even if he lacked an earl's intelligence. That broke my heart, because Marcus had spoken the truth. He's not stupid. He can be profoundly insightful, but he will never express a thought until he's sure of it. The result is that he appears slow, so he retreats into dignity."

"*You* are always so dignified," Dylan said, coming down beside her. "Maybe I am too. Marcus had a lot of writing supplies for a man living hand to mouth, Lydia. I suspect he's managing as a scribe and reader. The finest article in the whole room was a traveling desk that matches the one in your bedroom."

Lydia had seen none of that. She'd seen water-stained walls, a bare hearth, a sagging cot. A brother who'd gone to war barely old enough to shave, now several inches taller and worlds more serious.

"Is there any detail you miss, Captain?"

"Wesley knew exactly where Marcus was biding and seemed pleased with the results of his call. You don't truly plan to marry your cousin, do you?"

Would you care? "I cannot think clearly at the moment. I am too... too..." Sad, relieved, confused. "I thought the worst possibility was that Marcus was dead, but even his death would have been an answer of sorts. That he's alive and hiding from us, preparing to flee like some bigamist pursued by a mob of embittered wives... I cannot fathom what's afoot."

"Neither can I, and fathoming what's afoot is how I stayed alive for years. What do we know of Wesley?"

The vigilant pigeon was pacing back and forth on the opposite bench, while songbirds gilded the air with cheerful little birdy melodies. The sky above was for once clear, and sunshine dappled the walkway. Lydia noticed these small blessings only because Dylan had invited her to sit and share her thoughts with him.

She noticed something else too.

She would miss Dylan terribly. What she had initially taken as a lack of warmth in him was watchfulness learned in a hard school, and beneath that watchfulness was caring. Despite the differences between them, Dylan had found Marcus for her and even offered to help him. That mission accomplished, Dylan tarried with her on this bench, helping her sort out a situation that hadn't been at all what she'd expected.

"What I know of Wesley," Lydia said slowly, "isn't that much, considering I grew up with him. He's the family fribble, not quite the spare, but not without expectations. He games, he wagers, he flits through London when he has some blunt, I assume he has lady friends he would never introduce to me, and he was reasonably decent to Marcus. Marcus had no brothers and no father, but he had Wesley."

"He apparently still has Wesley, while Wesley has Hoby boots, a Schweitzer and Davidson coat, and an ebony tippling cane that cost more than your annual wages as my housekeeper."

"Tippling cane?"

"The upper part of the handle conceals a narrow cylindrical flask. Fashionable nonsense, and it comes dear."

Lydia was again impressed with Dylan's eye for detail. "I can think of three explanations for Wesley's finery. First, he got lucky at the tables, which has been known to happen."

"Second?"

"He's stealing Mama's jewelry and pawning it."

"Plausible, and because a retiring widow wears little jewelry, she hardly notices. What's third?"

"My mother has been buying my freedom with what wealth she still commands, and when Wesley has bilked her of all her jewels, he will expect me to turn over my settlements." This theory, while distasteful in the extreme, fit what Lydia knew of the people involved.

"He will expect you to surrender your settlements," Dylan noted, "and your person. Do you long to be Countess of Tremont, Lydia?"

No accusation colored the question, no judgment. "I would sooner keep house in hell than marry the man who is apparently exploiting my brother's bad fortune. I thank you for finding Marcus and for taking me to him. It will mean much to my mother to know Marcus is well and whole."

Dylan rose and offered Lydia his hand. "Marcus is not whole in spirit, Lydia. Whatever else is true, he believes he must flee the country and that doing so is the most honorable course before him. I can think of only one reason why the Earl of Tremont, who was nothing if not dutiful, would turn his back on his family."

Lydia took Dylan's hand and rose. "He fears some scandal worse than the dishonor of abandoning us and abandoning Tremont, and Wesley knows the details."

Dylan rested Lydia's hand on his arm. "Wesley knows the details, and if you or your mother prove difficult, Wesley will let Society know those details. Marcus will be held in contempt, whether he has earned that contempt or not."

They strolled in the direction of home. "You don't think Marcus deserves to be held in contempt? Don't you regard him as the worst excuse for an officer ever to disgrace a uniform?"

"Dunacre holds that honor. As for Marcus, even given his tender years, he was a bumbler, indecisive, unsure of himself, and a frequent target of Dunacre's ridicule. I nonetheless note that the men have been protecting your brother even at the risk of losing my good opinion of them. That is loyalty, Lydia. That is substantial, unwavering loyalty, and the average British soldier does not yield his loyalty lightly."

Another observation Lydia could not have made. "What are you saying?"

"I am asking for my orders. If you tell me to investigate the situation, I will do so and report back to you. If you tell me you need to borrow Goddard's traveling coach so you can return to Shropshire, gather up your mother and your jewels, and join Marcus on whatever ship he's taking, I will have a coach at your disposal and arrange your passage."

"Why make these offers, Captain? I lied to you, and were your sisters not underfoot, you'd send me packing."

They turned onto Dylan's street, and Lydia felt a sense of homecoming out of all proportion to the occasion. She had grown used to coming and going by way of the area steps rather than the front door, grown accustomed to having a cup of tea with Betty from time to time and listening for Dylan's footfalls on the floor above.

"You came to London on reconnaissance," Dylan said slowly. "Of all people, I understand the limitations inherent in such situations. I should not have spoken to you as I did, and I cannot in good conscience expect you to return to Shropshire when I know you are not safe there. At any point, Wesley could join you at the family seat, compromise you, and you would have nothing to say to it."

An honorable, if disappointing, speech, also just short of terrifying. "Have you added me to your collection of weary soldiers, Dylan?"

They reached the foot of the front steps, though Lydia had no intention of taking this discussion into the house where Dylan's sisters awaited.

"You said you were weary," he replied, "but not in the sense of needing more sleep. I am weary, too, Lydia, though I hadn't even realized it. The trumpet sounds 'Boots and Saddles,' and a soldier is on his horse without knowing how he got there. Your mother needed you to find Marcus and off you went, searching as best you could."

"And you found him."

Dylan gazed down at her, his expression solemn even for him. "And you found me. What you said, about wearing too many disguises, was the truth. The only part of me I have known to be real since coming home is the loyal officer, the loyal cousin, but that is not the sum of me. I was a good brother once. I can be again, and, Lydia—"

"There you are!" Marged stood in the front doorway. "Dylan, turn loose of Mrs. Lovelace and, for pity's sake, change into something presentable. You promised to take us back to the British Museum, and Bronnie is already muttering dire threats about brothers who cannot keep straight what day of the week it is. Mrs. Lovelace, good day. I'm sure you will be delighted to have us all out from underfoot for the day, and I, for one, am glad to see some decent weather."

Marged remained in the doorway, hands on hips, all but tapping her foot like an impatient governess. The Powell sisters had recognized "Mrs. Lovelace" as Lady Lydia. Well, fine, then, Lady Lydia she would be.

"Miss Marged, if you would excuse your brother and me for another moment, our business is not yet concluded."

That provoked a faint smile from Dylan. Marged looked from her brother to Lydia, sniffed, and withdrew behind a closed door.

"What are my orders, your ladyship?"

"Find out what Wesley is up to. I promise you this, Dylan, I will not marry that man. I will sign over my settlements to him, I will take Mama to live with Aunt Chloe, and I might even take ship with Marcus, but I cannot marry Wesley Glover." *Not when I love another.*

She left that part unsaid. Dylan had forgiven her for her subterfuges, and she had forgiven him for judging her, but sometimes, forgiveness was not enough.

He took off his disreputable hat and ran a hand through his hair. "I don't want to go to the rubbishing British Museum."

"Then refuse the assignment," Lydia said. "Tell the ladies to recruit one of your cousins, to impose on Mr. Dorning, to put off the outing until you are feeling more the thing. Tell them you need to rest, that a pressing business matter has come up. They are not your commanding officers, Dylan—*you* are your commanding officer now —and the British Museum will sit at the exact same location tomorrow."

Lydia kissed his cheek to soften the sting of her words. She longed to tell his sisters to leave him in peace, but Dylan would have to decide on his own when the time had come to muster out. Lydia took herself down the steps to the kitchen and left Dylan on the walkway, looking rumpled and thoughtful in the morning sun.

CHAPTER SIXTEEN

Dylan escorted his sisters to the blighted British Museum—also to the glovemaker's, Gunter's, and the parasol shop. Tippling parasols were apparently quite the rage in some circles.

Before he did any of that, though, he sent messages to his cousins, and even to Sycamore Dorning. As an afterthought, he included a message to Xavier Fournier, who seemed to have one foot on the genteel side of London's merchant community and another in all manner of unexpected locations.

For two days, Dylan squired his sisters about, though all the while he sought a moment to finish his discussion with Lydia, even as Lydia apparently sought to avoid him.

He had judged her too harshly when he ought not to have judged her at all. She had tried to convey her situation to him, and he had been too intent on charming his way into her bed. She was within her rights to hare off to Shropshire or Aunt Chloe or any bedamned where she chose to go.

Or to send Dylan figuratively to Coventry.

"For you, sir," Bowen said, putting a sealed missive on the blotter of the library desk.

The note was on heavy paper, in an elegant hand Dylan did not recognize, and the message was brief: *WG will be at The Aurora Club this evening as my dinner guest. You will join us. Pressing business shall draw me away from the table before the meal concludes. Fournier.*

The *F* in Fournier was a work of art, all flourishes and swirls, though clearly recognizable. Fournier had gained membership in the club through Goddard's good offices, though Dylan and MacKay had also supported the application.

A favor returned, which made the assistance trustworthy.

"Will there be a reply?" Bowen asked. He was looking more the part of the dapper man of business, less the gaunt and ragged former soldier. Lydia's good care and good meals had done that.

"Not a reply," Dylan said, "though I will send more notes to my cousins." Dylan still could not quite think of Dorning as a cousin, but he'd send word to him too. "I will go out tonight, supper at the Aurora."

"Should I put the men on alert, Captain?"

"No need," Dylan said. "This is a civil meal among gentlemen, and my family will take sentry duty. And, Bowen, you may tell the men that I bear Lord Tremont no ill will. He need not hide from me, and they need not worry that I will call him out."

Bowen looked about the library as if a lot of musty old books had acquired fascinating new qualities.

"The men will be glad to hear that, sir."

A silence arose that begged to be filled with truth. Dylan considered that his sisters knew Lydia's situation, his cousins knew—he'd told them—and Bowen was no fool.

"Tremont is Mrs. Lovelace's younger brother," Dylan said. "She is very concerned for him, and that means..."

Bowen turned his inspection on Dylan, his expression conveying only curiosity. "Yes, sir?"

"That means I have been an ass, and the only way I know to make amends to Mrs. Lovelace is to put things right with her brother.

He's determined to quit England under some cloud of scandal, and there's a cousin stirring the pot, and a title involved, and a bumbling uncle with his fingers in the family coffers... all quite muddled."

Dylan was explaining himself to a subordinate, which in the army never happened, except... He was no longer in the hellishing, rubbishing army and never would be again. Thank the merciful powers.

Stating that to himself changed nothing. He'd sold his commission years ago, but acknowledging the truth—the war was over, the time had come to muster out—left him feeling buoyant with determination. Lydia's brother was also apparently still fighting old battles, or perhaps he'd been taken prisoner by old scandal. Dylan would rescue the earl, and hope Lydia could sort matters from there.

"You'll have to go carefully, sir," Bowen said. "You're good at that, but, Captain?"

Dylan consigned Fournier's little note to the fire. "Yes?"

"You never dealt with Dunacre on his own terms. Never sent him out of camp with a bad map. Never dosed his flask with laudanum on the day of battle. You never lost your temper with him. All the skills you used to such good advantage in the countryside, you never turned on your own superior officer."

"I considered it, considered slow poison, ambush, jamming his pistols, anything to get him relieved of command."

"But you refused to play by his rules, even though he was clearly your enemy. You respected the uniform so much that you nearly let him kill you. Do you recall when Dunacre was laid up with a bout of dysentery?"

"About the happiest two weeks of my military life."

Bowen ambled to the hearth and poked some air into the coals, then added more fuel. "It wasn't dysentery. Will overheard our Frenchie doctor talking about some sort of local mushroom or herb that resulted in a bad case of the Jericho quickstep. As Tremont's batman, Will was in a position to see that Dunacre was laid up."

Dylan thought back, while the mantel clock ticked, and a kitten nosed her way around the library door.

"Dunacre fell ill right after I was stripped of rank."

"Dunacre was that angry you weren't hanged. He wanted you dead, and the men couldn't have that, so we gave your superior officer some time to settle his nerves. I'll send a footman by to collect whatever notes you need to send."

"The *men* decided to poison Dunacre?"

"He sent us into an ambush, Captain, just because he wanted to see you dead, wounded, disgraced, or captured. Something had to be done, and you were too gentlemanly to do it."

Bowen bowed and was halfway to the door before Dylan spoke again.

"Thank you, and please thank the men for me. I wish I'd thought of it myself."

"You had enough skulking about and lurking in haylofts to do. We felt giving you a few weeks' respite was a way to pay back a little of all you'd done for us. Dunacre is the least-mourned superior officer ever to fall on a battlefield. Enjoy your outing, sir."

Bowen left Dylan to the company of the kitten, though his confession wanted pondering. Why hadn't the men alerted Dylan to their scheme? Why hadn't Dylan thought of it? What would Lydia make of Will Brook's behavior, and what would Marcus's philosopher have said about it?

On the one hand, harming a superior officer was contrary to army regulations. On the other, needlessly putting soldiers in harm's way was clearly the greater crime.

Dylan roused himself from such philosophical conundrums and scribbled off notes to the requisite parties. As he wrote, the kitten clawed her way up onto the sofa and hopped to the reading table. The little beast nosed about the books stacked in the center of the table, then perched on her haunches and regarded Dylan with a basilisk stare.

"What?"

The cat closed her eyes. Dylan came around the desk, scooped up the intruder, and took a wing chair by the fire. The kitten was content to be petted, while Dylan needed to think.

"I intended to confront Wesley Glover tonight, ask his intentions, demand explanations, name my seconds if necessary."

Dylan would be honorable, in other words. Wesley Glover, though, was arguably a man who'd betray his cousins, manipulate his father, and extort valuables from a widow, all while presenting himself to Marcus as a loyal and selfless friend.

"Wesley will profess great concern for his aunt and for Lydia," Dylan murmured as the cat began to purr. "He will intimate that he's trying to stay his papa's inebriated hand and suggest that offering for Lydia is the generous act of a marital martyr."

Confronting such a man would be like confronting Dunacre. What followed would invariably be a display of lies from the party confronted, along with twisted facts and wounded dignity, all tied up with a bow of convincing outrage.

"You are absent from your post without leave," Dylan told the kitten as he rose. "I will march you back to camp, and you will suffer the wrath of your commanding officer. She will doubtless pet you soundly for your transgressions and sentence you to supper and a saucer of milk."

Dylan made his way to the kitchen, hoping to find Lydia bustling about as usual. He wanted to discuss the evening's agenda with her, and he wanted to finish what they'd started on the front steps two days ago.

The other kitten was dozing in the basket on the hearth, but Lydia herself was nowhere to be found.

❧

Wesley tried not to gawk, though The Aurora Club was a lovely venue. Understated, scrupulously clean, and both elegant and comfortable. The art was bland landscapes; the decorative scheme was Mayfair male preserve: burgundy red velvet draperies, dark wainscoting, and floral Axminster carpets.

The maître d'hôtel was a dapper fellow of apparent African extraction who projected both welcome and reserve, a skill Wesley would need when he was Earl of Tremont. This club was a wide cut above the glorified drinking venues that had admitted Wesley to their membership, which confirmed for him that matters were indeed moving in the right direction.

Finally.

"Monsieur Fournier awaits you in the lounge," the maître d'hôtel said. "We pride ourselves on our supper menus, Mr. Glover, and I am merely being honest when I tell you that our cellar is the equal of any club in St. James's. I hope you enjoy your evening."

The fellow bowed, not too low, but low enough—that was important—and gestured in the direction of a large, dark-haired gentleman who rose with an outstretched hand.

"Monsieur Glover, welcome. I am honored that you could join me. What is the sense of membership in a club if one cannot show it off to one's friends, eh?"

Fournier had charm, another skill Wesley needed to cultivate for when he had the title. Sybil found Wesley dear—she told him that often enough—but a peer needed to be able to charm his equals, and for a short time at least, Wesley would also have to charm dear Lydia.

Ambition required sacrifices, after all. Fournier introduced Wesley to the other occupants of the lounge. No titles, though some Scottish lordling's heir was among the offerings, as was Sir Orion Somebody, who looked somewhat worse for having served in the military. Sycamore Dorning was an earl's son, though a seventh son, so not much point in cultivating his acquaintance...

But still, the members were an improvement over the squires' puppies and gentry wastrels Wesley was used to hobnobbing about Town with. These were men to whom Wesley did not extend his hand in casual bonhomie. They outranked him socially—for now—and introductions to them were occasions for polite bows.

Even Fournier, who imported a luscious claret and owned at least a few acres, was arguably Wesley's social superior—at the moment. Sybil had introduced Wesley to him and hinted that volume discounts were offered to only the most respected customers.

The wine order of a future earl ought to merit a great deal of respect, not that Wesley would be discussing business over a social meal.

"And this is my dear friend Captain Dylan Powell," Fournier was saying. "Powell, may I make known to you Mr. Wesley Glover, late of Shropshire."

Powell extended a hand, the first to do so. "Come to the Old Smoke for your annual dose of wickedness?" he asked, smiling.

"You're Welsh," Wesley said, the first thing to pop into his head. Powell was a bit weathered, as many former soldiers were, and his handshake was firm and businesslike. He also had the merry eyes and friendly demeanor of the inveterate carouser.

"At least I'm not *French*," Powell said, his smile becoming a grin. "Or worse yet, *American*. I understand you appreciate a good claret, Glover. You must not bring that up over supper, or Fournier will bore you to tears rhapsodizing about grapes and barrels and whatnot. Quite tiresome. Have you treated yourself to a night at Dorning's club yet? If not, I must take you. Elegant surrounds, honest tables, fabulous food, and"—Powell leaned closer—"free champagne after midnight."

"And fine champagne it is too," Fournier said, "but might we continue this discussion at table? Powell, you must join us, lest I descend into rhapsodies about grapes. Lavellais signals us that the table is ready, and we disappoint him at peril to our digestion."

Wesley followed his host and the friendly captain to a private dining room. The door remained open, the better to allow a procession of waiters into and out of the room. The wine was quite good, the food exquisite, and the banter Powell and Fournier exchanged witty and ever so slightly naughty.

Wesley cut off another bite of perfectly delectable rare steak and congratulated himself on matters proceeding according to an excellent plan. By this time next year, Marcus could be declared dead, and Wesley would no longer be simply Mr. Glover, late of Shropshire.

He'd be the Tremont heir, complete with a courtesy title, and these lovely gentlemen would consider themselves lucky to have made his acquaintance. He'd acknowledge them—no need to be arrogant—but his companions of choice would become other heirs, peers, and the occasional comely Society widow with a good ear for gossip.

"Have some more wine," Powell said as Fournier excused himself to confer with a footman in the corner. "Fournier pays attention to who appreciates his vintages."

"Thank you, Captain. Why is it you're not enjoying springtime in Wales? I'm told the Welsh countryside is nearly as lovely as what Shropshire has to offer."

Fournier returned to the table and covered himself with apologies as only a member of the merchant class could. The press of business, an urgent matter having to do with a missing shipment, French effusions, a request that Powell take over the role of host, and then Fournier was gone.

"So dramatic," Powell said, filling Wesley's glass with first-rate claret. "Let's drink a health to Fournier's business, shall we?"

The captain lifted his own glass and winked, and the toasts began. Wesley kept pace with the former soldier, and soon the captain had ordered another bottle.

The mellow glow of good wine and good fortune spread over Wesley, for what in life could be more cheering than merry companionship, a happy and inventive mistress, and the prospect of a title looming close at hand?

❧

Dylan's old skills were still in good repair, much to his relief.

He knew which smile to give Glover, which innuendo to leave hanging in the air. He drank—or appeared to drink—at just the right pace to ensure Glover's good spirits, not fast enough to inebriate, and by careful degrees, he allowed silences to crop up in the conversation.

Wesley Glover bore a resemblance to Lydia and Marcus, around the eyes, about the nose. His bearing was that of the dandy, loose-limbed and subtly arrogant. Preening, always peering about to see who was looking at him.

"Let's move to the reading room, shall we?" Dylan said. "Let the menials tidy up in here while we get serious about our libation."

"You mentioned the Coventry," Glover said. "The hour approaches midnight. Shall we stop by?"

Dylan pretended to consider the suggestion. "One more bottle, then we'll collect MacKay and try our hand at the Coventry's tables. MacKay scares away the footpads, and he knows all the ladies."

This was true. Alasdhair MacKay was also ferociously protective of the streetwalkers and would cheerfully geld Dylan if he allowed Glover to bother them.

"I do enjoy the company of the ladies," Glover said, following Powell into the dim interior of the reading room. By arrangement, Goddard was pretending to nap over in a shadowed corner, while Dorning and MacKay would be in the lounge directly across the corridor.

"Life in the country can quickly grow tedious," Dylan said, gesturing to two chairs before the fire. When the footman came in to toss another scoop of coal on the flames, Dylan ordered a bottle of port. "All that goodwill in the churchyard, the quarterly assemblies, the interminable social calls. Give me a friendly lightskirts, and I'm a happy man."

"Oh, exactly," Wesley said. "And since when do hounds and crops ever qualify as interesting topics of conversation? An outlandish wager, a bloody cockfight, a curricle race with at least a crash or two, and I consider myself entertained."

Dylan remained silent until the port had arrived, then graciously offered the bottle to his guest. Glover was not hard to read, but then, he doubtless took himself to be in safe surrounds. Lydia's cousin was deep into enemy territory, did he but know it, and about to be taken captive by hostile forces.

"We occasionally have a bit of scandal back home," Dylan said, pouring himself a very scant portion of wine. "The squire's son is off to be a gamekeeper in Scotland because his attempt to compromise the local belle ran amok."

"And now the squire's son must always look over his shoulder," Glover said, taking a deep drink. "That's the best part of scandal, when you know the particulars, and know upon whom the scandal might land. This is quite good wine."

"The Aurora Club serves only excellent libation. Even the ale is impressive. Don't suppose there is a noteworthy scandal in Shropshire that sends you to kick your heels in London?"

Dylan saw the moment when Glover's shrewder instincts took exception to the question, followed by the next moment, when drink, overconfidence, and inexperience got the better of him.

"I will tell you a secret, Powell," Glover said, glancing at the supposedly sleeping Goddard. "Any man who has womenfolk—mothers, sisters, wives, daughters—is vulnerable to bad fortune. For those of us with some brains, that can mean good fortune."

Dylan arranged his features into an expression of slightly fuddled interest. "Because the ladies lead the unsuspecting astray?"

"They do, don't they? But I meant more than a lady's good name makes her vulnerable to threats of scandal, and that makes her menfolk vulnerable to all manner of stupidity."

"War is all manner of stupid," Dylan observed, peering owlishly at his drink. "Damned near got me killed twenty times over."

"War is useful," Glover countered. "I am all but heir to an earl because I knew how to use both scandal and wartime to my advantage."

If Dylan appeared too eager to hear details, Glover would grow reticent, and three hours of calculated bonhomie and careful manipulation would be for naught. If Dylan showed too little interest in Glover's boasts, Glover would similarly keep the details to himself.

Keep away, and come hither.

"You developed some clever strategy," Dylan said. "Any man who bought his colors appreciates effective strategy. Wellington is above all a brilliant strategist."

Glover leaned nearer, his breath redolent of spirits. "A fellow stood between me and my objective. Not a bad fellow, but not too bright. Honorable heart, empty head. You know the type. He would never have been happy with the title. I arranged a situation where the honorable fellow felt compelled to call another gentleman out. Unbeknownst to the dear boy, I'd provided the combatants with pistols that did not shoot precisely straight."

Glover gestured with his drink. "Poor lad thinks himself a dead shot to this day—and he is—but he also thinks he killed a man, which he did not. A bladder of chicken blood, an opponent clutching at his chest, a farce worthy of Drury Lane. It was utterly magnificent. Then I, exuding concern and woe, hustled my honorable friend off to buy his colors. He's still terrified that he's one step ahead of a murder warrant, and I am that much closer to the title. I should not be telling you this, but really, for the enterprising and the bold, these things are not complicated."

"I am impressed," Dylan said, summoning every ounce of his skill at duplicity. "How on earth did you provoke this poor widgeon into dueling?"

"Attend me, Powell, for I am about to explain my earlier claim." Glover's glance went to the open door, but he did not rise to close it. "Any man with sisters is vulnerable to provocation in this regard—any honorable man. This fellow had an older sister. Sheltered and yet, also virtually unsupervised, and pulling hard at the reins of propriety. We deployed a bit of strong punch—well, more than a bit—and some practiced flirtation. She succumbed in the manner of headstrong women since Eve sampled the apple. The hapless brother was allowed to catch wind of the dishonor to his sister, and the rest was child's play, my dear captain. Child's play for a future earl."

Dylan's heart broke for Lydia, whose fall from paragon-hood had been engineered for such a vile purpose. He nonetheless affixed an admiring expression to his features and saluted with his glass.

"What became of your accomplice in this little drama?"

Glover sat back and grinned. "Kicking his heels in Sussex, hoping nobody accuses him of rape while he waits for his papa to expire. The law will bring charges up to twenty-one years after an offense of that nature. I checked and suggested he might want to avoid Shropshire for what remained of his natural life. He'll keep his mouth shut, as will the young lady who inadvertently made my prospects so much more pleasant. I'll ruin her if she turns up difficult, and while she won't mind being ruined, her mama would be devastated."

Lydia would face marriage to Wesley or ruin at his hands, if Wesley's cleverness went unchecked. "What of the widgeon? Did the French dispatch him for you?"

"No, which is a mercy for my delicate conscience. He's off to America, gaining a fresh start and avoiding the near occasion of the hangman's noose, or so he believes. I'll have him declared dead in another year or two. He'll be much happier as a shop clerk or school-teacher, believe me. Always spouting Cicero or some other dead Roman. No fool like a learned fool, I suppose. He ought to be thanking me."

"You are ambitious," Dylan said. "I do admire ambition in a man."

"I'm ambitious, clever, and brave. Takes some nerve to execute a plan as I have. A military man ought to appreciate that."

"Oh, I do," Dylan said. "I commend you on your ambition, clever-ness, and bravery, but are you also lucky, Glover?"

"I must be," Glover said. "I ended up sharing supper with you, didn't I? You seem a good sort, Powell, trustworthy and so on."

"I was trustworthy to a fault in the army. Much given to following orders, observing protocol, and doing my duty. Thank God I've resigned my commission. What say we head to the Coventry and place some outrageous bets?"

"I'll drink the free champagne, you place the bets," Glover said, pushing to his feet and weaving a bit. "I daresay some cool night air is in order to clear my head, and where does a fellow take a piss around here?"

Dylan was tempted—so tempted—to indicate that a fellow stepped around to the alley, where—while his breeches were unbuttoned and his guard down—he'd have the piss beaten out of him.

But no. Lydia's orders were to get to the bottom of the situation. Dylan would, in this much, follow orders and report back to headquarters as he'd assured her he would. First, though, he would ensure Wesley Glover gambled away every groat the bleating scoundrel possessed. Dorning would buy up the resulting vowels, and Dylan would own them—and Glover—by sunset tomorrow.

Lydia stepped out of the post-chaise, every muscle and bone in her body rejoicing to be free of the conveyance. For two days, over the course of one hundred and fifty miles, she'd endured bouncing, bruising, and bad food.

She felt no sense of homecoming as she beheld the moonlit splendor of Tremont's stately façade, no relief. Marcus was leaving England in a week's time, and Mama at least deserved to wish her son farewell.

Mama herself came down the grand front steps, her step for once not quite graceful. "Lydia, my dear, you are home." Her hug was surprisingly fierce. "Are you well?"

"I am well," Lydia said, stepping back, "and I have much to tell you that I did not want to entrust to the mails. You must pack at once and prepare for a hasty journey to London. We leave in the morning." The thought of another two days in more post-chaises was daunting, but Lydia saw no alternative.

"Tell me of Marcus. Did you find him?"

Uncle Reginald emerged from the house, and in the short time Lydia had been away, he'd put on weight and aged. His progress down the front steps was careful, as if his knees troubled him, or as if his balance was unsteady.

"You are coming to London with me to shop for new frocks," Lydia said, keeping her voice down. "Time to catch up on the latest fashions and call on some old friends."

Mama studied her as Uncle reached the foot of the steps. "I would rather not leave Tremont, Lydia. Somebody must maintain order in your absence, and dear Reggie was relying on Wesley rather more than he should have been."

Mama was sweet and kind and quiet. She could also be prodigiously stubborn.

"If you ever want to see your only son again, you are leaving for London with me in the morning."

That got Mama's attention. "You've found him? You've found our Marcus?"

Either the coded letter Lydia had sent had yet to arrive, or Uncle had waylaid it. He appeared reluctant to set foot on the drive, or perhaps he needed to keep a hand on the banister to remain upright this late in the day.

"Come home at last, Lydia?" he called. "Your mama's been pining for you, and I daresay you've been on holiday long enough."

"I found Marcus," Lydia whispered as the post-chaise pulled away, "but he refuses to come home."

"I will write to him." Mama linked her arm through Lydia's. "I will send him an express. I am so glad to have you home, Lydia, and so pleased that you bring good news. I cannot convey to you clearly enough the weight you have lifted from my heart."

She began walking Lydia toward the house, while Uncle waited at the foot of the steps, a dark shape obscured by moon-shadows.

"Mama, you cannot tell Uncle about Marcus. You must not."

"Reginald is the acting head of this family for now. Maybe he can talk Marcus into coming home. He loves Marcus like a son."

Lydia freed her arm from her mother's grasp. "You do not believe that. You want to believe that, but you are lying to yourself."

Mama's posture became subtly more upright.

"Liddie," Uncle called, "are you haranguing your dear mama already? Do get inside, girl. The night air is not healthy for a woman of mature years. If you must be so rude as to show up at such a late hour, no notice to anybody, then you will at least have the decency to not tarry in the driveway."

"I will come tuck you in," Mama said, somewhat stiffly. "You will want a bath after your travels, and I will stop by your room to ensure you are well settled here at home."

Why won't you listen to me? Lydia wanted to shout the words and physically shake her mother, but Uncle Reggie had already started a ponderous ascent of the steps, and he would doubtless wait by the door until Lydia had accompanied Mama inside.

By the time Lydia was in the bedroom she'd occupied since girl-hood, and she'd had a short soak in tepid water, she had rehearsed a speech worthy of Mr. Burke on the subject of free trade.

Mama arrived a quarter hour later, already attired for bed. "I am glad to have you home, Lydia," she said, hovering in the bedroom doorway. "I missed you."

Mama looked as serene and pretty as always, but Lydia had learned to observe more closely and to listen more carefully.

"You worried that, like Marcus, I might not come back. I was tempted, Mama, but because of Marcus's situation, I betrayed the trust of a man for whom I might well have turned my back on Tremont. You are coming to London with me in the morning—I've already arranged for the post-chaise—and you will not go running to Reggie with what I have to tell you now."

"Did London turn you up churlish, Lydia?"

Had Lydia not kept house for Dylan Powell, had she not seen one soldier after another grappling with the challenge of life in London, had she not seen the mean little room where Marcus bided, she might have apologized to Mama and retreated into guilt. She instead advanced on her mother, and tugged her gently into the room.

"Wesley is in London, Mama," she said, pulling the door closed. "He's dressed to the nines, preparing to put Marcus on a ship bound for America. I saw Marcus, and he was adamant that he will not come home. Unless I miss my guess, your jewelry has been financing Wesley's excesses, and you never said a word to me or Uncle Reggie about what amounts to extortion. Why?"

Mama sank onto the bed. "Wesley is young. All young men over-spend their allowances. I never wear much jewelry these days."

"So you will allow an intemperate bully to inherit Papa's title? You will meekly hand over a fortune to Wesley while he ruins Marcus's future?"

"Marcus is doubtless doing as he thinks best, Lydia. I never wanted him to join up. Never thought he was suited to an officer's life. He was just a boy..."

Lydia paced before the hearth, steeling herself for Mama's tears. Mama had perfected the art of crying without turning all blotchy and sniffly.

"Marcus was older than some who bought their colors, Mama, and he came through the war safely enough. Toss his future away if you must, but please do not toss mine aside as well." The words and the determination behind them surprised Lydia—not so long ago, she'd been contemplating marriage to Wesley as a means of saving Tremont.

Dylan Powell had determination to spare, as did, Lydia suspected, his cousins and sisters.

Mama used the sleeve of her robe to dab at her eyes. "You have adequate settlements, Lydia. You will never want for anything. Why must you be dramatic? I'm sure Marcus merely wants a little more time to sort himself out. Travel can do that for us, give us a new perspective."

Lydia came to a halt beside the bed. "Mama, you and Papa had

some good years. He was the love of your life, and you were his
dearest lady. Wesley will use whatever he knows of Marcus's situation to force me to the altar. I want what you had with Papa. If I
could have even a few years of what you had with Papa..."

Lydia never would have that blessing. She'd used up that chance
when she'd abused Dylan's trust, but this argument alone might
inspire Mama to act.

"I loved your father so much," Mama said, staring at her embroidered slippers. "I ask myself, what would my John make of this situation? Reginald turning into a sot? Wesley demanding my jewelry?
You forced into service in an effort to find your brother? It's all quite...
wrong."

"For me to marry Wesley would be wrong, Mama. For Marcus to
run away from home is wrong. He's grown taller and more serious,
though he's still quoting his philosophers."

And those philosophers had not been any defense against
Wesley's schemes. Lydia sat on the bed beside her mother, the
memory of Marcus's sad little room landing like a blow to her heart.
The Earl of Tremont, reduced to that... Why? What had that bit of
ancient history with Finchly to do with anything?

Lydia thought again of Dylan, who'd found Marcus for her,
despite their differences.

"I liked being a housekeeper, Mama. Liked earning my own
wages, liked making a contribution to a household. I cannot marry
Wesley, and I cannot answer for what Wesley will do when I refuse
his threats."

Mama was quiet for a moment, and Lydia entertained the notion
that her journey back to London would be solitary, so why make that
journey at all?

"Do you know why I fell in love with your father?"

"He was handsome and charming?"

"He was not bad looking, true, and he had a good sense of humor,
but I fell in love with him despite myself. I was an heiress—*the
Lovelace heiress*—and thus I had offers, Lydia. My parents sorted

through those offers and decided on John. He was in line for an old, respected title, and he would come into this lovely family seat."

"But?"

"But I had danced with him exactly twice. He was so much taller than I that we were not ideal partners. He found that humorous, while I... I was mortified. Young people are easily mortified."

Why had Lydia never heard this story before? Why had she never asked for it? "You and Papa did not get on well?"

"We did not get off on the right foot, put it that way, but then the elders started matchmaking, and neither John nor I had any say in the matter, or so I thought. The settlement negotiations were well under way when John called upon me one day."

Lydia mentally clapped her hands over her ears, because an engaged couple was allowed significant latitude, and some things about one's parents should remain private.

"Papa swept you off your feet?"

"Not in the sense you mean. He sat a proper twelve inches away from me on a garden bench and told me that if the match was not to my liking, I was to refuse him. I was not to be bullied into marriage, or persuaded or herded or in any way coerced just because I was an heiress.

"English law does not allow forced marriages," Mama went on. "John told me what my parents and all the solicitors had failed to mention. He told me that much of my money was mine—tied up in trusts, but *mine*—and my parents could not control it. He told me the truth, Lydia. He alone told me the truth and took my part even when that might have cost him dearly in both coin and familial accord."

Mama dabbed at her eyes again. "I am like Marcus in some ways. Smart enough, but not quick, not confident of my conclusions. I nonetheless realized that John was the fellow I had to marry. He cared for me, he was honest, and he did *not* care about my money half so much as he valued his honor."

"And that swept you off your feet?"

Mama smiled, a hint of mischief shining through. "He was also charming, but after his little speech in the garden, I rather swept him off his feet. You should not have to marry Wesley, and I think I know how he's hounding Marcus from home. Do you recall a certain Lieutenant Finchly? Dapper young fellow in his regimentals, a friend of Wesley's?"

Oh dear. "He and Wesley were more than acquaintances?"

"Purported to be, though Finchly and Marcus got into some sort of disagreement, and there was a duel. Ladies are not supposed to know of these things. I was in the deer park having a morning constitutional, and one cannot ignore the sound of gunfire at close range. Finchly fell—Marcus was handy with a gun even at that age—and the next thing I knew, Marcus was buying his colors, and Reginald was allowing it. I suspected foul play on Wesley's part, and I always have."

"But that was years ago," Lydia said slowly. "Why do you think an old difference of opinion haunts Marcus after all this time?" Men dueled all the time, and titled men were practically immune from prosecution. "Did Finchly die?"

"I heard nothing to that effect at the time, and Mrs. Bloom would certainly have apprised me of such news."

"Then why would young men acting like fools years ago be relevant?"

"I suspect this unfortunate business still matters for two reasons," Mama said, "though it took me some time to puzzle them out. First, Wesley was Marcus's second. Seconds are supposed to try to stop the duel, with an apology, with some appeal to reason, any honorable way they can. Marcus held the title even then, while Finchly was a commoner. Had Wesley pointed that out to Marcus, there would have been no duel. Marcus believes in codes of honor, as his papa did, and seconds are expected to know and enforce the rules."

"And the *Code Duello* does not allow men of unequal station to duel," Lydia said slowly. "Wesley had come down from university by then. You are right that he would have known the rules, while

Marcus at that age would not. What is the second reason you suspect foul play?"

"Marcus would not have shot to kill, and yet, Finchly fell. Modern dueling pistols are more accurate than the antique variety, and your brother practiced his marksmanship incessantly. Finchly might have suffered a passing wound, but Marcus would never have intentionally taken his life."

"You think Wesley tampered with the guns?" A risky ploy, if the intention was to see Finchly murdered, but perhaps the intention had been to see *Marcus* murdered?

"I don't know what to think, Lydia, and as long as Marcus's name did not appear on a casualty list, I did not have to think anything. I could plan the village fete and miss your father, and life was bearable."

Bearable. Lydia was no longer willing to settle for a bearable life, if that meant more extortion, bullying, manipulation, and loneliness at Tremont.

"Before I left London," Lydia said, "a man I hardly know offered to serve as my reinforcements. He was sincere, if a bit... forward. I should have been your reinforcements, Mama. I should have stopped Wesley from bothering you. I should have forced Uncle Reggie to show me the books. You have worried for Marcus in ways beyond what even any mother with a son at war must bear, and all the while..."

Mama took her hand. "All the while, you have been running this house, quietly directing a staff that could not look to me for orders. You have been preventing the worst of Reggie's stupidity, and then I sent you off to London alone, because I did not dare... I am sorry, Lydia."

"You owe me no apologies, Mama. Marcus and Finchly were dueling over Finchly's behavior with me. I am nearly certain that this is all my fault." And with that conclusion came a crushing weight of guilt. This duel had to be what Marcus had meant when he'd alluded to Lydia not understanding the particulars.

"Don't be ridiculous, Lydia. I knew Finchly turned your head. I knew he was a rascal—all of Wesley's friends are rascals. I also knew you were a typical young lady with a lively sense of inquisitiveness, and sooner or later, you would indulge your curiosity. Had I been more vigilant... But I wasn't. Now you ask me to go to London, and it occurs to me that you need reinforcements too. That's why you came here, isn't it? Because you hoped I could convince Marcus to come home?"

Well, yes, though it was a forlorn hope in light of recent revelations. "I wanted you to see him again, even if only to say farewell. If Marcus killed a man in a duel, then we can hardly ask him to stay in England."

Mama was quiet for a time, while Lydia's thoughts ran riot. A duel... That explained much, but as Mama had said, it did not explain everything. How had Marcus learned of Finchly's lapse with Lydia? Finchly would not have been stupid enough to boast of such a thing to Lydia's own brother, would he?

The only possible conduit for that information was Wesley —again.

"To London, then," Mama said, rising. "We will be away hours before Reginald awakens, and that means I must pack."

"The post-chaise will be out front by seven of the clock," Lydia said, trailing Mama to the door. "You need not bring much, though a hamper of decent food would be a very good idea."

"To leave Tremont..." Mama regarded Lydia. "I suppose it's past time." She again hugged Lydia in that surprisingly firm grasp. "I always fretted over Marcus, because I know what it is to be surrounded by people who can think quickly and who seem to know how to go on. I should have fretted more over you, my dear." She slipped through the door and was gone.

In the ensuing silence, Lydia battled an unaccountable urge to cry—yes, she had longed for maternal reinforcements. Yes, she wished in hindsight that her mother's vigilance might have prevented that stupid interlude with Finchly. Perhaps she'd been trying to gain

Mama's notice with her outrageous behavior, but none of that signified now.

Morning would come all too soon, and the journey back to London would be wearying at best. Lydia ordered herself to bed, though she had much less success ordering herself to fall asleep.

CHAPTER SEVENTEEN

"Good morning, Betty." Dylan had come down to the kitchen after breakfast, determined to flush Lydia from her covert. "Might you direct me to Mrs. Lovelace?"

The kitchen maid paused in her kneading of a large, pale batch of dough. "Mrs. Lovelace is gone two days now, Captain. I thought she told you. She left me menus, all recipes I know how to cook."

"Gone?"

The kittens were curled up in their basket, the air was redolent of bacon and toast, and morning sunshine poured through the window. Dylan noted those details with the part of his mind that was always on alert, while another part of him howled in despair.

"Gone where?"

"Bowen might know. Something about a family matter. She left London, I know that much. Took a valise and left two days past at the crack of doom." Betty went back to her kneading. "She would scold you for being in the kitchen, sir."

Don't be insubordinate. Dylan kept that retort behind his teeth, because first, Betty was right, and second, she was not a recruit new to her uniform such that an accurate, factual observation should earn her a rebuke.

Dylan did an about-face, took the stairs two at a time, and shouted for Bowen, who emerged from his office with a cup of tea in his hand.

"What's amiss, sir?"

"Lydia—Mrs. Lovelace—has deserted the regiment." Or had she mustered out? Sold her commission? Put aside her caps and aprons once and for all? "Do you have any idea where she's gone?"

Bowen beckoned Dylan into his office. "I keep an eye on the post, because I hope to hear from Will. I almost hope he finds a good position in Portsmouth, sir, but you asked about Mrs. Lovelace."

"She's been gone two days," Dylan said, kicking himself for thinking Lydia was merely keeping her distance. She would not blow retreat merely to gather her composure. She seldom lost her composure, though Dylan was fast losing his. "How could I not realize she'd left the house?"

"Your sisters have kept you busy," Bowen observed. "All I can tell you about Mrs. Lovelace is that she sent a note to Mr. Dorning at the start of the week."

Dorning? Why *Dorning*? "Can you be more precise?"

"You'd come back from seeing Lord Tremont, I believe, and she asked me to post the letter for her. She has so little correspondence that I found her request somewhat unusual."

Dylan paced the small confines of Bowen's office, a cheery space, Lydia's touch evident in the bouquet of tulips on the mantel and in some flowery, golden and green embroidery along the hem of the lacy curtains.

"You are certain she did not correspond with Mrs. Dorning?"

"I know of only one gent named Sycamore in the whole of England, sir. The note was for Mr. Dorning."

Profanity came to mind in at least two languages. "Thank you for telling me. If my sisters ask, please inform them urgent business has demanded my immediate attention."

Bowen gave him the same look Dylan had often received from soldiers assigned to Dunacre's personal escort, equal parts resentment and resignation.

"Perhaps you can tell them that yourself." He pointed to the doorway, where Bronwen stood, a bonnet in one hand and a parasol in the other.

"We're walking in the park this morning," she said. "The day is too fine to spend cooped up inside, and Tegan and Marged are talking about a picnic at Richmond later in the day. You will escort us, of course."

Bowen maintained a diplomatic silence, while Dylan's internal stream of invective threatened to become audible.

"I'm sorry," he said, "I am not available to squire you ladies about today. Bowen will be happy to fulfill that office, I'm sure."

Bronwen advanced into the small office. "You are our brother. You are our host. Whatever gossip at the club, whatever damned horse auction, or—"

"Bronnie, Lydia has left."

Bronwen's ire deflated into an expression of consternation. "Of course she left. She's an earl's daughter, and she should never have been in service here in the first place. I gather you don't get on with her brother, and she loves her brother, so off she goes. *Some* people grasp the concept of sibling loyalty."

Dylan stared at his baby sister, who was spoiling for a fight, spoiling for a rousing set-to, when Lydia had all but gone missing.

Bronwen glowered at him, her parasol clutched in a tight grip. She'd whack him with it at the least provocation, but Dylan hadn't the time to indulge her.

"You wanted for nothing," he said. "You visit Town when you please to do so, and you fire off your disappointments at me as if they could not be put into a letter or conveyed by message. You are not cut off from all supply lines in Wales, Bronnie. You know where I am, and you know that I bide in London for reasons that matter."

"To carouse with Goddard and MacKay," she sniffed. "To gossip at Horse Guards, to—"

"That is not fair, miss." Bowen had spoken quietly, which spiked Bronwen's guns more effectively than had Dylan ranted at her.

"I was left for dead in an alley," Bowen went on, "half freezing in the dratted rain, the wits kicked out of me, but I knew there was one place I could go, for safety, for help. The captain doesn't gossip at Horse Guards, he doesn't carouse, he doesn't even have dinner at the club unless his cousins drag him out for a night. He remains here, on duty, and God be thanked for that, because Merry Olde England has little enough use now for the men who bested Napoleon."

Bronwen gaped at Bowen, who'd lost any pretense of the soft-spoken humble fellow grateful for his post. The sharpshooter who'd marched across Spain had taken aim at her, and she had sense enough not to return fire.

"I have felt useful here," Dylan said, "and I have missed my sisters, but I also knew I was needed in London. Right now, I need to find out where Lydia has got off to."

"Why?" Bronwen ask, though her tone was curious rather than accusing.

"Because..." Because Lydia was carrying on alone when she need not. When she should not and must not. "Because I have information she deserves to know. Important information."

Bronwen withdrew a folded and sealed missive from a pocket. "I found this on your pillow earlier in the week."

Dylan took the letter. "Snooping, Bronnie?"

"I wanted to see what art you keep in your bedroom, because I thought you might like a painting of the home place if you didn't already have one. You have no art in your bedroom at all, Dylan. What sort of Welshman are you?"

A lonely one. "I am a Welshman with much to do today. Please make my apologies to Tegan and Marged."

Bronwen gave him a brooding perusal. "Was Bowen truly in a bad way?"

Bowen gazed out the office window, having apparently said his piece.

"Most of my former subordinates have had a difficult adjustment to civilian life. Too many soldiers came home at the same time, after too long of an absence. They found no jobs, no place to live, many of their old trades have been obliterated by manufactories. Some fellows arrived home ill in spirit or dealing with old wounds... I have been needed here, Bronwen."

"You are needed at home too, Dylan." On that parting shot, she left.

"The ladies have their weapons, don't they?" Bowen asked. "Best read what Mrs. Lovelace has to say, sir."

"Right." Dylan took heart from the fact that Lydia had not crept away in the night, no word to him at all. He still wanted privacy to read her message. "Will you please see that my sisters don't start a riot in Hyde Park or storm Richmond?"

Bowen's lips twitched. "Miss Bronwen carries a sword parasol, sir. So does Miss Tegan. Miss Marged's parasol contains a peashooter. Some ducal fribble designed those fripperies, and they are all quite the rage."

Lydia would adore...

"Excuse me," Dylan said, brandishing her letter. "And, Bowen, my thanks. I was about to verbally cut loose with my sister, and she comes quite well armed to the battle of wits. That could not have ended well."

Bowen gave him a brisk salute. "Glad to oblige, sir."

Dylan crossed to the library, closed the door, and took the seat behind the library desk. He tried slowing his breathing. He tried picturing the rolling hills of the Welsh countryside. He tried reciting the 23rd Psalm in Welsh, but nothing would calm his racing heart.

He slit the seal on Lydia's note, having no idea what he'd find.

My thanks for all you've done for me and for my brother. I will send for my things when matters are settled with Lord Tremont. Love, Lydia.

A farewell, then. A polite, even gracious farewell. Dylan knew firsthand what it was to be kicked by a mule, and Lydia's good-bye had the same quality. Equal parts stunning and painful, with painful gaining ground by the moment.

Well, hell. Bloody, bedamned, perishing... Dylan sat in the reading chair behind the desk, seeing nothing, thinking nothing, while the sound of women bustling about came to him from elsewhere in the house. *I will send for my things...* That was something. Lydia would have to send for her things from somewhere, and Dylan could track her to that location and perhaps... but no.

She'd said thanks and good-bye as effectively as polite language allowed. Mustered out. Hung up her housekeeper's spurs and to blazes with stubborn Welsh captains too stupid to see...

Rubbishing, sulfurous, flaming perdition. He read the letter—so brief and unsentimental.

Then his eye caught on the final two words. *Love, Lydia.*

Love.

Love?

The great philosopher had had no particular wisdom to impart for when a man had made a complete hash out of everything and must—tail between his legs—leave the land and people he'd fought for. Marcus thumbed through his Latin version of *The Meditations,* searching in vain for some comfort, some perspective on the confusion that his life had become.

A thump on the door startled him half off of his chair, though at least nobody saw that reaction. No Dunacre on hand to laugh uproariously when Marcus had flinched at distant gunfire, to stick out a foot to trip him in the odd moment, to order him to empty the damned chamber pot like some spotty subaltern.

"Coming," Marcus called, noting the page number at which he'd stopped reading.

He opened the door without peeking, which William Brook had told him was the height of stupidity, but what did it matter if the watch, the archangel Michael, or Old Scratch himself had come to call? In a few days, Marcus would leave England, and that...

He was unhappy about that, and all the quotations in the world could not soothe his unhappiness away. He was leaving Lydia and Mama. Papa had told him that the whole of Tremont and the whole of England mattered naught, compared to keeping Lydia and Mama safe and happy.

"Wesley, good day." When had Wesley become such a dandy, and why didn't he know that fancy dress was a beacon for the pick-pockets?

"I know not what's good about it," Wesley said, sauntering into Marcus's room, "when I must call upon you at this detestable privy of a domicile, but such is my familial loyalty that here I am."

"And I am glad to see you." Marcus had been gladder to see Lydia, also horrified. Lydia had been her same self, entirely composed, articulate, and absolutely sure of herself. She should have been the earl, a thought that had plagued Marcus since her visit.

She had been herself, while Marcus had been a far less worthy brother than she deserved.

"You will be more glad to see this," Wesley said, producing a folded sheet of paper from a breast pocket of his morning coat. "This is your ticket of passage on the *Rebecca Louise*, bound for Philadelphia. You leave at week's end, assuming tide and weather permit. You will be done forever with this ghastly room in this beastly neighborhood and all the wretchedness that goes with it."

Wesley beamed at Marcus, while Marcus scanned the ticket. "I'm to travel in *steerage*?"

"It's only for a few weeks, dear boy, and you will attract less notice that way."

"I will attract foul miasmas and diseases that way, Wesley. Please see if second-class passage is available, and if not..."

Marcus considered waiting until another ship sailed, London being one of the busiest ports in the world.

"At this late date," Wesley retorted, "I can promise you no better berth will be available. Either you want to put the past behind you and start a new life, or you want to die in disgrace at the end of a rope, the title attainted, the earldom's wealth forfeited to that mincing buffoon we call our monarch. I'm profoundly sorry to be so blunt, but those are your options, dear boy."

Wesley's *profound* remorse was a subtle thing, if it existed, but then, Marcus had relied on Wesley far more than was typical even between cousins. Wesley was doubtless tired of dealing with Marcus and his troubles.

"Did you bring the coin?" Marcus asked, rather than antagonize his cousin further.

Wesley pulled a face. "That is taking a bit more time. Banks hate to part with the ready. Never fear that I'll have what you ask before you sail." Wesley unscrewed the handle of his ebony walking stick and extracted a tiny silver cup and an oblong silver flask.

He poured himself a portion, downed it, and offered a second serving to Marcus, who refused.

"Out of the habit of consuming decent libation?" Wesley asked, reassembling his accessory. "I suppose soldiering doesn't exactly refine the tastes, does it? And you will soon no longer be the earl, so what good are refined tastes to you anyway?"

Wesley offered a cheery smile with that observation, and Marcus remained silent. He had learned to remain silent around Dunacre, to avoid at least the verbal traps, unless Dunacre ordered him to answer. If the answer involved a regulation, Marcus could quote relevant military writ, chapter and verse.

If the answer involved anything else, Marcus had learned that only flattery and fawning distracted Dunacre from his tirades.

Wesley was reminding Marcus increasingly of Dunacre, oddly enough. Cheerful about the wrong things, very slow to attend to what few tasks he could not delegate, and disrespectful of protocol, as a mean boy breaks rules to see if anybody will scold him.

That bit with the cane-flask, for example. Wesley should have offered Marcus the first drink. Papa had said that manners were at heart a display of consideration for others, not just some list of rules to be memorized. Mama had said the same thing, probably quoting Papa.

"I have wondered," Marcus said slowly, "if the title ought not to be attainted. If I ought not to stand trial and endure the consequences of my actions."

Wesley looked up from screwing together his cane, his expression devoid of all good humor. "Have you parted with what few wits the Deity bestowed upon you? I care not what old Pompous Aurelius said about taking one's lumps, dear boy. He hadn't your mama and sister to consider, or an uncle who has spent years attending to your properties without a word of thanks from you."

Wesley stalked over to him, the cane still in two pieces. "And this great display of stupidity on your part would accomplish exactly what, Marcus? Finchly fell on the field of honor, as he deserved to fall. Executing you for the entertainment of the mob can't undo that. You can't undo that Lydia allowed him unspeakable liberties. You can't undo that your mama would die of mortification if she knew any of the details. Put away your childish yearning for drama and be grateful there's a place for you on the *Rebecca Louise*."

Once upon a time, Dunacre had come down with dysentery. He'd been too weak to leave his tent and too incapacitated by loose bowels to even don his uniform. He'd turned up all sweet and sincere for those two weeks, politely asking Marcus to read him the dispatches, to carry reports to headquarters that made no mention of Dunacre's illness.

He'd thanked Marcus and offered him confidences that had been, in fact, simply fears and opinions.

The day the illness had passed, Dunacre had gone back to his schoolboy nastiness, tripping Marcus, referring to him as My Lord

Lacypants, and comparing him with casual cruelty to the far more accomplished Captain Powell.

"Powell would never have missed that shot."

"Powell could have ridden straight though."

"The lady would have offered Powell much more than a smile."

Marcus would have hated Powell, except that Dunacre had hated Powell, and that was penance enough for any officer.

"If justice involves a certain element of drama," Marcus said, "then that is to better inspire proper behavior from those observing the punishment. I took Finchly's life, and I was denied an honorable death in Spain. I am troubled by the notion that I have avoided justice, Wesley, as any gentleman would be."

"You bloody choirboy," Wesley said, recovering his good cheer as he screwed together the parts of his cane. "Justice is what Finchly got for trifling with Lydia. I know you are easily confused, but do try to keep your facts straight. You were the instrument of justice when you dropped him, discreet justice, because a lady's good name was at risk. Stop thinking of your grand philosophies and think instead of Lydia and Auntie Caroline. Think of old Reggie, and if those good people cannot inspire you to take ship as you ought, think of me."

And there was the problem. Marcus longed to end this discussion and take himself down to the Goose, where he could order a pint and park his arse at a corner table, there to while away the afternoon with the whores and old sailors. When the post came, they'd all gather 'round while Marcus read them the latest news from somebody's nephew in Dorset or cousin in Nova Scotia.

The whores would steal half of Marcus's drink, and he'd pretend not to notice.

Wesley, sporting about in the first stare of fashion, with his fancy walking stick and French mistress, didn't need anybody thinking about him. Big Nan and the other streetwalkers, Old Blind Harvey, who refused a place at the Chelsea seamen's home, they needed thinking about.

They needed somebody to see that the pawnbrokers didn't cheat them.

They needed somebody to read those horrendously misspelled letters from far-flung family.

They needed somebody to help them write the replies, so cheerful and dishonest, but so full of genuine love and concern.

Wesley needed a few years marching under the command of a lying martinet, and Marcus was instead handing him an earldom.

"Bring me the money," Marcus said, "because there's no point my getting on the *Rebecca Louise* with empty pockets, Wesley. I'll surely starve in a foreign land without some means of making a new start. If I'm to die anyway, I might as well die honorably here in England."

Marcus mostly did not mean that, but he was beginning to suspect that Wesley, who could afford Bond Street finery *somehow*, was turning up miserly simply because he pleased to.

Wesley stared at Marcus as if he'd become a puzzle box, the solution not readily apparent.

"I do believe the Spanish sun baked your brainbox, dear boy. You owe me a final letter, I believe. On the eve of battle, farewell to mother dear, premonitions of death, and so forth. I will bring you some coin when I see you off and you will produce that letter. Then you shall make your new start, and all will be as it should be. You are getting cold feet, which is understandable before any ocean crossing. Keep your wits about you, and trust me to see the business through."

Wesley assayed a small bow, saluted with his fancy cane, and departed.

Marcus settled into the single, hard little chair behind the rickety desk and considered the ticket of passage before him. Wesley had booked that passage under the name of Marcus Glover, which surely had to be an oversight. They'd agreed that a pseudonym was in order, Mark Lovelace, an unremarkable name for an Englishman.

Wesley had provided Marcus no coin.

He'd booked passage for Marcus in steerage, the most uncomfortable and dangerous way to make a sea crossing—also the most crowded and thus the least discreet.

Perhaps Wesley wasn't quite as bright as Marcus had believed him to be, or perhaps what was lacking was the cousinly loyalty Marcus had always attributed to Wesley.

Marcus resumed reading *The Meditations*, but the words refused to penetrate his mind. The ticket of passage sat on the corner of his desk, putting Marcus in mind of one of Dunacre's more foolish and risky orders, the kind Dunacre had always assigned to the dauntless Captain Powell.

"Dorning was out all day yesterday," Dylan muttered, pacing Orion Goddard's office at The Coventry Club. "He was out all day today. I left word with his butler that I needed to speak with him, but the great man hasn't seen fit to respond to my note."

Dylan's host watched him with the same maddening calm Goddard had shown all across Spain and into France.

"Dorning and Jeanette were out at Richmond yesterday," he said. "They own a property there and are having it kitted out as a market garden. Today, they were off to sit for a portrait done by one of the Dorning brothers. Oak, I believe. He's in Town for the start of the Season to negotiate commissions while the missus does some shopping."

Dylan ceased pacing. "What the hell is Dorning up to now?" And why hadn't Dylan thought sooner to ask Goddard where Dylan's quarry had got off to? Goddard managed Dorning's fancy club, where Dylan had seen Wesley Glover relieved of a substantial sum at the gaming tables.

"Why are Sycamore Dorning's whereabouts abruptly of burning interest to you, Powell? You don't even like him."

One did not dissemble before Orion Goddard, but neither did one admit to having blundered enormously. "I need to shake your employer until his handsome teeth rattle, because Lydia has left Town for parts unknown. After four days, I have had no word from her, no note explaining where to send her things."

"You told us she'd piked off. MacKay has alerted his streetwalkers, and I have asked the urchins to be on the watch for her. What's the rest of it?"

"She took a perishing post-chaise, Goddard. One doesn't take a post-chaise to jaunt over to Southwark."

Goddard cocked his head. He had no need to threaten, bluster, or scold. He'd merely wait—until Lady Day twenty years on, if necessary—for Dylan to reveal what Goddard wanted him to reveal.

"The last person Lydia contacted before leaving my household was Sycamore Dorning. She could have asked me for anything, but she went to him instead. Why?"

"You can ask the man himself. Dorning came home over an hour ago—he sent across the street for supper from the buffet. Let's pay him a call, shall we?"

"I don't need you to nanny me," Dylan said, stalking for the door.

"No," Goddard replied, pushing to his feet, "but if Jeanette is from home, Dorning might need some supervision, and I am entitled to my entertainments."

They left the Coventry through the back entrance, pausing to give Goddard a moment to confer with his wife. Ann waved him off with a floury hand.

"Eclairs after midnight," Goddard muttered as he and Dylan crossed the garden. "This will be a brief call."

"I didn't know you were partial to eclairs."

"I like anything Ann makes, but the footmen lose all pretensions to decorum in the face of her eclairs and profiteroles. My stern presence is needed to prevent all-out insurrection."

"Do you like managing Dorning's fancy temple to idleness and vice?"

Goddard was silent until they emerged from the alley onto the thoroughfare. "The enlisted men passed many an hour dicing and playing cards. Officers bet on anything from how many petticoats the colonel's wife was wearing to the exact hour the first French cannon would sound. People need entertainment and diversion, Powell. What do you do for entertainment and diversion?"

Dylan could not stride across the street and pretend he hadn't heard the question, because a lone dray redolent of horse droppings lumbered past.

"I've been diverted half out of my mind this past week escorting my sisters to Astley's, various museums, Gunter's, and more bookstores than Napoleon had mistresses."

He'd played chess with Lydia once upon a time, but he kept that treasured memory to himself. He'd talked with her. Cuddled with her and argued with her.

"And you do so love to read," Goddard remarked, stepping into the street.

"I read poetry, mostly."

"What's the last poem you read?"

"Go to hell, Goddard." In his subtle way, Goddard had made a profound point. Dylan was still on forced march, stopping only to feed or water the horses, eat some dry biscuit, or tend to nature's call. His feet weren't aching, and he wasn't famished, but his heart was weary and sore.

As they approached Dorning's front steps, it occurred to Dylan that Lydia had been on a forced march, too, trying to find her brother, run Dylan's household, manage a family gone ragged at the seams...

Goddard rapped the knocker, and Dylan found himself involuntarily coming to attention. A youngish fellow in butler's sober attire opened the door.

"Colonel, Captain, do come in. I'll just have your coats and see if the family is still awake."

"No need, Bascomb," Goddard said, passing over his hat. "My stay will be brief. Powell and I will announce ourselves."

"But, Colonel..."

"I know to knock loudly on the parlor door and wait until I'm bade to enter."

Dylan passed Bascomb his hat and followed Goddard up the steps. "I still think of Jeanette as that quiet, busy sprite who tagged after us and tried to remain unseen. I don't think of her as Mrs. Sycamore Dorning."

"She very much is, and he is very much Jeanette's adoring husband."

"Like you and Ann."

"Like MacKay and his Dorcas. Like most happily married couples, which you would know if you weren't so blindly determined to remain at war with the past." Goddard knocked smartly on a closed parlor door.

Behind that door, somebody giggled, somebody else—male—cursed. Then a silence while Goddard smiled at the carpet. MacKay had that same smile sometimes, sweet, merry, naughty... A married sort of smile?

Jeanette opened the door some minutes later, her deportment entirely composed and gracious. Dorning, looking somewhat *hors de combat*—no cravat, hair less than tidy, jacket draped over a chair—stood behind her.

"What's amiss?" Dorning asked. "If you two are here at this hour, something must be amiss."

"Sycamore." Jeanette's tone held humor and gentle, wifely reproof. "I am always pleased to see my cousins." She drew back to admit them, while Dorning had the disgruntled look of a fellow who'd misplaced something, but could not recall exactly what.

"I apologize for disturbing you at this hour," Dylan said, "but I am concerned for my housekeeper. Mrs. Lovelace left Town with barely a word four days ago, and I..."

Dorning regarded him with surprising gravity. "And you have lost your mind. She promised me she'd leave you a note."

"Mrs. Lovelace left a brief word of parting, but no indication why she left now, where she's off to, or what's to be done about her brother."

"He's booked passage on the *Rebecca Louise*," Dorning replied. "Sails in a few days."

Would Lydia take ship with her brother? "How do you know that?"

Goddard spoke up. "I told the boys to keep a lookout for Wesley Glover around the shipping offices and docks. He rather makes a splash in those environments."

"He's begging for a beating," Dylan said. "But I'm more concerned that he's about to take Mrs. Lovelace to wife, and she will be helpless to refuse him."

A clatter of hooves on the cobbles below sounded unnaturally loud as Jeanette took Sycamore's hand, and some sort of marital discussion took place without anybody saying a word.

"She did not forbid you to reveal her plans," Jeanette said, eyeing her husband.

Dorning went to the window, Jeanette with him, still hand in hand.

"She did not forbid me, but unless I miss my guess, the prodigal has returned, and her journey was successful. She can explain her absence to you herself, Powell, and I suggest you listen to her as if your happiness depends upon it. If that doesn't suffice to silence your remonstrations, listen as if *her* happiness depends upon it."

Dorning eased his hand free of his wife's grasp. She held his coat for him, and he followed Dylan and Goddard down to the foyer.

Lydia and an older woman who resembled her were passing over wraps to Bascomb.

Goddard sidled around the ladies and departed before introductions could be made, promising to have more supper sent over.

Dylan laced his hands behind his back, lest other people witness him snatching Lydia into his arms. Her eyes were shadowed, her complexion pale by the light of the foyer's sconces, and Dylan had never seen her in such a wrinkled ensemble, but she was whole, and safe, and *here*.

"Captain Powell," she said, her bearing shifting into that of the housekeeper of unyielding dignity. She offered him a damned curtsey. "A pleasure to see you. Caroline, Lady Tremont, may I make known to you Captain Dylan Powell, a dear friend of mine and a former comrade-in-arms of Marcus's."

Dylan bowed over the countess's hand, for this had to be Lydia's mother, hauled in from the provinces literally posthaste.

"Your ladyship, a pleasure."

The countess considered him. "You found my son. I will always be in your debt, Captain, and I am pleased to meet you." A silent, ladylike *nonetheless...* hung in the air.

"His lordship has nothing to fear from me," Dylan replied. "He never did."

"Perhaps," Dorning said, "the ladies would like some food and—"

"I must retrieve my belongings from the captain's house." Lydia spoke quite firmly.

The countess paused minutely while drawing off her gloves. "At this hour, Lydia?"

Yes, at this hour. At any hour. Dylan had no idea what Lydia was about, but he knew that he and she needed privacy.

"I will be happy to escort Lady Lydia to her former abode. The rest of the staff will be delighted to see her, as will my sisters."

Lydia aimed an unfathomable look at Dylan, serious, patient... He realized what he'd left unsaid.

"Though nobody is more relieved or pleased to know her ladyship is well than I am. Her ladyship and I have matters to discuss, regarding Lord Tremont, among other things."

Not by a relaxation of her shoulders or a shift in breathing did anything of at-ease creep into Lydia's bearing, but her gaze softened.

"I will be safe with the captain," she said, "and you, Mama, will be safe with the Dornings. Mr. Dorning, my thanks for all your assistance. My regards to your wife."

Dorning passed Dylan his hat. "You are welcome. Until morning, Powell."

Dylan bowed. "Until morning, and my thanks as well."

"Take Lady Lydia over to the club for a decent meal," Dorning said, "and I'll have the coach sent around back. Ann and Jeanette will expect a full report tomorrow, and you should anticipate a call from MacKay and his lady as well."

Dylan wasn't sure what that was all about, nor did he care. Lydia was safe, he was her *dear friend,* and she was coming home with him for at least one night.

CHAPTER EIGHTEEN

After four days in a post-chaise, Lydia had developed the habit of letting her mind drift for hours on end, and for many of those hours, her thoughts had drifted to Dylan Powell.

She loved him, but she loved others as well, as did he. She most assuredly did not love Wesley Glover, though she did love Marcus. Mama loved Marcus, too, and Lydia desperately hoped that tender sentiment was reciprocated.

For the duration of a scrumptious meal in Colonel Goddard's office at the Coventry, Lydia and Dylan spoke little.

"Excellent ham."

"I believe these potatoes are mashed with both cheddar and sour cream."

"More Riesling?"

She was famished and exhausted, but not too tired to notice that Dylan was regarding her differently. His gaze, always so keen, had taken on a sweeter quality, as if he were preparing for a farewell. Soldiers became inured to farewells. Lydia hadn't acquired the knack.

"I might fall asleep on you in the coach," she said as she rose from an empty plate. "I never before grasped how sheer boredom saps the energy."

"You traveled from London to Tremont and back again in four days, Lydia?" Dylan draped Lydia's cloak around her shoulders, his touch merely polite.

Well, what had she expected? She loved him, but where had recent revelations left his regard for her?

"I thought if anybody could talk Marcus out of his plans to leave England, Mama could. When I compared notes with Mama, though, I realized that Marcus's entire situation is my fault."

Dylan escorted her down a hallway, then past a loud, hot, busy kitchen and into the cool night air.

"I missed the stars," Lydia said. "I had not even realized how much I missed the stars. London in winter has no stars at night. In Shropshire..."

A coach horse in the alley stomped a hoof.

"Outside of London," Dylan said, "you can breathe. You have true quiet and true silence. You don't move along at a near run, hoping to avoid footpads and pickpockets lurking in every doorway. Rambling along the country lanes, you know everybody you meet and they know you."

Dylan had apparently done some thinking, too, though to what end, Lydia did not know. He assisted her into the coach and took the place beside her on the forward-facing seat. A small, though encouraging, familiarity.

The coach pulled away, and Lydia's eyes nearly closed from sheer force of habit.

"You are not to blame for your brother's situation, Lydia."

She opened her eyes, prepared to defend her only sibling with the last of her energy. "Marcus was young, he was trying to be the head of the family, and he thought my honor needed defending. He engaged in a duel, killed—or badly wounded—his opponent, and galloped off to buy his colors in an effort to avoid scandal."

"You figured that out on your journey to Shropshire?"

"Mama puzzled through the general contours of the problem." And had kept silent about the whole of it until Lydia had taken the time to *listen* to her.

"There's more to it than that."

The coach turned a corner, and Lydia swayed into Dylan's side. She wanted to burrow against him and let sleep overtake her, but this discussion mattered.

"You are correct," she said. "There is more to it. Wesley was Marcus's second, and Wesley could have stopped the duel had he wanted to. I suspect Wesley made sure Marcus knew I'd been with Finchly, and Wesley may have tampered with the guns."

"Why do you say that?"

The coachman was keeping to a walk, for which Lydia was grateful. She'd been bounced so hard for so long in the post-chaises that she had become one big bruise.

"My father was a noted marksman, and from a young age, Marcus was determined to live up to Papa's memory. Marcus was a dead shot, and he would never have aimed to kill Finchly, and yet, Finchly was felled. The point of a duel is to satisfy honor, not commit murder."

A short silence followed that disclosure. What would Dylan think of Marcus now, when dueling had been added to the list of a young man's follies?

"I went on a short reconnaissance mission among Wesley's fondest memories," Dylan said. "Finchly did not die. He wasn't even wounded. Wesley set up the whole thing, and Finchly now bides in in the country, hoping nobody charges him with raping an earl's daughter."

Fatigue of body and mind hampered Lydia's ability to grasp the import of Dylan's words. She understood the plain meaning, but the rest of it...

"Wesley *schemed* to see me ruined and Marcus branded a murderer," Lydia said slowly, "and he has nearly succeeded."

"'Schemed' is the correct word, from telling Finchly to ply you with strong drink, to using some chicken blood to approximate the appearance of a mortal wound, to so helpfully aiding Marcus—a title-holder without an heir of the body—to buy his colors and go off to war. Wesley could not have Marcus convicted of murder, for that might see the title and wealth attainted, so he used Marcus's sense of honor as a weapon."

An odd combination of rage and relief seeped through Lydia's fatigue. Marcus had no need to flee—none—but Wesley's perfidy eclipsed all bounds.

"How do you know these things?" she asked.

"I treated Wesley to a few drinks at a club slightly above his touch. Asked the right questions, let the right silences linger. Wesley's besetting sin is arrogance. He must above all be admired for his cleverness, and he was sadly in want of admirers. I obliged with the boon he most craved—rapt appreciation—and he went willingly into the ambush."

Lydia did lean against Dylan then. She closed her eyes and sent up a prayer of thanks that Dylan had unraveled Wesley's scheme before Marcus had been hounded from home shores—again.

"Thank you," she said. "I must convey this news to Marcus, and to Mama. She knew something was amiss, and that was before Wesley was extorting jewelry from her."

Dylan's posture subtly changed, such that the muscle beneath Lydia's cheek became less yielding. "With Marcus gone from sight, perhaps permanently, what else could Wesley have held over your mother's head?"

"Me. My freedom. As long as Mama kept tossing her baubles into Wesley's lap, he would not press his suit. He doubtless planned to get his hands on every earbob and brooch Mama owned, and only then he would have come after my settlements. He is diabolical, and I don't know what to do about him."

"You need not make that decision when you are exhausted," Dylan said. "Never attempt to puzzle out strategy when fatigue clouds your mind. I will take you and your mother to Marcus in the morning, because whatever else you decide, Lord Tremont deserves to know the truth."

Lydia didn't know if she replied, but she did know that falling asleep tucked against Dylan's side was a sweet, sweet pleasure. She barely recalled stumbling from the coach into his arms. He carried her through the darkened house, not to her little housekeeper's apartment, but up to his bedroom.

He sat her on the bed, and Lydia bestirred herself to form a complete sentence. "What are you about, Captain?"

"You are at the end of your tether," he said, slipping off her boots and untying her garters. "I know that. I know you are upset and weary and muddled and sore. I have no designs on your person, Lydia, and if you tell me to sleep in the dressing closet, I will, but I want... I wish..."

He knelt before her, his gaze unfathomable.

"Tell me, Dylan."

"I would like to share that bed with you, to sleep with you, to hold you. Only that. I went half mad when you left, then Bronwen gave me your note. 'Love, Lydia.' Two words, but they restored a measure of hope to me. Tonight, you told your mother that we are dear friends, and you came home with me... I am babbling. You are consumed with worry for your brother, and I am blethering on about notes."

He peeled down her stockings and remained kneeling before her, rolling them into a tidy little ball. A minute tremor to his fingers was Lydia's only clue that Dylan Powell was not simply being his usual, conscientiously neat, considerate self.

Lydia had come home with Dylan intent on more than retrieving belongings that could easily have been boxed up and sent to Shropshire. He and she needed to discuss a few matters, as he'd said, but those matters would wait until morning.

"I am nearly too tired to speak coherently," she said, "but I will happily share this bed with you, Dylan, and I will hold you too. We can speak more when we are both back on our mettle."

He nodded. "After you have sorted out your brother's situation, you and I will talk. But you must not disappear again, Lydia. Until Bronwen gave me your note, I thought... Well, no matter what I thought. To bed with us."

If not for Dylan's assistance, Lydia would have fallen asleep where she sat. He got her out of her clothes and into one of his old shirts, then helped her to wash and to take down and braid her hair. He was more considerate and efficient than any lady's maid, and Lydia allowed herself to revel in his touch.

While he made use of the privacy screen, she climbed onto the mattress and nuzzled pillows that bore the spicy, citrusy scent she associated with Dylan. For the first time in years, she could put down a burden of worry that had grown enormous.

The bed dipped, and Dylan's arms came around her. Then all was peace, comfort, and oblivion.

Dylan lay awake, thinking about Lydia's situation, about her brother, about Wales... about much. When his thoughts eventually slowed, he simply savored the feel of Lydia in his arms and in his bed, and he came to some decisions.

He awoke with the soldier's ability to decide exactly how much sleep to permit himself and was waiting for Lydia when she joined him in the breakfast parlor. They had not made love, and the light in her eyes suggested they were about to make war.

"May I fix you a plate, my lady?" Dylan asked, rising and bowing. "You have to be famished, and the day will be taxing."

She frowned, suggesting she'd been willing to hide behind her Mrs. Lovelace uniform for one more day and hadn't anticipated that Dylan would challenge her decision.

"Eggs and toast please, and a cup of tea would not go amiss."

He heaped her plate with enough eggs to feed MacKay and Goddard for a week, set the plate and a toast rack at the place to the right of the head of the table, and held Lydia's chair for her.

"If your artillery are in place," he murmured close to her ear, "you may fire when ready."

Lydia took her place, scowled at him, and picked up her fork. Dylan sat as well, prepared to give as good as he got, though he also ensured the butter was beside Lydia's plate.

"I missed you," she said. "I asked Mr. Dorning to arrange the coach for me because I did not want you talking me out of fetching Mama. I also did not want you going yourself, because she would not have come at your insistence, nor could I tolerate even a day's delay with Marcus so intent on leaving the country. I asked Mr. Dorning to put Mama up because we haven't room here now that your sisters have arrived. Besides, your cousin Jeanette was married to a marquess, and Mama is a countess. They will get on as Mama and I never have."

Dylan set the honey and cream near Lydia's tea cup. "I missed you too. Desperately. I worried that you'd left... left London for good, or that Wesley had somehow threatened you, or Marcus had convinced you to sail with him."

Lydia took a bite of eggs. "You have a prodigious imagination, Captain. I put the note where you should have found it easily."

What a joy, to hear the starch back in her voice. "Bronwen found it first. She turned it over to me after seeing the torments I endured."

"Because one of your charges had gone astray?"

He heard both the dignity and the vulnerability lurking behind Lydia's question. "Because I love you, my lady, and if anything happened to you, I would be *undone*. I'd become as lost and confused as those old soldiers who can barely stumble from the street corner to the pub and back again. You have become map, compass, and canteen for me. The simple necessities that will bring me home. Without you..."

Lydia was giving him the same puzzled appraisal she gave a parlor in want of a thorough cleaning. Where to start, what to keep, what to toss?

"I smell bacon." Sycamore Dorning sauntered into the breakfast parlor, the Countess of Tremont on his arm. "You should hire a butler, Powell. Somebody to keep the riffraff out and send the trades around back. Maintain order on the male side of the domestic infantry. Lady Lydia, good day. How lovely, I see you were expecting us."

The extra place settings were for Dylan's sisters, who'd had the good grace not to interrupt Dylan's first real opportunity to propose to Lydia.

Dylan rose and bowed. "Countess, Dorning, good morning. You must of course join us."

"We can discuss strategy over the teapot," Dorning said, pulling out a chair for the countess. "Lady Tremont has intimated that there is trouble in Shropshire and a weasel on the loose in London."

"I did not intimate," Lady Tremont said, gracefully taking a seat. "I laid the situation out for you and your wife very clearly, Mr. Dorning. If Lydia trusts you, then I am bound to do likewise." She aimed a glance at Dorning that suggested her trust would be withdrawn without recourse if he didn't cease his strutting.

Dylan's heart wanted to toss them both out of the house. When his sisters decided to join the breakfast affray ten minutes later, he wanted to toss them out as well. The noise rose, the food disappeared along with the last of Dylan's patience. While Lydia silently sipped her tea, it was decided that Dylan would escort her and the countess to Marcus's dwelling, and Dorning and his liveried retinue would take guard duty.

The entire distance to Marcus's street, Dorning speculated aloud about how best to catch a weasel, and all the while, Lydia remained quiet.

"You are trying to figure out how to present matters in a light that doesn't make your brother feel like a fool," Dylan said as he handed her down. "Not every problem is yours to solve, Lydia. You were smart to fetch your mother, and I expect she'll do a lot of the talking for you."

Lydia took his arm after a quick glance at the surrounding street.

She was learning reconnaissance, and Dylan was displeased about that. The countess was at Dorning's side, though he would wait at the front door, keeping an eye out for one particular weasel.

Dylan escorted the ladies up the long, dingy climb to Marcus's room, rapped on the thin door, and waited for it to open.

"Tremont, you have guests."

To Dylan's great relief, the door opened. Marcus looked, if anything, more pale and gaunt than he had previously. No writing materials remained on the desk, and on the cot a battered valise sat open, neatly packed clothing arranged inside.

"Captain, good day. If you've come to... Lydia, and... *Mama?*"

Marcus's hands twitched, as if he'd reach for his mother, then fell back to his sides as he stood at attention.

"My lady, a pleasure." Marcus bowed. "Lydia, very good to see you again, though I really wish you had not come."

"We bring news, Marcus," Lydia said. "Good news."

"Mama, you should have the chair," Marcus replied. "It is good to see you, though I must apologize for the surrounds."

Marcus spoke stiffly, and because Dylan had been to war and because he knew Marcus somewhat, he realized that the earl was trying very hard not to cry.

The countess advanced on her son and wrapped him in a hug. "You are alive. You are alive and a bit skinny, but well enough. My relief knows no bounds, and, Marcus, your cousin Wesley has much to answer for."

Tremont patted his mother's back awkwardly, sent Lydia a helpless look, and when no aid came from that quarter, he gingerly hugged his mother.

"Wesley has arranged passage for me, and while I am glad to have this chance to make my farewells and apologies in person, I really must... Captain, it's not safe for the ladies here."

"Then it's not safe for you," the countess retorted. "Marcus, my dearest boy, you labor under the terrible misapprehension that you killed that Finchly fellow. You did not. He's kicking his heels at the Finchly family seat, probably growing portly and thinning on top."

Marcus's next bewildered gaze landed on Dylan. "Is this true?"

Dylan nodded. "Glover set you up. Chicken blood, drama, collusion. He turned Finchly loose on your sister and included a quantity of strong punch among the seducer's tools. Wesley wants your title and wealth, but he could not have you tried for any felonies. He apparently hoped Bonaparte's forces would put period to your existence, but the French instead obliged the side of decency."

Marcus turned loose of his mother and sank to the cot. "Wesley was so... so helpful. So concerned. I was an idiot."

"I am your older sister," Lydia said, quite crisply. "I was the bigger idiot, Marcus. You were trying to defend my honor, and all I wanted was to feel grown up, wicked, and sophisticated."

Marcus looked up at her as if he was having trouble following his native tongue. "You are my sister. You were innocent, until Finchly misbehaved with you, and Wesley said he did not want to tell me, but because I was the head of the family, he thought I had to know."

The Countess of Tremont took the place beside Marcus on the cot. "Wesley was your second. You were already the earl, and Finchly was and is a mere mister. You were prohibited by any rubric of gentlemanly conduct from dueling with him, and yet, your cousin doubtless planted the idea in your head and supplied the pistols you used."

Marcus stared hard in the direction of a crack running up the plaster of the opposite wall. "You are right, Mama. I ought not to have challenged Finchly, not the done thing for a peer to challenge a mister. I didn't grasp that until I was in Spain—duels were fashionable with a certain type of officer—but I supposed Wesley had been as vague on the rules as I had been. Finchly, though, was already in uniform. *He* should have known the rules even if Wesley..."

A silence spread, while Marcus stared, and his mama sat beside him, looking diminutive and hopeful.

"I did not kill Finchly?" Marcus put the question to Dylan.

"Truly? I aimed wide, but he went down like the hero of a Drury Lane tragedy, and there was that blood."

"He is quite alive," Dylan said. "I peeked at his record at Horse Guards. He was artillery. Mustered out before the Hundred Days and did not come back for Waterloo."

"I suppose that's something," Marcus said, rising and offering his mother his hand. "But, Captain, I must ask you to see their ladyships safely away, because your news does not change my plans. I'm off to Philadelphia, and I will promise to be in touch as best I can. Wesley booked passage for me..."

He resumed staring at the crack on the opposite wall. "Booked passage for me in steerage under my own name, the rotter. And he was doubtless going to give me tuppence of my own money with which to start a new life, assuming I didn't expire of lung fever before reaching the New World. I suppose it cannot be helped."

The countess was gaping, while Lydia's gaze had narrowed in a manner that did not bode well for dunderheaded younger brothers.

"You have committed no wrong," Lydia said. "Wesley lied to you, used you, manipulated you, intimidated me and Mama, turned Uncle Reggie into a sot... and you are still planning to simply take ship?"

Marcus nodded. "'Fraid so, Lydia. Needs must. Perhaps it's for the best that I'm officially alive, but I am still compelled by circumstances to quit this sceptered isle."

"I don't understand," Lydia said in tones that conveyed inchoate fratricide. "I do not understand why you would turn your back on the family who needs you. The tenant farmers and their families, the pensioners, the staff at Tremont... They are all suffering, and Uncle still has your power of attorney."

"I do not understand either," the countess said. "Marcus, you must explain your reasoning to us."

Tremont adopted his parade-inspection posture again. "I am not at liberty to do that, Mama, and you must trust that I am making the best decision for all concerned. I appreciate what you've told me regarding Finchly, and I will see Uncle's power of attorney revoked, but I must still be very much an absentee earl."

Lydia swiveled on Dylan like a man-o'-war coming about. "Is this your doing? Have you struck some sort of bargain with my brother that goes back to army days and more masculine stupidity prancing around beneath a garland of gentlemanly honor?"

Dylan expected Marcus to disabuse his sister of any such notion, but Marcus merely looked more pained than usual.

The trick to reconnaissance was to assemble a picture, as complete a picture as possible. The process wanted diligence. Skinny livestock might mean a drought, or might mean the French had just come through and killed all the fatted cattle. Only careful listening at the local tavern and a study of the terrain, the crops, the rivers, the sheep and goats, would put the one fact of skinny cattle into a meaningful context.

And that pained expression from Marcus, that failure to come to Dylan's defense, were the last pieces of information needed to unravel Marcus's motivations.

Dylan went to the door. "Dorning!"

"Here!" was followed by a rapid thump of boots, then the man himself, slightly winded but as obnoxiously self-possessed as ever.

"Please escort the ladies to the coach and see them safely to your abode. The earl and I have matters to discuss in private. Old business that need no longer concern anybody else."

Dorning's brows rose, but before he could stick his oar in, Lydia marched up to Dylan.

"I know you have little enough respect for my brother," she said, "but I love Marcus, and I love you, and I will not be forced to choose between the two of you. It's both or none, Dylan. The human heart was made to love widely, as you love your men, your cousins, and your sisters. If you send my brother to bedamned Philadelphia, I will never again polish your perishing *candlestick* or beat you at chess."

Dorning's expression was gratifyingly blank, while Marcus looked mystified and the countess bewildered.

"I love you too," Dylan said, smiling because he could not help himself. "Very much, and I assure you, I will use every resource I possess to talk your brother out of remaining distant from his home and family."

He kissed Lydia's cheek for good measure, then Dorning was shepherding the ladies from the dingy little room.

"Now then," Dylan said, closing the door and turning to Tremont, "tell me why you killed Aloysius Dunacre."

"The problem with philosophers," Marcus said, "is that they are too, well, philosophical. They haven't much specific advice for when a fellow has nothing sensible to say. I do wish I could offer you a seat, Powell, but then I'd have to stand, which is awkward when I've this earldom about my neck, and I haven't any port or brandy to offer you either. All quite lowering."

Quite confusing, in fact.

Powell regarded him with an unnervingly serious stare. That stare should have qualified the captain to interrogate prisoners, but instead, Powell had always kept to the more dangerous task of reconnoitering.

The captain sat himself on the cot. "You killed Dunacre. I'd like to know how and why, though I promise you, not a word of this conversation will leave this room without your permission."

How to put this, without insulting Powell? "You are a gentleman," Marcus said, "though as for myself, I've grown heartily sick of gentlemanly honor. If I tell you the particulars, you will be duty-bound to report them to Horse Guards or the Lords, or whoever has the present privilege of stretching my neck. If you keep mum, you become an accessory or an accomplice or some sort of villain along with me. This is why I could not tell Mama or Lydia why I'm leaving. If they knew, they would be implicated, and also be even more disappointed in me than they already are. They would protect me none-theless."

To have this conversation with Powell of all people—conscience of the regiment, guardian angel of the former soldier—surely ought to qualify as a fitting penance.

"Then don't admit anything to me. Just tell me why you did it."

Part of Marcus wanted to tell the story to somebody—to anybody —and here was Powell asking for particulars.

"I always envied you," Marcus said, though that had nothing to do with anything. "You always knew what to do. When Dunacre gave his stupid orders, when he insulted a man for simply trying to do his job, when he reported his staff for all manner of made-up infrac-tions, you never wavered, never backed down."

"While you," Powell said, with a smile even more unnerving than his doom stare, "played the fool. The jester."

"I am a fool." Marcus lowered himself to the cot as well. The hard chair was at the moment just too hard, and it rocked on its spindly legs. Marcus felt a passing temptation to smash it, but instead, he sat beside Powell on the marginally less-hard cot.

"You are a crack shot," Powell said. "Everybody notes this about you, and yet, I saw you nearly shoot your own foot."

"I missed by a good inch. My boots were never in any danger. Dunacre found my incompetence hilarious, and if he was laughing at me, he wasn't having anybody flogged, was he? If I bungled an order, he could not rage at the only earl on his staff, but he could ridicule me without limit and have a jolly fine time doing it."

"So you bungled orders, and nobody demoted you for it."

"Nobody sent me on patrols either, because in my case, they dared not trust such a one as I to read a map. I was fit only for staff duty—my handwriting is quite good—when all I wanted was to fight."

"Because you felt guilty for supposedly killing Finchly?"

"Because I wanted to be respected for *something*. Everybody talked about you, Powell. You were a wraith, a ghost, a chameleon. You'd become a bent-over old woman one day and a drunken Spanish drover the next. You read signs of passing French patrols better than any sniffing hound could, and you took a demotion rather than put the men needlessly in harm's way. I hated you, and I probably still do, except now I'm to swing for killing Dunacre, so what does any of that matter? Besides, the philosophers aren't very keen on hatred."

"They never took orders from the devil's aide-de-camp."

"Dunacre was rotten," Marcus said, surprised that he and Powell could agree on even this much. "He was the type to have shoved little boys' heads into the privy hole at school while the other small boys cheered lest they be next."

"He probably used his slingshot to aim stones at birds too," Powell said, "but he did something that even you, a man defined by your sense of duty, found beyond the pale. He offended your honor."

Marcus knew vaguely that he was being cozened with this little soldierly tête-à-tête on the cot. Powell's commiseration and understanding were in aid of gaining a confession, but Marcus had ceased to care. The commiseration and understanding were balm to his soul, and—not a detail—he *had* killed Dunacre, and—also not a detail—he did not want to run yet again for the convenience of a conniving cousin.

"I'd kill him again, if I had it to do over."

"I could never quite figure out how to get away with it," Powell said, "but if ever I held a man in low regard, it was he."

"I didn't want to kill anybody," Marcus said, hating the pleading note in his voice. "All I wanted was to take good care of Mama and Lydia, to know which tenant needed the loan of a team of bullocks and which neighbor needed a hand with his drainage. All I have ever wanted, Powell, is to do the right thing. I wanted to be a conscientious steward, a friend to mankind, but that's not enough, is it?"

Marcus was sniffling now, always a problem with the spring air. Even gave a man the sniffles in London.

Powell passed him a handkerchief. "Dunacre threatened one of the men, didn't he? When he really wanted to upset me, he'd go after the men. The older fellows, the ones too battered to hold up to the

long marches. He preyed on the weak and exploited their vulnerabili-
ties to prey on the strong."

"I wasn't strong, Powell. I was never strong."

"I think you were. I think you were, in your way, far stronger than
any of us, and certainly Dunacre or I, realized."

Well, Powell was confused at best, a comforting thought, to know
even the wily captain could become muddled.

"Waterloo was a mess," Marcus said. "Nobody had any maps,
and in low country, you can't precisely ride up to the hilltop and spot
the village spire, then reckon your bearings from that. Messengers got
lost or shot, generals fell, and we stumbled around, not knowing
whose cannon we heard. You were there."

"I was there, but my cousins got me an assignment out of
Dunacre's line of fire. You were not so lucky."

"I was finally to see action, Powell. Real action. My unit engaged
the enemy early and got the worst of it. No reinforcements, not
enough cannon, mud to our knees, the cavalry never where it was
needed at the time it was needed. You know how it went."

Marcus hated to think about that day, but it was never far from
his awareness, and a constant theme in his nightmares. This poky
little room and the lumpy cot were miles away from any battlefield
and not nearly far enough. Perhaps that was half the allure of Philadelphia—it was half a world away from Waterloo.

"How did the rest of the battle go for you and your men?" Powell
asked.

"We suffered heavy casualties and told ourselves the usual lies—
the French had suffered worse, by God, and we would show them, et
cetera and so forth. The typical rot soldiers rely on to keep morale up.
William Brook had been sent to relay our situation up the line, and he
came back with the news that we were to fall back to the nearest
woods. We were to rest and be held in reserve to provide reinforcements where needed later in the day."

"Dunacre wasn't having any of that?"

"He raised his pistol and was about to shoot Brook in the face, because Brook refused to recall any orders other than those he'd had from Wellington's very staff. Brook refused twice. Dunacre sat on his white charger and cocked his damned pistol, one foot from Brook's face. Then our glorious commander started yelling about insubordination and disobeying a direct order. He'd ordered Brook to tell lies, Powell, deadly, damnable lies. So I..."

Powell had to be the most patient man ever to sit on a worn cot and listen to a sad, old tale.

"Tell me the rest of it, Tremont."

"At that moment," Marcus said softly, "I had no more philosophy in me. I was on my horse a half-dozen yards away, and I put a ball through Dunacre's heart. I ordered the men to the woods. We took our fallen commander's remains with us, and the men later decided Dunacre had suffered a hero's death on the battlefield. French sniper was the official word. Was I a coward, Powell, to let the men make that choice for me?"

If anybody could answer that question, the conscience of the regiment could.

"*Dunacre* was the enemy, Tremont. The problem was never you or me, it was Dunacre. He was prepared to murder a loyal soldier so he could order more loyal soldiers to fling themselves at the enemy for the sake of his own glory. That is a great and unequivocal evil, to waste lives for the sake of vanity and personal gain."

A great and unequivocal evil. That sounded like something Aurelius would have said—both grand and accurate.

"Instead," Powell went on, "you put your own welfare aside and saved Brook's life, and probably the lives of most of the men still standing. Had it been a Frenchman or another enlisted man waving a pistol in Brook's face, you would not have hesitated to fire. A lieutenant colonel's uniform alone—a uniform Dunacre *bought*—should never have put him above the reach of justice."

Interesting word—*justice*. Powell had doubtless chosen that term on purpose. "Dunacre would have killed Brook in cold blood for conveying orders honestly. I believe that, Powell. I know it."

Marcus used Powell's handkerchief to blot his eyes. The linen smelled good, of sunny climes and spicy breezes. Of lives far from war and murder and despair.

"Every witness to the moment agrees with you," Powell said. "I know those men, Tremont. I've fed them, clothed them, given them places to sleep, found them jobs, sent some of them to Wales to work my land. Not a one of them has spoken a word against you, nor can I speak a word against you. In this matter, I am content to trust the judgment of the soldiers who saw the whole situation firsthand. They are judge and jury, and they have chosen to acquit you of wrongdoing. You prevented the greater harm by taking Dunacre's life."

Marcus folded up the handkerchief, damp now, and considered Powell's words. Marcus had of course tried that reasoning on for himself many times—saving many lives by taking one had to be the superior moral choice, right?

Except that a military court might not see it like that. Military judges were not known for a considered grasp of moral philosophy.

"You don't feel duty-bound to alert Horse Guards to my perfidy?" Marcus asked.

"I feel duty-bound to get you away from this place, find your sister, and see what she wants us to do about Wesley."

"I'm not shooting him," Marcus said. "I want to, but I haven't touched a gun since Waterloo and probably won't ever fire one again. He's family, Powell."

"Lydia might have some ideas." Powell rose and extended a hand. "I trust you will not be taking ship?"

Some part of Marcus, the part that had learned the relief of hiding in low places and giving up on happy endings, was tempted to get on board the *Rebecca Louise* and sail for the New World.

"What do you think I should do?" he asked.

"I think if Dunacre hadn't been so good at dividing his staff and sowing discord among us, we might have seen him relieved of command long before Waterloo—a proper court-martial with all the disgrace he deserved. I also think if more of us were concerned about being decent neighbors and doing the right thing—no small challenge —then fewer of us would ever have to march off to war again."

Of all the outlandish revelations... Dylan Powell was a philosopher. Marcus took Powell's hand and rose. "You won't tell Lydia or Mama?"

"Not my tale to tell, Tremont, and I owe you an apology for misjudging you."

Powell shook Marcus's hand, and that simple gesture effected a sense of absolution Marcus would probably not have found on his own, even if he'd searched the whole of Philadelphia for it.

"Apology accepted, though I've no idea what you're going on about. Lydia is sweet on you." An inane comment, given the ache in Marcus's chest. "Lydia is formidable. Witness, she found me."

"You wanted to be found," Powell said. "Most soldiers separated from their comrades do. Let's rejoin the ladies, and you can tell them of your decision."

Maybe that was a bit of cozening—Marcus had not announced any decision—or maybe it was Powell reading the signs most others missed, because Marcus *had* made a decision. He was not going to Philadelphia.

He was going to the solicitors' offices, where he would revoke Uncle Reggie's power of attorney and also cut off Wesley's allowance, effective immediately.

Lydia had hoped to slip in and out of Dylan's house without him being aware of her presence. He and Marcus had resolved matters between them two days ago—Marcus refused to yield details— and Lydia had spent all day yesterday at the solicitors' offices with Marcus and Mama.

Reggie's bumbling and Wesley's conniving had done some damage, but in time, with good management, Tremont would come right.

Not so, Lydia's heart. Dylan had not called at the Dorning residence in her absence. He'd sent no notes. She'd lost any ability to wait patiently on a man's whims weeks ago, to wait patiently for anything, in fact.

Lydia intended to retrieve at least her writing desk and perhaps chat up Betty about the doings in the Powell household. A little reconnaissance mission, nothing more.

She found the kitchen deserted, and beside her bed sat an open trunk, the same trunk she'd brought with her to London. Somebody had folded up her dresses and caps, tucked her slippers along the sides, and laid her Sunday gloves neatly atop the whole.

One of the kittens had curled up beside her gloves, and that sight —the bedraggled little feline now glossy and content—made her unaccountably sad.

"There she is," Dylan said, pushing away from the doorjamb. "We should name her Baggage if she's so determined to nap in trunks." He ambled past Lydia, scooped up the cat, and stroked her head. "My lady, good day."

I missed you. Lydia had already told Dylan that once—confessed that—and he'd said he loved her. Lydia had not imagined him admitting that sentiment, but where did that leave them?

"Captain, what brings you belowstairs?"

"You do. I saw Dorning's monstrosity of a coach stop at the corner and watched the footman hand down a very fine lady, whom he then escorted to my doorstep. Nobody knocked upon my door, though."

"I wanted to retrieve my writing desk."

Dylan set the cat down and gave her a gentle push in the direction of the parlor. The cat, of course, sat right upon her haunches and commenced licking her paw. Smart feline, to refuse direct orders when they did not suit a lady's agenda.

"I am preparing to ship your things to the destination of your choice," Dylan said. "Might we sit a moment, my lady?"

Dylan led her not to the bed, but into her sitting room—her

former sitting room. "I spent most of yesterday in a dead sleep," he said, "and my energy is still somewhat at low ebb."

Lydia took one of the wing chairs by the hearth, and when she was seated, Dylan took the other. That he'd been asleep yesterday suggested that while Lydia had been rattling her bones in all those post-chaises, Dylan hadn't exactly been picnicking in Hyde Park. He'd said as much, said he'd been upset, but the confirmation was reassuring.

"You and Marcus have resolved your differences?" she asked.

"We had a misunderstanding, not a true difference. The whole time we were in Spain, and I thought Tremont a bumbling toady, he was protecting me. He was protecting all of us."

"That is respect I hear in your voice." Dylan Powell was incapable of feigning such an emotion.

"I have tremendous respect for your brother, and I have apologized for misjudging him. I apologize to you for the same mistake. I used what skills I had to foil our enemies. Tremont used other skills. He was so expert at his tactics that I did not fathom what he was about. I suspect he has been fooling a lot of people for a long time, possibly even himself."

Lydia had no idea what all that meant, but she believed the sincerity in Dylan's words. "That is… good, that you and Marcus have cleared the air. Did he tell you what he has in mind for Wesley?"

Lydia did not give a filthy, mismatched pair of andirons what became of Wesley, but neither could she seem to bring the conversation around to more personal matters.

"I suggested that Wesley's fate should rest in your hands, my lady." Dylan was once again the correct, polite, self-contained officer, at least in his bearing. Only his eyes suggested a warmer regard.

"I need no say in the matter, provided I don't have to marry him. This whole imbroglio is my fault. If I'd resisted the temptation Wesley dangled before me—"

"Lydia, please stop."

Lydia got up to pace. "Well, who is the wronged party here?

Certainly not me. Wesley has intimidated Mama, Marcus, probably Uncle Reggie, and even that rotter Finchly. I was simply a headstrong girl indulging in a foolish, misguided, stupid bid for attention, and it solved nothing and created all of this, this—"

Dylan rose and took her hand. "Your mother was drifting about in a fog of grief. Your only brother was on his way to strutting young prigdom. Your uncle saw only your settlements, and what Finchly saw needs no elaboration. When you came to London, searching for the prodigal earl, you did not ask directly for my help at first because you've never been able to rely on anybody to take your interests to heart. Horse Guards sneered at you, albeit politely. The solicitors dared to pat your figurative head."

Lydia wanted to put her hand over Dylan's mouth, but she was too busy blinking at his cravat. A simple knot, a mathematical, and a pin tipped with lapis nestled among the folds.

"You overstate matters," she managed.

"I *understate* matters," Dylan said, drawing her into his arms. "Marcus did not have to issue a challenge over what you saw as your own, independent decision, one that materially affected nobody else. Reggie did not have to buy Marcus's commission—he could have sent his nephew off for a repairing lease on some Greek isle, where Marcus could have indulged in an orgy of philosophical studies. Your mother could have set aside the role of grieving widow enough to see you safely into adulthood. None of those people was truly concerned for you, Lydia, but I am. You have been scouting behind enemy lines on your own for too long, and now I ask you to come home."

He tucked her close, and Lydia went into his embrace and laid her head on his shoulder. She could not speak for the lump in her throat.

"What do you *want*, Lydia? What do *you* want?"

Something hot and wet trickled down her cheek. Dylan would wait forever for her answer, so she swallowed hard, mustered her will, and dredged up some words.

"Since you ask," she said, "I want my dunderheaded, impossible baby brother to take his place at Tremont. I want to never ride in a post-chaise again. I want peace and quiet and a home and a family. I want all your men settled. I want simple, honest, kind relationships, where we all try to look out for each other, and nobody is dueling or going off to war or trying to avoid murderous commanding officers or bemoaning the death of a good man who went to his reward nearly two decades ago."

Still Dylan waited, and now both of Lydia's cheeks were wet. "*I want you*, Dylan Powell, and *I love you*, and *I am tired*. Tired of marching and fighting and short rations and distant gunfire. I am so tired."

She descended into the sort of noisy sobs that ladies were never to indulge in, tears of exhaustion and heartache. Of sorrow and anger and bewilderment. Through it all, Dylan held her, tucking a handkerchief into her hand at some point and stroking her hair.

Gradually, Lydia's tears became tears of relief and then quiet shudders of mortification.

"Don't look at me," she said, her voice raspy.

"Looking at you has become one of my greatest pleasures," Dylan said, lips against Lydia's temple, "but I think what you mean is, I am not to *see* you. Too late for that, Lydia. I see you, and I love you, and when you speak of those treasures you seek—home, family, caring relationships—I want them, too, but mostly, I want you to be happy."

Lydia inventoried her emotions. "As best I can tell, I am happy right now. Also embarrassed beyond bearing."

"Could you be happy with me in Wales?"

Lydia did not need to inventory anything to fashion a reply. "Yes. But you have avoided returning home too, Dylan. Why go there now?"

"Will you marry me, Lydia? Become the lady of our manor and the companion of my heart? I am ready to look to the future—the men, the cousins, and the past are all settled enough—but I can't see a future without you."

His gaze had never been more tender. He let Lydia see to his depths, past the lonely years, past the courage, past the loyalty, to the man who'd marched alone for too long.

"You will make me cry again, and my answer is yes, Dylan. I have done what I set out to do, in large part thanks to you. Mama and Marcus will sort out Tremont."

She sank into his embrace in a different way, one that gave up the last shred of caution and wholly trusted the man in her arms. Lydia closed her eyes and knew a peace she'd sought but never expected to find, and a joy too precious for words.

Dylan seemed content to hold her, to stroke her hair, and to breathe with her, until the cat returned and began batting at Lydia's hems.

Lydia eased away from Dylan and picked up the cat. "May we take the kittens to Wales?"

"You need not ask me." Dylan scratched the feline's chin, which inspired predictable rumbling. "If you would like your palace tigers to accompany you to Wales, then accompany you, they shall. I would like for my sisters to bide here in London while you and I get settled at home. Tell me what to do about Wesley. Marcus has left the decision to you."

Lydia's first reaction was to demur, because she lacked the authority to decide another's fate, even the fate of her scoundrel of a cousin.

But Dylan *saw* her, the real, true Lydia, and so she must see herself and admit that she was in the best position to make the choice, and that Dylan had handed her the authority to do so. More than that, she *deserved* to pronounce sentence on Wesley.

"When does the *Rebecca Louise* sail?"

"Tomorrow on the morning tide."

Dylan put the cat out of the bedroom—he suspected he'd perform that little task often in the future—and locked the door.

"My sisters are off with Bowen terrorizing the milliners or mercers or some such. The house will be quiet until supper, and, Lydia, I have *missed* you."

He tried to will her to grasp the rest of it: She was an earl's daughter, and now that they were engaged, she would have to bide with damned Dorning, or somewhere other than Dylan's house, until the vows were spoken.

He was desperate to make love with her, but had no idea if a long-overdue fit of the weeps, hundreds of miles of travel, and a reunion with her prodigal brother had left her in the same frame of mind. She had seemed so self-possessed, so much on her dignity when he'd come upon her.

Captain, what brings you belowstairs?

"Do you know why I sought you down here?" he asked as Lydia closed the lid of her trunk.

"You saw me come down the kitchen steps?"

"Not only today. Why I always sought you down here." He sat on the trunk and held out his hand to her. "Because I wanted to behold you. To bask in the competence of a commanding officer who would never leave her wounded behind, never give quarter to the enemy, never abuse the sensibilities of her subordinates for her own convenience. I came to the kitchen to marvel at you and draw comfort from your very presence."

He hadn't admitted that to himself at the time, of course. Then, his stated motivations had been an empty belly or a nagging thirst.

Lydia took the place beside him and kept hold of his hand. "I delighted in your invasions and loved it when you'd sit at the worktable, demolishing a sandwich or a bowl of soup. I'd think, 'This much I can make right. I can make this one man less hungry, cold, anxious, and alone.' I drew strength from being a competent housekeeper."

For Dylan, it was enough to sit beside Lydia, hand in hand. The silence that took root was comfortable and sweet, and he could not have said who turned toward whom, but then he and Lydia were kissing.

And that was comfortable and sweet, too, for a time, until Lydia rose and began to undress him, and he was tempted to toss up her skirts and yield to the urgency her touch inspired.

But no. No need to hurry, no need to snatch like a thief at what should be shared and celebrated.

"Mama will expect me to join her at the Dorning household," Lydia said, draping Dylan's cravat over the vanity mirror. "I want a special license, Dylan. Promise me you will go to Doctors' Commons today."

"I promise, and I will call upon you at Dorning's every day for the next week, and he will have to be exquisitely gracious to me, or Jeanette will—"

Lydia stroked a hand over Dylan's falls, and every thought left his head save for those having to do with shedding his clothes and getting himself and Lydia beneath the covers. At least one button went flying across the room before he'd accomplished his objective. That provoked Lydia to laughing, and then the cat started scratching at the door, which inspired Dylan to fling his boot at the door, and that sent Lydia off into whoops.

The sight of her, overcome with mirth, kneeling on the bed and clad in only a chemise, etched itself on Dylan's heart.

"This is why I came so frequently across the lines to your domain," he said. "Because I hoped you would take me captive, and, Lydia, you have. You absolutely have."

Her laughter subsided to a smile. "We have captured each other, and I will never let you go." She held out her arms, and Dylan joined her on the bed. The lovemaking was profoundly tender, and profoundly pleasurable, and the peace thereafter wonderful.

Dylan slept, his arms around his beloved, and he dreamed of Lydia, kittens, and home. And at long last, his dreams were sweet indeed.

∽

"Today is the day," Wesley said, drawing a finger along the elegant curve of Sybil's naked back. "Today is the sweet, blessed day when my title becomes mine in all but name. How I wish I had time to tarry in your bed and celebrate with you for the next week."

Sybil rolled over to face him, her gaze amused. "You are too concerned that something will wreck your plan, and so you will abandon me to see your cousin banished. You are a very naughty man, Wesley Glover."

"You like naughty men," he said, rousing himself to sit up. Last night, darling Sybil had worn him out, bless her, and she'd put her dainty finger on the truth. Nothing and nobody would stop Wesley from ensuring Marcus was on that damned ship. He'd carry Marcus up the gangplank bag and baggage if necessary. He'd even pawned a pair of sapphire sleeve buttons to ensure Marcus would have a few pounds to start life in Philadelphia.

A very few pounds, which could not be helped after that debacle at the Coventry.

Sybil rose from her side of the bed and stretched, not a stitch on her fair person. The view of her bum was eye-crossingly delectable, but as the poet had said, time and tide waited for no earl.

Or something like that.

Sybil assisted Wesley to dress, and he was lacking only his coat when somebody knocked on the bedroom door.

"Breakfast, no doubt," Sybil said. She'd donned a dressing gown and was decently covered when she opened the door, though beneath that dressing gown she wore nothing at all. Wesley spared the clock a glance. Breakfast, or a reprise with Sybil, would take only a quarter hour.

But no. He would see Marcus off if it was the last thing he did— before a reprise with Sybil such as only an earl-in-waiting deserved.

"We have company," Sybil said, stepping back. "Colonel, Major, good morning. Fournier explained that I should expect a visit from you."

Wesley slipped into his coat, though for Sybil to welcome her next diversions into the very boudoir before Wesley had left was awkward, to say the least. Not well done of her.

"Gentlemen," Wesley said, nodding in an earl-ish fashion. "I bid you and the lady good day. I must be off."

"Orion Goddard," said the gent with an eye patch. "You are Wesley Glover?"

"I have that honor." Soon to be Earl of Tremont, at the rate Papa was drinking lately.

"Alasdhair MacKay," said the other fellow, who looked much too serious for a man contemplating an interlude with Sophie and the Goddard fellow, though something about Goddard and MacKay looked familiar.

Even the names rang a faint, slightly-the-worse-for-overimbibing, bell.

Too late, it occurred to Wesley that introductions under the circumstances were somewhat out of place. Gentlemen did not kiss and tell, and they certainly did not stand around in a courtesan's bedroom exchanging introductions. Moreover, Wesley had contributed handsomely to Sybil's household expenses with what ready cash he'd brought to London, and this whole situation was really quite—

"I like naughty men," Sybil said, wafting toward the door, "but I like having money more. Safe travels, Wesley, and I've packed a few bottles of Fournier's excellent claret for you."

She slipped out the door, blowing Wesley a kiss, and he had the sick, sinking feeling that she'd kept him abed until this appointed time and done so at the request of these two brigands.

"If you will excuse me," Wesley said, gathering up his pocket watch, "I have a pressing engagement."

"You will want that fancy walking stick," Goddard said, nodding toward the accessory Wesley had propped near the door. "And Sybil has kindly had your things packed and sent to the docks."

"As it happens, I am on my way to the docks now." Sybil had chosen a strange way to give him his *congé*, damn her. Women were all alike, always resorting to intrigues and guile to get what they hadn't earned.

The next thought to go crashing through Wesley's head was that trunks were sent to the docks for only one reason.

"What is all this about?" he snapped.

Goddard tossed a small leather bag at him, which clinked when Wesley caught it. "That is all the remittance you will ever see, a nod to familial loyalty from the earl whom you repeatedly betrayed. Don't expect another penny from Tremont. Don't think to come near his mother or sister in person or by letter or by intermediary. Your father has been pensioned and might well join you in Philadelphia, but that is not your decision to make. Now, Glover, unless you don't mind getting blood on that pretty cravat, *march*."

"March?" None of this was making any sense. "I am not some enlisted private that you—"

The other fellow, MacKay, smiled. "Keep talkin', laddie. For every word, I'll land a wee blow. For your widowed auntie, for your cousins, for the pure joy of pummelin' an arsewipe who deserves the noose."

Oh God. A cheerfully brawling Scotsman. "No pummeling necessary," Wesley said, snatching up his tippling stick. "I'm marching."

And march he did, right up the gangplank of the *Rebecca Louise*.

CHAPTER NINETEEN

"Jeanette reports that Marcus has the whole situation in hand," Lydia said, folding up the letter but not immediately passing it to her husband. Summer had fled, autumn had passed, and she'd spent her first Yuletide in the wild and beautiful Welsh countryside, but each and every day—and night—she still marveled that she and Dylan were husband and wife.

The sisters yet bided in London, having taken over Dylan's house, and they showed no sign of returning to Wales anytime soon. The kittens had made the journey to Wales in good health and now required separate baskets, as both were becoming rather majestic, considering their humble origins.

"Your brother has a talent for organization," Dylan said. "Marcus plays the dithering bumbler when he pleases to, but he's shrewd about what matters. If he set out to see that London's former soldiers have a place of refuge, then by God, he'll make a proper job of it."

Dylan sat at the library desk, a pair of spectacles perched on his nose. He'd opined that the glasses made him look elderly. Lydia found them arousing, particularly when he lay in bed reading, and spectacles were all he wore.

"You made a proper job of looking after those men, Dylan."

He smiled, and his smiles had the power to make Lydia's tummy fluttery. "I am not an earl, my lady. My version of a proper job is patchwork and pinchbeck compared to what Marcus is accomplishing. What else does Cousin Jeanette report?"

"I'm not sure you will like this next part," Lydia said, leaving her reading chair by the fire to deposit herself in Dylan's lap.

"Dorning is threatening to visit us?"

"Nothing so dire as that." She cuddled up and took a moment to wallow in the pleasure of Dylan's embrace. They were an affectionate couple, which had surprised her at first, but then, she'd realized that the ever-vigilant, relentlessly dutiful officer was not the real Dylan. That role was one Dylan had learned of necessity while serving in Spain under a foul excuse for a superior.

Nor was Lydia the overly serious, deferential, and dutiful aristocratic daughter trying to hold a titled family together by its tattered hems.

She was Dylan's wife, he was her husband, and life was lovely.

"Dorning isn't so bad," Dylan said. "He had the sense to marry Jeanette, after all, and he's made a place at the Coventry for Ann and Goddard. Few would have done as much. Sycamore is simply unignorable, and that puzzles a fellow like me who spent years learning how to avoid notice."

An interesting insight. "Sycamore has done something unignorable regarding you, Dylan. Or he and Marcus have, abetted perhaps by Dorning's titled brother."

"This is sounding dire."

Dylan did not seem worried, nor did Lydia sense any tension in him. He was, at heart, a man of the land, content to tend his acres and visit with the neighbors in the churchyard. He was patiently helping Lydia learn Welsh, though those Welsh lessons often devolved into lovemaking, for some reason.

"The honors list has come out," Lydia said, seeing no way to dress up the reality. "You have been made a baronet, in recognition for your service on the Peninsula and also to the former soldiers who found themselves in need of aid upon their return to London. We must all address you now as Sir Dylan."

Dylan's hand on her back went still, then resumed its slow caresses. "Sir Dylan. A baronet, not merely a knight. I must twit Goddard about this. Until such time as MacKay inherits his father's lordship, I am the ranking cousin. Do you know what the closest Welsh word is to baronet?"

And that, Lydia thought, was that. The *ranking cousin*, a smile, and back to snuggling. How she loved him and loved being his wife.

She was not yet toweringly fond of Dylan's native language. Like most Welsh words, the term for baronet was difficult for an English-speaker to pronounce. Dylan used the opportunity to expound on Welsh terms for various ranks in general, until Lydia, in defense of her wits, locked the door and led the new baronet to the library sofa.

Whereupon he stopped spouting Welsh—or much of anything else—for a good twenty minutes.